SILK AND STEEL

A powerful tale of bitter revenge and sweet retribution...

Mariah Bowes thinks that being alone and penniless is the worst thing that can happen to a woman, until she is the victim of a horrifying act of revenge. Daniel Thorpe is consumed with guilt, as it is his fault that Mariah endured such terrible punishment – he'd never realised the terrible consequences his affair with the beautiful Lily would bring. As Mariah pieces together the remains of her life she faces further horror – the terrible secret that her father, successful iron master and respectable member of the community Ezekiel Bowes, is determined to keep in the dark.

SILK AND STEEL

To the memory of Edmund Humphrey King

SILK AND STEEL

by

Catherine King

Magna Large Print Books
Long Preston, North Yorkshire,
BD23 4ND, England.

British Library Cataloguing in Publication Data.

King, Catherine
Silk and steel.

A catalogue record of this book is
available from the British Library

ISBN 978-0-7505-2836-8

First published in Great Britain in 2007 by Sphere

Magna Large Print is an imprint of Library Magna Books Ltd.

Printed and bound in Great Britain by
T.J. (International) Ltd., Cornwall, PL28 8RW

I should like to thank the staff and volunteers of Rotherham Archives, and the local history section of Rotherham Library, for enabling me to research the background to this book. Thanks, also, to my agent Judith Murdoch and editor Louise Davies for their sound advice and direction in its development and writing. The inspiration for the story is my great-grandmother, who came from a family of tailors in Stokesley, North Yorkshire.

Chapter 1

1840

The vicar read quietly from his prayer book, his soft hand gently touching the chalk-white skin of the woman's forehead. He traced the shape of a cross and those slight movements signalled the end of life for Amelia Bowes.

Tears ran down the cheeks of her daughter Mariah as she grieved silently for her loss. While they had each other, their hardships in this house had been bearable, but how would she survive without her mother? How could she continue to live here without the only person in the world who loved her?

She could not call this house a home. A home was where she would have been welcome. But her father had regarded them both as his servants, and treated them no better than he did his labourers at the ironworks. England may have a woman on the throne, but men continued to do the ruling.

Mariah inhaled with a shudder as she tried to repress her sobs. During her mother's long and painful illness, she had not thought beyond caring for her. They had not been separated in all her nineteen years and she could not imagine a life without her.

She heard the front door slam and her body went rigid. She knew who it was because she had

11

sent the stable lad to the works for him. Her father's heavy boots thumped on the stairs making the treads creak and groan. The door to the bed-chamber flew open and banged against the wall.

'She's gone then.'

Ezekiel Bowes stood in the middle of the sparsely furnished chamber in his working clothes. His face was streaked and sweaty and his once white neckerchief hung, stained and greasy, around his damp, dusty neck.

'It took her long enough,' he added.

His ruddy face, hot from the furnace, showed no emotion, but then it would not unless he was angry. Mariah and her mother always knew when Ezekiel had been crossed, but never when he was pleased. Happiness was not part of his life. Or theirs. Amelia's life had been an austere one as the wife of Ezekiel Bowes.

Mariah sat quietly by the bed and thought that her mother looked peaceful now – more so than she had for many years. The vicar drew a white sheet over the still, serene face and murmured words of condolence to Ezekiel. Mariah saw the discomfort in her father's face. Ezekiel Bowes was not a churchgoing man and this new vicar was taking more of an interest in him than the old one had.

She had sent for him against her father's wishes because it was what her mother had wanted. Ezekiel was angry to see him in his house, but Mariah guessed he would let it pass for the sake of appearances. Appearances mattered to Ezekiel, but only to the world outside this house.

'Aye, well. You can leave now, Vicar,' he replied,

with a surly nod.

The vicar added a few kind words to Mariah and hurried away. Mariah understood his haste.

'I suppose you sent for him?'

'Mother wanted him here at the end. You cannot begrudge her that, surely?'

Ezekiel turned on Mariah. He was a dark, swarthy man, toughened by years of manual labour. His hair was beginning to turn grey but he was still thick set and strong, for he still worked at the furnace with his men.

'I don't begrudge her anything now,' he said. 'Just get her out of here and clean up this chamber. I want everything of hers gone from this house. Do you hear me?'

'Yes, Father.'

'Get on with it, then!'

Mariah got to her feet and began to collect up the small comforts of nursing that had helped her mother through her last painful weeks. She knelt on the floor and piled the empty apothecary's bottles and soiled linen on a square of old calico and tied it into a bundle. She felt her father's domineering presence in the room and when she looked at him he was sneering at her mother's shroud.

Mariah's grief and anger rose against him. 'She was a good wife to you,' she cried.

'What would you know about it?'

'I know she was loyal to you, and you – you look as though you ... hated her,' she replied quietly.

'Hated her? I married her, didn't I? Aye, I did that. And with you growing in her belly.'

Mariah had not known this and was surprised but not shocked. Many a bride was wed with her first child already on the way. Indeed, any future husband would be pleased to know his betrothed was not barren. In a way, this knowledge cheered her and she remarked, 'You must have loved her once, then?'

He began to laugh, a low growling chuckle rumbled in his throat, but his brown eyes were hard. 'Is that what she told you?'

'Well, no. She did not talk of her – her early life.'

Ezekiel shook his head as though he had lost patience with her. 'Nigh on twenty years and she never told you.'

'It isn't a crime to be with child at the altar! Not if you loved each other–'

He let out a guffaw 'And I thought you two were close! Well, I'll be damned! She never said!'

'We *were* close,' Mariah protested. 'Especially as I grew older and–' She choked on a sob. 'When she became ill, she needed me.'

Ezekiel eyes glittered at her angrily. 'She needed *me*.' He spat out the words and his large frame towered over Mariah as she knelt by the bed.

'But you shunned her! You – you turned her away from your bedchamber, from your life, and treated her like a servant! What kind of marriage was that?'

'*Enough!*' Ezekiel shouted, closing in on her. 'You don't know what you're talking about! Don't you ever say things like that again! Do you hear me?'

Mariah's hazel eyes widened. He was standing right next to her and she could smell hot coal and metal on his leather boots and breeches. Anger

14

radiated from him like the heat from his furnace.

'Stop this hatred of her, Father! Stop it! She's dead now.'

This seemed to calm him. But for how long? Mariah wondered.

'What did she tell you?' Ezekiel asked.

'Not much. Only that you always took care of her and that whatever you did to us, to remember that underneath it all you kept your promise.' Mariah gathered up her bundle and rose. 'As I said, you must have cared for her once. And she did try to be a good wife to you.'

'What else did she say?' he demanded.

'About what?' Mariah was a full-grown woman now and not frightened of him as she had been as a little girl. If her father had something to say to her, it was best out in the open.

'About you!' he barked. 'Look at you. Carrot hair, white skin and freckles. Not dark like the rest of us.'

What was he getting at? Her brother Henry was like his father with brown hair and eyes. Her mother's hair had had a coppery hue when she had been younger and a skin like her own that freckled in the summer sun and reddened if she did not keep it covered. 'I have my mother's hazel eyes,' she muttered.

He leaned forward and his eyes looked directly into hers. 'Oh aye, you're *her* lass all right. Same stubborn way with you. But you're not *mine!*'

Mariah's jaw dropped, her eyes rounded and she swayed. 'Y-you mean you are not my father?' She did not believe it! Her mother had lain with another man and carried his child. 'Did you 'know this when you married her?' she whispered.

'Of course I knew!'

'She never told me,' Mariah murmured. 'Not about this. Who is he, then? If you are not my father, who is my real father?'

Ezekiel sneered at her again. 'Don't go getting any fancy ideas. Your precious mother disgraced herself and her family with some coal miner who got killed in a pit fall. And there was pretty little Amelia, left with no one to wed and a scandal on the way.'

'You knew about this and you married her?' Mariah thought it had been uncharacteristically generous on her father's part. There must have been some kindness in him all those years ago, although she had never seen much evidence of it in her lifetime. 'Then I was right, you must have loved her once.'

He did not answer but Mariah noticed his head shaking very slightly. Perhaps he had acted hastily and had regretted it ever since? Perhaps this was why he had spent most of his time at his ironworks, preferring to join his men for the heavy labouring in the yard?

'I never loved her,' he sneered. 'Not *her.*'

Mariah blinked as his face contorted to a sadness she had not seen before. 'Then why ... why *did* you marry her?' she asked.

He appeared to recover quickly. There was no grief after all; no sense of loss for her mother. He raised his voice, filling the stuffy bedchamber with his venom. 'Do you think I did it for nowt!'

Mariah tensed again. Her father was using the language of his earlier, younger years, language he usually kept for his men at the works. This was a warning sign that he was really angry, frustrated with his furnace or his suppliers, or simply with himself. She thought he was not a man at ease with himself and the successful ironmaster he had become.

'They paid me ter marry 'er! So long as I took 'er away and never went back to 'em for owt else!' he yelled. 'Paid me well, an' all. They were tailors, you know. Her family were all tailors in the North Riding. Doing all right for theirsenns, and her ma 'ad an uncle who was building cottages for a mine owner. How do yer think I got set up here wi' me own furnace, when I were on'y a labourer in a quarry and a forge?'

Mariah felt herself go cold all over. 'You married her for money?' she whispered. 'They paid you to take her – and me – away?'

'Aye. That's what folk with means do with their wayward daughters.'

Mariah found it hard to imagine her mother as wayward. She had been a warm and loving parent to her, and had more than made up for her father's coldness towards them both. She must have been in love with Mariah's real father. Perhaps they were planning to marry when he was killed?

'Mother never spoke of her own folk. She told me she had no kin.'

'Aye, she would say that. They wanted nowt more to do with her, so she turned her back on them an' all. It suited me too.'

'But surely they will wish to know of her passing?'

'Why? As far as they are concerned, she is

17

already dead. They were glad to see the back of her, let me tell you.' Ezekiel grimaced at the body of his late wife. 'And so am I.'

Mariah held her head in her hands. She knew her father could be unkind but to be this cruel to her mother's memory was too much for her to bear.

She cried out in anguish. 'She was your *wife!*'

'She was a whore with a bastard!' he retaliated. 'But she got me a share in the ironworks. That was the deal.'

'How can you be so disrespectful to the mother of your own child!'

'Aye. She bore me a son, all right. I'll give her that. He is all that matters to me.'

Mariah stood rigidly in front of him at the foot of the bed that cradled her mother's dead body. 'You *never* cared anything for her, did you? Never!'

'No.'

'Or me!'

'Even less for you! Some pit worker's bastard! I don't want you in my house reminding me of that!'

'What do you mean?'

'It's clear enough, i'n't it? Now your mother's gone, there's no need for you to stay here.'

'But you can't turn me out! I've nowhere to go!'

'You look all right, don't you? That carrot hair is not to everybody's taste, but you haven't got boss eyes or black teeth. Or a limp. And if you're like yer ma' you'll fall for a babby straight off to keep you out of mischief.'

Mariah was horrified. 'What on earth are you suggesting?'

'I am not suggesting, I am telling you. And if you value your mother's reputation you will do as you are told.'

'What do you mean?'

'I mean that if you do not obey me, I'll disown you for the bastard you are!'

'B-but people would think my mother was...'

'A whore? Aye, they would. So you'll do as I say and get yourself wed. And look sharp about it.'

'Be reasonable. I do not have a suitor.'

'I can find you one, don't you fret. A widower will do. One who won't be needing no dowry to have a bit o' young flesh in his bed of a night.'

'You cannot do that to me!'

His reply was slow and deliberate. 'I am your father, and until you are twenty-one I can do what I like with you and don't you forget it. Aye, I can find you a husband easy enough. And you'll marry him, by God. Before midsummer, or you'll be out on the streets selling yoursenn like your mother did afore you.'

'That is not true! How can you be so cruel? My mother would never have done such a thing.'

'How do you know she didn't? How do I know she wasn't at it here? She was never wanting for a new gown. Neither were you and *I* never paid for 'em. Where did they come from, I wonder?'

'What do you think she did all day while you were at work? Why do you think she kept the morning room for herself? You were never interested in anything she did!'

'Why should I want to know what women do with their time?'

'Why indeed,' Mariah responded wearily. 'All

19

you are concerned about is your precious furnace.'

'You listen 'ere to me, Mariah Bowes, and listen well to what I'm saying, because I mean it. I gave you my name, didn't I? You should be grateful for that alone. But while you carry that name, you make sure everyone in this town knows what a good husband I was to yer ma, and what a proper father I am to you. Did I send you out to service as soon as you were old enough? No. The both o' you had a roof over your head and food on the table.'

'We were your *servants!*'

It was then he hit her. He raised his right arm and brought the back of his hand hard across her face, sending her reeling. She grasped the iron bedstead to stop herself falling and stumbled over the silent, cooling body of her darling mother. It was then she realised the full extent of Ezekiel Bowes' hatred for his wife and herself.

'I was a good husband and father and don't you forget it!' he retaliated loudly. 'As far as this town knows, we were – are – a decent family! If ever I hear any different from you – or from anybody in the Riding – I'll tell them what a whore your mother was and expose you for the bastard you are!'

His dark eyes were angry and his hands were clenched into fists as he continued to shout. 'And if your husband turns you out because o' that, it'll be your own doing. You'll be on the streets then, because I'll not have you back here. D'yer hear me? Never. Things are going to be different around here with yer ma and you out o' the road.'

Chapter 2

Ezekiel watched the coffin as it was lowered into the ground. It's over at last, he thought, and soon the daughter will be gone too, away from my house and that part of my life will be dead and buried for ever. He was a widower now, respectable, with a profitable business and an educated son to be proud of.

He had friends at the Freemason's lodge and they had turned out for him today, in their best black and polished boots. He was glad of that. The church service had been an ordeal for him but he felt stronger with his friends around him. Their wives and daughters were waiting for them in their own homes, the best place for womenfolk at times like these. None of them knew of his early life, and now his wife had gone and the bastard was on her way too, he could erase all those memories from his mind, push them away for ever deep down into the dark recesses of his past.

'Ashes to ashes, dust to dust...' the vicar droned on.

He was anxious for it to be finished. Churchmen made him uncomfortable, and this one, this new vicar, more so than most. He had never known the old vicar very well and he did not want to know this one either. In Ezekiel's book, God was unforgiving. God had made him a sinner and God had made him suffer. For the rest of his life he would suffer.

His face contorted with the hurt of remembering as he stood by the graveside. He saw the vicar looking at him. What did he know? he demanded silently. What did he know of growing up at the beck and call of his betters? Uneasily, he wondered where this new vicar came from and hoped it was not the North Riding.

'Father?'

A hand took his arm. It was Henry. My, what a fine gentleman he had become, dressed in a new black coat and tall hat. His heart swelled with pride when he looked at him. Henry was his salvation. A fine boy, his son from his own seed, schooled and confident, moving among the straggle of mourners, taking charge.

There was sherry wine and shortened biscuits laid out in the dining room at home. Ezekiel was cheered by the thought of going back to his works as soon as this was over. He knew who he was when he was there. He was the gaffer and the men deferred to him. He could have taken greater advantage of them but he did not. He was no longer the troublemaker of his younger years, he was a changed man. A family man. Respectable. He would wear his black armband for the required length of time. Henry would advise him.

Ezekiel managed a weak smile for the vicar before moving away, thankful this necessary show was over. There was old man Smith from the ironmongers in town. A widower like himself. Well, no, not quite like himself. He had a big family of growing lads and lasses. But they were a handful for him and it was rumoured he was looking for a wife. His shop was prospering and he had a bob or two from rents as well, so he'd make any lass a good husband.

'Mr Smith,' he called. 'Mr Smith, a word with you, if you please, sir.'

'Do you know about Father's plans, Henry?'

'Of course, I do, Mariah. I am his son and heir. Father and I corresponded regularly when I was at school. The ironworks and this house are my future.' Henry sighed. 'It is a pity the house is so close to the works, for it is well proportioned and ideal for receiving callers.'

'It was very convenient for Father in the early days. I remember when Mother used to cook dinner for his labourers and feed them all in the kitchen. I helped her with the washing-up and cleaning.

'I did not know we used to have *labourers* in our kitchen.'

'No. You were away at school for most of the time.'

Mariah had served her father and brother their breakfast in the dining room. When Ezekiel left for the works, instead of returning to the kitchen, she drew out a chair opposite Henry and sat down.

'Tell me about Father's plans, Henry.'

Henry had come home from school for his mother's funeral. At eighteen, he had worn new black clothes for the occasion but now he displayed only a black armband on his finely tailored coat. It was a fashionable maroon colour, made of good Yorkshire wool, Mariah noticed, and he wore pomade on his dark hair.

He sighed again. 'Mariah, I have already said that you do not need to concern yourself with these matters.' He frowned and pursed his lips. 'And do remove your apron if you wish to join me at the table.'

Mariah ignored his request and watched him dispassionately as he picked an invisible speck of dust from his sleeve. He had grown into a handsome young man, with the dark hair and eyes of his father but without his swarthiness. Henry had inherited the smooth-textured skin of their mother. A feature he shared with her, except he had more warmth in his skin colouring and, of course, no freckles.

She felt plain and dowdy beside him. She had no money of her own and had sewn her mourning dress herself, from some black stuff already in her mother's workroom. She covered it with a large white pinafore most of the time as the cloth had been cheap and already showed signs of wear.

'But Father's plans do concern me, Henry,' she persisted, 'this is my home.'

'Not for much longer, I hear.' He measured out a small smile. 'Father has told me you will marry soon and become part of another family. That will be convenient for all of us. I know you are not a Bowes, and I no longer think of you as a sister.'

This was a shock for Mariah. Henry had grown apart from her in his years away at school and she no longer recognised him as her little brother.

'But I am your sister, Henry!' she protested. 'Your mother was my mother, too!'

'She was not a Bowes and never a part of Father's affairs.' He shrugged. 'She had no real claim to our family name. As Father's wife she was given it as a privilege.'

'Family name? What family name? Father was an ordinary labourer before he came to the South Riding.'

'If you take my advice, you will not let him hear you say that. He means to be a well-respected ironmaster in this town.'

Mariah thought he probably already was. As a young man he had invested his wife's generous dowry in a rundown furnace, repaired the crumbling brickwork and taken on men to labour alongside him. To give her father his due he had worked hard, but he could have done none of it without marrying Amelia.

She said firmly, 'It was my mother's money that bought him the ironworks!'

'No, Mariah. I think you will find that is not true. Women, generally, do not have money of their own. However,' he pronounced casually, 'your mother's father may have given her a dowry.'

Your mother? Mariah thought, not 'my mother' or even 'our mother'. She said pointedly, 'She was your mother, too.'

'Yes,' he sighed. 'Though Father did not wish me to be influenced by her. That is why he was so anxious for me to go away to be educated, and why he encouraged me to spend my time with young gentlemen from school, away from here.'

Well, thought Mariah angrily, go back to your expensive school and snobbish friends! She asked calmly, 'Then why have you chosen to stay at home now?'

'I would have thought that was obvious. Your

mother is dead and soon you will be gone too. Father and I have plans. I shall not go to university, but become a partner in the ironworks when I am twenty-one.'

Mariah despaired. She had thought Henry might be her ally against Ezekiel's wishes in this matter. Her childhood memories were of austerity mixed with occasional cheer, but she and Henry had been friends as children playing in the attic or the garden. And she remembered how sad she had felt when Henry went first to a local day school and then, at eight years old, further afield as a boarding pupil.

He had visited them rarely since then and, when he did, had little time for her or her mother. Mariah had put his aloofness down to his new schooling. Mother said he was going to be a proper gentleman when he grew up. She had wondered at the time why Henry, who was a whole year younger than she was, went for lessons before her, and had asked innocently, 'When shall I go to school, Mother?'

'Heavens, my dear,' her mother had told her, 'Mr Bowes will not pay for you to go to school. You must stay at home with me and look after the house. I shall teach you how to cook and clean and sew. You do not need to go to school for that. I learned from my mother and you will learn from me.'

But her mother could not read or write so Mariah went to Sunday school and learned her letters and read Bible stories there. Mariah had often wondered why her mother spoke so little of her own mother. She presumed she had died young and so did not ask. Now that Amelia was dead it was too late and she wished she had questioned her more. All Mariah had now was a likeness of her that she had kept in her workroom. It was a drawing, well executed by a travelling artist who had visited the beast market, mounted in an old silver frame. The features were recognisable as her mother's and, indeed, a little like her own. It was all she had of her past now; her mother had said she must have it when she was gone.

Mariah shook her head slightly at Henry's lack of sentiment for his own mother. His father and his schooling had taken him away from both of them. Henry pushed back his chair and his napkin fell to the floor. He did not pick it up but wandered over to the windows where tall glass doors led into the garden. He fingered the material of the curtains and looked at the walls.

'Between the two of you,' he remarked, 'you have neglected this house. Look at it! Dingy and unfashionable! What were you thinking of, letting it get into this state?'

Mariah had realised by now that her brother was not interested in replies to his questions. He did not want to hear about five years of illness and nursing and the small matter of her father's refusal to pay for paint or wallpaper, or even new fabric for window curtains. Father's usual response had been that all his profits were invested in raw iron for the furnace. Mariah thought this must have been true because Henry was right, the ironworks flourished while the house was run down.

It was a nice house to live in, though, and Mariah liked it. Situated, as it was, on the town

27

side of the ironworks, it was convenient for the High Street and the market square at the top of the hill, and had enough garden around it to grow fruit and vegetables. There was a carriage house, too, where Father kept his haulage cart and heavy horses for transporting the bars of steel his furnace produced. Father had his own horse, too, a large spirited beast that Henry also rode.

The stable lad, who slept next to the hayloft over the tack room, looked after the garden as well, so they always had fresh greens and such like in the kitchen. But for years her father would not employ a housemaid and it was a large house to clean without a servant. Built of local stone, it stood four square to the roadway, with a large front door and wide entrance hall. They had a drawing room, dining room, morning room and a large kitchen with a roomy scullery at the back. Upstairs were four good bedchambers with two attics above them.

When her mother was well, they were able to keep down the dust from the coal fires, wax the floorboards and furniture and cook meals between them. But when she became ill, Mariah could not manage the house and nurse her mother. Reluctantly, her father had agreed to occasional help in the form of Emma, a ten-year-old girl from down by the canal on the other side of the ironworks. She was a willing and cheerful child, but not used to a large house, and Mariah had to teach her many things before she could become a real help.

Mariah knew Henry did not wish to know any of this and said, 'Well, if Father will open an account at the draper's in town, I'm sure I can make new curtains and–'

'Really, Mariah! What do you know of fashion for houses? You have never been anywhere grand enough to see what can be done.'

Henry began to pace about, looking up at the ceiling and turning to survey the whole room. His new leather boots squeaked on the floorboards. 'This furniture is too light,' he declared. 'I want mahogany from the East. And red velvet for the windows. Yes. Dark red, I think, with gold tassels. That is much more fitting for a gentleman's residence, don't you think?'

Mariah stayed silent. She recalled her mother telling her as a child, 'When Henry comes home from school he will be accepted in the very best circles, and so will his father.'

'And what about us?' Mariah had asked.

'Well, of course, we are part of this family so they must accept us as well. Perhaps Mr Bowes will give me an allowance to buy new dress material and ribbons.'

Perhaps not, Mariah had thought; he is happy for us to forage for used and damaged garments at the market. To afford the clothes for their backs, Amelia Bowes sold surplus garden produce to buy straw bonnets that she trimmed with bits of lace and ribbons, and then re-sold or traded for lengths of cloth. If ever her mother caught sight of a fashionable traveller passing through the South Riding, every detail of her dress would be noted, memorised and sketched out on a slate as soon as she returned home, then her cupboards would be searched for remnants and trimmings to enhance their workaday gowns.

Henry brought her back to the present. 'I shall open up the drawing room,' he declared grandly, 'and have a carpet from Persia on the floorboards. And perhaps a pianoforte for soirées.'

Mariah wondered if her father knew the extent of Henry's dreams for his house and whether his one furnace was enough to make that kind of money. She found it difficult to keep the doubt out of her voice. 'Soirées? Gracious, Henry,' she said, 'this will mean a lot more work for me in the house.'

'But you will not be here! You will be married and caring for your own family.'

'Really? And who will look after you and Father if I leave?'

'Emma will,' Henry responded. 'She is fifteen now, is she not? I am sure she has learned everything she needs. She will know what to do.'

'You mean Emma will be your housekeeper?'

'As soon as you marry. Before if you wish.'

'And you, Henry? What will you do?'

'I shall assist my father in his business matters, of course. What else should I do?'

What else indeed? Mariah wondered how he would survive in the ironworks with his father. She could not imagine Henry working for Ezekiel, hot and sweaty in dirty, greasy clothes, labouring at a fiery furnace during smelting.

Henry went on, 'Father and I have been planning these changes for a year now. We have been impatient for your mother to die.'

Mariah felt as if she had been punched in the stomach. Even though her mother's passing had been a release from her constant pain and

30

suffering, Mariah had never wished to hasten her death. Henry's offhand remark appalled her and her voice was strangled as she said, 'How can you be so – so harsh and unfeeling!'

'Do not be so melodramatic, Mariah. It is not becoming in a woman of our standing. We all knew your mother was dying. I hope you will not behave like this should my friends, the Fitz-keppels, choose to visit, or I shall have to ask you to stay in the kitchen.'

Mariah stared at him. 'You are friendly with the Fitzkeppels? I am surprised you would wish to invite them here in the first place. This is a very small house compared to Fitzkeppel Hall.'

'Perhaps we shall move somewhere more gracious,' Henry mused. 'Father's investment in the works is paying off well for him now. Soon he will not have to oversee the men at all. He will be spending all his time with other ironmasters and men of substance at the lodge in town. You do see, don't you, Mariah, that neither your mother nor yourself could be a part of our future here?'

No, I do not see, Mariah thought angrily. It was her mother's dowry that had made all this possible! And she had been thanked with a position no better than a housekeeper. What kind of life had that been for her! Her workroom had been her only respite from the drudgery of being Ezekiel Bowes' unpaid servant. It had been Mariah's haven as well.

'But that does not mean I have to marry! I can run the household for Father and keep on Mother's workroom. She taught me everything she knew about garment making–'

31

'I want that room for a study. We shall need somewhere to discuss business affairs when gentlemen call at the house.'

'But we have an empty bedchamber I could use!'

'We do not! That is to be my dressing room. A gentleman needs space for his wardrobe and toilette. Oh, and would you move your things to one of the attic rooms forthwith? Father's new works supervisor will be sleeping in the bedchamber that you are using.'

'I did not know Father was taking on a supervisor.'

'Why should you? It is of no consequence to you. But I shall tell you this: he is one of the best iron workers in the Riding. Father wants him to live here, next to the works, so he can take full responsibility for the furnace. And then Father and I shall be free to spend our time mixing with the right sort of Riding people.'

'So – so – this – this new works supervisor can live here, but I cannot!'

'You must realise how important he will be to our success. He comes to us from the Fitzkeppel works and understands all the modern processes. He knows how to make the very best steel for the cutlers of Sheffield. We shall be rich, Mariah! If you are sensible and marry the man Father chooses for you, you will be able to visit us when we are grand and take Sunday tea in the drawing room.'

'And you, Henry? What will you do?'

Henry smiled. 'My education has not been wasted, Mariah: I shall help Father to become a gentleman. You will see how respectable we shall be now that I am home.'

'You are insufferable! You cannot order my life like this.'

'Of course I can. I do it on behalf of Father. You will move into the large attic. Emma will take the smaller one.'

'Emma? Emma is to live here in the small attic?'

'Of course. She may take over the running of the house immediately. Do not look at me like that. You will not be here much longer, for you will be marrying quite soon.'

Mariah swallowed hard and spoke slowly with an exaggerated patience, 'Henry, I am not yet betrothed to anyone.'

'Oh, but you will be! You must think of your future elsewhere now, Mariah. As a wife. Father is arranging a suitable husband for you.'

Suitable for whom? she wondered, but did not pursue the matter. 'I see. So when I marry, Emma will be living here with Father and you and – and – the new works supervisor? Henry, she is only fifteen, that is hardly respectable.'

'Mariah, do leave things like this to me. Father's new supervisor is Mr Thorpe, Emma's older brother. She can live here quite respectably if her brother is here, too.'

'And of course respectability is all that matters to Father! What will the ironmasters of the South Riding think if I refuse to marry his choice of husband, and he turns me out on the streets?'

'Do not be childish. Why should you not marry? I think you will find you will have no friends of consequence in the Riding if you disobey him.'

Mariah's anger turned to sarcasm. 'Well then,

Henry, you must help me find a suitor. Do you know any gentlemen I could meet? They, perhaps, will be a little young, but I am sure that, if you are acquainted with them, they will be men of means.'

Henry answered her seriously. 'Be reasonable. My friends have their sights set on much higher prizes than you. No one of any consequence will want to marry you. You have nothing from your mother to take to a marriage, and no proper education at all. Certainly no talent for music or singing. All you can do is cook and sew.'

'Thank you for explaining that so clearly to me. With such paltry talents where should I set my sights? A coal miner's wife, maybe?'

But the irony in Mariah's voice was lost on Henry and he replied airily, 'Well, you have all you need to be a collier's wife.'

'I am to be a coal miner's wife, then,' she responded angrily 'Is that how you see me? Would you come and visit your half-sister in her pithead cottage when she is a coal miner's wife?'

'Well no, of course not. If you marry a collier, our lives will part for good when you leave this house. But coal mining is a good living for a man. Emma's father was a collier before he got the – the – sickness that they get. I understand your own father was a pit man, too. You cannot set your expectations higher than that.'

'My expectations! What do you know of my expectations? Perhaps I'll marry Father's new works supervisor! I imagine that, if he is coming to live here, he does not have a wife. Have you met him yet? Will he do for me?'

'Do not be silly. You are, in reality, an orphan

34

and you would do well to take your situation seriously. Now the funeral is over, you must clear the house of your mother's things and leave.'

Mariah was beside herself with anger. 'But who will have me? As you have so kindly pointed out, I have no dowry or talent.'

'Oh, do not fret yourself so. Father knows of somebody for you. There's a man at the lodge who lost his wife to the cholera. You might know him. He is an ironmonger with his own shop in the High Street. His trade is good and he already has grown children to help you in the house. He needs a strong, healthy woman like yourself to look after him in his old age. He would be a much better choice than a collier. He would do for you.'

'No, he would not! I know who you mean and I've seen him around his lady customers. He's a greasy old man and he makes my flesh creep. I shall not marry him and Father cannot make me!'

Chapter 3

'I don't know, Miss Mariah, this dun't seem right to me.'

Emma was standing in the middle of the large attic room. A good north light streamed in through two large skylights onto an old oak side table littered with bits and pieces of Mariah's sewing. A horsehair-stuffed calico mannequin draped in a brown woollen cape leaned against the old iron bedstead in the corner. Where the sloping

35

ceilings met the floor, a line of limed wooden doors hid shelves storing travelling boxes and old clothes.

'What doesn't seem right, Emma?'

'Me moving in here to live and you going off, like. You should be 'ere with your family, not – not – where *are* you going to, Miss Mariah? Mr Bowes didn't say.'

'Well, I hear your brother is to run the works for my f-f–' Sometimes, Mariah found it difficult to call him Father. 'Er, for Mr Bowes and he needs to be here to do that. And you are more than capable of running this house as well as I or my mother ever did.'

'Oh yes, you've taught me well and I shall always be grateful. I shall get a proper wage, now. My mam and dad'll be right pleased about that.'

'And your brother's wage will be a help for them, too.'

'Oh yes, our Danny's money goes on rent and doctoring for me dad. He's got the miner's cough real bad now.'

'Your brother must be older than you, Emma.'

'Yes, Miss Mariah. He is.'

'And he does not have a wife yet?'

'Oh no, Miss Mariah. I had three brothers, you see. Only we lost two of 'em to the fever and then Dad got his cough and our Danny said he wouldn't wed and leave me mam with no money now only us girls is left. Mind, I know he's sweet on a young widow woman who lives near to us at home.'

'How many sisters do you have?'

'There are five of us now. The other four are all

younger 'an me. My older sister went to the fever, an' all.'

'How on earth does your mother manage?'

'Oh, she's right clever me mam. She makes her own bread and brews beer for me dad and scrubs out for the butcher's wife so we get butcher's meat every week. She even weeds the garden for Dad now. Daniel does the digging, o' course.'

'It is no wonder you have turned out to be such a good housekeeper.'

'Thank you, Miss Mariah. Can I ask you something?'

'Of course you can.'

'Where are you going to? Nobody seems to know.'

'Oh, er – I – I – er – I haven't decided yet, Emma. I – I may have to go away from here altogether.'

'You wouldn't leave the South Riding, would you, Miss Mariah?'

No, I would not, Mariah thought, and why should I? The South Riding is the only home I know and I like it.

'I have not decided yet. But I would like to store my mother's belongings in here with mine until I'm settled. Mr Bowes never comes up to the attics so he need not know they are here.'

'I'll help you,' Emma volunteered. 'Are there still some things of yours in Mrs Bowes' workroom? Master Henry says it's got to be cleared as he going to change it into a gentleman's study, like.'

They worked together diligently until the downstairs rooms were empty of all signs of Amelia Bowes and her daughter. When they had finished, they flopped on the bed in the large attic and took

37

off their boots until it was time to begin preparing supper.

'Emma, you have a split in the bodice of that gown.'

'Oh no,' she groaned, 'I'm growing outwards as well as upwards these days.'

'You are a young woman now, you can marry and have babies. Has your mother talked to you about that?'

'I'll say she 'as, miss! More about not having them, though! At least not until I'm wed.' She twisted round to examine the tear in the seam. 'Oh well, I can mend it and pass it on to one o' me sisters. I liked this one, though.' She fingered the material of the skirt. 'It's real good stuff, is this.'

'Yes, it was one my mother made for me. She had a good eye for cloth and never missed the beast market in case the traveller was there. When she could get the flannel she made shirts for the farmers' lads and exchanged them for all sorts of supplies.'

'She was real handy wi' a needle and thread, wasn't she?'

Mariah smiled to herself. Her mother had been the best seamstress in town and anyone who shopped in the market knew that.

'She was,' Mariah agreed proudly. 'Her mother taught her and she taught me.'

Mariah climbed off the bed and began to rummage in an old wooden chest. 'Look Emma, take one of Mother's skirts for yourself and I'll cut that gown to fit one of your sisters. I have several bodices I have outgrown, why don't you choose a couple of them to wear with the skirt?'

She began to lift the garments from their calico wrappings and hold them up to the light. 'These are hardly worn and the cloth is still strong.'

'Ee, Miss Mariah, I've never seen so many gowns all at once. Where did they all come from?'

'There used to be a travelling man from Leeds who came to the beast market from time to time. If my mother had money, she could not resist a bolt end of new cloth from him. We made it up together, mostly into skirts and capes to sell to the farmers' wives who came in for supplies. But sometimes we kept it for ourselves.'

Emma rolled to the edge of the bed and fingered the material of her newly acquired skirt. 'It's beautiful. But then you always look nice, Miss Mariah, even when you're in the kitchen.'

'Thank you, Emma. My mother said you had to start with good cloth. But it costs such a lot in the draper's shop. All ours was from the traveller.'

'I shall be the envy of my sisters.'

Mariah continued her rummaging. 'Why don't I cut them all down? I'll do one for each of your sisters.'

'Oh, I couldn't let you do all that needlework. If you show me, I'll do it.'

'I'll show you and help you as well. If you want we can make a shirt for your father and one for Daniel too.'

'Oooh, could we? I'd really like that.'

'We'll do the gowns first. I'll need to see your sisters. Oh dear, it's going to be difficult for them to come here now, without the workroom. Will you take me to meet them?'

'Oh – er – I don't know.'

'Emma?'

'Well, it's you I'm thinking of, Miss Mariah. It's only Canal Bank Cottages. It's not as nice as here, like.'

'You do not need to concern yourself with my sensibilities,' Mariah responded briskly. 'I am not at all like Master Henry with his airs and graces. Besides, I shall be leaving here soon to make my own way in life.' And heaven knows where I shall be, she thought. 'Does your mother have a sewing box with pins and chalk?'

'She 'as some things in a cupboard, I think.' Emma frowned.

'I'll take mine. Get my mother's old travelling box out and pack up these gowns for your sisters. They are all quite serviceable. And look at this one, it's really pretty. Mother liked a border or a frill, even on workaday skirts.'

As she sorted through the clothes, Mariah recalled how clever her mother had been at making trimmings from bits and pieces in her workroom. She made sure they looked their best when they went into town to market even though Ezekiel Bowes did not have an account at the draper's shop. She never complained that Ezekiel gave her no allowance and accepted that all his money was needed to pay the men's wages at the ironworks. But Ezekiel went to a good tailor for his own Sunday suits and now Henry did the same. Mariah and her mother had clothed themselves with what they could glean from good days at the market, while Ezekiel and his son had bespoke suits made of the very best wool.

If she stayed here much longer, she would

begin to despise both of them for their selfishness. She knew her feelings would fester into hatred if she continued to live in the same house as Ezekiel, and this would not be good for her. But she had no idea where to go, or indeed how to live without his support.

'There is one last thing I must collect,' she said at last. 'I shall not be long.'

Mariah hurried down the attic stairs to the spacious landing and then down the wide polished wooden staircase into the hall. She would miss this beautiful house with its well-proportioned rooms and large windows. Yes, it was shabby; she conceded that Henry was right in his assessment. But her mother had made it into a home although it was not the same now she had gone. Somehow, the warmth had disappeared and it was an empty shell. It no longer had a heart and she could not think of it as her home.

Since the funeral, Ezekiel had spent most of his time at his ironworks and Henry had taken charge of house refurbishments. Henry was growing more tiresome by the day. As Mariah nursed her grief, she tried desperately to make allowances for his youthful arrogance, born out of the expensive schooling that had given him such grand ideas about himself.

The morning room looked forlorn, its furniture stripped bare of any signs of her mother's presence. A few ornaments remained on the mantelpiece including her mother's likeness in its silver frame. She took it down and studied it. An attractive woman stared seriously back at her. Mariah could detect a family resemblance in her features, features that had passed to her. The ornate frame had become dusty and she rubbed it with her sleeve before pressing it to her bosom.

'What have you got there?'

She had not heard Henry's footfall in the hall. He stood in the open doorway, smartly dressed for town and sporting a new ebony cane with a silver top.

'What are you hiding, Mariah?' he repeated.

'I am not hiding anything. I am collecting my mother's things.'

'Let me see,' he demanded.

Mariah showed him the likeness. 'Our mother,' she explained. 'You must have noticed it.'

'Oh yes. That. Put it back, now you have looked at it.'

'Henry, this belonged to my mother!' Mariah protested.

'I ordered you to put it back.'

Shocked at his imperious tone, Mariah responded, 'I shall not. You told me yourself that – that Father said I may keep anything of my mother's.'

'Well, take the likeness out of the frame then and put the frame back. That belongs to Father. A rather fine frame it is, too.'

'Oh, Henry, why don't you just shut up and leave me alone! I am not taking the likeness out and I am certainly not leaving the frame.'

'I shall have to tell Father,' he warned.

'You may tell Father what you wish! I am sure he will think it is a small price to pay to be rid of us both!'

Mariah pushed past her brother and swept

across the hall and up the stairs, bristling with anger. She could not wait to get away from the pair of them and in her anxiety ran all the way up to the attics, so she arrived out of breath and coughing.

'What on earth is the matter? You are shaking!'

'It's nothing. Only the dust from the fireplace.'

'Are you sure you are well?'

'Perfectly well, thank you,' she replied firmly, 'although I shall not be if I stay here much longer. I need something to take me away from this house. Would you ask your mother when it might be convenient to visit and meet your sisters so I may make an early start on their gowns?'

Chapter 4

Ezekiel watched Daniel Thorpe from his works office. High above his ironworks yard, he had a good view of everything that went on in the name of Bowes. Even so, he preferred to be down in the yard where the furnace was, packing raw bar iron and charcoal into the stone chests and shovelling coal for the firing. Making blister steel was an art Ezekiel had perfected over twenty years.

He liked nothing more than to take off his jacket, roll up his shirtsleeves and labour with his men. They were good men, hard working and willing, and he counted himself their friend. But they were wary of him; he was their gaffer. He knew they thought he should be up here in the office, paying his invoices and filling his order book, not sweating with them at the furnace face. He continued to survey them as they toiled in his yard.

He had been the same as them once: young, strong, willing, happy to be grafting with his mates. It was what men did, what he did, what he wanted to do, until it had all fallen apart, until his young life shattered. Best not dwell on it, best the past was forgotten. He was a gaffer now and his future was here, in the South Riding, making blister steel, ready for the forge.

Daniel Thorpe was a piece younger than the other men who had applied for the supervisor's position. But his handwriting was good and he came with a top recommendation. He had been at the Fitzkeppel furnaces since he was a nipper and had nigh on fifteen years' experience of making iron and steel. He was a bright fellow who had been to the Mechanics Institute and knew all there was to know about smelting iron into steel.

Ezekiel watched him walk across the yard and nodded slightly to himself. That long leather waistcoat must have cost him a pretty penny. Hard wearing, though, and it set him apart from the rest. Thorpe had bettered himself, like he had as a young man. Well, maybe not in exactly the same way. Thorpe had more between his ears than most and you had to have brains as well as brawn these days to keep ahead in the ironworks business.

Aye, he was just what the works needed. Not wed yet, either. His mouth turned down at the corners into the smirk that signified approval. He listened for the young man's hobnailed boots ringing on the outside steps and knew he had made the right decision. Ezekiel straightened his necktie and stood up with his right hand out-stretched.

'Welcome, Mr Thorpe. Welcome to Bowes Ironworks.'

Daniel took off his cap and shook his new gaffer's hand. 'Thank you, sir. Where do you want me to start?'

'All in good time. If you are to be my right hand here, we need to get to know each other a bit better first.'

My, he's a fine figure of a man, Ezekiel thought. Like I was at his age. He straightened his back and pulled in his gut. I've not worn too bad, he mused to himself. Hard graft never hurt nobody and I'm a testament to that.

He said, 'You're not married, are you?'

'No, sir.'

Ezekiel raised his eyebrows. 'Five and twenty and not yet wed? A fine handsome fellow like you? Have you plans?'

'I might have,' Daniel responded warily.

Again, Ezekiel remembered himself, twenty-odd year ago; younger than Thorpe and in deep trouble. His gaffer, the ironmaster at the time, knew it. He gave him a way out of his trouble that Ezekiel was obliged to take. He was miserable for a time but it kept the law off his back. Who knows what might have happened to him if he had not been well in with his gaffer? It was who you knew that counted then. Still is, he thought. His son Henry was right. You had to have the right friends.

He said, 'A man needs a wife for respectability. I don't want any scandal at my works, d'you hear?'

'Yes, sir.'

'Do you get on with the men all right?'

'Well, I did at Fitzkeppel's. I don't know your gang yet, but I don't expect they'll be much different.'

'Did you know the Fitzkeppel men outside o' work?'

'A few of us with no wives to go home to sometimes shared a jug of ale at the Lion. Furnace work is thirsty work, sir.'

'Aye, well it's different now. Don't forget you're their gaffer. When you're outside the yard, stay away from the men.'

'If you say so, sir.'

'I do. Keep out of trouble.'

Daniel nodded. 'Sir.'

'Like I said, you'll lodge at my house next to the yard. My son Henry is seeing to the refurbishments and your bedchamber will be ready for you next week. You know how important it is to keep the furnace temperature right and I shall be relying on you to deal with anything to do with the works, night or day. Do you understand?'

'Yes, sir.'

Ezekiel handed Daniel a heavy iron key. 'This is for this door here. Keep it on your person at all times. You can use this office as your own. I'll show you the billing. Make sure it's kept up to date because I check the books every week. I have the keys to the safe and I'll give the men their wages, but you'll do the book work. Understood?'

'Yes, sir.'

'Good. Now, I've been thinking over some of your ideas. Sit down, will you?'

The office was dusty and grubby, with piles of

papers pushing open several wooden cupboard doors. Ezekiel's old oak desk had seen much better days but the worn leather chairs were comfortable enough, and Ezekiel watched Daniel's face as he settled in one by the fireplace. Ezekiel shovelled more coal on the fire, sat opposite him and said, 'We're a lot smaller than the Fitzkeppel set up.'

'Aye, sir, I know.'

'And I can sell all the blister steel I can make.'

'Aye, Mr Bowes, but for what price? Do you know what crucible steel fetches these days?'

'I'm listening to you.'

'Sheffield cutlers are crying out for the best steel. Crucible steel. Fitzkeppel's are building another bank of crucible furnaces to keep up supply.'

'Fitzkeppel's have got three cementation furnaces and word has it they're going to build more.'

'They'll always be the biggest smelters around these parts. But there's plenty of room for others. Sheffield knives goes across the ocean to the Americas. Now we have the railway from Sheffield to Manchester and the docks–'

'Yes, I know all that. But building furnace pits for crucibles costs a lot o' brass.'

'I reckon a yard this size could keep half a dozen crucibles going,' Daniel stated, adding, 'With extra men, of course.'

Ezekiel noticed a wariness in his eyes, which he did not let pass. 'And?' he prompted.

Daniel fingered the band of his cap. 'Well, you can increase your blister steel output an' all. You've got some slack here, Mr Bowes.'

'What do you mean – slack?'

'With the men–'

47

'They're good men down there.'

'Aye, but they need organising, Mr Bowes. They need more discipline. You don't want to have to watch 'em every minute.'

'That's why you're here,' Ezekiel responded. 'If I do put in crucible furnaces – and I'm not saying I will, yet – but if I do, then you'll have to show the men how to work them.'

'Aye, I can do that. You'll have to up their pay, though. It's dangerous work lifting out red-hot crucibles and pouring molten steel into moulds.' Daniel went quiet, wondering if he had said too much too soon. He'd been lead man on the crucibles at Fitzkeppel's and knew what he was talking about. He could make the best steel in the Riding at Bowes, and he couldn't wait to get started.

'Right, then.' Ezekiel stood up. 'You increase my output of blister steel from the cementation furnace and I'll look into costing up a crucible shed.'

The younger man's face beamed as he got up to leave. 'You won't regret this, sir, I promise.'

'Don't you forget I haven't got a bottomless pocket.'

'No, sir. I thought I'd make a start in the warehouse. See what stock you have.'

Ezekiel gave a nod and waved him away saying, 'Get on with it, then.'

As soon as Thorpe left the office Ezekiel moved to the window overlooking the yard and watched him clatter down the stone steps and stride across the cobbles. After talking briefly to the foreman of his furnace gang, he made his way back to the warehouse beneath the office.

Ezekiel should have been watching his furnace

workers to see how they reacted to their new gaffer, but he did not. He could not take his eyes off Daniel Thorpe and his confident swagger that reminded him of himself all those years ago.

It could be me, he thought. History repeating itself. If only Henry had turned out to be like him. There was too much of his mother in that lad. He was always thinking about the way he dressed these days. He was never going to make a proper ironmaster.

He swallowed a quick draught of whisky from his hip flask. This settled him down a little. He turned the key in the office door and went to the safe. The heavy door creaked as it swung open. He pushed aside his money bags and retrieved a thick packet of documents carefully folded and tied round with tape. He stared at it for a long time.

While he was alive the works would thrive. But how could he be sure they would do so after he had gone? He heard voices below, male voices, floating up from the warehouse beneath his office. Making steel was his life. He wanted his only son to reap the benefit of his labours. He had to find a way of keeping the works going after he had gone.

Chapter 5

'We have company for dinner today. What are we having?'

Mariah looked up from the pastry she was rolling out on the kitchen table. Ezekiel rarely came

49

into the kitchen when she and Emma were cooking. 'The butcher sent beef this week,' she replied.

'Got any horseradish to go with it?'

'Emma is just digging up a root in the garden.'

'Grand. You'll eat in the dining room with us today. I don't want our visitor thinking you're a kitchen maid. Make yourself look nice for him.'

'I am still in mourning, Father, and I have only this one gown in black.' Mariah was careful to wear her largest apron over her gown when cooking to avoid any unnecessary splash marks.

He grunted his annoyance.

'Who is your visitor?' she asked.

'You'll see. Be sure we have plenty of cream for the pie.'

'Of course.'

Mariah guessed the company would be one of his lodge friends and hoped Ezekiel would take him to see the ironworks after dinner. She was looking forward to a free Sunday afternoon to get on with her sewing. Emma would be off to see her own family as soon as the table was cleared and the pots washed.

When everything was ready, Mariah carried an oven tin containing a large Yorkshire pudding through to the dining room and Emma followed with the gravy boat.

'By gum, that looks good,' Ezekiel commented.

She slid the crisp ballooning pudding from the tin on a large oval meat plate in the centre of the table and stood back. Henry was pouring ale from a stoneware jug into a pewter tankard and handing it to the visitor. Mr Smith, from the hardware shop in town, looked up at Mariah and smiled at her. Mariah gave him a faltering nod in return.

'Take your pinny off and come and join us, lass,' Ezekiel ordered. 'Mr Smith wants to meet you.'

'I – I have to see to the joint and dish up the vegetables.'

'Nay, lass. We have Emma to do that now. It's Sunday and we have a visitor. Say good day to Mr Smith.'

Mariah bobbed a curtsey in his direction and muttered a greeting. He was a thin bony man with a lined face and knobbly hands. When she looked more closely at him, she thought he might have been almost handsome when he was younger, with a square jawline and eyes set well apart. But now, he looked like a crow, a carrion crow, perched at the dining table with his large hooked nose and his claw-like fingers on the white linen cloth ready to pounce on the food. A black coat, made of good cloth, hung loosely on his scrawny frame. She gave him a small smile. At least the black respected their mourning.

As she removed her apron and gave it to Emma to take back to the kitchen, she noticed his watery blue eyes dart over her, taking in her bright hair, pinned up in coils under a black lace cap. Up and down, his chin moved as he looked her all over until she thought there must have been a tear or something in her gown. His shrewd gaze made her feel uncomfortable as she walked around the table.

'Very pleased to meet you, my dear,' he said, adding with a nod to her father, 'Fine-looking lass, Ezekiel.'

'So I'm told,' Ezekiel answered shortly.

Mariah's heart sank. She wished she could say something similar about Mr Smith. His thinning hair was lank and long at the back. It should have been grey but he had blackened it with some oily substance that was rubbing off, making dirty smears on the collar of his white shirt. He smiled at her again, showing a gap in his tobacco-stained teeth.

Emma had disappeared to the kitchen and Mariah resigned herself to making polite conversation with a stepfather she despised, a half-brother she barely knew and a man whose appearance sent a cold chill down her spine. She knew why Mr Smith was here and she was having none of it! She would be obedient and civil over Sunday dinner, but that was all. They could not make her like him, so he was wasting his time!

All three men watched her as she took her place on her father's left opposite Mr Smith. She cut up the pudding and forked it onto plates. They ate silently for a few minutes, then Mr Smith spoke.

'Very nice, Ezekiel. Your daughter is a decent cook too.'

'Aye. Takes after her mother in a lot of ways.'

'I am sorry about your mother, Miss Bowes,' Mr Smith continued, looking directly at Mariah. 'You must miss her.'

'Yes I do, Mr Smith,' Mariah replied.

'My own daughters, too, have lost their beloved mother. But we have to go on with our lives, do we not?'

'Yes.'

Mr Smith turned to Ezekiel. 'And how are you getting along, my friend?'

'I am well, sir. Henry is home from school as you see. Isn't he a fine gentleman now? He is taking charge of my house refurbishments. I have a supervisor at my ironworks, too. You may have heard of him. He was at the Fitzkeppel works before and was one of their best furnace workers.'

Mariah concentrated on her Yorkshire pudding. She was hungry, having been up at five with Emma to get the kitchen range going for hot water and the Sunday joint. Besides, she was tired of hearing about all the changes at the ironworks and the wonderful Mr Thorpe who knew how to handle the men and was going to make them a fortune from crucible steel. He may be Emma's brother, but he was Ezekiel's underling and she knew very well where his loyalties would lie. Then Henry started on about his new furnishings for their house. Their house. A house bought and paid for with her mother's dowry.

Clearly she was no part of it any more. They had decided her future was with Mr Smith. Well, she was going to have a say in this. Father could not get rid of her so easily. But even as she thought it, Mariah knew he could, for he did not make idle threats. She could not let him sully her mother's reputation. No, the answer was to make sure Mr Smith did not like her. But she had no idea how to do that.

Emma came in and out, taking away the York-shires' plate and fetching the joint and vegetables.

'We always use the same plates for our meat, Mr Smith,' Ezekiel commented as he carved the ribs of beef.

'We do too. The gravy is too good to waste.' Mr

Smith handed up his plate to receive several steaming slices of tender juicy meat.

Mariah leaned forward to pass Mr Smith a tablespoon for the vegetables.

'Did you cook this joint, Miss Bowes?' he asked.

'Yes, sir.'

'And everything else to go with it?'

'Emma helped me with the preparations.'

Mr Smith turned to Ezekiel. 'The late Mrs Bowes did a good job with this one.'

'I told you. She's nigh on twenty years of age and can look after you as good as any house-keeper to the gentry.'

'Father!' Mariah dropped the spoon.

'Steady on, Miss Bowes,' Mr Smith said. His gnarled bony fingers rescued the spoon and he brandished it at her in a friendly fashion. 'I'm looking for more than a housekeeper, y'know.' He paused. His watery eyes began to roam over her again. He added, 'That's a pretty gown you're wearing, even though it is black. A husband likes his wife to look nice when she goes with him to church.'

Mariah's mouth opened to respond but Ezekiel got there first. 'Sews them all herself, don't you, Mariah?'

'Yes, Father.' She resigned herself to being picked over like a heifer at the beast market. She wanted this meal and Mr Smith's visit to be over and done with as quickly as possible.

Henry added, 'Quite a fashionable gown too, Mr Smith. For the South Riding, anyway.'

Her father added, 'I've been telling Mr Smith how clever and thrifty you are. A man with several daughters needs a wife who can be of use to them.'

Mr Smith simply nodded quietly to himself and piled baked potatoes and greens on his plate. Mariah stayed silent. She was inwardly fuming and could not trust herself to say anything civil. The conversation soon turned to how the Riding was prospering and how fortunate this was for their businesses and she was forgotten for a while. She tried to enjoy her dinner, for the meat was very good and the horseradish fresh and tangy. But every time she looked across at Mr Smith's lined and drooping face, large hooked nose and flaccid mouth chewing his food steadily, her stomach lurched and knotted.

Was Ezekiel serious about her marrying this man? He was well over twice her age, though that would not have bothered her quite so much if he had been personable and she had felt an attraction for him. As she grew older Mariah realised her mother had not known love in her own marriage. But Mariah could not imagine ever even liking Mr Smith, let alone loving him. He was creepy. He always stood too close to his lady customers, making them hot and flustered with embarrassment. The idea of him near her made her backbone go shivery and the food become dry and tasteless in her mouth. She sat back and took a swallow of her dinner ale, but did not feel any better.

Emma came in with pudding and cleared away their plates. Her father droned on about the price of coal and transport. Henry told them how an old farmhouse on the road out of town had been bought by a glass manufacturer and was being totally remodelled. They would soon need a larger meeting place for their lodge friends, now there were so many gentlemen of means moving into the Riding. Mr Smith drank and ate heartily, and looked at Mariah for a good deal of the time. She was more than ready to scrape back her chair after the apple pie and say, 'I'll leave you gentleman to your cigars.'

'Where will you be, Mariah?' her father asked.

'In the scullery. Helping Emma with the washing-up.'

'Not today, it's Sunday. Bring us another jug of ale and then wait in the study for Mr Smith.'

Mariah nodded silently, stacked the plates and picked up the empty jug. She drew the ale from a barrel in the scullery. Emma would be off to see her family as soon as she was finished at the sink.

'Everything all right with you, Miss Mariah?' Emma asked.

'Yes, of course.'

'You look a bit pale and strained. Was the dinner all right?'

'Yes, Emma, you did very well. Don't forget to take that new bonnet for your mother.'

'No, I won't. Thank you, Miss Mariah. I'll be back just after dark.'

'There's no rush. I'll put out the tea later.'

She carried the ale to the dining room, leaving quickly to return to the kitchen and stack the dried crockery on the dresser. Then she riddled the kitchen fire before banking it up for the afternoon, delaying as long as possible the inevitable time when she would have to wait for Mr Smith in the study – the room which had once been her mother's special place. She rehearsed what she would say if he offered for her hand today: I thank you for your attentions, sir, but I am unable to return your affections and therefore, in fairness to your good self, I must decline your offer.

Short. Civil. She hoped he would accept her decision and not make a fuss with Ezekiel. There would be enough of that after he had left. Perhaps she would try and explain to her father that she was not against marriage, but that she wished to have a say in who her husband would be.

The study had a carpet on the floor now, a fancy one, imported from the Orient, with a beautiful pattern of exotic birds. The whitewashed walls, too, had been covered with embossed wallpaper giving the room a more sombre appearance and making it look smaller. A few pieces of drawing-room furniture had been moved in and although a fire had been lit, the room was distinctly chilly after the warmth of the kitchen.

Henry had arranged for a carpenter to make mahogany bookshelves and a large desk with a leather top, which would fill the remaining space. Mariah conceded that the room would look nice when it was finished. She sat in a comfortable leather chair by the fire and waited. When the door opened, her father came in first. He had his Sunday-best cloak about his shoulders, with his hat, gloves and cane in one hand. Henry hovered behind him, also dressed for outdoors. Mr Smith was directly behind them and came straight into the room.

Mariah stood up quickly. 'Where are you going?'

He ignored her question and said, 'Mr Smith wants to talk to you. You be nice to him, Mariah.

Do you hear me?'

'Yes, Father.'

Ezekiel pursed his mouth and gave a very slight nod. She doesn't look too happy about this, he thought, and she can be stubborn, that girl, just like her mother. He'd never understand women. Mariah ought to be fawning at Mr Smith's feet. He was a well-set-up family man with money in the bank. His business was good, he had a decent house to live in and was not overly fond of the drink. Perhaps he *was* a bit old for her but, by all accounts, he could still keep her well satisfied in the bedchamber. Proud of himself in that department, Mr Smith was.

Ezekiel wondered if Mariah was like her mother in that respect as well. Amelia must have lusted after men, the bastard was testament to that. And she had wanted *him* in the bedchamber. At first, any road. Well, he was giving the bastard a better life than her mother ever had with regard to that. She should be grateful to him.

'Henry and I are taking a walk,' Ezekiel said, 'we'll be back for tea.' When he saw the alarm in Mariah's eyes, he added, 'You'll not come to any harm with Mr Smith. Will she, Mr Smith?'

'No, sir. I'll look after her for you.'

Ezekiel closed the study door as he left and a moment later Mariah heard the heavy thud of the front door slamming. She remained standing, acutely conscious that she was the only person left in the house with Mr Smith. He stood in front of her and held out a small object wrapped in calico.

'This is for you, Miss Bowes. Best that Sheffield makes and very popular with my ladies in the

58

shop.' He spoke carefully, as he did to his best customers. It was an affected way of talking that did not help Mariah to like him.

Mariah's heart sank. She wished she could say she did not want any gift from him, but did not know how, and, anyway, her father would be angry if she refused it. His hand jutted out further.

'Go on, then. Take it.'

Reluctantly she did and unwrapped the calico carefully. It contained a pair of scissors, brand new, with long sharp blades. They were not fancy but well crafted and would be very useful for her sewing. She appreciated the thought. She hoped he would not take her refusal of matrimony too hard.

'D'you like them?' he demanded.

She nodded and put them on a side table. 'Yes, sir. Thank you, sir.'

He seemed to relax. He crossed the room to the fire, turning his back to it and lifting his long jacket to warm his rear. Mariah felt the room become even cooler as he blocked out the heat.

'Well, sit thissen down, lass. We 'as ter get ter know each other proper like, now.'

Her eyes widened in alarm as he so readily made himself at home in their study. She had not detected such a strong local dialect when he spoke at dinner. But then, that was before he had drunk several tankards of ale. She backed away towards the door.

He raised his voice, 'We'll have no running away now, shall we? Where's there to go, any road? You heard what yer pa said. You 'as ter be nice ter me. So why don't yer sit down here, like

59

the good lass you are, an' we can talk.'

Talk? Yes, talk. In a civilised way, and then he would see the nonsense of it all. She wondered if her father would give her a beating for turning down Mr Smith's offer. Her father had never thrashed her when she was growing up. Not a proper thrashing with a belt or a beating with his cane, though he had slapped her when she answered him back.

'Well?'

Slowly, she returned to her chair, pushing it back a little to increase the space between them.

After a short silence, Mr Smith remarked, 'That wa' a fine dinner you put on today, lass.'

'Emma did most of it. And we are a small family.' She paused. 'Not like yours, sir. I shouldn't fare very well in a large household, I'm sure.'

'Yer don't have ter put yerself down. What tha' dun't know, tha'll learn soon enough. Tha'll 'ave to, wi' my lot.'

'How many children do you have, Mr Smith?'

'Too many now their ma 'as gone.' He grunted sourly. Then he appeared to think better of his comment and added, 'But that dun't mean I'm against having any more. Young lass like you, there'd be no problem wi' that.' He stopped and coughed.

Mariah held her breath as her cheeks went hot; she did not know where to look. She kept her eyes on her hands folded in her lap and examined the signs of wear in her black mourning gown. It would soon be past repairing.

Mr Smith coughed again, loosening the phlegm in his throat, and then turned around to spit into the fire; the coals hissed and sizzled.

Mariah saw her chance. 'But I could not care for your family properly, Mr Smith. I have never looked after children or been a nursemaid or anything like that. I would be of no use to you, sir. You need a wife who has had her own infants and knows what to do.'

'Nay, lass. All mine are growing up now. The youngest is nigh on eight and the eldest lad is older than you. Got a lass, too, your age, so you'd have some company when me and my boys were at the shop all day. And the lasses'll help wi' the cooking an' the scrubbing.'

'But I wouldn't know what to do for such a lot of you! There were just the four of us and Henry was away at school for most of the time. I would be a disappointment to you, Mr Smith. Truly, I would not do for you.'

'Aye. Yer pa said you might need a bit o' persuading.'

Mariah's mind raced. What had she rehearsed in the kitchen? The words had flown from her mind, but her feelings had not: she did not like Mr Smith, let alone love him.

She inhaled deeply and looked up at him. 'Mr Smith, I am ... er ... privileged you should consider me in this way, but I do not return your compliment. I have no feelings for you, sir.'

'Feelings fo' me, is it, that yer lack?' He stared at her so intently she was obliged to return to examining her skirt. The silence lengthened until, eventually, he moved away from the fire and picked up the coal tongs.

'T' fire needs making up, lass.'

He stretched out his arm and handed the tongs to her.

He did not give her much room to get by him and her full skirts brushed against his legs as she moved towards the scuttle at the far end of the hearth. His head was on one side and he was smiling at her. She caught a whiff of the ale he had drunk and the cigar he had smoked at dinner.

She leaned over with one hand on the mantelshelf to pick up the coal. As she bent to her task, she was startled by the rough touch of a bony hand reaching up her skirts and over her stockings and garters. Quickly, his fingers moved upwards and under the leg of her drawers to grasp the soft exposed flesh of her thigh.

She dropped the tongs and coal in surprise and attempted to turn round. 'Mr Smith! What *do* you think you are doing?'

'What does that do fer yer feelings?'

She could barely believe this was happening to her. She struggled to break free, but he held her by her waist while his fingers continue to press into the naked skin of her leg. He was a surprisingly strong man and she was thrown off balance, only just saving herself from a nasty blow on the corner of the mantelshelf.

'Let go of me!'

He ignored her plea and tightened his arm about her waist, pressing her against him so she could feel his hot breath on the back of her neck. 'I can show you how ter 'ave feelings fer a man. You need have no worries there. A fine well-grown lass like you and not yet wed at nineteen years of age. It's not right, that.'

62

'Mr Smith! Take your hands off me this minute!'

'Oh, tha' 'as ter say that. All maids 'ave to say that. But I know better. I know tha' likes it all the same.' He made a soft grunting noise in his throat.

'No, I do not! I insist you let me go this instant!'

'Ee, fiery little thing, aren't yer? Don't you fret none, my little maid, I'll not hurt thee.'

Mariah raised her voice. 'I am not your little maid. Get away from me at once! At once, I say!'

'Yer won't be saying that if yer stop yer struggling. Yer got some pleasures to come wi' me, I can tell thee.'

'Lord, no!' she cried out desperately 'Never! Take your hands away. You are too forward, sir, and you mistake my meaning. How can you ever think I should want you to...' She could feel the heat of the fire on her face and Mr Smith's thin hard body pressed up against her back as he held her so tight she thought she might faint. How dare Ezekiel leave her alone with this vile man? She coughed and choked in her anger and tried to kick his shins with the heel of her boot.

The groan in his throat turned into a chuckle. 'Tha's got a bit to learn yet, lass, if tha' gunna wed me.'

'Wed you? I haven't said I'll wed you!'

His voice took on a serious edge. 'Your father has, though, and that's good enough fer me. We don't want ter be wasting no time, do we?'

Ezekiel had already promised her to him? No, it was not possible, she had not agreed. She hated this horrible creepy man forcing himself against her and breathing down her neck. She tried again to push away his hand but his fingers continued to play with the skin of her thighs, stroking and squeezing as he said, 'Ee, lass, that dun't half feel good to an old widower like me, let me get me other hand round thee an' all.'

'Get off me! Help me someone! Get him off me!' She made a futile attempt to lean further away from him. The glow of the fire was beginning to burn her cheeks, but the heat was nothing compared to the hatred she felt for Ezekiel and this man. And Henry! He, too, had left her alone to endure this humiliation. She hated all of them!

'Steady on,' he muttered. 'We don't want yer falling in t'fire afore we're wed, do we? Come over 'ere where we got more room.' He pulled her away from the fire, removing his hand from her thigh, but he did not let her go. Roughly, he turned her around so she was backed against the study wall.

Her cap had come loose and her hair was beginning to fall from its fastenings. This man, truly, must have lost his senses and she feared what he would do next. She raised her voice. 'Mr Smith! You must not touch me. My father will be very angry! I have told you I am not going to marry you!'

Again he chuckled, a low growling sound. 'Ee, yer pa didn't say I'd 'ave a fight on me hands. We don't want ter be scrapping now, do we, lass?'

'No, we do not.' Mariah sighed thankfully. He stood squarely in front of her. He was so close she could feel his breath fanning her forehead.

'Well now, that's better, isn't it? I know what you young 'uns need. I'm not that old I can't remember what young lasses like you want.'

Mariah's breath was coming in shallow bursts. He had no idea what she wanted! Certainly not him. She had refused him clearly enough, so why could he not accept that and then all this would be over? Her father would be disappointed but, surely, *surely*, he never really believed that she would marry Mr Smith?

'Y-you said we should talk,' Mariah suggested. 'Shall we sit down?'

Mr Smith seemed to recover his composure a little, but he did not move away from her. He said, 'No, no. We're best off here. You thinks 'cos I'm an old man, I'm past it, don't you?'

'No, it's not that.' Flustered and embarrassed, Mariah said the first thing that came into her head, 'I do not love you, Mr Smith.'

'Not yet, you don't. And I understand that. A young maid like you needs a bit o' learning when it comes to love.'

'It is not your age, sir, it's just that—' Oh what is the use, she thought, he had made up his mind about her and would not listen to reason.

'If we are to be wed, it's on'y natural that yer wants ter know what yer getting.'

She was puzzled by his change of tone. 'Well, yes,' she answered, 'that is why we have to talk. But I have already given you my answer, sir.'

'Yer don't know me yet.' He smiled lopsidedly. 'Y'ought ter try out the goods, proper like. I promise yer, yer'll not be sorry.'

'I don't understand what you're talking about.'

'Oh, I think you do.'

As she caught the leer in his eyes, she suddenly did understand. Oh God, no. Was this what he

65

meant by getting to know one another? Her mother had warned her that some gentlemen could be very persuasive and give all kinds of reasons why they should lie with you before they wed you. But Mariah had not been interested enough to ask her questions at the time.

It was now very clear to her what Mr Smith wanted. He wanted to lie with her to show her he would not fail her in the marriage bed. Dear heaven, she thought despairingly. If she were wed to him, his failure in that respect would be her only salvation! She could never give herself to a man she did not love, and she could never love Mr Smith.

Her rage and resentment simmered. How could Ezekiel do this to her! Did he know how Mr Smith would behave and had no care for her feelings at all?

'No, sir, you misunderstand me. I mean it when I say you must not touch me! Step away from me at once!'

'Just look at them eyes flashing at me. And that wild hair o' thine. By gum, I'll bet that looks a treat when it's spread across the pillows. Well, don't thee worry, lass, I can keep thee satisfied like a young 'un. An' if tha dun't believe me, I'll show thee.'

'No! Let me go!' she wailed desperately 'What are you doing to me?'

But he was not listening to her. He hardly seemed aware that she protested. He was breathing heavily and there were beads of sweat on his brow. His words came out rushed and anxious, 'I'm on'y gunna show thee, lass. Don't fret theesenn so. Gi' us thee hand.'

'No!' She flung her arms above her head, but he forced one hand down to where the front of his breeches bulged with his need for her.

'Feel that, then,' he breathed 'as hard as a young 'un's and a grand big 'un, even though I do say it mesenn.'

His fingers began to fumble with the buttons on his flap. Shocked beyond belief she squeezed her eyes tight shut. She had to get away!

Trapping her with his arm, he pushed his body against her again and again and muttered incoherently under his breath. She squealed and then her voice sank to a grunt as she desperately tried to yank herself free from his grasp. Her stomach, full of Sunday dinner, knotted into a lump and she thought she was going to be sick all over him.

'Get away from me, Mr Smith. I do not want you near me and I shall not marry you!'

But he did not seem to hear her and, when she opened her eyes, his face had slumped into slackness and his eyes were half closed and glittery. His body ceased its rhythmic movements and he released his grip on her, but he was grasping at her skirts as though he were holding them for support. His breath was coming in short gasps and then, quite suddenly, he let out a strangled groaning sound and relaxed his hold.

Horrified and shocked into stillness, she held herself rigid as he fell flaccidly against her. He groaned again and then whispered, 'Tha'll not want for owt when tha weds me, lass.'

She struggled from his grasp and ran out of the room, through the kitchen and scullery, across the

67

back yard and past the ironworks to the scrub land next to the canal until her legs were tired. She could still feel Mr Smith's breath fanning her face, hear his panting and smell the ale and tobacco on him. Exhausted, she slowed down and coughed. It was then that she noticed the sticky damp stain on her skirt and she retched on the rough grass.

She wished desperately her mother was here. She would never have let this happen. She would have spoken up for her, made Ezekiel understand. What on earth was she going to do? She could never marry Mr Smith. He was a coarse, vile man and she hated him. She shivered in the cold and wished she had snatched her shawl before she fled. She was determined not to return before Mr Smith had left.

She waited until daylight began to fade before going back home and crept in the back door. Hurriedly, she lit a lamp in the scullery and poured water from a ewer into a bowl. She had to get the stains out of her gown before anyone saw them. As she mopped at them with a cloth, a dark patch of water spread over her skirt. She prayed that the marks would be gone when it dried.

The house was quiet and she hastened through to the hallway. Her foot was on the bottom stair when the study door opened.

Ezekiel called out loudly, 'Get in here this minute, Mariah. I want an explanation.'

The fire was dying and he had already lit a lamp. His face was like thunder. Mariah breathed in raggedly. Best get this over with, she thought.

'What do you think you're doing? Mr Smith came here courting and you throw it in his face.'

'I do not want to marry him.'

'I'm not having this. I'll not have it round the town that my daughter disobeyed me, do you hear?'

She stood silently in front of him.

'Nothing more to say for yourself? Too ashamed, are you? I should think so, running off like that!'

She took a deep breath. 'Father, he tried to ... that is he...' She started again. 'He showed me no respect.'

'Rubbish! He told me about that. He was courting you, that is all! Good God, woman, he will be your husband within the month. He has a right to court you!'

Mariah had no idea what Mr Smith had said about his approaches towards her, she simply replied, 'I cannot marry him. I cannot.'

'Don't talk daft! Silly woman! You'll want for nothing as his wife. And he is keen to have you, so you *will* wed him. You'll wed him as soon as the banns are read.'

'Don't make me do this, I do not love him,' she pleaded.

Ezekiel's anger simmered. 'Not love him? You will learn to love him. Besides, you don't know what love is!'

'I know you did not love my mother and she suffered from it.'

'What about me?' he yelled. 'Didn't I suffer too, from being manacled to that whore?'

'Don't call her that!'

'Why not? It's what she was! She came from a good family, well off they were, and she carried a

69

miner's bastard.'

'You may call me what you will, but my mother was a faithful and dutiful wife to you and I think your own good name in this town would suffer if you sullied her memory with your accusations.'

His silence told her that she had scored a hit. Respect was everything to Ezekiel. He must realise that ruining his wife's reputation, or indeed his daughter's, would have a damaging effect on his own standing in the Riding. Mariah bit her lip and wondered if she had gone too far. She became nervous of his mounting rage and turned to leave the room.

'Don't you turn your back on me!' His heavy hand struck her across the head, knocking her sideways. 'I haven't finished with you yet,' he went on. 'You will do as I say and wed Mr Smith.'

She rubbed her stinging ear and scalp, but stood her ground.

'No, I shall not.'

He hit her across the face with the back of his hand. Her head spun. She stumbled and fell against the door, sinking to her knees. She felt a hot trickle of blood running down her cheek.

'Don't you dare disobey me! I'll not have it. I'll not be the laughing stock of the Riding. Get up on your feet and listen to me. You'll do as you're told and wed him or it'll be the belt for you until you agree. D'yer 'ear me?'

'Yes.'

'Good. Now get off up to bed and think on what I say.'

Mariah sat in the dark for a long time. The cut below her eyebrow was small, but her face and head were smarting. The damp spot on her gown had dried but, in the light of a candle, the stain was still evident. She had to get it out before Emma saw it and asked her what it was. As she remembered how it got there, the corners of her mouth turned down and saliva ran into her mouth. She felt the vomit rise in her gullet. She could not face another moment in the company of Mr Smith. Nor could she continue to live in Ezekiel's house. He did not want her here and she had no wish to stay. If she left she was sure he would consider his own interests first and not spread the truth about her birth; he had too much to lose. She should leave before he locked her in and beat her into submission. Tonight perhaps. Or tomorrow. She had to go soon. But where could she go? And how would she survive?

Chapter 6

'But our Daniel is moving in today! Mr Bowes said he would be eating with the family and I'm making meat and 'tatie hash. I want you to meet him, Miss Mariah. You'll like him, everybody likes our Daniel.'

'I know, Emma, and I am sorry. I cannot stay. He may be your brother but he is Mr Bowes' works' supervisor. It would not do to draw him into my affairs, so it is best that I do not meet him.'

'You had a row with Mr Bowes last night, didn't you, Miss Mariah? I heard him shouting at you when you got back in from your walk. It doesn't mean you have to go, though, does it?'

'I am afraid it does. I shall stay up here until Mr Bowes has left for the works. Is he at breakfast now?'

'Yes. Master Henry was there, too, all dressed up to go out.'

'That's good. He is usually gone all day. I'll wait until they have both left and then carry my boxes downstairs. Are they coming back for dinner?'

'No, not until teatime. Mr Bowes said to take a jug of ale and two meat pies over to his office at dinner time.'

'Two meat pies?'

'One for our Daniel.'

'Oh yes, of course. Do you think you'll manage here on your own?'

'I should hope so! There's eight of us at home to look after.'

Mariah grasped one of the rope handles to test the weight of her mother's old travelling box. She had packed it, determined to move out immediately. 'We can manage this down the stairs between us. I'll leave it in the wash house and come back for it later.'

'What about the other one?'

'It's got those gowns in for your sisters. Perhaps Daniel could take it to your mother's on one of the carts?'

Emma tested the weight of the second box. 'We could carry it down home together. I'll make the pies first thing and take them to the works on our way. Then I can show you where I live and you can meet my sisters.'

'All right. I'll make the pastry for you.'

When they were putting on their cloaks to go out, Mariah stood for a moment in the kitchen, looked about her and said, 'I shall miss this house. But it is not a home for me any more. I cannot come back here.'

'Where will you go?'

'I shall take lodgings in the town. I have a little money from selling my baby linen. Mother made some beautiful things for me and Henry when we were infants. She was saving them for her grand-children, but Henry did not want them and I, well, I am sure it will be a long time before I have any infants.' She added wistfully, 'If ever.'

As she said this, Mariah felt a pang of regret for her actions and vowed that if she did have any children, she would make new baby linen, just as beautiful as those tiny gowns she had been forced to sell.

Emma grimaced sheepishly. 'You don't have to leave today, Miss Mariah. You can creep back up to the attic. Mr Bowes won't know.'

'Henry would! His bedchamber is right under-neath mine. No, Emma, I do not wish to stay here. I am no longer wanted as part of this family and Mr Bowes' ideas for my future are not to my taste. I'll find lodgings for tonight and look for a position somewhere.'

As Henry had so clearly pointed out to her, she could cook and sew. There must be suitable work for her somewhere. But her immediate problem would be finding lodgings that would take her in as an unmarried woman with no male companion and no obvious way of supporting herself. Word would soon spread that she was Ezekiel Bowes' daughter, so if she stayed in town he would, no doubt, drag her back to avoid a scandal. She might have to travel to Sheffield or even further. She began to feel anxious about the small amount of money she had.

'But where, Miss Mariah?' Emma repeated.

'Emma, I am no longer your mistress. You need not call me Miss Mariah now. Mariah will do. Just Mariah.'

'If you say so, Miss – if you say so, Mariah.'

The two young women smiled at each other, heaved up the tightly packed box by its strong rope handles and set off for Canal Bank Cottages. The Thorpe family lived in the middle of a terrace of little houses with long back gardens that went down as far as the towpath. They belonged to the canal company which leased them to the local pit owner for his colliers. They were situated next to a foundry that had prospered and expanded and was now surrounded by a high brick wall with iron gates opening onto the towpath.

The foundry had bought the land behind the cottages and built a large store for its heavy iron output, effectively cutting off the cottages from the town. The only way to market was through the narrow alley between the works and its warehouse. Mariah shivered in its dankness as they clattered down the slope. At the bottom of the alley lay the canal with its constant traffic of bar iron, coal and manufactured goods from furnaces and forges. On the opposite side of the water she could see scrubland, more ironworks and, in the distance, gentle hills that led to the Fitzkeppel and Grassebrough estates.

A soft breeze rippling the water surface cheered Mariah. It whirled playfully around rows of vegetables in the cottage gardens on her right. To her left, in front of the foundry, the towpath gave way to a stone cobbled wharf littered with spilled coal and pieces of rusting iron. The wharf provided good overnight mooring for any passing barge on its way upstream through the water meadows to Sheffield. A pair of huge cart horses plodded by, diligently drawing a tandem of laden vessels bound for the Tinsley basin.

The scattered spoil crunched under their boots as they walked and Emma explained that Mr Thorpe's bad cough had stopped him from working down the pit and he would have had notice to quit his cottage if the mine had needed men. But the thin coal seam was nearly worked out and the pit owner was laying workers off so, as long as they paid the rent, the Thorpes could stay.

They staggered through a squeaky gate and up a long brick path in the middle of a garden. The path widened into a yard outside a lean-to scullery at the back of the cottage. They stepped into a busy noisy kitchen that seemed to Mariah to be full of squabbling children. Mrs Thorpe stirred a blackened cooking pot over the fire. Mr Thorpe sat in a rocking chair by the fire, humming softly to a fractious infant who was wailing pitifully in his arms. The rest of the room was filled by pushing and shoving children.

Mariah, used to a much bigger house, was stunned by so much activity in such a small space. She realised quickly there were only three other girls apart from the baby, it just seemed like so many more as they crowded around the box wondering over its contents.

After very brief introductions Mrs Thorpe took charge of the chaos. 'Meg, help our Emma take their cloaks and that box through to the front room. There's no space in here for it. Liddy and Lizzy, you two set the table and no squabbling.' She turned to Mariah and smiled. 'You'll join us for some broth, will you?'

'Thank you. I'd like that.'

The front room was small, neat and tidy with a couch, an old polished table and a bed in one corner. The bed was covered with a counterpane that matched the window curtains. Emma and Mariah set the box on the fired-clay floor tiles in front of the hearth.

Meg took their cloaks and laid them over the couch. 'What's in the box?' she demanded impatiently

'Meg, be quiet! It belongs to Miss Mariah.'

'Oh, but it concerns all your sisters, Emma,' Mariah responded. 'Shall we show them now?'

'Ooo, yes, yes,' Meg squealed.

They unpacked the gowns and draped them over the bed and table. Meg, who was just ten and growing fast, stared at them for a while and then approached warily and fingered the skirts. 'Are these all yours, Miss Mariah?' she asked quietly.

'They were. Which one do you favour?'

'This one, I think. No, this one. Or maybe that one over there, or...'

'Stand over by the window where I can see you properly.' Mariah looked steadily at Emma's

younger sister for a minute. 'I think the red woollen one will need the least alteration and the
colour will suit you. What do you say, Meg?'

'Really? For me?' She picked up the red gown,
held it in front of her and danced around the
room. 'Oh, thank you, Miss Mariah.'

'Mariah will do, Meg. Just Mariah.'

Meg stopped and looked at her older sister who
gave her a nod.

The front-room door opened and Mrs Thorpe
stood in the doorway with her hand on the knob.
'I wondered what was taking you so long.' She
gazed at her front room as Liddy and Lizzy, who
were close behind her, darted underneath her
outstretched arm.

'Look, Mam!' Meg, still holding the red gown,
twirled around.

'It's beautiful,' Mrs Thorpe commented, raising
her eyebrows at Emma.

'I've been helping Mariah to clear her mother's
workroom,' Emma began to explain.

Mrs Thorpe turned to Mariah. 'I was very sorry
to hear about your mother, Miss Bowes. She was
a kind and gracious lady. You must miss her very
much.'

'I do.' Suddenly overcome by the warmth that
pervaded this household, Mariah's grief rose to
the surface. Tears filled her eyes and she sank
onto the edge of the bed. 'Did you know her?'

'I met her once, when I took Emma along to
start work. And I saw her in the market place
occasionally. You too. You were often admired for
the cut of your gowns.'

Mariah's voice shook a little as she pulled

77

herself together. 'Thank you, Mrs Thorpe. I – I thought these might be of some use to your daughters. One or two are hardly worn and I can easily alter them to fit.'

Mrs Thorpe looked around her front room again. Emma was already wearing one of the gowns and it really did suit her. Meg, clearly, had set her heart on the red one and Liddy and Lizzy were watching anxiously for their mother's reaction. She said, 'I usually make alterations myself–'

'As a gift, Mrs Thorpe,' Mariah added hastily. 'Emma has been such a help to me, I should like to give something in return.'

'Very well. Thank you, Miss Bowes. Your gowns are most welcome.'

'Perhaps you would care to choose ones for Liddy and Lizzy now, and then Emma can pack the rest away for another day?' Mariah suggested.

'You are very kind. I shall leave the choices to all of you. Dinner is almost ready.' Mrs Thorpe returned cheerfully to her kitchen.

Lizzy and Liddy, at seven and eight were almost the same size and tussled over a checked cotton gown with pretty ribbon insets on the bodice until Mariah intervened.

'It's far too big for either of you,' she said. 'Besides, you need something warmer for the winter. The brown ones are much more serviceable.' She searched in the bottom of the box. 'When I was little I put these lace collars and cuffs on for Sunday school.' She arranged them on the gowns and added, 'I'll show you how to attach them, if you like.'

This seemed to please the younger girls and

they dashed off with their choices to show their father. Emma and Mariah exchanged a smile and re-packed the box, stowing it under the bed.

'Have you decided where you are going to sleep tonight?' Emma asked.

Mariah shrugged. 'I don't think a lodging house is a good idea.'

'Me neither. You get all sorts in them. Why don't you go back home? Make it up with Mr Bowes.'

'Never. I can't do that, Emma. Please don't ask me why.'

'But you'll be on the streets!'

'Who will be on the streets?' Mrs Thorpe was standing in the open doorway.

Emma jumped up. 'Mam! I didn't know you were there.'

'I came to tell you the broth is ready. Now, who will be on the streets?'

Emma gave Mariah a hurried glance, 'Mariah. She's got nowhere to sleep tonight.'

'Emma! Be quiet about it.'

'Is this true?' Mrs Thorpe asked.

'She's had a row with Mr Bowes and he's turned her out. That's right, isn't it?'

'Mrs Thorpe, please believe me, I did not know Emma was going to tell you this.'

'My Emma tells me everything, lass. Has he really turned you out?'

'Not exactly. But he has made it impossible for me to stay, I'm afraid.'

There was an awkward silence until Mrs Thorpe said, 'You'd better come through for your broth, now.'

As they walked past the bottom of the stairs to

79

the kitchen, Emma said, 'I can't stop, Mam. I've got to get back and put the tea on for Mr Bowes. Mariah will stay, though, won't you?'

'Of course she will. She has already said so,' Mrs Thorpe responded. 'Sit down, dear.'

Emma left through the back door and Mariah joined the girls at the table. Mrs Thorpe ladled her meaty soup into earthenware bowls and handed them round.

Mr Thorpe, who had been gently rocking his youngest to sleep, got up and laid the infant on the chair to doze by the fire. 'Well, Miss Bowes,' he said, 'I'd like to thank you for your kindness. I've never seen my little girls so pleased with theirsenns.'

'It's a pleasure for me, Mr Thorpe.'

Mrs Thorpe finished serving and said, 'Arthur, things are difficult for Miss Bowes at home.'

'Oh aye? It's nowt to do wi' our Daniel, is it?' he responded.

'No, Mr Thorpe,' Mariah replied. 'It's between me and my father.'

'Well, we know about Mr Bowes and his ways, lass. Our Em 'as told us.'

'We'd like to help you if we can,' Mrs Thorpe added. 'I won't see you out on the streets.'

''Ave yer nowhere else ter go, lass?'

'Well, no, but–'

'That's settled then,' Mrs Thorpe concluded. 'You can have our front room. What do you say, Arthur?'

'You're more than welcome to stop with us, lass. We're only working folk, though. I were a coal miner afore the cough took me down.'

'I know, Mr Thorpe,' Mariah replied. 'My father was a coal miner, too.'

Mrs Thorpe's eyes widened. 'Mr Bowes was a miner? Oh! I didn't know.'

'No – er, I mean, er, I should explain...'

'Either he was or he wasn't.'

Mariah considered her position. She had left Ezekiel's house for good and there was no going back. He was glad to be rid of her, she was sure, and she reasoned that if she stayed silent, so would he in the interests of his own reputation. But she could not lie to these good people. Nor did she wish to compromise their livelihood, vested in their only son at Bowes Ironworks.

She said, 'I think everyone in town will know soon enough that Ezekiel Bowes and I have quarrelled. They will not know why and I am sure they will talk. If I am to stay here then you should know the truth about me. But only if you promise to keep it to yourselves. I mean that, Mrs Thorpe, because, well, it's about my mother and I do not want her memory sullied. I would rather folk think ill of me.'

A silence fell round the kitchen table. Mr Thorpe broke it by saying, 'That's a fine speech you made there, lass.'

Mrs Thorpe looked wary. 'We're good-living folk here, miss. We may be poor but we don't have no time for idle chit-chat.'

Mariah looked straight into Mrs Thorpe's eyes and said, 'Then you should know everything about me before you allow me into your home.'

Mrs Thorpe frowned slightly and addressed her daughters who were being unusually quiet and

81

listening intently to the conversation. 'Liddy and Lizzy, if you've finished your broth, wash your hands and go with Meg into the front room to try on your new gowns. Arthur, why don't you take the little one upstairs to her crib?'

All three girls left dutifully and Mr Thorpe carried the sleeping child upstairs.

Mariah began. 'Ezekiel Bowes is not my true father. My true father died before I was born. My mother's family – er – persuaded him to marry her when she was carrying me to avoid a scandal. Now that Mother has passed on he no longer wishes to support me and I have nowhere to go.'

Mrs Thorpe sat down. 'Well, I'll be. Has he really told you to leave?'

'Not exactly. He has decided that I shall marry Mr Smith from the hardware shop in town. Mr Smith wishes that also, but I do not.'

'Mr Smith! Nay, lass, he's far too old for a young lady like you!'

'His age would not be such a great concern to me, if – if I cared for him. But I find his ways so – so repulsive.'

She saw Mrs Thorpe watching her intently as she said this and looked down into her empty bowl. Mrs Thorpe said, 'His ways around the womenfolk are well known hereabouts. I wouldn't wish him on any o' my girls.'

'Quite. My father has insisted that I obey him and marry Mr Smith so I have left his house. I would rather make my own way in life – if I can. But you do understand that, for the sake of my mother's memory, I do not want people asking too many questions?'

Mrs Thorpe nodded. 'Aye, I see that all right. But you've got your own reputation to think of as well. Folk round here can be spiteful, I can tell you.'

'I shall understand if you do not wish me to stay in your home.'

'Nay, lass, none o' this is your fault. Not your mother's neither, and I should know. I know how men like their way with womenfolk. I've had more babbies than I can count on me fingers and my Arthur still hasn't lost his liking for the bedchamber – if you know what I mean. Sorry, miss, if I've made you blush, but some men are like that. And I fall for a babby as easy as blinking. I'm lucky I've got my sister over at Keppel to put me right, else I'd have had even more. What happened to your real dad then?'

'He was killed in the pit.'

'Round here?'

'No. My mother came from the North Riding. Mr Bowes too.'

'Have you thought of going back there?'

'They made Mr Bowes swear not to return.'

'That's families for you. I couldn't do that to any of mine. Mind, as soon as they're old enough, I do drum into each o' my girls not to let any man near 'er afore she 'as a gold band on her finger.'

My mother said the same to me, Mariah thought. Though, apart from that dreadful Mr Smith, she had had little opportunity. Nursing her mother and looking after the house had been a full-time occupation and the only gentlemen she met were delivery boys from the butcher and grocer in town. Even her father's labourers were kept well away from the house nowadays. If Mariah went down to the works she was only allowed in his office, which was over the warehouse and away from the furnace. How could you start a courtship on that basis? Assuming that I wanted to, Mariah thought grimly.

She began to fret. She had no regular income and she could not impose herself on the Thorpes for more than a night or two. They were overcrowded as it was. She had a small amount of money that would pay for a few weeks in a decent lodging house. But when that ran out, she would need some kind of work to pay for rent and board or she would end up starving. Or in the poorhouse. Or, heaven forbid, really on the streets! She had seen it happen to other women who had become destitute through no fault of their own. For the first time in her life she realised why there were so many ladies of the night frequenting the ale houses in town. They had no other option. It didn't bear thinking about.

Mrs Thorpe watched her closely as she fretted. Miss Bowes was her mother's daughter, a good, kind woman who did not deserve the grief and unhappiness that she had suffered. She said, 'You are welcome in this house for as long as you wish, Miss Bowes.'

'I am most grateful. I should like to stay. Thank you.'

Chapter 7

'How do I look, Henry?'

Ezekiel Bowes stood quite still as his son walked around him slowly and silently.

'Well?' He ran a forefinger inside the stiff collar that cut into his neck. This was the most uncomfortable part of his evening dress. But the shoes, the dress shoes that Henry had insisted he wear, felt like a pair of slippers. Their shiny patent leather was featherweight in comparison to the heavy boots he wore at work.

Henry took his hand and examined it closely, turning it over and running his palm over the hardened skin and rough edges of the nails. He gave a sigh. Ezekiel snatched it away.

'What's up? They're clean, aren't they?'

'Keep your gloves on, Father.'

'I can't do that! Not to eat my dinner!'

'Then try and keep them out of sight. Bow your head to the ladies with your hands behind your back.'

'I know about that, lad. I have been to grand dinners before.'

'Not at Fitzkeppel Hall, you haven't.'

'No. I grant you that. I wasn't good enough for them when old Fitzkeppel was alive and this young 'un 'as never tekken an interest in local folk before now.'

'If you mean Master Nathaniel,' Henry

85

responded stiffly, 'he is only just one and twenty. If this evening goes well, there will be other invitations to the Hall.'

'Aye, well I 'ope he knows there's nowt wrong wi' a bit of muck under your fingernails,' Ezekiel muttered sourly.

Henry sighed again and corrected him. 'Nothing wrong, Father. Nothing.'

'There'll be other ironmasters there? And engineers? I want to know more about these crucible furnaces.'

'You will be acquainted with some of them from the lodge. I expect you will be seated next to one of their ladies. Do remember to converse with the ladies on both sides of you at dinner.'

'Do I have to?'

'Yes, you do!' Henry sounded irritable. 'Speak to the one on your right for the first course and then the one on your left for the second and so on. And try not to talk about the ironworks. Ask them about their sons and daughters.'

Ezekiel groaned. 'I don't know why we have to have womenfolk there at all. We don't have 'em there for dinners at our lodge meetings.'

'This is different. You can talk about the ironworks when the ladies have left us to our cigars and port.'

The evening wasn't the ordeal Ezekiel had anticipated. The first part wasn't, anyway. The men there were better placed in the Riding than his usual business friends. These were forge and factory owners, not the usual shopkeepers and dealers he knew from the lodge. His lawyer was there, too; Abel Withers was chairman of the parish poorhouse board and Fitzkeppel was his major benefactor.

'Good evening, Mr Withers.'

'Mr Bowes! A very good evening to you, too. Is that young Henry over there?'

'It is, sir. He has finished with schooling now and is joining me in my ironworks. I am thinking of moving into crucibiles.'

'Indeed? We should have a talk. Not here, of course.'

'A talk? What about, Mr Withers?'

'Your will, Mr Bowes. Henry is not of age, yet. You need a trust for him.'

'A trust? I don't know anything about trusts.'

'As I said, we should talk. Come into my office next week.'

Ezekiel nodded thoughtfully and moved on. Lawyers could be useful when you wanted 'em. There was a churchman there, too. That new one who had been at Amelia's deathbed. At her funeral as well.

'Good evening, Vicar,' Ezekiel said politely as he shook his hand and attempted to move on straightaway.

'Are you well, Mr Bowes?' he asked.

Ezekiel nodded

'We never see you in church on a Sunday, sir,' the vicar added, holding on to his hand.

Ezekiel's back went rigid and he pulled his hand free. Quickly, he took up a glass of sherry wine from a footman and walked to the other side of the anteroom. It was a small oval chamber, over-crowded and uncomfortably warm. He swallowed the wine, hoping to push down the memories with it. He saw the vicar watching him and hated him for it. He hated churches. He grew hot and angry as he remembered – it was all so long ago.

He took another glass of wine from a passing silver tray held aloft in a white gloved hand. He was hardly aware of going in to dinner. There was an old lady on his arm and they followed the procession. She seemed to know where to sit and he was next to her. He was glad to see the vicar was seated at the other end of the table and he calmed down.

My, he thought, the dinner table was laid out fit for a king. Well, I suppose you had to say fit for a queen now this young Victoria girl was on the throne. The polished mahogany glowed and the lead crystal sparkled. This is where young Henry was getting his ideas from. He caught his son's eye as another footman pulled out a chair for him, and smiled. Henry smiled back and settled nearer to young Mr Fitzkeppel at the top of the table.

Ezekiel was next to the hostess, *Miss* Fitzkeppel. She was Fitzkeppel's older sister, Henry had told him. Well, he couldn't ask *her* about her sons and daughters. She smiled at him and he gave her a stiff bow before he settled in his chair.

'Tell me about your ironworks, Mr Bowes,' she asked.

So he did and she seemed genuinely interested when he told her about his new supervisor and plans for expansion into crucible steel. He talked so much his soup went quite cold.

The old lady on his other side was Mrs Withers, the lawyer's wife. Her father had made his brass years ago through the Canal Company. He was dead now, though. Just as well, seeing as the railways were taking most of the canal transport. She prattled on all through the fish about her sons at university. Ezekiel did not care for the pike stuffed with chestnuts and he was glad when a footman took it away so he could turn back to Miss Fitzkeppel.

The wine was plentiful and strong. An elderly butler carried in a roast haunch of venison and carved it at the sideboard, layering steaming slices on plates that were hot to the touch. Ezekiel liked a good joint on his own table and he relished this feast. A footman served him currant jelly and gravy; the meat was well hung and tender, the best he had ever tasted. Henry was right. This is where they should be. Dining with the gentry.

After the ladies had left for the drawing room, he moved up the table to sit with the other gentlemen. The glossy wooden surface was littered with broken cobnut shells and smears of ripe Stilton. Fitzkeppel's old butler brought round a box of cigars and Ezekiel took one, passing it under his nose to inhale the aroma. The conversation became more interesting and he engaged with his companions about the price of coal and iron and how much money there was to be made in smelting steel.

Fitzkeppel and Henry looked bored and Ezekiel noticed them exchanging glances. He resigned himself to the fact that Henry would never have a real interest in his furnace. He wished he was more like young Thorpe in that respect. But his son's schooling had not been wasted; Henry was already making powerful friends in the Riding. Besides, the profitability of his ironworks was safe in Thorpe's hands.

The vicar was on the other side of the table and he tried several times to catch Ezekiel's attention. He managed to avoid his eye until the vicar stretched across with the decanter of port. Ezekiel fumbled as he took it. The churchman nodded briefly and smiled, making him feel hot and uncomfortable. After that he concentrated on his port and withdrew from the conversation. He had had enough of this. He wanted to go home.

Memories had been stirred and he struggled to suppress them. He was torn between wanting to remember and the pressure of needing to forget; to put it all behind him. He wished he was back in his works yard, labouring with his gang, not here, not dressed up like the butler, making polite conversation with the gentry and their womenfolk.

'You went very quiet in there, Father,' Henry murmured in his ear as they went upstairs to the drawing room. The ladies looked rich and beautiful all together in their silks and satins, drinking coffee out of tiny gilded cups.

'I'm tired, lad,' he explained. 'It's all a bit of a strain.'

'Take some of the coffee, then.'

'Aye. I think I will.'

Ezekiel hoped no one would notice him, alone by the window. He had to do this, to be here, to be part of Riding gentry. He was going on all right until that new vicar – oh no, he was coming over–

'Mr Bowes,' the vicar began, 'please allow me to apologise to you. I had no wish to upset you earlier. I was merely making conversation.'

'I am not upset,' he replied stiffly.

'Forgive me, sir, I believe you are. You are, perhaps, of a different persuasion.'

'I am of no persuasion, sir.'

Clearly, the vicar did not believe him. 'You are not comfortable with my Church I take it. Are you, perhaps, of the Jewish faith?'

'I was baptised in the Church of England.'

The vicar looked surprised. 'But you no longer worship with us? I should know if you did.'

'I do not wish to talk about it, if you do not mind.'

'But I think you should. Clearly, my presence here causes you much concern.'

'How would you know what concerns me?'

'It is my calling, sir. As making iron is yours.'

'Steel, actually.'

'I beg your pardon.'

Ezekiel stared at him uneasily He wasn't gentry because he wasn't a rector. Old Fitzkeppel never had a brother or a second son, so there was a stipend available for a vicar. Ezekiel gave him a curt nod and turned away. His evening was ruined. He hated himself for allowing his past to intrude like this, for not being able to put it completely out of his mind. That vicar was shrewd, though. Shrewd enough to spot a troubled soul when he saw one.

He felt the man's eyes on him as he moved about the room and was thankful when the first carriages were announced. Henry had arranged for them to travel with a glassmaker who lived at the far side of the Riding and they talked of trade and politics during the ride home. But Ezekiel felt unsettled as he prepared for bed.

Long after the house was quiet he lay awake. That vicar knew something, he was sure. No, how could he? He had come here from the south of England and Ezekiel's past was in the North Riding. No, the past was dead and gone; it could not be revived. But as he lay in bed he realised he wanted to remember. He wanted to relive the agony, because there had been joy among the pain. Forbidden joy, wicked joy and sometimes, just sometimes, he wanted to go back.

He turned restlessly in his bed, unable to sleep. Finally, he lit a candle and went downstairs for a sleeping draught, shivering in his nightshirt and felt slippers. He poured a few drops into a glass of port and tossed it to the back of his throat.

That should work, he thought. That should take away the memories and allow me to sleep.

'I'll take those in for you, Em.'

Daniel had come into the kitchen from the works yard as usual to wash and change into his jacket for breakfast. He had been living in the Bowes household for a few weeks now and had settled well. He carried the warmed platters of fried eggs and toast into the dining room and placed them on the sideboard next to a heated chafing dish of kidneys and mushrooms.

'Good morning, Mr Bowes. Henry.' He nodded in their direction. 'Shall I put some of this on a plate for you, sir?'

'Aye.' Ezekiel was dressed as he was, in tough moleskin trousers, flannel shirt and thick jacket, an indication that he planned a day in the yard.

'Two eggs?'

'Aye.'

'Henry? How about you?'

Henry was in his dressing robe. It was an ornate affair of heavy wool, edged in braid and with a gold embroidered crest on the breast pocket. He had tucked a linen scarf around his neck and throat.

'Not now,' he responded tetchily. 'Father and I are talking.'

Daniel handed Ezekiel his breakfast and sat down to his own. He was hungry. He had been up since six o'clock – over two hours ago. As he ate, he glanced at the papers on the table between father and son. They were invoices and not for coal or bar iron. He recognised the supplier's names. These were bills for the changes Henry had been making to the house, for new furniture and carpet for the study and Henry's dressing room.

Ezekiel gathered up the papers and brandished them at Henry 'Well, if you say you have bought these things, then I'll pay for 'em. But it seems a lot o' brass to me.'

'You want the best, do you not, Father?'

'Aye. I do.'

Emma came in with a pot of coffee and poured them all a cup before placing it in the centre of the table.

'Where are my eggs?' Henry demanded.

Emma looked puzzled.

'Boiled eggs,' he added impatiently. 'I want boiled eggs this morning.'

'Very well, sir. They'll only take a few minutes.'

Daniel avoided her eye as she left the dining room. 'The blister steel will be ready today, Mr

Bowes. We can start to cool down.'

'I thought it would be. I'll check it myself first, though.'

'Yes, Mr Bowes. Will Henry be with you?'

Ezekiel turned to his son. 'What do you say, Henry? Do you want to come and learn about what earns the brass to pay for all this?' He stuffed the bills into his jacket pocket and picked up his knife and fork.

'No I do not. I have things to do here.'

'The works will be yours one day, son. At least find out what goes on down there.'

'You buy iron, make steel and sell it to the forges. There, you see. I know.'

Daniel ate silently. The field mushrooms were tasty and his kidney very fresh.

'You know there's more to it than that,' Ezekiel retaliated sharply. 'It won't do you any harm. Put on your outdoor clothes and come down to the furnace with us.'

'My outdoor dress is for riding or shooting. As yours ought to be. I really do not think we should have working clothes in the dining room. The kitchen is a more suitable place for your work-men to eat, surely?'

Daniel put down his knife and fork, picked up his coffee and sat back in his chair. If he had had any respect for Henry Bowes, he might have been offended. But he thought that the boy was an over-educated, underdeveloped excuse for a man and Ezekiel indulged him far too much. A couple of weeks at the furnace face would set him right, thought Daniel. But that was never going to happen.

'I am not wearing a good suit for the yard, Henry,' Ezekiel replied.

'I don't see why not. You don't have to shovel coal any more.'

'I am not a clerk. I am an ironmaster.'

'*He* isn't,' Henry said petulantly.

'If you are referring to Mr Thorpe, he is as good as. Mr Thorpe is my works supervisor and without him there is no way Bowes Ironworks can make enough steel to keep you in the style you require.'

Daniel reached for the butter and kept his eyes on his plate. He didn't want Ezekiel dragging him into this exchange. Neither did he want Henry Bowes anywhere near his furnace, distracting the men with his foppish manner. Besides, he thought Henry was more use doing what he preferred to do, dressing up and hobnobbing with the local gentry.

Emma came in with two boiled eggs and some thinly sliced bread and butter. She placed them on the table next to Henry and smiled at Daniel, who returned her silent greeting cheerfully.

Henry looked at the eggs disdainfully. 'I do not want them now,' he said. 'You have taken so long my hunger has passed. Father, do make haste and pay those bills. I wish to order more furnishings.'

'I shall call on my bankers *after* I have checked my steel,' Ezekiel responded.

Daniel sought to ease the tension between father and son and asked lightly, 'Will your daughter be returning home soon, sir?' A barely suppressed squeak from his sister made him look sharply in her direction and he noticed the alarm in her eyes.

'I have no daughter, Mr Thorpe, and I'll thank you to remember that.'

'Sorry, sir. I thought–' He saw Emma shake her head and stopped.

'She has shamed us both by refusing to marry the suitor that my father has chosen for her.' Henry smiled. 'We are glad she has gone, aren't we, Father?' He stood up, took two pieces of the bread and butter and left the room.

'Shall I pour you more coffee, Mr Bowes?' Emma asked, reaching for the pot.

Ezekiel nodded. 'Mr Thorpe, while I am down in the yard today, I'd appreciate your opinions on the siting for a crucible shed.'

'Right, sir. I have been thinking about that. We've got to leave space to get the drays round.'

They discussed the layout of the yard as they finished breakfast. Afterwards, Ezekiel went upstairs to fetch his outdoor coat and Daniel carried the coffee pot and eggs into the kitchen.

'You said the daughter was away visiting. What's going on, Em?' he asked.

'She's left. They had a terrible argument. It was after Mr Smith came for his dinner. Mr Bowes hit her. I saw the blood on her face.'

Daniel looked shocked. 'Why didn't you tell me?'

'I don't want to cause any trouble. You saw how he was about her.'

'Where has she gone, then?' His sister looked pained and pursed her lips. 'Come on, Em, I ought to know. I don't want to upset Mr Bowes again by saying the wrong thing.'

'Promise me you won't tell him.'

'Of course I won't.'

'You'll find out soon enough, anyway. She's staying with me mam.'

'What!'

'It's true! I took her down there. I knew Mam wouldn't turn her away.'

Daniel frowned. 'Her father would want to know she is safe, surely?'

'Don't say anything, Danny! If he finds out I helped her, I'll have to leave!'

'All right, I won't. But it doesn't seem right for father and daughter to argue like that.'

Chapter 8

'Daniel!' Mrs Thorpe was sitting on a kitchen chair outside the back door, nursing baby Victoria and enjoying the fresh air after a morning spent cooking Sunday dinner. She was delighted to see her only son striding along the towpath to their garden gate. Mr Thorpe was in the garden, too, showing Lizzy how to weed between the bean plants.

'Danny! Danny!' Meg and Liddy stopped what they were doing in the kitchen with Mariah and ran through the scullery into the yard.

Mariah watched them through the small kitchen window and thought what a happy close-knit family they were and how lucky she was they had welcomed her as a friend. She had been there for several weeks now and this was the first time

Daniel had come home. Emma came down when she could, with money and a message that he was busy at the works learning his new job and would see them soon. She also carried messages for the widow in the end cottage, but no one else knew about those.

Mariah had settled well in these happy, homely surroundings. She slept and sewed in the front room, altering her outgrown gowns to fit the three older girls, and showed Emma, when she visited, how to make a shirt for her father. Today, all three girls still had on their new skirts and bodices, which they had worn that morning for Sunday school and which were now almost completely hidden by their calico pinafores. However, they still twirled around in the full skirts to show them off to their beloved brother.

Mariah went back to making pikelets for tea in the kitchen. She busied herself at the fire, dropping spoonfuls of batter onto an iron plate over the coals. But she could hear a chink of coins and subdued conversation through the open door.

'Take it, Mother. Get Father what he needs from the apothecary and some of that salve you like for your hands. Emma has sent the extra money for the girls, and here's a bag of spice for later. Mmm, something smells good.'

'It's the pikelets for tea. Can you stop?'

'Not for long. I've got people to see and Mr Bowes is expecting me back for supper. Emma says their Mariah is staying here. Is that right?'

'Aye. She's in the kitchen if you want a word with her.'

'I do.'

He stepped inside and peered into the darkness that contrasted sharply with the bright sun outside. 'Miss Bowes?'

'Yes.' Mariah straightened and turned to him. Her cap was pushed well back from her brow to prevent it scorching in the fire and her face was pink from the heat.

She had not expected him to be so striking. She had imagined him to be a dreary, serious kind of man who had worked hard at his studies to escape being an ordinary labourer and rise to the position of foreman and then works supervisor. She had thought he would be younger, nearer to her own age. But, of course, she realised that a working man did not get to be a supervisor by nineteen or twenty, even of a small works like Ezekiel's.

No, Mr Thorpe was older than that, middle twenties, Mariah thought. Attractive too, she conceded, and not dreary at all! There must have been many a girl set her cap at this one. He was a well-built man dressed in his Sunday best of a brown jacket and trousers, clean white shirt with a high collar and a dark red necktie.

Mariah noticed that his shoulders filled out the jacket well and his dark curling hair grew thickly. In the small cottage kitchen his height and breadth blocked the daylight from the window.

'Daniel Thorpe. At your service, Miss Bowes.'

As he spoke his teeth flashed white against his skin and his deep voice resonated in the limited space. He stood quite straight and gave her a brief bow of the head. She thought it was an incongruous gesture from a working man in the informality of his mother's kitchen but realised he was rising in the world and learning the ways of his betters. She appreciated his civility; it made her feel valued and that was something she had not felt since her mother had died. That is, until she came to live with the Thorpes.

She returned his compliment with a smile. 'Sir.'

For a moment they simply stared at each other. Mariah wondered what it was about him that she found so attractive. He was handsome, to be sure, but then so was the traveller from Leeds who came to the market, and she did not find him particularly attractive. Mr Thorpe was different. He had an air about him she could not fathom. It was an air that appealed to her, and she warmed to his presence.

She still held the spoon and bowl, now empty of pikelet batter.

He stepped forward. 'Shall I take those?' He removed them and carried them into the adjoining scullery, reflecting on his surprise. So that is Mariah Bowes, he thought. He had expected her to be dark, like her father and brother, not – not this young woman with the remarkable colouring. He supposed that Emma or his mother must have mentioned her to him at some time. But he and his father were often discussing other things when his sisters chattered on and he probably had not listened.

He had first seen her years ago, when he had started his night-school studies at the Institute. A young girl, out with her mother at the end of the working day, seeking bargains from the market stalls. Who would not notice hair the colour of burnished copper? He did not see her often, for there was no reason why their paths should cross. But on rare occasions, when his eye caught a glimpse of flame beneath a bonnet, he took a second glance and recognised her features.

Latterly she had visited the market alone and now he knew why. Why had he never made the connection? He knew of Mariah Bowes' existence before he went to work for her father, but not that she was this fiery-haired girl he had noticed grow into a comely young woman.

'I'm afraid I have interrupted you,' he said.

Mariah glanced at the iron griddle over the hot coals. 'Oh, they're fine for a few minutes.' She wondered how much he knew about her. Since Henry had told her about Mr Thorpe's position in the works, she had asked Emma about him.

Daniel Thorpe had been spotted at an early age as a bright and enquiring boy, learning to read at Sunday school and, from there, invited to join a group of boys tutored by the preacher. He had gone out to work at the age of ten, though he did not follow his father down the pit. His interest in natural sciences, mathematics and engineering led the preacher to recommend him for a job at the big Fitzkeppel ironworks, and more learning at the local Mechanics Institute where his potential was evident and quickly exploited.

His hard work and diligence impressed Mariah and she admired him for it. As she considered that this might be why she found him so attractive, she experienced a small shiver down her back. It was not an unpleasant feeling, but it was one that was unfamiliar to her.

'Are you comfortable here?' he asked.

'Oh, yes. Thank you.'

'I fear the bed is a little hard.' It had been his bed and it suited him. But he had discovered how much softer feather mattresses were since he had moved into the Bowes household.

'Yes. More than I am used to.'

'I am sorry. I prefer a firm–' He stopped as her face became pinker.

He had embarrassed her by reminding her he had previously slept there. He blinked as his imagination took over and in his mind's eye he saw her at rest in his bed, neatly tucked in with the sheets up to her chin and her brushed and burnished hair spread over his snowy-white pillow. For a moment it was an image he savoured until he mentally rebuked himself. He swallowed, trying desperately to think of something else to say.

Mariah felt herself blushing and raised the back of her hand to her brow. 'Oh, it's so hot by the fire. Shall we sit?'

'May I speak with you on a personal matter?' he asked as they pulled out chairs from the table.

'Of course.' Something about Emma, she guessed.

His expression became serious. 'I did not know that you had left your father's house until I asked Emma where you were. She told me you had quarrelled with him. I am sorry about that, Miss Bowes.'

'Oh!' She had not considered the conversation would be about her and became alarmed. 'Does my father know I am here?'

'I do not think so. He has not asked Emma about you and she has not told him.'

'Then he truly does not care what has happened to me.' Mariah got up and went back to her pikelets, testing them lightly with a knife.

'Oh, I'm sure that is not so!' Daniel responded with concern in his voice. 'He is a hard taskmaster, I know. And proud. No father would want his daughter to disobey him.'

'He has said that I disobeyed him?'

'No, he has not spoken of you at all. I – I heard about Mr Smith's visit from Emma.'

'What did she say to you?'

'Very little. Only that you argued with your father after Mr Smith left and that she brought you here.'

'She did not say why?'

'Henry mentioned you had refused a suitor. I can only guess it was Mr Smith.'

'It was,' she said over her shoulder.

Daniel blew out his cheeks. He wouldn't have wanted any of *his* sisters saddled with Mr Smith, no matter how prosperous he was. 'Perhaps Mr Bowes will relent when he has had time to consider your objections?'

Mariah remained silent.

'It is not unknown for fathers and daughters to disagree. Fathers and sons, too.'

Mariah heard a sigh in his voice as he spoke the last few words and glanced at him. Was he referring to Henry? Or to himself and Mr Thorpe? He was frowning at her, in a sympathetic, appealing way, as though he really cared for her welfare.

He added, 'I am sure your father will welcome you back if you can mend the differences between you–'

103

'No, sir, you are wrong. You do not know him.'

'He is your father. He wishes only the best for you.'

'Then why does he not seek my return? I shall tell you why. It is because the best for me – and him – is for us to stay far away from each other. He knows that and so do I.'

'Surely this is some misunderstanding?'

'No. He will not own me. Of that I am sure.' She took a thick cloth, moved the pikelets to a cooler spot on the range and returned to her chair.

'Miss Bowes, please reconsider,' he begged. 'I have your father's confidence. I believe he will listen to me and I can speak for you if you will let me.'

'Do not trouble yourself. It is of no consequence to me because I shall never return to that house while he lives there.'

This seemed to shock him and he responded quickly, 'Those are harsh words, Miss Bowes.'

'Ezekiel Bowes is a harsh man! I have told you he will not own me. He wanted rid of me and I have obliged him!'

It occurred to her that, although he was a Thorpe and the Thorpes had been good and kind to her, he was also Ezekiel Bowes' right-hand man. His first loyalty after his own family would be to his employer and therefore she could not count on Mr Thorpe as a friend.

She asked bluntly, 'Has he sent you to speak on his behalf?'

He answered her with an equal frankness. 'Of course not.'

She sensed she was annoying him with her forthright manner and did not want to cause unpleasantness in this cheerful household. She had a sincere respect for Mr Thorpe's concern, but she did not wish to recall those last unpleasant days with Ezekiel. She felt an urgent need to close this conversation before she became more agitated.

'Do not be drawn into my affairs, Mr Thorpe. They are not of your doing and I am capable of dealing with them myself.' She would like to have felt as confident about the latter as she sounded.

She saw a flash of anger darken his grey eyes. He did not speak for a second or two. His mouth pursed slightly, then he nodded briefly. 'As you wish. I trust you will be safe and well here.'

'Thank you. I am sure I shall. Your family are good people.' Mariah returned to the fire and slid the cooked pikelets onto a warm metal plate.

The appetising smell brought the rest of the family in and they all sat around the table eating the still warm tea bread spread with honey Daniel had brought from town.

Shortly after tea, he stood up to leave. 'Miss Bowes, I am pleased to have met you at last. Should you change your mind about your father—'

'I shall not,' Mariah replied firmly. She saw Mr and Mrs Thorpe exchange a glance and added, 'But I thank you for your trouble.'

Mrs Thorpe put her hand on her son's. 'Do you have to go so soon?'

'I – I–' Daniel glanced at his father, 'I have some plans to read for tomorrow. Mr Bowes has already started to build new furnaces – crucibles, to make better steel – and you know how things are. I'll call next Sunday if I can.'

As he left, Mariah collected up the knives and plates and took them into the scullery to wash up. Mr Thorpe began to wheeze and cough and Mrs Thorpe went to the cupboard by the range for his linctus. 'Calm yourself, Arthur. He's a grown man and can take care of himself.'

'It's still not right.'

'Arthur, be quiet! The girls are listening.' Mrs Thorpe waved a hand in their direction. 'Meg, take the little ones and give Mariah a hand with the pots.'

When they had gone she said, 'Leave it, Arthur. He is a single man and she is a widow.'

'Then he should wed her!'

'Perhaps he will one day.'

'Not while he can have his way wi'out. All that we drilled into our lasses about wedding afore bedding and he goes an'–'

'Keep your voice down. They'll hear you.'

But Arthur was not to be quietened. 'He lets hissen down when he goes there. I'm right proud of our Danny for everything he does apart from that.'

Meg had closed the door after her when she went into the scullery and the clattering of pots effectively prevented Mariah from hearing the details of this exchange.

'Take no notice,' Meg sighed, 'they're on'y going on about our Danny and Mrs Cluff in the end house.'

Mariah wondered who Mrs Cluff was and why his father was so upset by her. Was this what Daniel had meant earlier about fathers and sons disagreeing? Mariah tried to concentrate on her

106

task. It was none of her business yet she wanted to know more and this irritated her.

Later, as she went through to the front room with Meg to do some sewing, she could not look at the bed without remembering Daniel's conversation earlier. She was unable to forget that this bed had been his. Where she slept, his body had also rested and her pillow had once supported his head. The image filled her mind and unsettled her. He was a man she could not ignore. He was an achiever, a man to be reckoned with and one she found attractive in spite of his allegiance to Ezekiel. She busied herself with shirt seams and pondered on this dilemma.

Chapter 9

Daniel Thorpe was in a pensive mood as he let himself out of the back door of his parents' cottage and turned towards the end house. The differences between Mr Bowes and his daughter ran much deeper than he had imagined. Emma's concern was justified. She, like him, hated arguments in the family. He had tried to help, but there was little he could do if Miss Bowes was unwilling to accept his support.

He reflected on her strong will, a quality he admired. She intrigued him with her forthright ways, but he considered she had acted foolishly. However, she was safe with his family; he felt easier in his mind about her when he remembered that. He feared she was right about her father. If Mr Bowes ignored her wishes so readily, then he did not hold his daughter in very high esteem. Coming from a close and loving family himself, Daniel found this difficult to comprehend. But if father and daughter were determined to oppose each other, he could not see a solution.

He walked down the garden along the towpath and through Mrs Cluff's untidy garden to her back door. How different Mariah was from Lily, he thought. Where Mariah was proud and independent, Lily was compliant and clinging. He could not imagine Mariah behaving towards him as Lily did, but he found himself imagining what she would be like if she did. He had to rein in his thinking sharply and compose himself before he rapped on Lily's back door. Lily would be waiting for him and, tonight, he wanted to talk about their future.

Now he was in charge of the old cementation furnace and looked forward to making crucible steel he knew Ezekiel Bowes would soon be a wealthy man. And Daniel knew, also, how much Ezekiel relied on him for that success. His son Henry was no use at the works, and never would be. Henry was more concerned with spending his father's money on fashionable clothes and buying new furniture for the house than with the price of bar iron and coal. Ezekiel was becoming more and more like his son now, dressing in fancy waistcoats and going to dinner with the gentry.

Daniel shook his head as he thought about his employer. Henry Bowes might be able to pass himself off as a gentleman, but Ezekiel had little chance. The man was too rough round the edges and had an abrasive nature. He was not happy with himself somehow, Daniel thought. Ezekiel was a man who was closed up to others, as though he was keeping himself on a short leash. Perhaps, he thought, he had a foul temper on him and had to control himself in front of others.

Still, a fine house, even one next to the iron-works was welcome when it came to impressing customers. New crucibles meant new trade and new money. And the more money Daniel could make for Ezekiel Bowes, the better he would be paid for his labours.

Strange, he thought, that Mariah Bowes was so different from her father and brother. She had no artificial airs and graces and possessed a kind of courage about her that was unusual in a woman. His mind slipped back easily to their meeting earlier that day. Interesting woman, Mariah Bowes, Daniel thought, I should like to know her better.

He grinned to himself. But perhaps not in the way he knew Lily! Mariah was not a bit like Lily. Soft, submissive Lily who had no hidden depths and whose mock surrenders he relished. He raised his clenched hand to knock on Lily's door and it opened in front of him.

'Danny! Oh Danny, I thought you would not visit me any more, now you are living over at Bowes.'

'And why would I not call on you?'

'I thought you would not have the time.'

He took her pretty face, framed by light brown curls and white lace, in his hands and kissed her on the lips. 'And leave my little Lily all alone on

Sunday afternoons?' he asked, drawing out a parcel from his jacket pocket. 'Look, I've brought you some satin ribbons from town.'

Lily took the small package and opened it excitedly, dropping the frayed muslin wrapping on her kitchen floor. 'Oh,' she breathed, 'they are such a lovely blue.'

'To match your beautiful eyes.' He smiled. He looked into them and thought they were, indeed, the prettiest eyes in town.

Suddenly, he was hungry for her and stooped to kiss her again, this time more urgently. He felt her body open to him, curvaceous and yielding, and he wanted her. He gave a low growling noise in his throat, probing her sweet delicious mouth with his tongue.

She made a slight, squeaky noise in her throat, her own familiar, feminine protest that she knew excited him and he felt his arousal pushing inside his Sunday best trousers. Her delicate fingers crept around his neck and climbed through his thick dark hair, tangling and teasing it at the roots.

She pulled away from him tantalisingly. 'Oh!' she squealed softly. 'You are such a wicked man, tempting a poor defenceless widow woman with your charming ways!' She twirled across the room, her full skirts lifting slightly as she moved, so he caught a glimpse of a shapely ankle and a felt slipper. She wore no stockings and the sight of her naked white skin inflamed his passion further. Lily was such a perfect name, pure white and delicate, a flower waiting to be plucked and adored.

'Temptress,' he breathed, darting across the room and catching at her small hands.

Again, she twisted and swirled away from him, opening her china-blue eyes wide in mock fear and simpering, 'Oh, sir! You mean to have your wicked way with me!'

This always made Daniel smile, because they both knew she had been the one to seduce him on that sultry Sunday afternoon last summer when he had been stripped to the waist in the garden and she had called for his help to open an upstairs window. The window was warped and had been stuck fast for years, but he offered to return and repair it the following week and that was how it had all started.

He caught her again, pulling her hard against his body, taking her chin in one strong hand and capturing her mouth again. She slipped away from him through the door to the stairway dividing the two small cottage rooms. He knew when he climbed the stairs after her she would be waiting for him, her eyes as hungry as his.

The bedchamber was quiet, its window shut tight against the gathering dusk and the only sound was their laboured breathing as he peeled away her gown and she unbuttoned his shirt. When he was naked, his muscled labourer's body tense with desire, Lily lifted her chemise over her head and stepped out of her drawers so they stood face to face, as naked as Adam and Eve in their own private paradise.

He marvelled that she understood his needs. He liked to wait, to prolong the pain of passion, until he could barely contain himself. It made their eventual union all the more pleasurable. She had taught him that, as she had taught him how her

111

own body worked up to that same level of desire.

She stood before him, lily white with a skin as delicate as petals. Her full breasts drooped towards a small rounded belly, and, as she turned towards the bed, her plump behind made his fingers curl with the desire to grasp that soft white flesh.

He stretched out beside her on the wide bed and she fondled him, smoothing on the sheep's gut cundum for him. He kissed her breasts and belly and explored her hot wet hunger with practised fingers. He knew that when her arms or legs made those small involuntary jerks she was ready for him, and that, before long, she would abandon any control and be his to tease and tempt until neither could restrain their passion any longer.

His name came from her throat as a strangled cry, and her body convulsed in an arching spasm. He pulsed inside her, closing his eyes and relishing every second of exquisite pleasure, until they lay side by side, spent and sweating in the gloom. Her arm was flung across his body. He took her small left hand in his and fingered her slender gold band.

'Do you still miss him?' he asked.

'I used to. But not since I met you,' she murmured.

'How long were you wed before – before you lost him?'

She hesitated. 'Well, I were wed at sixteen so it must have bin twelve year.'

'That long? And no children?'

'He – he were away from me a lot of the time, wi' 'is brother and their lad. Working on the railway line took them all over.'

He kissed her lightly on the lips and asked, 'Do you love me, Lily?'

'What kind of question is that for a woman lying beside you in a bed?'

'No, I mean more than this. I know we are good for each other like this, but do you love me as a man as well?'

'Of course I do! What woman wouldn't? You are strong and handsome with a good job and a regular wage.'

He pushed her away playfully. 'So it's my good job and regular wage you love?'

'You know it's not!'

'What is it, then?'

She stroked his hard chest, roughened with hair and drew light fingers down over his firm flat stomach to fondle him gently. 'It's this,' she said quickly 'It's being with you like this. I need you, Daniel.'

They were two of a kind, he thought. She craved the possession of his body as he did hers. He wondered whether it would be enough for them together.

'Could you live with me?' he asked.

Lily sat up promptly. 'What is this, Daniel? What do you mean, "live with you"?'

'Well, I'm earning good money now. And it's two years since you were widowed, you could wed again if you wanted.'

Lily looked surprised at first and then wary. 'Are you asking me?'

'Yes,' he replied firmly. 'Marry me, Lily. Make all this legal and respectable.'

'I couldn't! Er – that is–' Lily stuttered. She

shook her head. 'I thought you just wanted – well – just wanted this.'

'We live in a small town. We cannot carry on as we are. People are beginning to talk.'

'Is that why you want to marry me? Because now you're a fledgling ironmaster people might talk about us?'

'I am worried about you,' he snapped. 'Folk round here know about us and they can be hard on women they see as sinful.'

Lily was quiet. All the other women in Canal Bank Cottages were wives and two of them were her age. But none of them spoke to her in the street and even Mrs Thorpe ignored her. But she did love Daniel.

'I didn't know you thought like that about me.'

'You know I love you.'

'Well, you say you do when we do this, but–'

'If you were prepared to walk out with me on a Sunday afternoon, others would see that I do!' He was becoming irritated with her. He was five and twenty. He had a future in this town and she was a childless widow. He had thought she would be pleased he was prepared to offer for her. But she was shaking her head.

'I can't do it. I can't marry you.'

'Why ever not?' he demanded.

She looked desperate, almost frightened, and he began to wonder what her husband had been like to her.

'It's – it's too soon after... It's just too soon. My brother would not approve.'

'You're thirty years old, for God's sake! Who is this brother of yours? Let me talk to him.'

'He's – he's my – my late husband's brother. He looks out for me.'

This was the first Daniel had heard of him and he became alarmed. 'Is he some kind of benefactor to you? Or does he want you for himself? Do you have an understanding with him? Is that it?'

'No. Nothing like that. He has his own wife and grown-up son.'

'What then?'

'I told you, he looks out for me. He's family.'

'You're independent, Lily. You said your husband left you money.'

'A little. His brother looked after me at first but I – I had to get away from – from the memories.'

'So? I can look after you now. I can pay your rent. Why don't you let me do that for you?'

'Oh no! You can't do that!'

'Why not? If we love each other and we are going to wed–'

'But we're not. If you paid my rent I would be a–!'

If she could not bring herself to say the word, he would say it for her. He did not understand why she had rejected him and he was angry with her. If she did not love him she ought to say so. But he knew she did love him, so why wouldn't she marry him?

'Whore?' he finished for her. 'Is that what you mean? If I pay your rent, it makes you a whore? Well, let me tell you something, Lily. Every time I visit you I leave you money for food and coal! And if you don't love me, if you don't care for me, then that does make you a whore!'

'Stop it! I do care for you, I do love you. It's just

115

that we can't – can't marry. Not just yet.'

'I don't understand. There is nothing to stop us. I have a good position at Bowes and it is difficult for me to keep coming down here like this.'

She rolled over and clung to him, her heavy breasts pushing against his chest. 'Don't leave me. Danny! Please say you won't leave me!'

'I don't want to, Lily. But you're making it tough for me.'

'I need you, Danny.' She began to whimper and her wide blue eyes glistened with unshed tears. 'I've done my best to please you. I do please you, don't I?'

'You do. You do. Oh, come here.' He began to kiss her tumbled hair and then her eyes and nose and lips. She had taught him such a lot and he thought she did love him really. Perhaps it *was* too soon for her to wed again? Perhaps her late husband's family felt she needed their protection? Perhaps he had been too hasty? He decided to talk to her brother before he mentioned marriage again.

He began to stroke her skin, tracing the shape of her breasts and waist and the roundness of her rump until she relaxed, then he fondled her between her thighs until she, once again, began the slow climb to abandonment.

It took her longer this time so he pulled her on top of him, watching the rising ecstasy in her face and her sheer pleasure as she controlled their movements. He hoped she would be quick because he wore no protection. She was, and she cried out as she rocked and then flopped back onto the bed, spent and exhausted. She was

116

unaware she had left him unsatisfied but she had forgotten their quarrel and that made him happy.

He could not keep visiting her now he was working for Ezekiel Bowes. There was already too much gossip, and Mr Bowes would not tolerate any scandal. Daniel had a good position and did not wish to lose it.

Besides, he wanted to marry Lily. She was the first woman he had seriously courted. If what they had could be called courting, for she never let him take her anywhere they would be seen together. She was the only woman he had bedded. But she was true to him, he was sure. He would have found out if she had been with anyone else.

He had to wed Lily soon! He would not give her up.

Chapter 10

'That's him!'

Daniel heard the thud of heavy boots behind him as he cut through a narrow alley that led from the canal wharf past the forge. The weather was overcast and gloomy and the track was quiet as the works closed on the Sabbath. High iron gates secured the yard fronting the canal, and a blank brick wall formed the alley boundary.

'What the–!' Daniel turned and was met by two angry men, roughly dressed. They rushed at him with clenched fists, and started to throw random punches at his head and body.

117

Taken by surprise, he shielded his head with his arms until a well-placed fist in the middle of his body winded him and his knees buckled. The younger of the two men grabbed his arms and pinioned them behind him while the other positioned himself squarely for a further attack.

Daniel saw a consuming rage in the older man's eyes and felt a sudden sickening fear. The man drew a knife from the waistband of his trousers and approached Daniel slowly. Terror sent Daniel's pulses racing. These men were not just a couple of drunks looking for sport. They had a killing in mind. But why him? He did not know them. He had not seen them before in town.

'I'll teach you to mess with one o' the Cluff women,' the man growled menacingly. 'You'll be lucky if you can shove your cock in a greased pipe by the time I've finished with you.'

Daniel did not wait to reason with him, or to argue the mistaken identity he was sure this was. His woman was a widow and a willing mistress. Had one of their women been set upon and degraded in some way? Was the ruffian holding his arms a vengeful suitor? He could smell drink on both men and, mistake or not, they meant to do him harm.

He twisted round sharply, bending his strong back to throw his captor off balance, flinging him bodily against the other attacker, following through with a kick that made the younger man yelp with pain. Both men fell heavily on the cobbles and he heard one call, 'Mind the knife!'

Daniel used those few seconds to search around for a weapon, an old fence post, an iron bar, anything to even the odds of two against one. He found nothing and fear gripped his stomach as the ruffians untangled themselves. These were not men who gave in easily. They were a couple of thugs, toughened by the struggles of surviving the harsh world of industry.

Daniel was taller and broader than either of them and did not doubt he could lick each one soundly in a one on one fight. But two of them together? And one of them with a knife! He feared for his manhood if not his life.

He aimed a couple of kicks at both men as they struggled to their feet, effectively flooring them again and shouting, 'You've got the wrong man, mate!' Then he ran for all he was worth along the alley and away from these snarling, snapping villains.

As he ran, he heard one of them call after him, 'We'll get you, Thorpe. We'll find a way. You see if we don't. No one fucks one o' the Cluff women and gets away with it!'

Daniel continued to run, up the hill and away from the canal, his breath coming in fits and starts as he darted across the square to the back of Bowes Yard. He slowed down, breathing heavily as he approached the gates. They knew who he was and they talked of Cluff women.

Lily's husband was a Cluff but he was dead, taken by the fever. The same fever that had robbed him of his own brothers a few years back. It had hit most of the industrial towns. Surely they could not mean Lily? She and her late husband came from Manchester. Besides, she had told him that there was no one else. He let out a sigh. It must be another Cluff. There were a few by that name down Mexton way and somebody had got it wrong.

As he unlocked the gate and let himself into the yard, he reflected that this was a nasty outcome of the gossip about him and Lily. The sooner she was Lily Thorpe the sooner they would still the wagging tongues. He reckoned he could persuade her to wed him eventually. Perhaps he would be firm about courting her more openly, walk out with her on the Sabbath and be proud of themselves as a couple.

He wondered again why she was so against wedding him. Emma constantly reminded him that he was quite a catch now for an ordinary working lass. Women! He was a slave to Lily's body, but he would never understand her reasoning! The thought of her delicious soft curves waiting for him at his next visit to her cheered him as he leaned against the warehouse door to recover his breath before he went into the house.

The following week Daniel had trouble with the old brickwork in the cementation furnace and had to let it cool right down so the fault could be repaired. He stayed at the works all weekend overseeing the repair. He was anxious to have the furnace ready to load again when the men arrived for work on Monday morning. Ezekiel and Henry were at the country-house home of the biggest ironmaster in the Riding and would not be back until after dark. Emma roasted a hand of pork for herself and Daniel and he came in from the works yard to eat it with her at the kitchen table.

'That was very good, little sister,' he said, as he finished off her rhubarb pie. 'As good as our mother's.' He got up from the table. 'Sorry I can't stay and talk. I have to get back to the furnace.'

'Will you be going home for tea?' Emma asked.

'Not today. Here, take this money for Mother and tell Father I'll try and get down to see him one evening after I've got the furnace going again.'

Emma washed the pots, then laid out some bread, cheese and pickles on the kitchen table for Daniel's tea. She saw to the fire, damping it down to keep it in until she got back. Then she cleaned herself up in the scullery and went up to her attic to put on the new gown Mariah had given her and helped her alter. It was made of lovely reddish brown cloth and fitted her perfectly. She twirled around the room making the full skirts flounce out about her, showing her brown boots and thick stockings and the frill on her drawers underneath.

The sky was cloudy again and she needed her shawl to walk down the hill to Canal Bank Cottages. They were all pleased to see her and spent the afternoon talking and laughing in the kitchen. After tea, Emma and Mariah went through to the front room to work on the shirt Emma was making for her father. They wouldn't let the little ones in because they were using the best white linen from the market and wanted to keep it clean. They sewed by the window until dusk, when it became too dark to see the tiny stitches even by the oil lamp.

Emma got up and stretched. 'I must be getting back to put out a cold supper for...' She stopped, glancing at Mariah.

'It's all right, Emma. You can talk about my half-brother and his father without upsetting me. They are nothing to me now. I hope they are paying you well.'

'Ooh yes, Mariah, and Master Henry lets me have Meg in to help clean up while the alterations are being done.'

'Alterations?'

'Mr Bowes is having two big doors made leading from the dining room to the drawing room. And the bedchambers are having paper on the walls! Master Henry has been buying new furnishings and everything. I've never seen anything like it!'

'This is to entertain their new friends, I presume. How will you manage?'

'Oh, Master Henry said they would be getting in a proper cook and housekeeper and I would have to do what she says when she's there.'

'Their new friends must be quite important people in the Riding, then?'

'Oh, yes. They are visiting the Fitzkeppels again today. Fancy that, eh? The Fitzkeppels.'

'Yes, indeed,' Mariah responded wryly. Mr Fitzkeppel was the wealthiest ironmaster in the Riding and owned land with coal underneath it as well as the biggest ironworks in the area, located in a prime spot between the river and the canal. Henry must have worked hard to get such an invitation, for, most certainly, the Fitzkeppels would never have entertained his father.

'I should get back before it's pitch black. I hate going past the forge when it's dark.'

'I'll walk with you to as far as the square. You'll be safe from there.'

'But what about you? You'll have to come back along the towpath on your own!'

'Oh I don't mind that. There's usually a barge moored with a lamp glowing on board and some wife taking in her washing off the bushes. It's just the alley by the works that's creepy. It's so dark.'

'We'd better get a move on, then. You'll need your shawl. It's chilly out.'

The cottages were quiet as families settled in for a Sunday evening around the kitchen fire, reading Bible stories and talking. The end house was different. The back door was open and there was a commotion going on. Two men and a woman were standing outside shouting at each other. The woman was crying.

Mariah slowed and put her hand on Emma's arm. 'Shall we go the long way round?'

Emma peered through the gloom as they passed the end of the garden. 'Ooh, what's going on there? It's not our Daniel, is it?'

'Isn't he at work today?'

'Aye, you're right.' The two girls stopped, unsure of which way to go. But the shouting went on. 'That's Mrs Cluff from the end cottage who's crying. He's sweet on her, you know, our Daniel.'

'We'd better get on. It's none of our business.'

'It might be our Daniel's business. I wonder who those men are? Can you see them?'

'Don't stare, Emma.'

'I can't make out their faces. I expect they're strangers 'cos Mrs Cluff's from Manchester. Our Daniel said she came here to stay with a cousin over Mexton way.'

'Mexton?'

'It's rough over there, isn't it? Danny said it was a distant cousin of her husband and she'd gone there to get over his death.'

'Shush, they might hear you.' Mariah tugged at Emma's shawl. 'We'll carry on this way. Hurry, it's getting dark.'

As they walked by the end cottage, the shouting stopped. Mariah began to feel uneasy. Mrs Cluff was still hiccupping and sniffing, but the men were silent. Mariah kept her head down and her eyes firmly fixed on the dirt path beneath her boots. But she was sure they were watching her. Her and Emma.

Emma's head turned towards the cottage when they passed the garden gate. 'I don't like the look of them at all,' she whispered.

'Just ignore them.'

They hurried along the towpath in silence. Mariah heard a garden gate creak and her heart began to beat a little faster. Then there was a crunch of heavy boots on loose stones behind them. She took Emma's hand in hers as they reached the high iron fencing and turned up the alley towards town.

Mariah thought she would not come back this way. There was another way round. It took longer and came out at the front of the cottages, but it avoided the alley.

'I think they're following us.' Emma moved closer and linked arms.

'No,' she reassured the younger girl, 'they're only taking the same way home, that's all.'

But Mariah's voice shook and, when she looked behind her, she saw the men were catching up quickly. They jostled Emma as they overtook the two women and then stopped, barring their way forward. The two girls backed away until they were hard up against the high brick wall.

'What do you want?' Mariah demanded. 'We don't have any money.'

They were full-grown men but one was thicker set and older than the other. Close up she saw they were ill-dressed ruffians with heavy boots on their feet. The older man bared his teeth and leered at her.

'Well, my lad, I think our luck is in tonight,' he said. 'We got two o' the Thorpe lasses together 'ere. D'y' think we can handle two on 'em?'

The younger man began to chuckle. 'Oh aye, Dad. One each, like.'

Mariah sensed Emma go rigid beside her. Her hand tightened on Mariah's arm and the younger girl said, 'Our Daniel is coming to meet us. He's on his way now.'

The older man stepped closer. 'Your Daniel! Oh aye, we know all about your Daniel. Thinks 'e can tek what 'e likes when 'e likes, 'e does.'

'What do you mean?' Mariah demanded. She sounded much more confident than she felt.

'Don't tell me y' don't know what your Daniel gets up to in t' end 'ouse on a Sunday a'ternoon.' The older man sneered.

His son added menacingly, 'An' we're gunna teach him not to tek what's not 'is. See how 'e feels when it 'appens to 'im!'

Fear stiffened Mariah's back as the men circled them, looking them up and down and moving closer. She released Emma's arm, took her hand

and whispered, 'When I let go of your hand, run for your life and get Daniel. Run as fast as you can, Emma.'

The older man was taking a particular interest in Mariah. He was so close to her that she could smell the stale sweat and grease on his clothes and see his broken, blackened teeth as he threatened them.

'Think you're 'andsome, you Thorpe lasses, don't you? Living in a pit man's house and prancing about in your fancy frocks? Well, we'll make whores o' you like your Daniel's done ter our Lily. You see if we don't!'

Mariah face froze in horror but she saw her chance as the younger man moved away from his father. She dropped Emma's hand and yelled, 'Run, Emma. Now!'

Emma darted between the two men and fled up the alley towards the square. Mariah, confident that their real quarry had escaped, faced the two men squarely and declared, 'You are wasting your time with me. I am not a Thorpe.'

Chapter 11

The younger man swivelled round to run after Emma but his father stilled his progress.

'Let 'er go, lad. This 'un'll do fer starters. We can gi' young Thorpe a warning, like, wi' this 'un.'

'I am not one of the Thorpe sisters,' Mariah said firmly.

'D'y' 'ear that? This 'un lies an' all.' He leered at her. 'We seen yer come out o' the Thorpe 'ouse. We knows yer lives there.' He grabbed her roughly by her arm and dragged her down the alley towards the canal.

Mariah pulled and struggled but was no match for the two of them. In fear of her life she opened her mouth to scream for help. A grimy hand stifled her and the older man breathed in her ear.

'We ain't gunna kill you. There's no fear o' that. We wants yer ter go back to yer jumped-up gaffer of a brother and tell 'im what's 'appened. We wants 'im ter know what's it's like to 'ave 'is sister turned inter a whore. Cos whoring is all you'll be fit fer when we've done with thee.'

As soon as he removed his hand Mariah inhaled deeply and tried to scream again. But this time a corner of her shawl was stuffed roughly into her mouth until she almost choked on it, and then they wound it about her head so she could not see and could barely breathe. They took hold of her arms and hauled her bodily along the towpath away from the cottages.

The hard stone under the toes of her boots told her they were dragging her past the forge loading wharf. Their hands gripped her arms so tightly they hurt. She attempted to struggle free and shout for help but fragments of wool from her shawl caught in her nose and at the back of her throat making her cough.

They pulled her through the scrubby bushes bordering the towpath and she heard her skirts tear on the branches and thorns. Then the ground became softer as they lugged her across

127

the hummocks of the water meadows. It seemed a long way across the bumpy grass until they stopped and she heard the older man say, 'This'll do. It's far enough away to let 'er scream to 'er 'eart's content and nob'dy'll 'ear.'

He sounded out of breath and both men loosened their hold. Mariah took her chance and tried to break free, tearing the shawl from around her head. It was a hopeless attempt. They grasped her skirts and the fabric ripped away further as she fell head first to the ground.

'Eh up, Dad, she's a bit of a fighter, i'n't she? D'yer think she fights dirty like her brother?'

'Maybe she does, maybe she doesn't, lad. Either way we can 'ave usselves a bit o' fun finding out. A man likes a bit o' fighting spirit in a wench.'

They rolled her over on to her back and bent over her, laughing at her cries and attempts to escape and pinning her easily to the cold damp ground. The moon has risen giving an eerie silver light that was reflected in her frightened eyes as she cowered there, terrified of what they might do.

'Handsome woman an' all, i'n't she, lad? A man likes a pretty face to look at when he's fucking 'er.'

'No, please no,' she cried. 'You are mistaken. I'm not a Thorpe. I'm not.' She shook her head from side to side and lifted her feet off the ground to try and kick them as they leered at her. Both men grinned.

The younger one said, 'I'll wager she's a maid an' all. Word 'as it in the tavern that all the Thorpe lasses are maids and will be maids until they wed.'

'This 'un won't be.' The older man's voice had taken on a hard edge. 'An' she'll be lucky if any man wants to wed 'er after we've done wi' 'er. I'll teach that young Thorpe stallion to mess wi' one o' the Cluff women. Tek 'old of 'er arms and keep 'er still.'

'I'm Mariah Bowes. Bowes–' she wailed. But her throat was closing with fear so her voice weakened and they did not hear her. She struggled and kicked as the older man tore away her skirts and pulled down her drawers until she felt the cold night air on her naked thighs and stomach. Her strength to fight was sapping away. She clenched every muscle in her body, drawing up her insides as tight as she could and crossing her legs rigidly as he took off his jacket and unbuttoned his trousers.

His heavy body on hers squeezed her breath out of her lungs. She smelled the oil and grease on the coarse cloth of his waistcoat and the foulness of his breath so close to hers. He did not try to kiss her. He fumbled around his open trousers and then, with both his hands, gripped her thighs pulling them wide apart. Her sinews tightened against him. She tried to push her back into the ground to get away from him as he jabbed at her until he found his way into her. Thorns and nettles scratched and stung her naked skin but it was nothing compared to the pain of his assault, stretching and tearing her virgin flesh as he shoved and grunted and, finally, pulsed inside her until he was spent. His sweating face, roughened with coarse stubble, fell against hers, smothering her cries, which were now reduced to feeble whimpers of protest and pleading with them to stop.

'Thy turn now, lad,' he mumbled.

The younger man tore away the tattered remains of her gown and chemise exposing the full extent of her skin to the elements. He had already rolled down his trousers and he knelt over her, his hands pinching at her breasts and then his teeth nipping at her until she yelped with pain.

He laughed. 'Tha likes it, really,' he said, and probed between her legs with his fingers before invading her as roughly as his father had done before him.

She was past struggling now, worn out by the effort, numb with shock and whimpering with pain. Lord, help me, she cried silently. Lord, where are you? Help me. Someone must be there. Anyone. Please help me. But no one was listening to her in that isolated ditch away from track and canal. No one came to rescue her as they invaded her body and humiliated her in the most brutal manner.

She began to pray they would kill her, for then it would be over. But they had said they would not do that. They wanted her to live, to tell Daniel Thorpe what they had done and why. But she would rather die and wished only for it to end, and for them to leave her alone so she could fade away. She would rather be dead than endure any more of this most personal of tortures.

But endure it she must. She realised they had not finished with her and meant to continue to raid her body, forcing themselves into her, one after the other. The pain and despair brought on tears. She squeezed her eyes tight shut and held her breath. If she stopped breathing she would faint. She hoped, again, that she would die quickly. She did not know how long they were there with her, in that cold wet field, worrying and sporting with her as a terrier does with a frightened, cornered rabbit.

When she roused, she could feel nothing except the heavy weight of a man on top of her and the cold night air on her exposed skin. Her wide-open eyes stared straight up at the sky. There was a moon, bright and silvery, playing hide and seek behind fast-moving clouds. She thought she heard a distant voice calling her name. No, she was wrong. The voice was here, above her, rough and grunting, like a boar on heat. It was not a nightmare. It was real.

He climbed off her and she saw the older man's face, leering triumphantly in the moonlight. Vomit rose in her throat and she twisted her body to spew on the grass. She grasped at the tattered remnants of her gown to wipe her mouth as he bent down towards her.

'Listen 'ere, you little whore,' he breathed menacingly, 'tell that fuckin' brother o' thine that if he don't stay away from our Lily, next time it'll be his *little* sisters.' He buttoned up his trousers. 'Come on, lad. We're finished 'ere now.'

She was dimly aware of them crashing through the hedges, making their way further across the fields, away from the canal and town. The taste of vomit burned the back of her throat, her feet were icy in her boots and cold crept through her veins. Her last conscious thought, lying there alone and in that dark and freezing field, was that, soon, it would be all right, soon she would be dead, and then everything would be all right.

Chapter 12

As Emma ran away leaving Mariah to face the two
thugs alone she heard her protest that she was not
a Thorpe. Mariah could stick up for herself and if
it was a Thorpe they were after, she would be all
right. Even so, Emma was frightened and wondered what all the fuss was about. No matter.
Daniel would sort it out. He always did. Since
Father had come down with the miners' cough he
had been the strength behind their family, able in
mind and body. Emma relied on him to know
what to do.

'Danny! Danny!' Emma ran across the works
yard, past the half-built crucible shed to the old
cementation furnace where two or three men
were standing talking.

'Where's Danny?' she demanded.

'Danny? Who's Danny?'

'The supervisor here.'

'Oh, you mean Mr Thorpe? Sorry, miss, we
don't work here, we're only masons doing the
repairs.'

'Do you know where he is?'

'Inside t' furnace. Checking it out wi' our boss.
Hey. Steady on, you can't go in there. It's not for
womenfolk.'

Emma ran to the base of the huge brick structure and yelled into the gloomy interior. Her voice
echoed through the empty space. 'Danny. Come

out here quick. It's Mariah, she needs your help.'

He loomed in front of her with a lamp. 'What is it, Emma?' he began irritably. 'I've told you before not to come down to the works.'

'It's these two men. They came after us for summat and Mariah told me to run and fetch you. They were rough-looking and said they knew you.'

'After you? Why? What did they want?'

'Summat about you and Mrs Cluff, I think.'

'Who were they?' An urgency began to run through his blood. He hoped they were not the same ruffians who had come after him, but he feared they might be.

'I don't know. Oh, please hurry, Danny. I left Mariah talking to them in the alley.'

'Men like that don't waste their time talking,' he said grimly. He turned to speak to the builder who had appeared behind him. 'I'd better go and sort this. I had a bit of trouble myself the other day. Mistook me for some other man.'

'Get yourself off, then,' the mason replied. 'We've done all we can here for the time being.'

'Right you are.'

Ned stepped forward from the dark interior. 'I'll come with you, Mr Thorpe.'

'Thanks, Ned. Follow me with a lantern. And hurry. Emma, go in the house and stay there. *Do as I say!*' Ned could be trusted. The Thorpes had known him since he was a nipper.

Daniel sprinted on ahead, out of the yard towards the alley, but when he got there he was met by a silent blackness in the narrow passage. He could not see or hear anybody. He slowed to

133

a jog, clenching his fists in readiness. Ned caught up with him by the time he reached the end, where the alley met the towpath. Still they saw no one. The night was quiet apart from the scuffling of animals in the undergrowth and the occasional screech of an owl or a vixen.

'There's a barge moored over there, we'll try them.'

Daniel banged on the cockpit door and the bargeman's head appeared at the open flap. 'Clear off, will yer?' he said, angrily. 'We got youngsters asleep down 'ere.'

He was not one of the thugs and Daniel apologised. 'I'm looking for a young woman. Bright coppery hair. Maybe with two men.'

'None o' my concern,' he replied gruffly and shut the flap.

'Try the other way,' Ned suggested.

'The cottages are that way. Maybe she ran away from them and went home. We'll go there. Hurry.'

Daniel burst into the kitchen of his parents' house. 'Is Mariah here?' he demanded.

'Hey, steady on, lad,' his father replied, nursing baby Victoria by the fire. 'Calm yoursenn down.'

'Where is she?'

His mother replied, 'She went to see Emma up the alley.'

'Yes, I know that! But how long ago?'

'Quite a while, come to think of it. Afore it got dark. Should be back by now. I wonder what's happened to her? Who's that with you, Daniel?'

Daniel inhaled deeply to calm himself. There was no sense in worrying his mother. But he had a nasty feeling in his gut. 'It's Ned from the ironworks. You remember? The poorhouse sent him down the pit when Father was there? We can't stop now, we have to find Mariah. She can't be that far away.'

She was a sensible woman, he thought. But she had a tendency to speak her mind and to deal with things that faced her. If the thugs had threatened Emma because of him, Mariah was likely to have given them what for instead of running off. So where was she now? He hoped to high heaven she had got away from them. But an uneasy fear gripped his stomach. There was something not right about this business. Lily's name had been mentioned. Perhaps she knew what was going on? Perhaps those thugs had taken Mariah there?

Daniel turned to Ned. 'Those ruffians seem to have gone to ground, but I know where they might be and where I can find some answers. Follow me.' He went out of the kitchen door and headed for the end cottage.

It was a long time before Lily came to the door with a candle and when she did he could see why. Her face was bruised and there was bleeding about her mouth. Her delicate skin was blotchy from weeping and her pretty light brown hair was all over the place.

Daniel let out a cry. 'My God, Lily, what have they done to you?'

Lily fell into his arms and began sobbing hysterically. Behind him, Ned exclaimed. 'Did those men do this? They must be evil beasts to take it out on a defenceless woman!'

'We must find Mariah quickly! She may have got away from them and be hiding somewhere in

135

fear of her life. Or–' Daniel stopped, unable to contemplate that they may have treated Mariah in the same way as Lily. 'Take the lantern, Ned, and search the towpath and the alley again. Go all the way back to the works. If you find her, take her to Emma and tell her to stay put until I get back. Make sure the yard gates are locked up for the night. Mariah may have gone there for safety.' Even as he said it, he remembered Mariah's vow never to return to the Bowes' house, but she was sensible, he reminded himself. Clear thinking too. He desperately hoped she was safe. She had to be.

'You gonna be all right on your own, Mr Thorpe?'

'Aye. I think I've found the root of the problem.'

Poor Lily. She was all over him, clutching at his leather waistcoat, weeping and wailing and choking on her words. He held her close, smoothing her tumbled hair. He hoped that if Lily had been their target then Mariah must be safe and that made him feel better. Emma and Mariah had got away from their attackers and the men had come after Lily instead. He took hold of her shoulders gently and held her head away from him so he could see the extent of their beating. His teeth clenched in anger. 'Are they still here? Let me get my hands on them. I'll make them pay dearly for this.'

Lily shook her head, coughing and hiccupping through her sobs. 'Th-they've g-gone.'

'I'll get them back for this, don't you fret.' He pushed her away as carefully as he dare, grimacing at the angry bruising on her delicate features. 'Now tell me, who are these men?'

But he could get no sense out of her as she continued her weeping. He closed the door behind him and sat her down by the dying kitchen fire. He added a few coals and drew up a chair next to her. 'Is this your brother's doing? You have to tell me what's going on. They've been after my sister today.'

This news heightened Lily's weeping to hysteria level again. Daniel got up and rummaged in her kitchen cupboard until he found a small bottle of brandy she kept as a medicine. He poured some into a chipped cup and stood over her until she had drunk it.

When she had calmed he turned up the lamp and took a good look at her, wincing at what he saw. Those thugs had really given her a pasting. He said, 'I'll get some water and clean you up first.'

He took off his waistcoat and did his best with cold water and linen strips, but even the lightest touch on her face made her squeal and recoil with pain. What kind of men were they, for God's sake? he thought.

After giving her another gulp of brandy, he ventured, 'There were two of them, Lily. Two men. They came after me the other day. And now this. Who are they?'

'M-my brother, and – and his son.' She hiccupped shakily.

Daniel frowned.

'He lives in Manchester. But he's – he's come over to – to stay with his cousin. He – he is my hus – late husband's brother. He – he d-does not like me seeing y-you.'

137

'But why not? You must tell me, Lily. Your husband has been dead for two years now.'

She began weeping again and he took her in his arms as tenderly as he could, for they had beaten her about the arms and body as well. These people were not men, they were no better than beasts of the fields! 'Hush now, Lily, my love. Do they want you to marry someone else? Is that it?'

She shook her head against his chest, snuffling wet tears on his flannel workshirt. 'I-I c-can't see you any more.'

Daniel frowned. 'Why not? You're a grown woman. If there is no one else, is it money that's the problem? Do they think I cannot look after you?'

She had finished the brandy so he fetched cold water from a ewer in the scullery for her to drink. 'You must tell me, Lily,' he insisted quietly.

She inhaled deeply, and let out a long juddering sigh, burying her face in the folds of his shirt. Her muffled voice was soft and quiet. 'He's n-not d-dead. M-my husband is n-not d-dead. H-he's in gaol.'

Daniel's arms dropped away from her and he stepped back, horrified, astounded and shocked as a host of unanswered questions seethed through his mind.

'Tell me that is not true.'

She shook her head. 'I-I was lonely and – and I – I missed him.'

'You *missed* him! Your husband is in gaol and you missed him? While he languished in a prison cell, you used me to keep his bed warm? Lily? How could you?'

She flung herself at him, gripping the fabric of his shirt. 'Don't hate me, Danny. I love you. I do.'

'And what about your husband? Do you love him as well?'

'Not like I love you. Honest.'

'*Honest!* Honest? Do you know what that word means? You lied to me!'

'I had to! You would not have come to me otherwise! And we have such fun – we are good together, you and me. Oh Danny, you do still want me, don't you?'

He collapsed into a chair and held his head in his hands. 'Have you any idea what you have done?' he groaned.

No wonder those thugs came after him. And as they were no real match for him they had opted for a softer target in Emma. My God, thank goodness she was safe, for what kind of revenge would they have extracted from her? His anger rose and spilled out. 'You stupid, *stupid* woman!' he shouted.

'I am sorry. Truly I am. I had to have you. I need you–' In the flickering firelight she caught sight of the contempt on his face and stopped mid sentence, adding in a small voice, 'Emma wasn't hurt, was she? Or your other sister?'

'What other sister?' he demanded roughly

'There were two of them. Two Thorpe lasses, they said, who came out of your house and my brother and his lad followed them.'

Mariah! They thought Mariah was his sister, too. And Mariah had stayed behind to face them when Emma ran for help!

He stood up. A cold hand was gripping his

heart. Emma had left Mariah with those thugs and they thought she was his sister. He did not know where she was. What if she had not escaped them and run after Emma? He made straight for the back door, stopping only to turn and say, 'I never want to see you again, Lily Cluff. Never. Go back to your husband's family and wait for his release. As any good wife should.'

He closed the door on her and did not look back. Mariah was out there somewhere and God only knows what had happened to her.

Chapter 13

Daniel did not need a light for his search as the moon was high and the clouds were clearing. There would be a frost on the ground before dawn. Was Mariah already lying beaten in a ditch somewhere? Or had they kidnapped her for sport? Had they taken her back to Mexton where they were staying?

His heart was thumping in his throat and his mouth was dry. Why had he gone running to Lily first? Why had he not realised sooner that they could have taken Mariah? That they *had* taken Mariah! Please God let her be all right!

Would the Lord listen to him? He regretted he no longer went to church to pray. Sunday school had taught him to read and write, and going to church with his parents had taught him right from wrong. He knew his regular visits to Lily were wrong. His father had always disapproved and told him no good would come of it. Why hadn't he listened? Daniel had ignored the warnings and now he was reaping the consequences.

He retraced his steps to where the barge was moored, then carried on searching the hedges frantically, expecting to find her, beaten up and discarded. He examined every broken twig and flattened stem until he saw the gap. A new break in the hedge, recently pushed aside and – and – his heart stopped in his breast. His body went cold all over. A strip of cloth torn from a dress, quite a long strip of woollen cloth and some shreds of lighter cotton. Further on he saw a trail of flattened grass through the meadow.

Daniel clutched the torn fabric in his fingers and hurried on. Please, Lord, he prayed, please let Mariah be safe. I have never asked much of you, but now I do. Keep Mariah safe. Please. Do this for me and I swear I shall repent my ways.

He searched every inch of the meadow, then the next one and the next until he found her. When he saw her, lying motionless on the wet grass, moonlight reflecting off her naked white skin, her gown and undergarments stripped from her body and in shreds about her, he realised this was not just a beating. This was worse, much, much worse. This was rape.

His anguished cry echoed through the night air. Daniel's face contorted in horror and despair. *He* had done wrong, not her! Why had the Lord not punished him? Why Mariah? But, as he sank to his knees beside her, he realised this *was* his punishment: to see an innocent woman, a *chaste* and respectable woman defiled in this way because of what he had done. This was his fault. He was as guilty as the men who had done this awful thing.

She was freezing cold. He tried to rouse her; he lifted her head and it flopped back like a broken doll's. Her bruised and battered body was limp but she was breathing. The moonlight revealed the bite marks and weals on her skin. He searched about for pieces of clothing to cover her. His jaw set rigid, twisting his features into a bitter grimace and saliva crept slowly into his mouth as he controlled the urge to vomit. Sickened by the sight and smell of this unholy deed he bowed his head, ashamed of being a man with a man's desires; tears filled his eyes.

'I am sorry, so sorry. It's all my fault. My fault. I am so, so sorry!'

He hugged her close to him, rocking her gently backwards and forwards. He would never forgive himself for this. He prayed for the Lord to punish him and let her live.

He did not know exactly when her eyes opened. Only that they stared. When he spoke to her to reassure her she was safe, she did not acknowledge him but continued to stare straight ahead, silent and unseeing.

He took off his thick leather waistcoat to cover and warm her, and then removed his shirt and vest. He did not feel the cold night air, he felt only the pain in his heart, a pain he had not known before. Guilt, despair and anger mingled with an overwhelming anxiety that she might die. He could not let that happen. This independent and courageous young woman was worth ten of

Lily and she must live. He sat her up, supporting her back, easing her arms into his shirt, hardly daring to touch her damaged body.

He fashioned some drawers for her, gently wrapping her torn petticoats around her lower body and legs, and was forced to stop a moment, squeezing his eyes tight shut to stop the tears, when he saw the bruising on her thighs. And there was blood, fresh blood, sticky on her skin and on his hands as he tried to clothe her.

He buttoned his heavy waistcoat securely around her, protecting her from the night air and prying eyes of any prowler on the towpath. Then he lifted her up as gently as he could and carried her across the cold dark meadows, through the hummocks and hedges, and to home.

She grew heavy in his arms but he did not stop. He kicked open the garden gate and kicked again, hard, at the kitchen door. His father un-locked it, started and stared at the sight before him, then opened the door wide.

'Take her through to the front room. I'll get your mother.'

Daniel laid her on the bed that used to be his own. 'You are home, now, Mariah. Safe at home,' he whispered. Safe, he thought, but not sound. She was broken and bruised in mind as well as body. He felt her pain and anguish tearing through his own body and he wept. 'We'll look after you, Mariah, and make you well again. You will be well again, you will.'

But she only stared. And not at him. As he moved away her eyes did not follow him. They stayed, fixed on the ceiling, motionless and still.

143

The ceiling creaked. His young sisters had heard the noise downstairs and were curious. His father and mother came in to the room, anxious to help.

'She's in a bad way, Ma. What can we do?' They all heard the wooden stairs creak and Daniel continued, 'Keep the girls out of here. They should not see this – or know about what happened.'

Fanny Thorpe retreated, calling softly, 'Back to bed now. All of you. And quietly, I say.'

Arthur Thorpe looked at his son and asked, 'Did you see what happened?'

Daniel shook his head, choking on the words. 'She took a beating, and – and – oh, Father – they raped her. Those animals raped her – both of them and more than once, by the look of it.' He sank into a chair with his head in his hands, his broad shoulders shaking as he tried to repress the sobs. 'They thought she was my sister. It was me they were after. They wanted revenge on me and took it out on Mariah. Oh God, it's all my fault!'

'You'd better tell me what you did, son. Why did they want revenge on you?'

Daniel heaved a sigh and tried to control himself. 'I am to blame. I was too full of myself and vain. I believed a liar. I let a pretty face – and a – a pliant body – turn my head – and – never again will I allow that to happen. I won't ever get over this. I'm finished with women. Finished.'

'I take it the liar you speak of is the Cluff widow, then? What has she been telling you?'

'Sh-she is not a widow. Her husband is still alive. He's – he's in prison.'

'Good God, no!' Arthur Thorpe grimaced. 'So the man's brother came after you? And if not

144

you, your sisters? An eye for an eye, eh?'

He was tempted to say, 'I told you no good would come of carrying on with that Mrs Cluff', but he did not. His son was suffering enough for the evil that had been done this night. The Lord had taught him a lesson. But even Arthur's faith was tested by what he had seen. Why choose Mariah for this deed? She did not deserve this.

Fanny Thorpe was standing at the front room door with a bowl of water and some strips of linen. 'I heard what you said, Daniel,' she whispered angrily. 'Does that mean no daughter of mine is safe because you could not keep your breeches buttoned? You are just like your father!'

'Fanny! That's enough!'

Daniel looked from his father to his mother in surprise. They were the closest of couples and this was the first crack in their loyalty to each other he had seen in all his years. From a young boy he had been aware of his parents' passion for each other. He was the eldest of nearly a dozen children and a regular birth in the family had been part of his childhood. This spat between his parents was caused by something he did not know about, he felt sure.

'Out of my way, both of you,' Fanny went on irritably, 'and let me see to Mariah.'

'I'll make her a toddy,' Arthur said and went off to the kitchen. 'And you, my lad, put some clothes on before you catch your death. We've enough with one invalid in the family.'

'What can I do?' Daniel pleaded. 'It was all my fault and I feel so helpless.'

'Nay, lad. You didn't do this damage to her. But

145

for her sake you have to keep quiet about this, or the poor lass's life will truly be ruined. There is enough talk going on around her without adding to it.'

Daniel lifted his arms to encircle his head, as he paced frantically about the room. 'I feel so useless. There must be something I can do!'

'You can leave me alone with her, that's what you can do. Light me another lamp and go and help your father. Ask him to make some of that Indian tea. Here's the key to the bureau.' Fanny lifted her skirt to find the pocket in her drawers.

Daniel hovered, reluctant to leave until his mother said, 'Go on, then. Mariah does not want a man around for this.'

Fanny Thorpe set about tending to Mariah's injuries, removing her makeshift clothing as gently as she was able. She grimaced at the bruising on her face, and again as she uncovered her breasts. She almost choked when she removed Daniel's wrappings around her hips and legs, sticky with fresh blood.

'You're safe now, you'll be all right, Mariah,' she murmured as she worked. 'I am just going to wash you all over with this warm water and then put some salve on your cuts and bruises. Tell me where it hurts most.'

But Fanny could get no response from the young woman. She lay there, awake, eyes staring straight ahead and said nothing. Fanny thought it was like tending an infant's rag doll. Her limbs were compliant and moved, unresisting, as she washed them. But, when she had finished, they fell back, flaccid and lifeless. Lifeless, like her eyes.

Fanny began to frown as she worked. She padded and wrapped her like a baby, making her as comfortable as she could in the hard narrow bed. 'I am just going to get you a drink to help you sleep,' she murmured, before leaving to join her menfolk in the kitchen.

Daniel and his father busied themselves fetching fresh water from the pump at the end of the row, and stoking the fire to heat it.

'What was all that about?' Daniel asked.

'I don't know what you're talking about,' Arthur replied gruffly.

'Yes, you do. That spat between you and Mother.'

'It's nothing, son. It happened a long time ago, before you were born. But women never let you forget these things.'

'Who was she?'

'I said, it's all in the past!'

His father was angry and Daniel let the matter drop. It would only start his father coughing if he pursued it. His mother came through with the bowl of water, stained red with blood and both men grimaced.

'I'll empty that for you.' Daniel took the bowl from her. 'There's more water warming on the fire. How is she?'

'Not good. Not good at all.'

'Will she get better?'

Fanny let out a sigh. 'Who can tell? I've not seen anything like this before. I reckon her body will heal. Don't get me wrong, it's nasty all right. But Mariah is a strong young woman. No, it's not her body that I am worried about, it's – it's – oh, I don't know. She won't speak to me. Didn't say a word all the time I tended to her. She been living here with me like a daughter for weeks now, and all I get from her is a blank stare.'

'She was the same with me,' Daniel added anxiously.

'It's the shock of it all,' Arthur said. 'I've seen it afore, when I was down t' pit. Remember that roof fall? One of the lads got a badly mangled leg and he went like that. He wouldn't talk to anybody for days on end.'

'Did he get better?' Daniel pressed.

'Depends what you mean by better. The surgeon took away most of his leg and it wa' months afore he wa' right in the head again.'

Daniel sagged into the nearest chair and covered his face with his hands. 'She needs looking after. Can you do that for her?'

'I'll do my best. But tomorrow is my day for the butcher's wife.'

'Meg or Liddy? You can tell them what to do.'

Fanny shook her head. 'I don't want any of my girls going in there, doing nursing duties and finding out what happened.'

'What about Aunty Dora?' suggested Daniel. 'You always go to her when one of the girls is ill.'

Daniel saw his parents exchange looks.

Arthur spoke. 'Can you have a lend of a cart from the works, Daniel, to take Mariah over there?'

'She can't travel all that way, Arthur,' Fanny argued. 'Not in her state. There's no proper road to speak of.'

148

'I don't want Dora over 'ere.' Arthur's voice was firm.

'I can't deal with this on my own. I need our Dora,' Fanny pleaded. 'She can help the lass, proper like.'

'Aye, I know. You allus go to her, though. She's out o' the way o' tittle-tattle over there.'

To hell with them, Daniel fumed silently. If Mariah needed Aunty Dora, he would fetch her himself. He stood up and said, 'Why can't she come here? Mariah needs her! She's mother's sister and she can sleep on the couch in the front room.'

But his father continued to grunt his objections.

Daniel grew angry with his father's stubbornness. 'Aunty Dora will know what to do with – well, with women's things like this. She's the best around here!'

His father swivelled round and challenged, 'And what do you know about your aunty's doings?'

'Oh come on, Dad. Men talk in the works. Mind, they always have something good to say about her. I don't let on she's my aunt, but if any of their wives or daughters needs that kind of help, they always send her out to Aunty Dora.'

This only served to make Arthur more angry. 'So Dora Barton's the talk of the works now, is she? Thank God the both o' you are Thorpes.'

Daniel's eyes rounded at this outburst and he was surprised his mother did not spring to her sister's defence and retaliate. Instead she put out a hand on her husband's and said quietly, 'Arthur, our Dora can help Mariah.'

Daniel lost his patience and stood up. 'I'm not

149

listening to any more of this. I'm fetching her now. I'm going to saddle one of Mr Bowes' horses and go over there tonight.'

'Arthur?' Fanny Thorpe was looking intently at her husband.

'All right then. The lass needs her so you'd better fetch her,' he agreed.

Fanny jumped into action and went to a pile of clean laundry on a chair. 'Here you are, Danny. Put on one of your father's shirts, and your waistcoat. Your other things'll need a good wash before you can wear them again.'

As Daniel prepared to leave he heard his father say, 'I don't like having Dora in the house, Fanny.'

'I know you don't,' his mother responded, 'but it was twenty-five year ago. Things were different then.'

'I don't want to talk about it,' Arthur muttered.

'We're lucky to have her; she knows a lot about doctoring.'

'Aye, well, it isn't right for an unmarried woman to do what she does,' Arthur responded.

Fanny answered firmly, 'Mariah needs our Dora. Mariah has to come first for now.'

'I can see that,' Arthur agreed. 'Daniel'd best be off for her then.'

Daniel wondered about the family squabble his aunt had caused in the past. Whatever it was, they had to put it behind them and look to getting Mariah well again. He ran along the towpath and up the alley towards the stables behind the house, panting heavily as he roused the stable lad to saddle one of the lighter beasts. The lad came down from where he slept next to the hayloft with his breeches over his nightshirt. Before long Daniel was on his way.

Daniel liked his Aunty Dora and had looked forward to his childhood visits to her with his mother and younger brothers and sisters. Father was never with them. He was always working down the pit when they went. Daniel remembered it being a tiring walk for little legs, out of town and up past Keppel village, but the journey seemed much shorter on horseback.

Aunty Dora was in her nightgown, but not asleep. Daniel explained as best he could and helped pack a couple of saddlebags for her while she dressed. She hitched up her skirts and rode astride the horse in front of him.

'Will you get word to Mr Shaw to feed and water my pig?' she asked.

'Don't you worry. I'll see he knows. You don't think it'll be too much for him?'

'He'll get one of the Home Farm lads to do it. He's kept an eye on my patch since your grandfather passed away. He promised him, you see. In return for the help I gave his wife when she was badly.'

'Do you mind if we go a bit faster, Aunty?'

'Ee, lad, I do. I'm not as young as I was. You'll make the horse nervous if you don't ease off those reins.'

Daniel swallowed and tried to relax. Maybe some of his aunty's tales would take his mind off Mariah. 'How old were you when Grandpa died?' he asked.

'Nineteen. Our Fanny was just one and twenty. And she, being the elder, decided she was in

151

charge of me. I thought different, though. Ee, now I think back, I was a handful, all right. I wanted to know everything and do everything.'

'Is that why Father doesn't like you?'

'What has he been saying?'

'Nothing. He doesn't approve of what you do.'

'Well, it kept the home going when me and your mother were left on our own. And the vicar and his wife visited us regularly to see we were all right.'

'Weren't you lonely, though? Young women, stuck out here in the wilds with only old Mr Shaw next door for company?'

'We walked over to Keppel church on a Sunday, if the weather let us. Fanny was contented looking after the house and I was out and about tending to folk. They never had much money round here but they always paid me with something, a fowl or a brace of rabbits. I remember we used to save any silver I got in an old crock to pay for my boots. Fanny made sure I had good boots for turning out on a winter's night. Even so, it was touch and go that first winter after Father went. When he was alive we had logs from the estate and he kept the coalhouse topped up for us. We just about got through that winter, but we both knew we'd have to earn more in the following year.'

'So what did you do?'

'Well, the Fitzkeppel estate was losing its farm labourers to the works in town so the trustees went round the Dales offering work on the land, and these newcomers needed lodgings. We thought it would keep us off the parish and out of the poor-house if we took a lodger. We'd have help with chopping wood and digging the garden, too.'

'And did you?'

'Oh aye. That was when your father came along. He was twenty-three and a single man. Ee, do you know, Daniel, you're the image of him, as he was then.'

Daniel managed a smile in the darkness as the horse plodded on. 'We're nearly there.'

Dora stood alone by Mariah's bed.

'I'm right sorry this has happened to you, lass,' Dora began. 'Our Fanny's done her best, but she wants me to have a look at you. I won't hurt you, I promise. Just you relax and lie back on the pillow. There. Put your feet on these cushions...'

Mariah heard what she said but could not move. She had no control over her limbs. They were dead weights hanging from her body, a body that would not shift for her, no matter how hard she tried. She stared straight ahead, unable to form the words on her lips.

Dora continued, 'I'm Dora Barton, Fanny Thorpe's sister. You can call me Dora. You're Mariah, aren't you?' Dora frowned when she could draw no response from her patient. Still, the lass was compliant enough as she examined the bruising and bleeding, grimacing occasionally and tending to her wounds.

Mariah was dimly aware of stinging pain and the mingled smells of soap, wintergreen and camphor. Dora lifted her to a sitting position and she took the drink that was offered. Warmth seeped through her veins. Her eyelids drooped and closed. It was peaceful now and there was a warm glow in her head...

153

Dora waited until she was sure Mariah was asleep and went through to the kitchen where Daniel was hopping about impatiently.

'How is she?'

'Her body will mend given time and the right tending. But she needs rest and understanding more than ointments and salves. Do you know the men who did this to her? It's not right, Daniel. You should get the constable onto them.'

'They'll only deny it. Or even worse, say she was one of the street women from the tavern. Don't worry, I can find out who they are and they'll not get off lightly.'

Dora sat down in the rocking chair opposite her sister. 'Has Arthur gone to bed, Fanny?'

'Aye.'

'I still make him feel uncomfortable, don't I?'

'Aye, but don't you worry. It's him, not you. Do you want a drink of this Indian tea?'

'Don't mind if I do.' Dora took the cup gratefully. 'He's a fine lad, isn't he?'

'Our Daniel? Aye. A credit to the whole family.'

'I'm not a lad,' Daniel interrupted. 'I'm–'

'Five and twenty,' Dora finished for him. 'Aye, I know. But you're still just a lad to me and your mother. This is nice tea, Fanny.'

'Will she get better? She's had a bad time. She's not long since lost her mother. And her father – well he's just wants rid of her.'

'I don't know. She's still not said a word, and she turns away from all my questions. It's like she's blanked it all out of her mind. It might take her a while to come round.'

'What can I do to help her?'

154

Dora shook her head and grimaced. 'Nowt, really. But she needs a close eye kept on her. I'll stay until she's healed enough to travel and then take her back home with me. Country air'll do her good and there'll be no prying busybodies asking questions. Can you borrow a cart from work, Danny?'

'I think so. Just tell me when. I'll take you both back when Mariah's up to it.'

The two women nodded to each other in agreement.

Daniel added, 'I can ride out and see you both on a Sunday.'

'Best not, love,' his mother responded quickly. 'Your father wouldn't like that.'

'He's not still upset, is he?'

'Your mother's right,' Dora answered. 'Besides, Mariah won't want any men around her, reminding her of what happened.'

'Especially you, my lad,' his mother added. 'Your father knew that Mrs Cluff was trouble as soon as she moved into the end house. He told you to stay away from her.' She saw Daniel slump in the chair and stare at the floor. 'Why didn't you listen to your father?'

'How much does Mariah know about you and Mrs Cluff?' Dora asked.

Daniel shrugged. 'Just that we were sweethearts. Emma said she told her.'

'Sweethearts! Huh!' his mother exclaimed.

'All right, Fanny,' Dora said. 'Leave it for now. He's been through enough tonight.'

But Fanny was not to be put off. She turned to her son, leaning forward to reinforce her opinion.

'Don't be surprised if Mariah blames you and never wants to speak to you again!'

Again Dora soothed her anxious sister. 'It's not his doing, Fanny He didn't do those horrible things to her.'

'Lily lied to me,' Daniel said quietly. 'She lied to everybody. She said she was a widow and I believed her. I'd even asked her to marry me,' he finished miserably.

Dora placed her hand on his arm. 'Your mother's right about Mariah, though. She won't want you around. You found her, you saw what happened to her and saw her as she was and she'll know that. It's best you stay away, like your mother says.'

'If you say so. As long as you let Mother know how she's getting on and send word to me and tell me as soon as she agrees to see me again.'

'*If* she agrees to see you again,' Dora added quietly.

Daniel looked shocked, but stayed silent.

Fanny said, 'Shall we all get some sleep, now? Daniel, you'd better get that horse back to its stable and make sure you are up for work on time tomorrow.'

After he had left, Dora said, 'Daniel has been asking me about the old days, when Father died.'

'What did you say?'

'Only how hard it was to manage before Arthur came along.'

'Aye it was. I remember that bad winter before he came down from the Dales after lambing. He said he was only staying the year to work on the Fitzkeppel estate.'

'It caused talk in the village, though, us being spinsters, like. He was a right handsome young fellow in those days.'

'There were the two of us! And Arthur was a good, God-fearing man. He went with us to Keppel church as regular as clockwork.'

Dora grimaced. 'Even so, the church folk didn't approve of him lodging with us.'

'Aye, if we'd have let it go on, we would have ruined our reputations for good.'

'Yours, maybe. I was a lost cause any road, doing what I did with the nursing and such like.'

'You were a lively young thing, weren't you?' Fanny reached across to take her sister's hand. 'Any regrets?'

Dora shook her head and gazed into the dying embers of the kitchen fire. She was remembering the old vicar and his wife, and how they had taken it upon themselves to invite the three young people to the vicarage one Sunday teatime before evensong. And while the reverend invited Arthur to talk in his study, Fanny and Dora drank tea and ate bread and butter and jam with his wife in their drawing room.

That afternoon visit had changed their lives for ever. The Reverend and Mrs Judd had decided that Arthur could not continue to lodge with them. He must marry one of them and they had chosen Fanny as his bride. Arthur was delighted. He worshipped her. Dora had not realised until then how much he truly cared for Fanny.

But Dora had loved Arthur. He knew it and Fanny did not. The banns were read for the following three Sundays and Fanny became Arthur's

157

wife on the fourth. Dora was her bridal attendant. They wore their best Sunday dresses and put early primroses in their hair. Mrs Judd gave a small tea party for them in the vicarage drawing room.

Not long after that a new coal seam opened up near town and the pit owner was looking for men. There were cottages by the canal for men with wives and Arthur was taken on.

The sisters sat in silence with their memories of twenty-odd years ago as the fire grew cold. Eventually, Fanny said, 'Best get to bed now. Will you be all right on the couch?'

Dora nodded. 'I can keep an eye on the lass in there. Goodnight, love.'

Daniel stabled the horse himself and threw pebbles on the house roof to wake Emma to let him in. He fended off her questions. He was so full of remorse he could not trust himself to talk about Mariah without breaking down. He wondered whether he should tell Ezekiel about his daughter. But Ezekiel was determined to disown her and Mariah herself had begged him not to interfere.

He wrestled with this dilemma until he decided to keep silent. Mentally and physically ex-hausted, he fell onto his bed without undressing, but he could not sleep and was glad when the first streaks of dawn lit the morning sky so he could go down to the yard and make a start.

He could not get the sight of Mariah's damaged body out of his mind. Everywhere he looked he saw her still, ivory form, blemished by blood. What had he done to her? Even if she recovered, how was he going to live with this on his conscience?

Chapter 14

'Are you ready, Mariah?'

She nodded silently and pulled the hood of her dark winter cloak forward to shield her face. It was early and the morning air was chilled by mist. Dora had been away from her cottage for two weeks now. Fanny and Arthur stood at the open front door and the curious faces of their younger daughters peered out of an upstairs window.

'You go first.' Dora stood by while Mariah negotiated the step into the dog cart and sat facing her box and a basket of food on the opposite seat. Then she climbed in beside her and the horse whinnied and shied as she arranged herself on the seat beside Mariah.

'Steady, boy.' Daniel, in his best Sunday suit, held the horse's bridle and stroked his nose. 'All set?'

'Yes, love. Take it slowly.'

'Aye.' Daniel took the reins and climbed into the driver's seat. He looked behind him with a worried frown on his face. Mariah buried her head deeper in the folds of her cloak. It was as though she were trying to make herself disappear, he thought. She had not said a word to him or looked at him since he had arrived with the cart.

His mother had warned him that Mariah was having a hard time getting over her attack. Anger and self-loathing bubbled through him. If only he could turn back the clock! Why had he ever allowed himself to be taken in by that whore Lily Cluff? That's all she was. A whore who had married into a family of rogues. By God, he was going to make those Cluff ruffians pay for what they did! He was going to give the pair of them the hiding of their lives!

The horse plodded on through the morning mist as Daniel tussled with his mounting rage. Before long the docile creature picked up his tension and began to whinny and fret.

'There, boy, calm yourself now.' Daniel spoke as much to himself as to the horse. This anger was no good to man or beast. He had to do something soon or he would burst with fury!

The sun's rays began to push through the morning mist. Daniel forced himself to relax his grip on the reins and make his voice sound normal. 'Nice day for a drive.'

'I hope my house is all right. I don't like leaving it empty for too long.'

'I looked in the other day. Didn't Emma tell you?'

'No. When was that?'

'Mr Bowes had some papers to go to Fitzkeppel Hall.'

'I thought you'd send Ned on errands like that?'

'They were important documents for his son to read. Master Henry is staying at the Hall and Mr Bowes said I had to deliver them personally. It didn't take long on horseback so I had time to call in and see if everything was in order.'

'And was it?'

'Aye. A bit chilly without the fire going, and the

garden needs weeding. But everything was safe and sound as far as I could see.'

'Was my pig all right?'

'He seemed happy enough. I took him some stale bread from the house. But he had fresh greens and potatoes in his trough.'

'That'll be the lad from Home Farm. A good 'un, he is.'

'He still doesn't have a name, then?'

'Who? The lad?'

'No, Aunty. Your pig.'

'Oh no, no, no, no, no. How could I eat him if I gave him a name? He's just the pig.'

The first smile of the day crossed Daniel's face. 'That's a nice little house you've got.'

'Your granddad built it, you know.'

'Did he?'

'That's what your grandma told us before she died. He was a farm labourer on the Fitzkeppel estate. When he married, old Fitzkeppel gave him a plot of land on condition he built a house on it in a day. He did it for all his young farm hands when they wed. Saved building them himself, I suppose, cos he had to have the men there to work his fields. The other labourers helped my father build it, so they had their own house from the beginning. Old Fitzkeppel gave him stone from the quarry an' all. Mind you, your grandma said it only had the one room then.'

'On good land though. And near to a spring for water.'

'Your granddad had laid wooden boards between the roof trusses within a year, and put up a ladder so they didn't have to sleep on the

161

earth floor.'

'You've got stone flags now, haven't you?'

'Nice, aren't they? Mr Shaw put them down for me after I'd looked after his son's wife when she...' Dora glanced at Mariah and changed the subject. 'Your granddad built the pigsty next and I reckon the Bartons have had a pig in there ever since. We never went short of a bit o' bacon.'

'Is Mariah all right back there?'

'Just the same. This fresh air will do her good, though. Ee, lad, I know there's brass to be made from them furnaces by the canal, but the smoke that comes out o' them chimneys fair makes your eyes water.'

'Aye, it gives Father a real bad cough on some days and nothing we get from the apothecary's can calm him.'

The small cart trundled on in silence. They left the works and terraces behind and slowly climbed a small hill on the Grasse Fell road, went through Keppel village with its neat rows of stone-built workers' cottages and an ale house at the end, and skirted the Fitzkeppel estate to the edge of the woods.

Daniel negotiated the horse and cart down the narrow lane leading to Dora's house. 'Nearly there. How is she?'

Dora peered at the tiny amount of Mariah's face visible under the hood of her cloak. 'Still too pale for my liking. Are you all right, Mariah?'

Mariah nodded silently.

'I laid a fire when I was there,' Daniel added. 'Just needs lighting. I'll chop some more wood for you before I go. How are you for coal?'

'Enough for me, but I reckon I'll need more with company to cook for.'

'I'll get Mr Bowes' carter to bring over a load. He can bill me for it at the works.'

'Thanks, love. You're a good lad.'

Daniel helped his two passengers out onto the overgrown track outside Dora's house. Mariah grasped his outstretched hand but still would not look at him. She took Dora's arm to walk down the garden path. Daniel grimaced silently and went ahead to open the front door. He led the way down to the back kitchen and continued his conversation with Dora.

'When was the front room and this hallway built on, then?' he asked.

'Just after old Fitzkeppel put up that folly to celebrate the end of Napoleon. His ironworks had made him a pile of money from the war and he paid his men well to build that monstrosity. There was plenty of stone left over. Good stone an' all. His labourers shared it out and your granddad bought timber for the stairs with his extra pay. Me and your mother were just little 'uns then.'

'I'd like to have known my granddad.'

'Aye. You're a lot like him in some ways. You get on with things.'

Daniel took off his coat and smiled. 'I'll fetch water from the spring first.'

'Let me do that. It's women's work.'

'No, you keep an eye on Mariah. I'll not be long.'

As soon as the fire was drawing, Dora boiled some water and made porridge for Daniel to ease his hunger. Mariah would not eat any. She sat silently at the table in her hooded cloak and prepared the

163

vegetables that Dora put in front of her.

Daniel sat across from her and frowned, glancing from Dora to Mariah and back to Dora. Finally he pushed back his chair and said, 'I'll chop that wood and bring in more coal.'

Mariah did not even glance in his direction. When Daniel came back inside, his arms loaded with logs, she pulled her hood forward again and avoided looking at him. Then she got up silently and went down the garden to the privy.

'I'll just bring in some buckets of coal from the outhouse, Aunty, and then I'll get off.'

'Aren't you staying for some broth?'

'No. Thanks all the same, but I don't think Mariah likes me being around.'

'She needs time to herself, that's all.'

'She's had enough of that recently, but I suppose you're right. You usually are about these things.'

'She doesn't want you near her, Daniel.'

The strain of Daniel's pent-up feelings twisted his handsome features. 'She blames me, doesn't she?'

'I don't know She might not be thinking about you at all. It's herself she's having trouble with.'

'I don't follow you.'

'It was an evil deed those men did to her that night. It was their doing but Mariah blames herself. She feels dirtied by it and is ashamed. She'll not forget it, you know.'

'But none of it was her fault!'

'That doesn't make any difference to the way she feels, love. She is going to need a lot of time to get over this. A lot of patient tending.'

164

'You will give her that, won't you?'

'I'll do my best, but I can't work miracles.' Dora's own heart was torn apart by the anguish on his face. He felt so guilty for his involvement in the attack on Mariah. But nobody could turn back time and he had to deal with his own part in this as Mariah was dealing with hers. 'Look to sorting yourself out, lad. You can't do anything for her, now.'

'Yes I can!' he yelled. 'I'll get my revenge on those Cluff bastards, if it's the last thing I do!'

Dora stared at him. She had never seen him so angry. 'Be quiet, will you? She'll hear you. I know how you feel—'

'No you don't! It was my fault. My fault! Mariah will never forgive me! Never!'

'She won't if you keep going on like this! She needs a bit of peace!' Dora retaliated sharply. 'All this shouting and blaming yourself will not do her any good at all! I think you'd better get off home now. Before she comes back inside.'

Daniel clenched and unclenched his fists. He wanted to make things right for Mariah, but he could not. He felt so useless. How was he going to live with himself? He pulled himself together and made an effort to calm down. 'I don't want to leave her. I want to help her get better. She will get better, won't she?'

Dora pursed her lips. 'Time will tell.'

'You send word to me if she needs anything. *Anything.*'

Dora reached up to give him a hug. 'I will, lad. I will. Look, it's a nice day out there. Why don't you go back home and help your father in the garden?'

165

He grimaced and Dora's heart ached for his anguish, but eventually he agreed with her and shrugged. 'If you think it is for the best. I'll call back next Sunday.'

'Best not. I'll let you know when she's ready to see folk from town.'

Mariah heard Ezekiel's cart rattle away down the track towards town and came in from the garden.

'There you are. You can come back inside. He'll not be back until I ask him. Why don't you take off your cloak? The fire's going well and it's warming up a treat in here now.'

Dora watched as Mariah obeyed. She hoped the fear in her eyes would go. It wasn't only when Daniel was around. Mariah shrank from looking at and talking to anybody except her. Dora had seen it before. Mariah could not get over her disgrace.

She was such an attractive young woman, Dora thought, with that striking coppery hair and upright stance. A bit too thin now, though. That gown was hanging off her. The dark grey colour seemed appropriate for her sombre mood and it was very well made with a separate bodice and skirt. Dora had selected it from Mariah's box when she had been unable to salvage her tattered black mourning gown.

Dora persevered. 'There's a hook by the back door for your cloak. You'd better put a pinny on over that nice travelling outfit. Here's a clean one for you.'

Again, Mariah did as she was bid without a word. Dora continued, 'Sit yourself down. This

166

broth won't be long. It's only vegetables today, but Fanny's given me a nice shin of beef for tomorrow.'

Dora was used to Mariah not speaking by now. She nodded and shook her head and, sometimes, her eyes lit with an expression that gave Dora hope for her recovery. But it never lasted. It was as though Mariah was climbing out of a deep pit. She took two steps up and one step back, and then, suddenly, for no apparent reason she dropped back into the abyss.

Dora resolved to carry on as normally as possible until she came round. She put some of Fanny's new bread to warm in the bake oven at the side of the fire. 'Ee, with the two of us here, it'll be just like when me and our Fanny were younger. Afore she wed Arthur and went to live in town. We had to fend for ourselves then, y' know, after our mother and father passed on.'

Dora watched Mariah's face carefully as she talked, looking for signs of what cheered her. Clearly mentioning their loss of parents was exactly the wrong thing to say. But Dora rallied valiantly and pressed on.

'Of course, we were grown women. But we had the garden and hens, as well as pigs in those days. Do you know, I might start keeping a few hens again, if the henhouse down the garden is still any use. I don't know why I stopped having them in the first place.'

Yes I do, Dora thought, the fox got in one winter and killed them all. But Mariah's face had brightened at her suggestion and she continued. 'I'll ask at Home Farm if they've got a few laying

167

pullets to spare. They won't take too much feeding. What do you think, Mariah?'

Dora saw a vestige of a smile cross Mariah's face. She stirred the broth as it simmered in her blackened cauldron suspended over the kitchen fire. A large, similarly blackened kettle rested on the swing hob. She'd make some proper tea for them both later, and fry some of that black pudding Fanny had fetched her from the butcher's in town.

'Well now, lass. Why don't you take yourself off upstairs and unpack your box? I've put you in the front room. There's a nice little window that looks onto the lane.'

The broth was ready when Mariah came downstairs, her woollen shawl wrapped tightly about her. Dora ladled it into deep stoneware bowls and sawed at the warmed bread.

'This knife needs a sharpen,' she muttered with a tutting sound. 'Ee, when our Fanny and me were on our own, and Arthur came to lodge, he used to see to all that for us. Cleaned up our garden tools, tidied the outhouse, shovelled the coal – the lot.'

Silently, Mariah broke her bread and dropped the pieces into her broth.

'After we've had this,' Dora suggested cheerfully, 'we'll walk down the garden and look at the old henhouse, if you like.'

Dora was relieved to see a light in Mariah's eyes and the hint of a nod. Poor lass, she thought, I'll just have to keep trying but it was going to be a long journey for both of them.

Mariah pulled a few weeds with her in the afternoon sun and then they went inside for their black pudding and potatoes, and drank tea by the fire as the daylight faded. Mariah clasped her mug in both hands and stared silently into the flames.

'It is nice having you to stay. I miss our Fanny sometimes. You couldn't separate us then. Not until Arthur came along.'

Mariah turned her head towards Dora, so she continued, 'We worked hard, o' course. There was money to be earned from helping out at the Hall. In those days there was always building work going on and the parkland being altered. And they had times when the Hall was full of visiting gentry for the hunting and the shooting. And sometimes there'd be a ball, with grand ladies and everything. We'd be up there for days on end, sleeping on straw pallets in the barns to save the walk there and back every day.'

But after the scandal with her ladyship, Dora thought to herself, the visitors stopped coming and the work dwindled away. Best not talk about that now. She leaned forward in her chair and picked up the brown teapot from the hearth. 'Would you like a drop more of this, Mariah, love?'

Mariah, sitting on the other side of the fireplace, held out her mug while Dora poured the hot liquid carefully. 'Thanks,' she said quietly.

Dora gave a half smile and nodded. That was the first word she had heard Mariah utter since Daniel had left. It was a start. Tomorrow they'd have a nice walk over to Home Farm to see about the hens.

Daniel saw to the horse and cart himself when he got back to the Bowes' house. Being a Sunday, the stable lad had had his dinner and gone off to

169

see his mother and father. Daniel cleaned up the cart and rubbed down the horse thinking all the time about Mariah. She was in the best place with the best person. Aunty Dora was the finest there was around here for tending to womenfolk.

Daniel remembered visiting as a nipper, not quite understanding at first why they always went when his mother was swollen with child. He was sent to Mr and Mrs Shaw's house further down the lane when the baby started coming. And afterwards, they stayed on until Mother was strong enough to walk back to town. Aunty Dora came with them, but never stayed at the cottage. She'd have a bite to eat and a sit down until it was time for Father to get in from the pit, and then set off back on her own.

Daniel knew his father did not like his aunt coming to the house even though she was his wife's sister. He said she was ungodly. This shocked young Daniel because his parents had brought their family up to be decent church-going folk. All the children went to Sunday school and learned to read the Bible and write their letters.

As he grew older, he stopped going to church every Sunday and sometimes visited Dora instead if the weather was fine. She had told him about the cundums and even gave him some, making him promise not to tell his father who didn't hold with that sort of thing; he thought it was unnatural to use anything like that in his marriage bed. And his father liked the marriage bed. As the eldest child in a small cottage, Daniel knew everything his parents did in their bedchamber.

He realised now how much he was like his father

in that respect. He should have heeded his father's warnings about Lily. But she was a mature and comely woman and he had been unable to resist her advances. He did not need any persuasion to climb into her bed. Once he had tasted the pleasure of her soft body he could not get enough of her.

He had not talked to his parents about Lily. After their first disapproving row, they maintained an uneasy silence about her. But Dora was different; she did not discourage him. She said he was a grown man and he should not resist his urges. It was not good for men to contain their urges. She knew about these things.

Oh Lord, what had he done? He could not blame anyone else for his passion for Lily, or for what her menfolk had done to Mariah. He let out an anguished growl that startled the horse into a whinny. He meant to get his revenge on those evil men for Mariah's sake. He had made up his mind, and his anger simmered. He had to get it out of his system. He'd ask the men in the works about those Cluff thugs. Somebody would know where to find them. And when he did...

He shook out some fresh hay for the horse and then went indoors to the kitchen where Emma was clearing the remains of Sunday dinner.

'You're back early. I thought you were staying at Aunty Dora's for your dinner.'

He shook his head wordlessly, and reached for his leather waistcoat that he kept hanging by the back door.

'How's Mariah? Mam said she was on the mend when I called last week. She wouldn't let

171

me see her, though.'

'Mariah has to rest. She be all right with Dora.'

'Those men beat her up, didn't they?'

'Who told you that?'

'Nobody. I was there, Daniel, when they came after us. I was scared stiff. I locked the kitchen door as soon as I got back. Ned told me they beat up Mrs Cluff.'

Daniel stared at his sister silently, desperately trying to suppress his mounting rage. His stomach knotted with anger. Why had he ever taken up with that whore?

'It shouldn't have been Mariah, should it? It should have been me,' Emma added quietly.

'It shouldn't have been either of you!' he yelled. 'It should have been me!'

'Don't shout. Sit down and have your dinner. There's some roast mutton still warm, and left-over 'taters.'

'I – can't eat. I can't.'

'I'll leave it on the hob for later. Shall I make a pot of tea?'

He shook his head again. 'I'm going down to the yard.'

'On a Sunday?'

'Yes, on a Sunday,' he replied sharply.

Emma turned back to her plates. He was very upset about Mariah. They all were. But Daniel seemed a different person these days. Not the big brother she knew and loved. He was always at work and no fun any more. Ever since that business with Mrs Cluff and Mariah. She heaved a sigh. She hoped he'd get over it soon.

Chapter 15

'You don't have to do this, Ned.'

'Yes, I do, Mr Thorpe. After what I saw they did to Mrs Cluff. They need some o' their own medicine.'

'It could be dangerous.'

'What? More dangerous than working down a coal mine? Or at the furnace face when the fire's at its height? I done both, Mr Thorpe, and look at me now!'

'Aye. Look at you, as tall as me and just as brawny. How old are you, Ned?'

'Seventeen. It's been seven year now since I left the poorhouse and went down the pit wi' your dad.'

'Are you still lodging with Dad's mate?'

He nodded. 'We get on all right, we do. Let me come with you, Mr Thorpe. There'll be two o' them.'

'Saturday night, then. They're staying in a farm shed near their cousin in Mexton and going to the cock fight over that way. I'll follow them afterwards and pick 'em off when they've split from the rest of their clan.'

'*We*, Mr Thorpe. *We'll* foller 'em and pick 'em off together.'

They took the towpath out of town, past Fordham down towards Mexton Lock. But before

173

they reached the Navigator Inn, they cut across the fields to a tumbledown farmhouse outside one of the new pit villages. The farm had been one of the best around until the local landowner had discovered a coal seam running underneath it and now all the trappings of the pit dominated the land. The men worked under ground instead of on top of it and the farmhouse had decayed. A winding house and spoil heap scarred the pasture. But there were rows of new cottages nearby for the labourers, and an ale house, and even talk of a chapel.

Skirting the farmhouse, they followed the noise and glow of light from a broken shutter of the big old barn at the back. The fight was underway when they arrived. Daniel and Ned slipped unnoticed into a crowd of spirited men baying for blood.

The screeching and scrawing of fighting cocks as they flapped and scrabbled in the dust, pecking each other to near death, set Daniel's teeth on edge. But he understood the rivalry and it fired his own blood for revenge.

They climbed on an old cart, abandoned in the shadows, to get a better look and Daniel wished it were him and Cluff in that half circle enclosed by a brick pen against the back of the barn. He felt his pulse begin to beat and his fists clenched involuntarily. He had never been more ready than now to give Cluff his dues. The fighting pit was lit by oil lamps standing on straw bales and flares hoisted on poles sent grotesque shadows against the walls.

'Are they here?' Ned whispered.

Daniel scanned the jeering crowd of men enjoying their sport of a Saturday night after a week of grinding labour at the furnace or coal face. But they were not all working men swigging ale from stone jars. He recognised one or two, better dressed, friends of Mr Bowes, in a group around the bookie, flashing purses jingling with coins, and even banknotes, as they wagered. They drank spirits from small flasks and in the flickering light, their eyes and teeth flashed in their flushed sweating faces.

'We should've brought a nip to drink ourselves,' Ned said. Daniel reached inside his jacket and drew out a small leather-covered metal flask. 'Try this.'

'You first.'

'I have no need of it.'

Daniel's blood was up already. He wanted no prop from any bottle. Cluff and his son were there, he recognised their wild eyes and harsh grinning faces showing rotten and crooked teeth. They called and sneered at the birds and their owners. The bookies pocketed their gains as the broken, bleeding cocks were packed away in wicker cages and fresh ones presented to the baying crowd.

The air was rank with the smell of old straw and horse droppings, fresh chicken blood and human sweat. Between bouts, a couple of rouged women with their bodices half open, crept around the back of the crowd, picking off men they knew were good for a tanner, and leading them away outside.

Daniel and Ned stayed in the shadows, watching, until there were no more cocks to fight and the noisy crowd began to disperse, some to

175

carriages that loomed out of the darkness for their gentry owners. They followed the Mexton bunch until they saw the two Cluff men turn off the main cart track. Then they cut across the scrubland and, a few hundred yards on, stepped out in front of them.

'What the–!'

'Ned, you take on the young 'un. Just a pasting. Understand?'

Ned was already laying into the surprised son, who took a few seconds to rally and give as good as he got. Daniel, confident that Ned could lick him, turned his back and faced the father, the instigator, the evil one. He saw a knife blade glint in the moonlight and heard him call out.

'Come on then. I know who you are and I'm ready fer yer. Think yer can fuck our Harry's missus and get away wi' it, do yer?'

Daniel ignored the taunts and leapt forward, kicking the knife from the other man's grasp. He heard it clatter as it fell on the rocky track. Cluff was surprised, but quick to respond and lashed out with both his fists. Daniel fended him off, taking the blows on his raised arms and then set about the man with a vengeance that had simmered in him for days.

One heavy punch after another, first to the man's head and then his body. He ducked and dodged Cluff's futile retaliation. Thump. Thump. The sickening thuds of fists on flesh sounded good to his ears, the tortured gasps and cries from his opponent were sweeter than music. Cluff was on his knees and still he hit him, lifting him by the collar to punch his jaw until he was nothing more

176

than a bleeding, groaning heap on the rocky dirt track.

He felt a tug on his jacket sleeve. 'Mr Thorpe. Mr Thorpe. That's enough. You'll kill him,' Ned tugged harder, pulling him away.

Daniel straightened and tried to calm himself. Cluff's son was lying motionless on the ground. 'What about him?' he asked.

'Knocked out, that's all.'

He heard a groan and scrabbling noise behind him and turned to see the older man recovering, on his knees, the knife back in his hand. 'I'll get you back for this, Thorpe. I'll get you where it hurts. You see if I don't. You'd better watch them little sisters o' thine, cos I'll 'ave 'em afore I'm through wi' you. I'll 'ave 'em all.'

Cluff lunged forward, throwing the knife at Daniel. His swift reactions saved him from injury and the knife whistled by him and fell to the ground. Cluff tried to stagger to his feet but collapsed back into a heap on the track. 'I'll ruin 'em like I did that carrot top,' he croaked. 'They'll all be whores like 'er, afore I'm finished.'

Daniel caught sight of the knife, its glinting blade signalling, beckoning, no, summoning him to pick it up. And as he picked it up, it was Mariah's bruised body he saw through the red rage that engulfed him. Dear sweet Mariah, who was a friend to everyone and so misjudged by her own family.

'No, Mr Thorpe. That'll be murder. Chuck the knife away!'

Ignoring Ned's pleas, he slashed at Cluff's breeches, splitting them open at the front.

177

Cluff yelled and desperately struggled to roll over and scramble to his feet. He called over to his son who was stirring from his stupor. 'Gerron yer feet, lad!'

'Stop it, Mr Thorpe!' Ned pleaded. 'Just fists, you said. Fight fair. Man to man.'

'Do you think he fought fair with Mariah?' Daniel's voice cracked and broke into a hoarse whisper. 'Kind, innocent Mariah, who had no part in any of this.' He straddled Cluff as he tried to escape and pushed him back to the ground, tearing away the shreds of his clothing to expose his private parts.

Pinned on his back, Cluff struck out with his fists, finding strength through fear.

Daniel fended off the blows, keeping the knife well out of reach and breathed, 'This is for Mariah.' He angled the knife to slice.

He could not move his arm.

Ned had stilled his wrist with an iron fist as strong as his own.

'I thought this fight was about Lily Cluff,' Ned said quietly.

'Leave me be, Ned. He deserves this. You don't know the half of it.'

'I know you could end up in gaol or worse if you carry on like this.'

'It would be worth it!'

'And then what good will you be to this Mariah? Locked up wi' men no better than he is, and not able to help those who rely on you. You're not thinking straight, Mr Thorpe.'

Daniel wrenched his arm away. Ned was right. But, more than that, in his anger he had said too much about Mariah. He did not want Ned asking questions. What had happened to her was a secret Daniel would keep to his grave.

He had wanted to make Cluff suffer and by God, he had! He had frightened him half to death. Cluff really thought he meant to castrate him there and then. He was groaning as he squirmed, his punches weakening as Daniel's greater strength overcame him. "Ow many sisters 'ave yer got?' Cluff goaded him hoarsely, and choked on his laughter.

'Shut up!' Daniel shouted. He bent over Cluff, grasping his chin in his hand and brandished the knife. 'If I ever see you or your vile clan around any woman again, I'll finish you. I'll cut off your scrawny balls and stuff them down your evil throat.' He flung the knife as far as could into the scrub. Then he marched over to the son and yelled, 'Let this be a lesson to the pair of you!'

He surveyed the scene in front of him. The Cluffs would recover; Mariah might not. He felt better for extracting this revenge but it did not assuage his guilt. It was his own greedy passion for that Cluff woman's body that was at the root of all this. He was as bad as they were and he hated himself for it! He stood there, breathing heavily, watching the men squirm on the ground and wondered what good he had done for Mariah by this deed.

'Come on, Mr Thorpe,' Ned said quietly. 'They'll not forget that in a hurry. Let's get off home.'

Wordlessly, Daniel followed Ned back to town.

Chapter 16

'What's been going on? Did that happen in my yard? Because if it did, my lad, you can leave right now. I'll not have fighting in my yard.'

'It was nothing to do with here, Mr Bowes. It was a private matter.'

Ezekiel looked more closely at Daniel Thorpe's face. A bit of swelling and bruising around the eyes and jaw. Not much. Just a scuffle probably. Then he caught sight of his hands. The knuckles were red raw. Thorpe was a strong man. He was tall and muscular and Ezekiel reckoned the other fellow had not fared so well. Poor sod, he thought. He remembered when he had been on the wrong end of fists like Thorpe's. It had only happened once and he hadn't deserved it. But he remembered it.

'You'll not do it again, Thorpe. Do you hear? I am not having my supervisor, who lives in my house, brawling in the streets. Now, who else was with you?'

'No one you know, sir.' Ned had had an easier time of it, seeing off Cluff's son in the fight. Men at the furnace face were often getting knocks and bruises, but to avoid any questioning Daniel had sent Ned off that morning with a delivery to Sheffield. 'It happened outside town.'

'Are you going to tell me what it was about?'

'No, sir.'

'I have a right to know!'

180

'It was over a woman, sir.'

This seemed to anger Ezekiel. 'Womenfolk!' he exclaimed. 'They always cause you trouble. Not your sister, lad! Not this one living in my house, I hope?'

Daniel's face was set in an angry grimace and he wanted to shout, 'No, it was your own daughter, you imbecile! The one you threw out because she would not marry that smarmy friend of yours!' But he knew the less Ezekiel knew about what happened to Mariah, the better. He simply said, 'No, sir.'

'This is not a good start, my lad, but this time – mind you, only this one time – I'll give you the benefit of the doubt.' He got to his feet and raised his voice. 'I mean it, though. If you bring any trouble to my yard, you're out!'

'I know that, Mr Bowes. It'll not happen again, I promise you.'

Ezekiel grunted. 'Sit yourself down a while. I have something to discuss with you.'

He watched Thorpe as he settled in one of the worn leather office chairs. He noticed the thick leather on his boots. It was worn and scuffed as he expected, but they were well-made, from the best cobbler in town – he recognised the workmanship. Thorpe had on tough moleskin trousers and a grey flannel shirt that was protected by his long leather waistcoat.

Thorpe wore that waistcoat every day and it carried the scars of his trade. It set him apart from the rest of the men and gave him authority. Ezekiel wondered if Thorpe realised how much he did not want to row with him, or get rid of him from his yard. By heaven, he wished his son Henry was more like this fellow.

Ezekiel stood up and walked around his desk to sit opposite him by the fire. Thorpe was sitting rigidly upright, with a straight back and his shoulders squared. He was staring intently at Ezekiel, with a neutral expression on his face. He was his own man, this one was, Ezekiel thought. That's what makes him a good gaffer to the men. As long as he's on my side.

'You're a capable fellow, Thorpe. One of the best. Any man would be proud to have you as his son. You think on that when it comes to women-folk.'

'Aye, Mr Bowes, I will.'

That seemed to relax him a bit, and Ezekiel felt better too. The last thing he wanted was any kind of scandal about his works supervisor. Although a fight over a woman might give Thorpe some credibility with his gang, so it was not such a bad thing. A bit of a reputation with the ladies would do him no harm as the works gaffer. It gave the men something to talk about as long as none of their own women were involved and Thorpe would know better than to cause that kind of trouble. Even so, Thorpe was five and twenty, too old to be a bachelor without causing talk.

'It's high time you got yourself a wife, man,' Ezekiel said. 'I run a respectable shop here and I'll not have any miner's son bringing us down. A fine well-set-up fellow like you should have no difficulty finding himself a good woman! You do have a lady friend, don't you? Didn't you tell me you were thinking of getting wed?'

182

'I said I might be.' Daniel did not care for the way this conversation was going. He felt uncomfortable, closeted in that small office with Mr Bowes. He had his own father to advise him without Mr Bowes pitching in as well. The fire radiated its heat onto his face. He did not want to lie to his employer, but he could not possibly tell him the truth, not about himself and Lily and his own daughter.

'She hasn't turned you down, has she? I don't know! Some o' these young lasses don't know when they're well off. Have you talked to her father?'

'It's not like that, Mr Bowes. My father has the miner's cough and I'm the only son left now, so most of my wages go to keep my mother and sisters.'

'I see,' Ezekiel responded. 'Well, that's right responsible of you, lad. They said you were a good 'un when I asked about you at the Fitz-keppel works. It saves the parish a shilling or two when families can look after their own.'

Daniel became more uneasy in Ezekiel's presence with each passing minute. He said, 'I thought you wanted to talk about the works, sir. I need to keep an eye on the furnace out there...'

'This won't take long.'

Daniel shifted his position in the worn office chair.

Ezekiel stood up but remained in front of Thorpe, with his back to the fire and said, 'What you need is a lass with a bit of dowry behind her. Don't you agree?'

'Well no. I...'

'Don't be daft, man. I reckon you could have your pick of one or two decent lasses round about here. What about one of Smith's daughters from the hardware shop in town?'

Ezekiel watched Thorpe's face closely. He had been trying to think of a way of getting back into Mr Smith's favour and this might be it. Mr Smith was powerful in the lodge and Mariah's behaviour towards him had caused Ezekiel a lot of embarrassment. By God, if she had been his own flesh and blood she would never have disobeyed him like that! He was glad to be shut of her and good riddance!

But it had not done his reputation at the lodge any good. Since then, he had been trying his damnedest to think of a way to make up the lost ground with Mr Smith. His youngsters were getting to be a real handful since his missus had passed away. Taking one of Smith's unruly lasses off his hands and marrying her to his ambitious young gaffer was the least he could do for him. By heaven, that would mend the rift between them, all right!

He went on, 'You know of Mr Smith, don't you? His eldest girl would do very well for you. He's got property, has Mr Smith. His late wife brought a row of houses with her when he wed her. In town they are, not far from here. His daughter'll be bound to come with one o' them to live in, and a dowry besides.'

Daniel swallowed. He knew about the Smith family. Everybody in town did because they were well off and Mr Smith's business was one of the best. But he had never met any of them, except in

184

their shop. Nor had he any wish to. He was more than capable of finding his own bride when he was ready, and she would be of his own choosing.

When he did not reply, Ezekiel pressed on, 'I can arrange a meeting with Mr Smith, if you like. He's got five daughters to wed, you know.' After a further silence, he raised his voice, 'Well, man, I can do this for you. What do you say?'

Daniel stared at Mr Bowes uneasily, not sure what to make of this unsatisfactory exchange. He knew from the works gang that Mr Smith's eldest daughter had her eyes firmly set on the farrier's son from Keppel village.

That did not matter to Ezekiel Bowes, he thought. He was a harsh and unfeeling man when it came to women. After what he had heard about Mr Smith's visit to the Bowes household, he was in no doubt as to why Mariah had left home. Daniel began to realise the difficulty Mariah had faced with her father's wishes for her.

He said, 'No thank you, Mr Bowes. I have my own plans.' He wasn't even sure himself what they were, but he knew they did not involve one of the Smith girls. God, his life was in such a mess. How had he let it happen? How could he make things right again?

'What plans?' Ezekiel demanded irritably.

'I can't say. Not yet.'

'You think on about my offer, lad. It's a good one. And get yourself sorted out. I want no trouble sticking to my yard.'

'Right, sir.'

'Get back to work, then.'

'Yes, sir.'

Daniel was glad to escape from the office and back to the furnace. The last thing on his mind was getting wed. He'd had his fingers badly burned with Lily and he was damn sure he wasn't going to let that happen again. But he did not dwell too long on these thoughts. He'd produced a decent amount of blister steel from the furnace last week, and it was already sold. Once the new crucibles were installed he'd get an even better price for Mr Bowes and his fancy son. Now he was in charge, Daniel was going to make his name here. The men worked hard for him, and Mr Bowes, for all his faults, was not mean about paying his men, especially now the output was rising.

Daniel stopped as he went out of the office door. 'I thought that, when I've got the furnace loaded and going again, I'd show one of the men how to make the crucibles. I learned that before I did the teeming. We'll need a full-time potter when the new crucible shed is finished.'

'Aye. Do that.'

'When will the new furnace be ready, Mr Bowes?'

'You'll know in good time. Just concentrate on keeping the men working and yourself away from the fighting for now.'

'Yes, sir.' Daniel nodded, closed the door behind him and clattered down the stone steps.

Chapter 17

'I've collected some mushrooms for your breakfast.'

Dora Barton stopped stirring a pot of porridge on the hob and looked round. She smiled. 'Ee, Mariah love, I thought you were still in your bed. It's grand to see you up and about with a bit of colour in your cheeks. Come and sit by the fire.'

'It's your careful tending that's helped me, Dora.'

'I wish I could do more, lass. But it's really down to you to get over this now.'

Mariah gave a brief nod and chewed her lip. Dora Barton had looked after her as a mother does her own child, soothing her sleepless nights and talking to her. She could not remember the things Dora said, only that her words had been comforting and they had helped her recover a semblance of her self-respect and she would always be grateful.

She wished, oh, how she wished her own mother was still alive, to hold her and comfort her and tell her everything was fine. But she wasn't and everything was not fine. None of this would have happened if her mother had lived. A knot began to form in Mariah's stomach. She tried to ignore it and managed a smile for the woman whose unfailing kindness and generosity of spirit had helped her through. 'You have been so gentle and understanding towards me. I do not know what I would have done without you.'

'What happened was not your doing and I don't hold with womenfolk suffering like that. But it did happen and there's no turning the clock back,' Dora responded briskly. 'This porridge is ready if you're hungry.'

'Oooh, not just yet.'

'Shall I fry the mushrooms in a bit o' bacon fat instead?'

'Give me minute or two, Dora. I felt a bit queasy early on and it seems to have come back.'

'You need to eat more, lass. You've gone ever so thin since – well, these last few weeks.'

'I've lost track of how long it's been now. Just getting through one day at a time has been the best I could do.'

'Don't you fret about that, you take all the time you need,' Dora said soothingly. But a suspicion began to form in her mind. 'How do you feel in yourself?' she asked.

'I-I don't know. A bit strange, really.'

'You've healed well enough.' Dora frowned. 'You should be getting back to your normal self by now. I've some sweet milk fresh from the farm dairy, if you fancy that with your porridge.'

'Perhaps later.'

Dora's frown deepened and she went back to the fireplace.

Mariah made an effort to talk and said, 'The pig is looking nice and fat now. Did you get him some of the skimmed milk while you were over there?'

'It's in a bucket in the scullery. Why don't you take it down to him? You can pull some greens for the hens, while you're at it. And see if there are any eggs to make a Yorkshire for dinner.'

Mariah tipped the bucket of milk into the pig's trough and stayed, leaning over the low stone wall of his sty to scratch his back with a stick while he sucked and lapped. Then he snuffled and grunted, searching for some of his favourite turnips in the corners of his trough. She scattered the greens and crumbled some stale-bread crusts under Dora's fruit trees at the end of the garden. Two of her hens had gone through the hedge into the woodland and she shooed them back to the orchard. The bread should keep them there now. You couldn't be too careful with foxes at this time of year.

Mariah took refuge in the isolation of Dora's cottage. The only living soul she had met since moving here was Mr Shaw, who had a bit of land on the edge of the wood. He had known Dora's father well, having worked with him on the land, but he was a very old man now. Mind you, he was still sprightly for his age, Mariah thought. In his younger days, when he was a labourer on the Fitzkeppel estate, he had kept a farrowing sow and a flock of geese as well as hens. And he'd had ferrets for flushing out rabbits in the hillsides.

She found a clutch of small pullet eggs and considered herself lucky now the days were getting shorter. There were plenty for one of Dora's Yorkshire puddings, to go with the stew she was making. They had meat today, scrag end of mutton with plenty of onion and barley. It ought to have smelled appetising to Mariah when she went indoors from the garden, but it did not.

Something about her was still not right.

'How is Mr Shaw keeping?' she asked.

'He'll be all right as long as his cough doesn't come back this winter.'

'He has you to keep an eye on him.'

'We've allus looked out for each other.'

'You must have missed Fanny when she went to live in town.'

Dora looked wistful for a moment. 'You couldn't separate us until Arthur came along. He changed everything. We'd never had a man except our father living in our house before.'

Mariah raised her eyebrows. 'Mr Thorpe lived here with you?'

'He took lodgings with us one spring to work on the Fitzkeppel estate. We were glad of his help, I can tell you. But he was laid off after autumn ploughing with no hope of any more labouring until the following year. He had paid us rent at Michaelmas, but when it came to Candlemas he had nothing left. We didn't want to turn him out, so we asked him to do repairs on the sty and hen-house, and gardening and the like for us. Just like Father had done. That way we all got through the winter warm and well fed.'

'Even so, unmarried ladies living with an un-married gentleman...'

'Oh, Reverend Judd kept a close eye on us. He took it upon himself to act as our guardian after Father died, and he made it his business to call on us regular. His wife too, if she was round this way on her visits to the sick.' Dora smiled and gave a chuckle. 'Good old Mrs Judd. She used to say she was only doing what our dear mother would have wanted when she asked to look over our housekeeping.'

'What, your account books and such like?'

'No, Mariah. The bedchambers. She would straighten the window drapes and run her finger over the mantelshelves for dust. But really she only wanted to see our sleeping arrangements, just in case we were not being truthful about our domestic activities.'

'I expect she was worried for your reputations,' Mariah suggested.

'Well, Fanny's anyway. I think I was beyond help by carrying on Mrs Shaw's work. Nursing and the like was not considered a fitting vocation for an unmarried lady, but I didn't care. Looking back now, I can see how they would be concerned. Arthur was a real handsome fellow and one or two of the maids at church had their heads turned by him.'

'Shall I mix the batter for the pudding today?' Mariah volunteered.

'Go on, then.' Dora sat at her kitchen table and chatted to Mariah as she measured and stirred. 'Mrs Shaw was the midwife round here. She did all the doctoring for the poorer folk as well.'

'What happened to Mrs Shaw?'

'She died the same winter as Father. There was a fever that year that took a lot of folk from round here.'

'That must have been hard for you and Fanny. And Mr Shaw.'

'We helped each other through. I had been going to see sick folk with Mrs Shaw, reg'lar, before she caught the fever. I knew all her doctoring ways. I still turn out when I'm called on, and I can get to the village quicker than anybody from town.'

'Don't you ever get lonely?'

'Not me, lass. I like it out here on my own, away from prying eyes and loose tongues.'

'Me, too.'

'Aye, I know,' Dora responded sympathetically.

'Did you never want to be married?'

'Oh, I did that! Mrs Shaw had told me I should get wed and have my own babbies if I was going to be of any use to others. But there weren't many suitors to choose from around here. Those we didn't lose to soldiering went off to ironstone pits or coal mines in other parts, or to the foundries in town. There were plenty of lasses for them to pick from in town.'

'Your sister seems happy with Mr Thorpe and their children.'

'Born to be a wife, she was, baking bread, salting down the pig, pickling vegetables.' Dora sighed and looked around her. 'The house always looked nice when she was here.'

Mariah glanced up from her mixing, at the framed samplers hanging on fresh whitewashed walls, and a mellowed wooden dresser stacked with pretty china. 'It looks nice now.'

'Not bad, I suppose. Mostly our Fanny's doing, though, when she visits. I have always been more interested in looking after the animals – and the doctoring and nursing, o' course.'

'That's lucky for me – and for a lot of other folk, I'm sure.'

'Me and Fanny helped out at the Hall from time

192

to time. When they had their shooting parties to visit. But not long after Father died that stopped because her Ladyship upped and left and we had to find something else to make ends meet. When Father was alive he used to keep a sow and I lent a hand when she farrowed. Right from being little I was into all that. Not our Fanny, though. She liked the indoors, like our mother.'

Mariah smiled. It cheered her to listen to Dora talk about her younger days and her family. 'My mother was a good housekeeper, too,' she said, 'but she liked doing her sewing more than anything. She taught me all she knew.' Mariah lifted the spoon from her mixing bowl. 'This batter's ready now. Shall I put a tin in the oven?'

'Let it stand for a bit first.'

Dora bent over the fireplace to give her cauldron a stir and went on. 'I learned more from my father and Mrs Shaw. If there was a runt in the sow's litter, my father let me fetch it inside to see if I could rear it. Ee, I was full of questions in those days. I wanted to know everything about how the piglets got inside the sow and how she knew when they were ready to come out.' Dora laughed lightly. 'Mother told me it was God's doing and our Fanny knew no better. I never swallowed that, of course. I knew it was something to do with the season and the boar. But Father was really strict about us girls staying out of the way when the boar was here.'

'Did Mrs Shaw have any children?'

'Oh, aye. Three lasses and two lads.'

'And none of the girls wanted to follow their mother's calling?'

Dora grimaced and shook her head. 'They wanted better for themselves. Nursemaids and lady's maids to the gentry. No, it was left to me to go with Mrs Shaw when she had to turn out in the middle of the night in winter. Besides, after seeing to the sow and the lambing every spring, helping the midwife came natural to me.'

'Where are her girls now?'

'Long gone. All three. They went off into service in Derbyshire. Big house there, three times the size of the Hall. And very proper they were, too. They had royalty to visit and everything. Still do, but all the Shaw girls have left now, got themselves wed and settled over there.'

Mariah thought how wonderful it must be to have sisters. Like the Thorpes. They may be poor and living in a miner's cottage, but they had each other. Oh, how she missed her mother! She missed her so much, it hurt. 'Don't you miss your sister, Dora?' she asked.

'Yes, I do. But she has her Arthur and that's that.'

Dora's sharp tone made Mariah look up at her face and the older woman went quiet for a moment. But she recovered quickly and smiled. 'You look tired already, Mariah. Why don't you bring your mending and sit by the fire for an hour before dinner?'

Mariah sighed. She felt ill most of the time, she could not remember feeling this way before and her energy flagged easily. Dora said her flesh had healed well and she kept herself busy around the house and garden. But the feelings and images of that night were still strong in her mind and they ate away at her reason. Sometimes she felt so

194

angry with those men she could not deal with it and wanted nothing more than to sweep all the pots off the table so they smashed on the floor. She never did, of course, and her resentment festered.

Sewing soothed her. It reminded her of happier times and helped her to think of other things and calmed her mind. But such calmness was usually temporary.

After a while Dora said, 'I think you can put that tin in the oven now. This stew is about ready and I'm feeling peckish.'

Mariah put aside her mending and got up. 'I'll set the table. I'm hungry, too.'

'That's a good sign.'

After dinner, when the washed pots were lined up on Dora's kitchen dresser and they had fetched fresh water from the spring, they sat by the fire for a rest, waiting for the kettle to boil on the hob.

'How are you feeling now?' Dora asked.

'Better. I just hope the queasiness doesn't come back.'

Dora pursed her lips, fearing it would. 'Shall I make some of my mint tea for you? It might settle your stomach a bit.'

'Thanks. I'll get the cups and you can tell me more about when you and Fanny were younger.'

When they were seated again, sipping the hot tangy liquor, sweetened with honey, Dora resumed her tale.

'The winter was the worst. The days were short, always overcast with heavy cloud, and the weather was bitter cold, so none of us ventured out much except for church. But we survived. Our Fanny always had a good fire to cook our dinner, and the washing and mending to fill her days. Arthur was there for the outdoor work. We'd killed the pig before the winter set in and it was salted down in a lead trough in the outhouse. He cleaned out the empty sty and whitewashed it ready for a new piglet in the spring. I was called out quite often, too, for my medicines, and usually came back with something for the table. Arthur built that big wooden cupboard in the back scullery for me to keep my lotions and potions in.'

That was the start of it for me, Dora thought. That was when I knew I had fallen for him. Best not talk to Mariah of courting and such like right now. It might upset her and set her back again.

Mariah pulled her shawl closer about her shoulders and thought how cosy this little house was and how lucky Dora and Fanny were to have each other. The fire warmed her face and her eyelids drooped.

Dora drank her cooling tea and thought she would let her doze a while. Mariah had eaten a good dinner today and it was clearly making her sleepy. It was nice to sit quiet by the fire and remember. As Mariah dozed, Dora thought back to earlier times, when she was Mariah's age, Fanny was one and twenty and Arthur just two years older, and those stolen times together.

Chapter 18

Dora watched her fire burn down. The flames flickered low and the glowing embers fell quietly. She decided not to add more wood. It might spit and crackle and wake Mariah. Besides, what had happened that winter was as clear to her now as though it were yesterday, and she might say too much if Mariah woke.

Dora did not plan it. It just happened. It was before Arthur had asked Fanny to be his wife. Dora had been out to see a sick child and, on the way back, called in to look up a treatment in one of Mrs Shaw's books. Arthur was there. He often went over to look after Mr Shaw and read the news sheets to him as his eyes weren't so good. When Dora saw Arthur tending quietly to the old man, in his waistcoat and shirt sleeves, she felt desire shoot through her like nothing she had experienced before.

She had some knowledge of men from Mrs Shaw's books and the widowers she had helped tend when they were dying and had no family to see to them. But this was different, an overwhelming need to explore Arthur's manliness and strength in a much more intimate and personal way. A way that was forbidden until a man and a woman were wed. In that isolated cottage, watching him move quietly about his tasks, she was overpowered by such a yearning for him she did not know what to do.

She wanted to lie with him.

She had seen the way he looked at her, sometimes covertly, in the kitchen at home. If she caught his eye, he turned away and went outside. Mrs Judd was right to be concerned about them living under the same roof. Men had these urges; Dora knew that Arthur had these urges.

But Mrs Judd had not warned her that she might have these urges too.

When it happened, it was all her own doing. Mr Shaw had taken to his bed early with a sleeping draught. Arthur and Dora were tidying round, damping down the fire and laying the breakfast table. They did not say much. But they kept bumping into each other as they moved about Mr Shaw's kitchen. Dora held onto Arthur's arm, first to steady herself, and then to stop him moving from her. She did not let go and, when he tried to pull away, she tugged at his sleeve.

'Arthur, I've seen the way you look at me.'

'Stop this at once, Dora.'

'Why?' Her hands reached around the back of his neck and she pulled his head towards hers and kissed him briefly on his lips, pressing her body against his, wanting him.

Taken by surprise, Arthur wiped the back of his hand across his mouth and exclaimed, 'Good God! What on earth do you think you are doing?'

'Kiss me, Arthur. Put your arms around me and kiss me. Please?'

'Certainly not! You shock me with this behaviour.'

'You want me, too! I know you do! Why do you

198

deny it?'

'This is nonsense. Now, move aside so I can pass.'

'No. I love you. No one will ever know. Not even Mr Shaw. Come on, Arthur.' Her heavy winter shawl had suddenly become a hindrance and she pulled it away to reveal her throat.

'You must stop this now.'

But she had wanted this since the first day he had stepped over their threshold. 'I won't. And I won't let you run away from me.' She put her arms around him to hold him close.

His shoulders were sagging forward, his head bending to hers. She raised her mouth to his again, this time opening her lips and seeking his tongue with hers. Her knees buckled and she sank to the floor, pulling him down with her.

'Dora, Dora, what are you doing to me?'

But he no longer resisted her and her aching body melted for him.

'Hush. Here, come closer to the fire.' Hastily she bunched up her skirts and scrambled out of her drawers, discarding them on the rag rug by the hearth. She remembered her need at that time, her young, desperate need to know what it felt like to be possessed by him. No one had told her how much *she* would want this.

'This is what you want, isn't it? Say it is. Say it, Arthur.'

His voice came out a strangled, sorrowful moan. 'No, it's not right.'

But as he said it, his actions told a different story. 'Do it. Do it now,' she whispered urgently.

Her veins were throbbing in her head and her

199

body opened up to him. He cried out, in a soft, throaty, satisfying moan that made her want to weep with joy. She felt so wonderfully fulfilled she thought nothing could spoil that moment.

But Arthur was distraught and angry. He scrambled quickly off her, pulling up his clothes and scolding her. 'Get up and dress yourself at once! You are a wanton woman, and you should be ashamed of yourself!'

'I love you.'

'Nonsense! You've behaved no better than a harlot. I can see you've been allowed far too much freedom since your father passed on. You know far too much for an unmarried lady of your young years. This will not do!'

'But you wanted me, too.'

'I am a man. It is different for a man. Did not Mrs Shaw tell you that? You seem to know all there is to be known about these things!'

'Please do not say that. Do not spoil it for me.'

'Spoil it! What are you talking about?' He shook his head and then held it in his hands. 'Oh God! What have I done? I have ruined you. What on God's earth shall I say to your sister?'

'Oh, you mustn't tell Fanny! Please don't tell Fanny. She'll send you away!'

'After this I am sure I should leave anyway.'

'No!'

They sat on the rag rug, in the darkness, dishevelled and silent, watching the fire burn low until Arthur took a deep breath and said, 'We must forget this happened. I am sorry, Dora. I have wronged you. The fault is all with me. The Lord presented me with temptation and I gave in to it. I shall pray to the Lord for forgiveness. We shall both pray for forgiveness.'

But all Dora could think about was that he had not told her he loved her.

'Whatever you do, you must not tell Fanny either. Promise me.'

Of course she promised. She did not want to have Arthur sent away. It was the first secret she had kept from her sister. Dora was not proud of what she had done but she did not regret it, whatever Arthur might think of her.

Arthur avoided being alone with her from then on. If they did find themselves in the same room without other company, he made excuses and left. He would not even look her in the eye and shortly afterwards, he and Fanny were betrothed.

As Dora watched Mariah dozing by the fire, she thought back to that stolen time with Arthur wistfully. Her illicit passion had been short lived but it caused repercussions for the rest of her life.

Mariah's eyes shot open suddenly. 'Did I fall asleep? I am so sorry, it must be the heat of the fire.'

'Do you good, dear. It's getting cold outside now. We'll shut up the hens early tonight and put bricks to warm for our beds. I don't want you catching a chill now you're on your feet again.'

'You were talking about your younger days, Dora. Tell me some more.'

'Oh, nothing really. Just that when Arthur came to lodge with us, I fell for him real bad.'

'But he married Fanny? He married your sister?'

'Aye, he did. Our Fanny was always more closed

up than me, so you couldn't really tell what she was thinking, but I reckon she loved him more than I did. Mine was like many a young passion that flares out of control and then dies when – when it isn't returned.'

'Did Fanny know you had fallen for him?' Mariah asked.

'Not then. I thought when they were gone it would be an end to the matter.' But I was wrong, she thought. Arthur did not forget, or forgive, in spite of all his praying. Neither himself nor me. I think he would have got over it if Fanny had not found out.

'Did you tell her?'

Dora shook her head. 'Neither of us breathed a word at first. But she found out all right. She might be quiet, our Fanny, but she's clever with it.' Dora stood up and stretched. 'It caused a split between us for a while. Fanny and me made it up eventually, but Arthur will never forgive me.'

'That seems a bit harsh on you.'

'It's another story, Mariah my dear, another story.'

Besides, thought Dora, I don't want to let anything slip. Family secrets are best kept in the family. She got up and took the teapot through to the scullery.

'I'll go and shut up the hens and see to the pig before the light goes,' Mariah volunteered.

Dora watched her walk down the garden and sighed. She had told Mariah about her love for Arthur but not that she had lain with him, or the consequences. Mariah was not family. Dora must watch her tongue in future.

Chapter 19

The following morning Mariah sat on the edge of her bed holding her stomach as the nausea crept over her. Saliva trickled into her mouth and bile rose in her gullet.

'I'm going to be sick!' Her voice was strangled as she reached under the bed for the chamber pot and sank to her knees on the floor, helplessly retching and choking.

But there was nothing in her stomach and it was soon over. Dora came into her room and Mariah took the cup of water she had brought, pulling herself awkwardly to her feet and sinking gratefully onto the mattress.

'I had a bad dream,' Mariah explained. 'I saw those men again, they tried to–' She choked on the words.

'Don't get up too quickly. Take things slowly for a while.' Her own heart was sinking. She had seen women in this condition too often to mistake it. Oh Lord, she thought, I cannot tell her yet, not until she is stronger. It will be too much for her to bear. 'I'll mix you something to settle your stomach. Then get a bit of fresh air, but don't stay out in the cold for too long.'

Half an hour later, Mariah dressed and, refreshed, carefully ate some porridge and said, 'I feel better now, thanks, Dora. A little walk might do me good this morning.'

'Good idea, lass. I'll come with you and show you the way. There's a footpath through the wood and over the fields to Keppel village. It goes across the parkland in front of Keppel Hall, but the present master doesn't mind village folk using it. Not like the old squire. He was a right tartar. His son's different though. Nice fellow. A bit of a dandy, but nice with it.'

Mariah wrapped a woollen shawl around her shoulders and put on her cloak. It was heavy on her thin body and it made her feel weaker than she was. She gritted her teeth and resolved to fight this decline! She must get well again!

She hated those men for what they had done to her and she would never be able to understand their actions, let alone find a scrap of forgiveness. Never. She could not. She could only believe, with Dora's wise counsel, that she had to get on with her life, a life that would be different now. She did not know how, just that it would, for she was a different person from the one who had lodged in Mrs Thorpe's front room.

Dora buttoned on a gentleman's long hunting coat over her dark brown working dress. It was made of thick waxed cotton and was old and worn. She tied a leather belt tightly around her waist and her skirts pushed out through the front opening and the back vent. It kept out the wind and the rain, and Mariah realised it was much more serviceable than a cloak against the brambles and undergrowth.

As they walked, an idea began to form in Mariah's head for a coat, a proper ladies coat. If only she had some cloth. The more she thought about it, the more she liked her idea. She would make a Sunday best coat for Dora, as a gift. The plan occupied her mind and cheered her.

The family resemblance between the sisters was strong. Both Dora and Fanny had large grey eyes, good cheekbones and healthy complexions. Arthur, too, had robust features with a straight nose and square jaw. Mariah realised, now, where Emma and Daniel got their strikingly handsome looks.

It was a bright, cold autumn day and Mariah inhaled its freshness, bringing a spot of colour to her pallid cheeks. They followed a pathway through the woods, and then a worn footpath over the meadow past grazing sheep and rabbits. Eventually they crossed a wide track that led away from Keppel Hall to the distant park boundary. A rider was cantering along it, heading towards the gatehouse and onwards to the village. As he drew closer, he reined in his horse and slowed.

Mariah clutched at Dora's arm and whispered, 'Who is it? What does he want?'

'It's all right, love. It's only the master on his way to town.'

He waited for them to reach him, then lifted his tall hat and bowed his head, 'Good day to you, Mrs Barton.'

His hair, Mariah noticed, was fair and curly and his face had an aristocratic delicacy not weathered by outdoor labours. She looked down and pulled the hood of her cloak closely around her head, hiding her hair and most of her face.

'Good day to you, sir,' Dora replied. 'A fine morning for a ride.'

'Yes indeed. And for walking too.' He looked at Mariah, raised his eyebrows and smiled. 'Why does your companion hide from me?'

Dora took her cue. 'Mr Fitzkeppel, may I present Miss Bowes, a – er – a friend of my niece. She is staying with me for the present.'

'Sir.' Mariah glanced up at him and dropped a curtsey. His skin was pale but not freckled like hers and his eyes pale blue. He had fine-boned features and sat tall and straight in the saddle carrying his dress well. They were garments that caught her attention. From the high polish on his chestnut boots and his soft doeskin breeches to the cut of his jacket and the frilled trim of his silken shirt. Mariah's expert eye recognised good tailoring when she saw it. A gentle approving smile lit her eyes.

Mr Fitzkeppel responded with a brief nod and murmured, 'Miss Bowes. Miss Bowes? A cousin, perhaps, of Henry Bowes? Of Bowes Ironworks in town?'

'We are related, sir.'

He replaced his high hat, a well-made hat with a cashmere finish if she were not mistaken, Mariah thought. 'Enjoy your walk, ladies.' He spurred his horse and rode on.

'So that is Mr Fitzkeppel,' Mariah murmured.

'Why? What do you know of him?'

'My half-brother, Henry, is acquainted with him. They went to the same school, though Mr Fitzkeppel is several years older than Henry, I believe.'

And now I know where Henry gets his notions of grandeur, Mariah thought. Henry would be very comfortable in the surroundings of Keppel

Hall, with the friendship of its young master. But she wondered how Ezekiel would fit in there, away from his gang of labourers and his furnace. Oh well, it was none of her concern now, thank goodness.

She said, 'Back there, he called you Mrs Barton.'

'Every one does and most folk think I am a widow.'

'You had a husband?'

'I was never wed, lass. Mrs Shaw thought it was for the best if people thought I was a married woman. They don't hold with their midwife being a maiden lady round here. So one day I said I was Mrs Barton instead of Miss Barton and I have been ever since. I wear my mother's wedding ring and none o' the younger folk question it. Not too many of the older ones who know different are still alive now. Mr Shaw does, and a few in the village.'

'What about the master?'

'No, he's too young to know about the Bartons.'

'Young, too, to be master of the Hall. But a fine-looking gentleman if I may say so,' Mariah commented.

Dora agreed, adding, 'His sister, too, is very pretty. Fair-skinned, like he is, and with hair the colour of honeycomb. They deserve better, poor mites.'

'Poor mites?' Mariah glanced around at the Hall and parkland. 'Is all this not theirs?'

'Oh yes. Master Nathaniel is one and twenty now and has just inherited. He is unmarried, so his sister Miss Christobel acts as mistress of the Hall.'

'They are not exactly poor, then.'

'No, I do not mean they lack wealth. Heavens, no! But they might as well have been orphans for most of their childhood. The pair of them were brought up by schoolmasters and governesses, and latterly, the lawyers who were their guardians.'

'Yes, I remember hearing at the beast market when their father died.'

'Seven years ago, now. Master Nathaniel was fourteen and Christobel just sixteen. Old Fitz-keppel was in his seventies then and had been ailing for years. He was a crusty old bachelor when he married and got steadily worse by all accounts.'

'I see. What about their mother?'

'Mrs Fitzkeppel? She ran off with her Italian lover. She came from the Dales. She was a pretty little thing when she arrived at the Hall. Barely nineteen and him in his fifties; he could have been her grandfather. When Fanny and I helped out at the Hall we heard tales of what went on, enough to make your hair curl!'

'What on earth do you mean? Did he beat her or something?'

Dora gave a low laugh. 'Ee, lass, no. Nothing like that. Antics in the bedchamber.' She stopped suddenly. 'I've said too much. Unmarried ladies are not supposed to know about such things.'

'No,' Mariah agreed quietly.

'I'm sorry, lass. I shouldn't have talked like that.'

'Of course you should. There is no sense in treating me as though I shall break in two every time I am reminded of what happened to me. I do not know why those evil men did what they did to me. But it is over and I am alive. Alive and – and I shall be strong again. One day. I shall.'

'Strong in body, I am sure. But you must look to purging the memories. I know they still plague you and that's not so good. You do not want that dreadful night haunting you for ever.'

'How do I stop it, Dora? I have tried to blank it from my mind but it is still there, as clear as yesterday. I don't believe I shall ever forget it.' Mariah added bitterly, 'Why are men so evil? Why?'

'Nay, they're not all like that, love.' Mariah was clutching tightly at her hand. 'You will have to put it all behind you, though, or else the memories will eat you up and spoil your chances of finding yourself a decent man to–'

'Decent man! *Decent man*,' Mariah retaliated scornfully. 'What decent man would look at me now?'

'No no, don't talk like that. You are still raw and hurting. But you will get over it. You will.' Dora wished she felt as confident as she sounded.

'I'll never get over it,' Mariah muttered.

Dora stayed silent. She kept a hold of her hand until they reached the boundary wall near the village and she suggested, 'Shall we sit and rest a while?'

Mariah nodded and leaned against the cold stone. 'Where is Mrs Fitzkeppel now?'

'Abroad somewhere. She has no contact with her children and even her own parents disowned her. Her husband didn't care about anything except his heir and the family name. She wanted to take Miss Christobel with her, but old Fitzkeppel was going to have her locked away in an asylum and she had to flee the country. So, you see, Miss Christobel and Master Nathaniel were more or less left on their own from a very young age.'

As I am now, Mariah thought. Poor things. Dora was right. No amount of wealth could be a substitute for your own mother. Mariah was aeons apart from the Fitzkeppels in her position in life but felt a bond of deprivation between them. Oh, how she missed her mother!

She thought of Arthur and Fanny Thorpe in their overcrowded cottage, a cottage that Daniel and Emma returned to at every opportunity. Mariah knew why. They didn't have land or wealth, but they had each other. Suddenly, Mariah felt very lonely.

She stretched out both her hands towards Dora and said, 'Thank you, again, for all you have done for me.'

Dora gave her a wry smile. 'You're a good lass. You never deserved what happened to you.'

The two women sat in silence for a moment each with their own thoughts, then got up to retrace their steps back to Dora's little house.

'My, it's turning chilly. We're in for a cold one this winter.'

'That coat is perfect for the rain, but you need something warmer when it's frosty. Shall I make a nice Sunday coat for you, Dora? A proper tailored one with a lining and a shoulder cape and everything.'

'Ee, lass, can you do that?'

'Oh yes, my mother taught me.'

'Where would I get the cloth, though? I can keep my little house warm and dry and put food on the table, but I couldn't run to buying that kind of cloth.'

'I've thought about that. I shall sell my silver picture frame. That will fetch enough.'

'And more besides, I should think. No, I can't let you do that for me.'

'But you have to let me do something to thank you.'

'Not your silver frame, though. It has your mother's likeness in it.'

'I shall keep the likeness, for that *is* important to me. But, truly, Dora, my mother would have approved of putting the frame to such good use. I shall have enough to buy cloth and notions for making other things, things I can sell at the market in town. I can begin to earn my keep. It is what I need to do, Dora, to get along. To get better. I need to do what I have always done when Mother was alive. And, eventually, pay my way with real money. If I may stay, of course.'

'Of course you may. Stay with me for as long as you wish. Are you sure about the frame?'

'Yes.'

'Well then, we can take the carrier into town next market day.'

Mariah inhaled sharply. 'Oh no, not me. Not yet. What if I see those men at the market? I am not ready to face that yet. Would you go for me, Dora? Take my frame to the silversmith in the High Street and get as much as you can for it. Then go next door to the draper and choose some good woollen cloth, and some satin for the lining.'

'A satin lining? You'll be giving me airs.'

But Mariah was not listening. 'Oh, and I shall need my sewing things from your sister's house as well. It will be too much for you to carry on

211

your own.'

'We-e-ell,' Dora began, 'I could ask our Daniel to bring them over on a Sunday.'

Mariah's heart lurched. 'D-Daniel? Over here? Oh no, I should be too ashamed to see him. He knows about the attack. He found me in that field–'

'I shan't ask him if you do not want him here,' Dora added hastily. 'It's just that he, well, he is always asking after you and he – he is so distressed about what happened to you.'

'I do not see why *he* should be so distressed. It was not Daniel who attacked me.'

'No, but he blames himself, you see, because he was carrying on with–' Dora stopped, unsure of what Mariah knew.

'With Mrs Cluff. I know Emma said she was his sweetheart. Dora, she's a married lady! How could he?' Mariah's heart was beginning to pound in her breast. 'I am not stupid, Dora. I have been ill but I have not lost my wits. He must have lied about her to his parents!'

'But *he* did not lie! It was Lily who lied. She told him she was a widow and he believed her. We all believed her, even her neighbours at Canal Bank Cottages. Her husband is in gaol and she took some of the money he had stolen and moved to get away from his family. She lied to them as well. She told them she had to look after her dying cousin in the next county.'

'I didn't know about that,' Mariah said quietly.

'Her husband's family were suspicious and came looking for her. They had heard rumours and when they demanded to know where her money

212

was coming from if it wasn't her husband's, she told them our Daniel had given it to her.'

'He really did not know Lily was married?'

'No, he did not. Our Daniel is not a philanderer. He's a good lad. He could have wed any of the lasses from round here years ago and he did not. He worked hard and looked after his family. But he's like his fa–.' Dora faltered. 'He – well, he wanted his own woman. He had asked her to marry him, you know. When he got the supervisor's job with your father, he asked her to marry him.'

'Where is Mrs Cluff now?' Mariah asked.

'Went off back to Manchester. The end cottage is empty now. Good riddance if you ask me.'

'Yes, indeed,' Mariah echoed with a sigh. 'I expect that's what people think of me, now. A disgraced woman. Unworthy.'

'Why should they?'

'People talk about these things.'

'Only when they know about them.'

'Of course they know! Like everyone knows about Mrs Fitzkeppel!'

'No. The Fitzkeppels were different. Their servants talked, as servants do. Everyone thinks you were knocked sideways by a cart horse on the towpath!'

'Not quite everyone – there's your sister and her husband, and Daniel, and Lord knows who else.'

'I have not breathed a word to anyone, I swear.'

'And the others who know what really happened to me? What about them?'

'There's only Daniel, Fanny, Arthur and me. That's all.'

'Not Emma? Meg and Liddy?'

Dora shook her head. 'No. Fanny would not tell them. As far as anyone else is concerned, you were thrown off your feet.'

'I see. I'm sorry, Dora. It's just that, oh, I don't know, it is all so dirty and humiliating. I feel soiled by it all. And worthless. I am – I am so ashamed.'

'I know. But you must try not to let it consume you like this. It was no fault of yours.'

Tears welled in Mariah's eyes. Dora noticed them and began, hurriedly, to talk of different things. 'Look, this sewing idea of yours is a good one. It will help to take your mind away from all this. Why don't we go into my front room when we get back and see if we can make space for you to sew in there? My mother's old oak dining table might be just the thing.'

Dora's table was a solid heavy piece, darkened by years of waxing, and it took pride of place under the window, graced by a white lace runner and burnished brass bowl.

'The only thing is,' Dora explained, 'it's got a rickety leg and it wobbles a bit, but I'm sure our Dan–' Dora stopped suddenly.

'It's perfect.' Mariah ran her fingers over its smooth polished surface and as she did it rocked noticeably. 'Apart from this corner,' she added. 'You were saying about the leg?'

'One of the legs is a bit loose. At the back. It has always been a bit wobbly there. Piece of soft wood gone rotten in the joint, I reckon. I...'

'Yes?'

'I was thinking of asking our Daniel to fix it.

214

Will you mind?'

'Of course not. Why should I?'

'I mean, ask our Daniel to come round here. But not if you don't want to see him.'

How would she overcome her embarrassment? How could she face a man who had seen her naked body? Who had touched her most intimate parts when he had wrapped her and carried her home? A man who knew she had been defiled by not one but two men? How could she face him knowing that, like her, he would be remembering that night?

Dora continued, 'If you really don't want him here, I'm sure I can wedge the joint somehow and stop the wobble.'

Mariah heaved a sigh. She would have to face him sooner or later. 'No, Dora, ask Daniel to come and mend it.'

'Not if he upsets you so much. When I go to market, I'll ask him to send Ned instead.'

'Daniel is your nephew, and he ought not to stay away on my account.' She straightened and inhaled sharply. 'I can keep out of his way for a day, I am sure.'

'You will eat your dinner with us, surely? It will seem strange if you do not.'

Mariah resigned herself to this. 'All right. I cannot hide for ever.'

Disgrace and shame weakened her resolve. It seeped into her heart, and she resented this enforced intrusion. She tried desperately to suppress her anger, but it would not leave her. Why did Daniel have to come here, reminding

215

her again of that night and those despicable men?

She wished she could rid them from her mind, but she could not. She wished they were dead, but they were not. Sometimes she could smell their sweat and foul breath in her face, feel their hands holding down her arms and legs and worst of all, feel the scratching of their coarse hair on her vulnerable skin as they invaded her. God forgive her, but she wanted to kill them for what they had done to her. *She wanted to kill them.*

She took herself off to the copse and screamed as loudly as she could, long and hard until there was no breath left in her body and she fell into a crumpled heap on the damp leaves of the woodland floor and wept. She knew that Dora had followed her and was grateful she did not comment. She was thankful when Dora took her hand silently, led her back to a comfy chair by her kitchen fire and made her tea. Real Indian tea, with a splash of brandy.

Mariah pulled herself together, stood up and said she was well and occupied herself with mending. There was plenty of mending at Dora's. Dora was good with the sick and with women's ailments, but hopeless with a needle and some of her sewing efforts around the house raised a smile on Mariah's tear-stained face. She looked forward to making Dora a new warm coat for the winter.

Chapter 20

Ezekiel took off his hat and wiped his brow with the back of a grimy hand. 'That's a grand job done, lads. The fire's pulling a treat now. Thorpe, make sure you keep the heat up.'

'Aye, Mr Bowes. Steel'll be ready by next week, don't you worry.' Daniel surveyed the yard. His men were busy moving more coal in barrows, ready to be shovelled into the furnace.

Ezekiel sucked his teeth and gave his head a shake. 'Chimney'll be smoking on the Sabbath, though.'

'It won't be on its own in this town, sir.'

'No. I never kept the Sabbath meself. But many do. You'll have to keep an eye on it yerself.'

'I wanted to talk to you about that, Mr Bowes.'

'Oh aye? Let's get away from this heat, then.'

Daniel picked up Mr Bowes' jacket from the mounting stone near the office steps. 'I'd like some time off this Sunday, sir.'

'Going courting, eh?'

'No, sir. I've a few repair jobs to do at my aunty's cottage.'

'Can't be done, lad. I'll not be here. I'm invited out to dinner with Henry.'

'I've no need for you, sir. Young Ned over there is more than capable of watching the fire and keeping it hot. Look at him working, sir. Got a good head on his shoulders an' all.'

217

'Ned?'

'Aye, sir. He knows what to do. I'll see to everything before I go and be back before tea.'

Ezekiel thought for a minute. Thorpe was producing better steel than he ever had, and more of it. He was getting a good price, too. 'Are you sure you can trust him?' he asked.

'I wouldn't leave him with the furnace if I couldn't, sir.'

Ezekiel knew this was true. 'It's your responsibility. If owt goes wrong it'll be your fault.'

'I know. I'll be back even quicker with a horse,' Daniel ventured, and added, 'One of the cart horses.'

'Aye, I suppose you will. Don't you touch my hunter, though.'

'No, sir.' Daniel helped Mr Bowes into his jacket and watched him walk back to the house with a smile.

Aunty Dora wanted her table mending so Mariah could sew on it. He was to carry some cloth over at the same time. His heart lifted as he realised Mariah must be feeling better. Dora wouldn't have asked him over if she had thought it would upset her. He'd be able to see for himself how she was, and do something to help her. Something useful that would please her. It was only a small thing, but it was a start. He felt a pleasure coursing though his veins and looked forward to the Sabbath.

'He's here!'

The following Sunday, Dora was pulling grass from between the tansy and feverfew in her little front garden. She saw Daniel leading one of Bowes' heavy draught horses up the lane. Laden with bundles and boxes and Daniel's carpentry tools, the gentle beast plodded slowly, as though enjoying his country outing. The weight of this burden was nothing compared with his usual haul of raw iron uphill from the canal to the ironworks furnace.

Mariah heard Dora call and jumped, startled into a sudden nervousness. She was in the kitchen, preparing vegetables for a Sunday dinner they would eat together when Daniel had finished mending the table. Quickly, she gathered up the corners of her jute apron and scraped the vegetable trimmings into this makeshift bag.

'Just taking these down to the pig,' she called and hurried out through the scullery to tip them over the sty wall. Mariah dawdled as long as she dared, until she heard Dora call her name from the door.

'All right.' She smoothed down her apron, straightened her back and forced herself to go into the kitchen.

Dora's face was a picture of pleasure. She was clearly so delighted to see Daniel that Mariah felt guilty about being there and the cause of their separation. She must try to behave normally, for Dora's sake. She would make conversation, be civil and polite, and not sink into one of the depressions that overcame her when she was reminded of that dreadful night.

It was easy to see why Daniel's family was so proud of him. Tall and straight with broad shoulders, strong arms and good features, he seemed to fill Dora's kitchen with his presence. He was not in his Sunday suit and looked ready for country work in a flannel shirt tucked into moleskin trousers under a riding jacket that had seen better days. His riding boots, too, were well worn and mud-splattered from leading the horse. He was smiling, easily, openly, naturally, at his aunty who he was so obviously pleased to see. Until he became aware of Mariah's presence.

Then he turned to her and his expression became more serious, his voice softer. 'Mariah. Dearest Mariah, how are you?'

'I – I am – I am quite well.' She swallowed, feeling a blush rise in her face. She resisted the urge to turn and run and added, 'Thank you. And you?'

'Very well, thanks.' He took a step forward. 'I am so happy you are up and about at last and that you are staying on here.' His arms moved towards her, just a fraction.

Mariah, instinctively, took a step backwards. She was relieved to see he let his hands drop to his sides and then put them behind his back. He was looking at her so intently she felt herself go hot all over. What was he searching for? Some outward sign that she was a defiled and disgraced woman? Was not her shame and degradation clear enough for all to see? Well, she would not stay to be stared at like the freak show from the travelling circus. She took off her jute apron, picked up her workbox and a pair of stockings from the line under the mantelshelf and said to Dora, 'I have finished the vegetables. I am just going upstairs with this darning.'

220

'Mariah?' She heard the query in Daniel's voice as she hurried from the room.

Dora put her hand on his arm. 'Leave her. It's hard for her to see you. It brings back the memories. She – she is an angry young woman.' Dora frowned as she saw the anguish contort his face, and suggested, 'Will you take a tankard of ale?'

Daniel grimaced at Dora's words. He had believed that Mariah was much improved, but what he saw told him otherwise. Lord help him, what should he do? How could he ever repair the damage he had done her? How could he ever make it up to her?

He said, 'I'll unload the horse and feed him first. I have a box of things for Mariah, from Mam's house. Emma packed it for me. And the new cloth you bought the other day. I hope I have brought everything Mariah needs...' He faltered. He had no idea what Mariah really needed to help her through her trouble. Except, perhaps, for him to leave.

'I'll come and help you unload,' Dora interrupted briskly. 'Fanny said she would send some butcher's meat for dinner.'

'Oh yes. A good piece of beef brisket for boiling. And some fresh suet for dumplings.'

'Best get it on then, if we want it done for dinner today.'

'This parcel from the draper's is heavy. He delivered it to Emma like you asked him to. Where shall I put it?'

The cloth, Dora thought suddenly, that will cheer Mariah. 'I'll take it upstairs while you're working in the front room.'

'Let me. It's too heavy for you.'

'No! You stay down here!'

Daniel slumped against the wall and lowered his voice. 'Does she hate me so much that I cannot even carry her boxes upstairs?'

'It's – it's not that she *hates* you.'

'But she won't talk to me! She won't even look at me!'

'Hush, she'll hear you.'

He groaned anxiously. 'What can I do? Tell me what I can do?'

'I don't know. Truly, I don't. But do not show you pity her. That will make her humiliation worse.'

Upstairs, Mariah listened to the sounds as Daniel carried in his tools. She realised this was going to be much more of an ordeal than she had imagined. It was not until after Daniel had finished unloading, and his horse was munching oats contentedly from a nose can, that Mariah moved to her chair by the window to do her darning.

A creak on the stairs made her stop and hold her breath. It was Dora.

'Daniel has brought over the cloth from the draper's. Will you come and unwrap it now?'

'When the table is mended. After dinner, perhaps.'

Dora sat on the edge of the bed and watched Mariah's nimble fingers as she mended her stockings. 'You will come down for your dinner, won't you?'

Mariah nodded. 'I said I would.'

'He means well, Mariah.'

'Does he? Then he should stay away from me. I

do not wish to face him, knowing what he knows and – and what he saw.'

'He wants to help you.'

'There is nothing he can do! There is nothing anyone can do.'

Dora sighed. Mariah was right. But that did not help Daniel, and Dora was obliged to watch her beloved Daniel suffer as he tried to make amends for his part in Mariah's tragedy. Dinner time was a travesty of the friendly meals they had shared at her sister's house. They talked of the weather and the garden and the pig. Daniel was polite and Mariah was civil. They ate the last of the eating pears for pudding, with a wedge of crumbly cheese from the Dales, and then got up to clear away.

Mariah washed the pots in the scullery. Daniel went outside to chop wood in the back yard. Dora made some tea and began to wilt from the effort of keeping a smile on her face.

When Mariah came into the kitchen from the scullery with a stack of clean crockery, Dora commented, 'Daniel has finished my table.'

Mariah continued to arrange the china silently.

'Would you like to see it?'

Mariah nodded. 'Yes.'

'Why don't you ask Daniel to show you what he has done? He did it for you.'

Dora's comment made Mariah feel churlish at her truculence and she could not think of a reason why she should refuse the request. 'All right,' she said.

Although there was a chill in the air, he had taken off his shirt and under-shirt so she could see he was sweating freely as he swung the axe to split logs for the fire. She watched his muscles knot and flex as he worked and she became entranced for a second by his suppleness and strength. She remembered the admiration she had felt for him in his mother's kitchen, and how it had attracted her. What did she feel for him now? she wondered. Nothing? Only a numbness borne out of suffering? Was a void of affection within her to be the legacy of her ordeal?

Daniel concentrated on his task, trying to empty his mind of his grief and frustration. He did not notice Mariah watching him.

She hesitated, unsure of how to proceed, and hovered in the shadow of the house until he flung the axe with a final resounding thud to lodge in a tree stump. He walked over to the water butt and cupped his hands, drinking freely and then sluicing the cold water on his head and shoulders, smoothing it over his chest, arms and face.

Mariah frowned. Seeing him like this, he seemed unknown to her, a different man. She had not thought of him as a – a man like this, before. The earlier appeal she had felt for him had been for his achievements. And he was Dora's nephew, Emma's brother, Ezekiel's supervisor. Yes, that's who he was, Ezekiel's supervisor, not this strong, attractive man who was unsettling her fragile healing. She turned quickly and went back into the scullery.

'Mariah, is that you?' Dora called from the kitchen.

'Yes. I – I – er – I – Daniel needs a drying cloth.' She picked up a folded square of linen from by

224

the sink and went outside again.

He was walking towards her. 'Just the thing,' he said, taking the towel and wiping it over his face and neck and shoulders and chest.

'Dora says you have finished her table,' she said. She felt strangely unsure of herself, stupid and shaky, and she wondered if he'd noticed.

He slowed his drying. She was too pale, he thought. Yet her pallor enhanced her beauty giving her delicate features a waiflike appearance. He wanted to stay around and help her recover. He wanted that so much it hurt and he frowned as he remembered his aunty's wise counsel to keep away.

She was looking in his direction and he tried to fathom her expression. But her eyes had a wariness in them and she did not meet his gaze. There was a brittleness about her that ate away at his heart. He understood why she was guarded in the company of men. But for her not to trust him? When his prime concern was for her well being? He replied gently, 'Yes, I have. I'll show you, shall I?'

'Please.'

'Let me get my shirt first.'

He turned away and so did she.

The three of them gathered in Dora's front room. As Daniel bent over the table, Mariah caught sight of damp patches from water or sweat darkening the shirt on his back. The seam of his sleeve strained as he stretched.

He pushed down hard on the surface of the table with his hands and said, 'There you are, ladies. As good as new. That joint will hold an ox.'

He retrieved the heavy, calico-wrapped draper's parcel from the floor at the back of the room and placed it on the table.

'For you, Mariah.' He watched her and was rewarded by a light in her eyes that he had not seen since before the attack.

'My cloth! At last. Oh, thank you!'

Daniel stepped back as she untied the wrappings. He was so overjoyed to see her smile again that he hardly knew how to respond, and the sheer pleasure on his face brought a tear to Dora's eye.

'We'll have that drink of tea now,' she suggested.

'Good idea. And then I must get back and check on the furnace.'

'Shall I see you again soon, Daniel?'

'I don't know. My time is taken up by the ironworks and, well, Father does not like me to come over here too often.'

Dora smiled, a rueful curve of her mouth that made her look more sad than happy.

After tea, Mariah stood with her hands clasped in front of her and said goodbye to Daniel as he led away his horse down the lane. She was relieved his visit was over. His presence had disturbed her more than she cared to own. It had been an ordeal for her in a way she had not expected. His careful concern for her had stirred at the black hole within her and by doing so had caused her further anxiety. She had only begun to relax at the very end of his visit when she knew he would soon be leaving.

She gave herself a mental shake and turned to Dora. 'Will his father ever come round?' she asked.

Dora shook her head and thought, He'll not forgive himself, so how can he forgive me? She said, 'Our Fanny got over it years ago, but not Arthur. I hope our Daniel is not going to turn out to be as stubborn as his father.'

'I always thought there was a rift like that between my mother and Ezekiel. He never liked my mother. He despised her, and me even more. But she had actually lain with another man and I suppose I was a constant reminder of that.'

'Men are different creatures from women, that's for sure. Oh, enough of this self-pitying! It's the harvest supper in a few weeks and the Fitzkeppels are holding their usual barn dance. It's always a good do, that is. What will you wear?'

'Oh, I'll stay at home if you don't mind, Dora.'

'No! You need to get out and enjoy yourself. It'll cheer you up no end.'

Mariah shook her head. 'People may have heard rumours about me. They'll shun me and gossip about me in corners. I couldn't stand that.'

'Nonsense! They don't even know you.'

'I don't want to go out. Not yet.'

Dora didn't argue with her and waited a couple of days before raising the matter again. They had finished their household chores for the day and eaten a good dinner. Dora had given her kitchen table a scrub and was drinking tea by the fire.

'Will you help me get my gown ready for the barn dance?' she asked. 'It might need a stitch here and there.'

'Yes, of course. Bring it down. The table is nearly dry.'

Together, they examined the checked cotton

gown and repaired weakened seams and loose bows.

'Are you going to let me go on my own, lass?' Dora ventured.

Mariah grimaced silently.

'People in the village know I have someone staying with me, and the master has met you already. What shall I say to them if you're not there?'

Mariah gazed out of the kitchen window. 'The light's going. We'd better finish this for now.'

'Well?'

'Tell them I'm ill.'

'I can't do that. They'd expect me to stay at home with you. They're good folk, Mariah. I won't lie to them. Master Fitzkeppel will be there in all his finery; at least, he will call in for a short time.'

Mariah brightened. 'Oh, he takes an interest in his village events, then?'

'Aye, he's not too bad as a landlord. But farming is not what it was now with all the pits and ironworks taking the labour. He leaves it all to his estate managers and legal people. Mind you, we still have the harvest festival in the village church, and he gives the best harvest supper around here at the barn dance. Everybody joins in. It's tradition.'

'Oh, all right! I'll go, then.'

Dora smiled. 'Champion. What will you wear?'

'This, of course.' Mariah looked down at her dark grey gown.

'I think you should wear something really pretty. You want to look your best for when I present you to the village.'

'I shan't be dancing, Dora. I am still in mourning. I shall stay by the wall and watch the others.'

'If you say so, dear.'

Dora cheered up. She wondered how Mariah would be in the company of other gentlemen. The barn dance would tell. A bit of dancing, a good supper and a cup of punch might be just what Mariah needed to get her back to rights again. She had been much better since she had started sewing and Dora had plenty of time to make sure she looked her best on the night. Her cheeks had a bit of colour in them now. Dora wondered if she had been wrong about her condition. If she was, it was a good job she had kept it to herself.

Chapter 21

But Dora's worst fears were realised when she heard Mariah being sick in the garden the next morning.

Mariah straightened up and looked directly into her eyes. 'Is this what I think it is?' she asked nervously.

'I'm afraid so, my dear. I guessed as much a few weeks ago. When did you last bleed?'

'I have not had any since – since the attack. Well, not my monthly bleeding, anyway.' Mariah sighed heavily and held her head in her hands. 'It cannot be so! I was a maid and it does not happen to maids, does it?'

Dora did not answer directly. She asked, 'Did you get a regular show before the attack?'

'Yes.'

'And definitely none since?'

'No.' Tears welled in Mariah's eyes. She began to feel afraid. 'I am not wed. I cannot be with child.'

'Yes, you can.' Dora nodded ruefully.

Mariah's felt her knees go weak. Her eyes grew wide and round as she contemplated Dora's answer. 'But what shall I do? Where shall I go?'

'Come back inside and sit down. I have suspected this for a while now.'

'Why didn't you say?'

'You were bruised and torn by the attack and I thought, well, there was a chance you might lose it early on.' Dora looked pained.

'Dear God, Dora, this is too much to bear. Have I not suffered enough? Do I have to carry a child as well?'

'Try not to distress yourself.'

But Mariah wasn't listening. She felt fear creep around her heart like the cold hand of winter. A child? A child resulting from that vile act? A child who would not even know which of those men was its father? This was indeed a cruel, cruel hand for the Lord to deal her.

She looked up at Dora and pleaded, 'How can I have a child conceived out of hatred and violence? How can I care for such a child? It does not feel like mine! It feels like – like the devil himself growing inside me! God is as cruel and evil as those beasts that did this to me!'

'Hush, Mariah. Do not blaspheme so. You must stay calm. Come inside and I'll make you an infusion to help with the sickness. You must get used to how you feel and think what you will do.'

'Do? Do? What can I do? I am ruined! I am an

orphaned spinster with no means of support. A defiled woman whom no decent man would want for his wife. And now, with a bastard child growing inside me. Oh, Dora, I'm frightened!'

'There's no need to be. I shall look after you.'

'But I cannot stay here and bring more shame on you!'

'We are isolated here. No one need know.'

'Until the child is born! And then how shall I live? I cannot be a burden on you for the rest of my life!' Mariah felt desperate. What kind of life would it be anyway? One of more humiliation and disgrace? She had had enough of that already! She breathed quietly, 'I do not want a life with a child borne out of sin.'

'What do you mean?'

'My life is worth nothing now. I might as well end it.'

Dora took her by the shoulders and shook her. 'Stop talking like this, Mariah. Other women have suffered this fate and survived. We shall find a way for you.'

'How? I cannot stay here! I shall end up in the poorhouse and be condemned to a life in the laundry to pay for my keep!'

'Do calm yourself. It is not good for you to become so agitated. Your child will suffer.'

'What do I care for this child? I would as soon it was taken from me and brought up as a pauper. It is no child of mine. It is the devil's child.'

'Do not say such things. It is your child. When it is born you will surely love it?' Dora ventured gently.

'How can I? It is not possible! I shall not listen

to you! What do you know of bearing an infant? You know only of others in this matter. You have had none of your own!'

'Yes, I have,' Dora replied quietly. 'I had a child.'

Mariah stopped and turned to her, wide eyed. 'You had a child?'

Dora nodded.

'You were married?'

Dora shook her head. 'I had Arthur's child.'

Mariah's eyes rounded and for a moment she forgot her own troubles.

'Oh Lord! I should not have told you. It happened before he and Fanny were betrothed. At Mr Shaw's house one evening. I loved him! At least, I thought I loved him then.'

'Did Fanny know?'

'Not at first. We did not see much of each other in the first months after they were wed. Arthur was working long hours at the pit and Fanny was busy with her new cottage. But she fell for a baby straightaway, I could tell as soon as I saw her. She was quite poorly with her first, so she came over here to rest in her final months and stayed for a while. Mine was well on the way by then and Fanny was quite overcome with shock.'

'What happened to your child, Dora?'

'My child? My – my–' She choked on the words, took a deep breath and steadied her voice. 'He was born too early, poor little mite, and I – I – I lost him. He's in the churchyard with my parents.'

'I am so, so sorry.'

'It was all a long time ago.' Dora sighed. 'But, you see, I do have some knowledge of your situation. You will love your child, Mariah. As soon as

232

you hold it in your arms.'

'No! Never! My situation is different. This seed inside me is the devil's work! I could never care for a child borne out of such evil! Your child was conceived in love, at least on your part, but mine is not. It is made from revenge and hatred and every time I look at myself in the glass I am reminded of those unspeakable men and the unspeakable things they did to me. My growing belly will only serve to make it a hundredfold worse.'

Mariah began to sob, her tears spilling uncontrollably. 'I was getting better,' she wailed, 'and now this – this *thing* growing inside me. I cannot do this, Dora! Not a lifetime of reliving that night every time I looked at my child!'

Saliva crept into her mouth and her stomach knotted. She retched and dashed again for the garden, holding her stomach and weeping. She was on her knees among the grass and dock leaves, sobbing and shuddering, when Dora caught up with her.

'It is punishment enough for me to face the world as a defiled woman. But to be branded for ever as a whore! It will kill me,' she whispered. 'As sure as any cancer will. And if it does not, I shall surely kill myself. I cannot live with this.'

'You must not speak this way. It is a shock, I grant you. You need a little time, that's all.'

'Time for what?'

'To get used to the idea of a child. Your child.'

Mariah choked on her words. She covered her face with her hands. 'Their child, those evil thugs. Not mine.'

Dora's frown deepened. 'You are overwrought.

Come inside. I'll make you something to calm you down.'

But her ministrations did not reassure Mariah and Dora was forced to watch her sink back into the depression she had fought so hard to overcome. She worried about leaving Mariah alone in this state, remembering girls before her who had harmed themselves. There was a limit to the number of knocks any woman could take and Dora believed this was one too many for Mariah.

She thought about it for three days, three whole days of anxiety and despair until, finally, she said, 'I can take it away, if that's what you want.'

Mariah had not slept properly. She had tossed and turned, dreading the future and wondering how she could end it all. She was exhausted, at the end of her tether and snapped, 'It will be taken from me anyway. The poorhouse will see to that.'

'I mean...' Dora inhaled deeply. 'Before it is born. I can take it away.'

'What!' Mariah was aghast. Surely she had misheard?

'I'm a midwife. I know how to do it.'

'But – but – you *can't* do that! You'll be damned in hell.'

Dora shrugged. 'I think God might understand.'

'But, Dora, you can go to prison!'

'Who will find out?'

'I – I...' Mariah did not reply. She was too stunned by the idea.

'I've often thought that if the men who made the laws had the babies, the laws would be different.'

234

Mariah pondered on this wearily. 'It's still a wicked thing to do.'

'I don't see it that way. The men who did this to you are the sinful ones. They get away with it and you've to suffer. You don't want to suffer for ever.'

'No,' she agreed. Dora could give me my life back, she thought. Instead of poverty and hatred in the poorhouse, I could have a life worth living. 'Would you really do it for me?'

Dora nodded. 'If that is what you want. Yes.'

Mariah tossed and turned for another long, sleepless night. There was no other way, she fretted. No other way.

'Have you finished that drink?'

'Yes. It was very bitter. What was it?' Mariah was sitting by the kitchen table dressed only in a muslin chemise that came down to her thighs. Her feet were cold on the stone flags, but her face felt the glow of the fire, banked high to heat water.

'A tincture of herbs.'

'What for?'

'To help you relax. You must keep very still.'

'I'm frightened.'

'I know.'

'What are you going to do?'

'I've already said. You'll be all right. I've done this before. Stand up now for me.'

'Will it hurt?'

Dora hesitated. 'Yes, it will. Afterwards. But not for long. And you'll have a nice hot bath by the kitchen fire.' She watched her, patiently, with a wise and practised eye. 'How do you feel now?'

'Kind of – kind of – floating.'

Dora smoothed the boiled calico covering her scrubbed kitchen table. 'Climb up on the table, now. That's right. Lie back and close your eyes.'

'Whass happening to me, Dora?'

'It's the poppy juice. It makes you dream. Close your eyes and dream, Mariah. Dream of nice things. Dream of trimming your gown for the harvest supper. I am just putting these pillows under your back.'

'Wha' for?'

'Bring your knees up. Both of them. Right up. Good girl. Now drop them to the side. Nice and wide. Try and relax, now, good girl.' Dora picked up her silver probe from the spirit and ran it back and forth through a candle flame.

'Whass that?'

'Close your eyes, I said. Go to sleep and dream. How is that gown coming on?'

A quiet strangled groan rumbled in Mariah's throat as Dora's gentle, cool fingers pushed aside her flesh. And then the probing, like the probing of her attackers, invading her, hurting her. This was different though, a deeper hurt, a dull uncomfortable hurt. Mariah's thoughts floated in the space above her head. It was not natural what those men had done to her. But neither was this... This was not natural... Her mind drifted as Dora probed.

She felt drunk and her eyelids were heavy. There was an uncomfortable feeling in the pit of her stomach. Through her sandy eyelashes she saw Dora standing by her head, watching her. 'Iss that it?' she slurred.

'No, my dear. It is not over yet. We must wait now.'

She did not know how long she waited, drifting in and out of sleep. Her discomfort escalated as she lay there, emerging from her dreamy stupor. But Mariah knew this was no dream and the ache spread into a sharp stabbing pain that made her cry out in agony, turn on her side and curl into a ball. Someone was carving away her insides, stripping them out, killing her! Someone was killing her!

She yelled and reached out, clutching at Dora's clothes with iron fingers that would not let go. 'Help! What have you done to me? I'm dying!'

'No, you are not dying.' Dora eased her arm underneath Mariah's shoulders. 'Try and sit up. Look, I have a nice hot bath for you by the fire. Let me help you down from the table.'

'Aarghh!' Every movement Mariah made seemed to make the pain much worse. Leaning on Dora she lifted one foot over the rim of Dora's tin bath. 'It's too hot! I can't!'

'You must. Slowly now.'

Mariah stood in the water, bending over double to support her aching innards. She rested her hands on the metal rim, watching her feet blush with the heat. Cautiously she lowered herself into the tub. The prickling of her skin as she sat in the hot water took her mind from the pain in her belly. The edge of her chemise floated to the surface and then sank as it soaked. There was a strong smell of wintergreen and the salve her mother had used on broken knees when she was a child.

Oh Lord! She wished her mother was here with her now. Why did she have to die and leave her? If her mother had lived she would never have gone to the Thorpes' and been mistaken for one of them. She would never have suffered that degrading invasion of her body. She would never have lain with the devil! Where are you, Mother?

Her pain eased and the water cooled to a comfortable warmth. For a while she felt normal, soothed by the warm water, the banked-up fire radiated heat onto her face and muslin-clothed breasts. Dora busied herself refilling kettles for the bath and mixing another tincture which she offered to Mariah as she soaked.

Mariah shook her head. She knew it was laudanum and she had seen its effects on the street women who frequented the taverns in the market square.

'Drink it, Mariah.' Dora sounded stern. 'This is just the beginning. The pain will come back.'

'I don't want that stuff.' Mariah had made shirts as she sat with her dying mother and sold them to buy her laudanum for those last painful months of her illness. It had hastened her end she was sure. But for her mother that end had been a welcome release from her pain. 'Take it away,' she added.

Dora returned with a bottle of spirits. 'You do not have to suffer. I'll leave this here on the floor, it may help you.'

'I don't want that either. Save it for cleaning your ribbons.'

'At least take this.' Dora handed her a short rope of knotted linen. 'If the pain becomes too much for you, bite on the linen.'

'Thank you. You won't leave me, will you?'

'No, of course not. If you change your mind about the laudanum...'

'I shan't.'

When the pain returned it was worse than before, worse than anything she had experienced in her short life, worse than the attack that had caused her to be like this. She screamed once, gritted her teeth and finally reached for the knotted linen.

She was sweating with heat and felt wearied by the pain. Her head flopped down to her breast and it was then she saw the red stain seeping through the water, spreading slowly and insidiously, at first making patterns between her legs and over her thighs, and then as she twisted in agony and the water became more bloodied she realised what she had done and screamed again.

'It is for the best,' Dora soothed. 'It will soon be over now.'

No, this will never be over, Mariah thought. This was not her life's blood that was ebbing away, it was her child's. A child that was part of her, her own flesh. Yes, a child conceived in brutality and rape but the child had done no wrong and yet it was the child's blood that darkened the water, spreading, swirling and soaking into her chemise.

She began to weep, silently at first and then with shuddering sobs she tried to repress but could not. Gradually her grief took over until she was crying vociferously and then hysterically, uncontrollably, her shoulders heaving with hiccups and coughs, her tears running down her face and falling into the water, mixing with the blood of her dead baby.

Her fingers tangled with her hair as she held her head in anguish. The pain was relentless. A tearing, searing pain that she deserved. She threw the knotted linen aside in contempt of herself. She had to suffer. She must suffer for her wickedness. This was an evil compounding evil. Her baby was innocent and her baby had died. She had murdered her own child and she screamed again. 'Murder! Murder! I am a murderess!'

Dora watched her silently She had seen as many reactions to this as she had the women that she helped. Some were simply grateful, glad to endure the pain and get back to normal. Some were mortified and secretive and took spirits or laudanum readily. Others, like Mariah, took it badly and these women worried Dora the most.

The worst would soon be over; the pain would ease and Mariah would stand and allow Dora to rinse off the blood with a ewer of clean, lavender-scented water, then dry her, wrap her and put her to bed.

Brutal rape was always the worst, women suffered in their heads as well as in their bodies. Now Mariah was grieving for the loss of her child on top of the loss of her mother. She was a strong lass, strong in mind as well as resilient in body. But, Dora wondered, was she strong enough to withstand all this?

Only time would tell. A good lass like Mariah deserved a better chance in life than the one she had been dealt. When this was over, the harvest supper would be a new start for her. New company and good food to build her strength. Her time of mourning would be over. It had to be. If Mariah was to come through this ordeal she had to have distraction. People and music and perhaps dancing to cheer her.

Dora fervently hoped she would pull through.

Chapter 22

Mariah cried every day for a fortnight. She went about her household chores silently and took solace only in her needlework. Dora tended to her as best she could, but even she did not have lotions or potions to help this time.

Mariah worked away, fashioning Dora's Sunday coat on her mother's old mannequin. Dora helped with the seams, under Mariah's watchful eye. It was a beautiful coat and Dora thought she hardly deserved such luxury, but she looked forward to wearing it in the cold weather to come.

'Have you decided what to make with the remnants?' Dora asked as they sewed.

'Hand muffs for the winter. We have a flour sack full of wool-gatherings from the hedgerows for warm linings. The farmers at the beast market will buy them for their wives and daughters.'

'Will you take them into town and sell them yourself?'

'When I am ready.' Mariah heaved a sigh. 'At present I do not think I shall ever want to go back there.' She put aside her sewing for a moment. 'Oh, Dora, what shall I do? I am ruined, totally ruined. How shall I look anyone in the face again?'

'You are not the only woman to have suffered

241

what you have gone through,' Dora replied quietly.

'No,' Mariah responded bitingly. 'I suppose it happens to street women all the time. Is that what I have become? A woman fit only for work on the streets?'

'Do not compare yourself with them! It is unworthy of you.'

'*I feel unworthy.*'

'But you are not!'

'I let you take away my unborn child.'

'It was the right thing for you.'

'Fanny once said to me that she would have had more children if it hadn't been for you.'

The querying tone in Mariah's voice made Dora look up sharply. 'You don't think I do that for anyone who asks, do you?'

'I don't know. Do you?'

'No, I do not! Only for women like you, who had no say in the act. Never for a woman who is wed. When you get wed it is your duty to bear children, everybody knows that.'

'What? To have a child every year until you're too old and worn to care for them?'

'As a wife you have to give your husband his rights. And some of them are like our Fanny's Arthur. They never tire of wanting their wives in the bedchamber.' Dora looked at Mariah. 'Your family was different from mine and Fanny's. I suppose your mother did not speak of such things. Mrs Shaw told me.'

'What do you mean *such things*? I could tell *you* about men wanting – no – *taking* what they see as their dues!'

'Mariah, calm yourself. Those men had no

rights as far as you were concerned. But it is possible to lie with a man and not make a child.'

'That is God's will. Sometimes you do and sometimes you don't. My mother told me the only way not to get with child was not to lie with a man.'

'Yes, well, try telling that to the menfolk around here. Besides, Mrs Shaw taught me it's not good for men if they do not lie with their wives when they have the urge. That's what wives are for. And rich men's wives know what to do to stop the babies coming.'

'I know. Separate bedchambers. Mother told me.'

'And more. I'll show you.' Dora put down her sewing and went to a polished oak chest in a corner of the room. She retrieved a key from a hidden pocket in her skirt and unlocked the top drawer. Carefully, she lifted out a plain wooden box. Dora placed it on the table and opened the lid.

'Before I show you what's in here, you must promise me you will not talk of this to anyone. There are folk around here who don't approve of these things and if the vicar's wife ever found out I had them, I can't think what she'd say. But I know for a fact that her ladyship at the Hall used them.'

Dora held up a piece of sea sponge, a very small piece of the kind Mariah used when bathing. It had a piece of narrow ribbon firmly attached at one end. 'I gave Fanny one of these to use.'

Mariah frowned. She had seen nothing like it before.

'Some folk make them out of folded muslin,' Dora explained. 'But the sea sponge is better. You soak it in vinegar and push it right up inside you before he comes to you in your bed. It has to be afore he is anywhere near you and you have to use strong vinegar. Mrs Shaw told me it stops the seed before it can make the child.'

Mariah's eyes rounded. 'I had no idea that there were such things. That means a woman could lie with her husband every night and – oh! Oh yes, I can see why the Church would not approve.'

'Some folk say it's all right and some folk don't. Mostly those who don't hold with these say they lead to wicked ways.' Dora glanced furtively at Mariah. 'Y'know, outside of wedlock. But I reckon folk around here have their wicked ways with each other any road.'

'Is that what I am, Dora? A wicked woman?' Mariah asked quietly.

'No, just the opposite. You are a good woman. You were an innocent, you *are* an innocent, and nobody can tell me otherwise.'

Dora noticed a frown gather on Mariah's forehead. Hastily, she closed the box and locked it away again.

'Are you still set on wearing that gown for the harvest supper?'

'I'm really not sure about going. After–'

'No one will know. Or even guess, if you act normally.'

Mariah fingered the cloth of her skirt. It had been her best gown, but she had worn it every day at Dora's house and the wear was beginning to show at the elbows and edge of the skirt. She would have to put a darn in it and re-stitch some of the seams. 'If I do go, I ought to wear black,' she commented.

Dora disagreed but did not say so. 'Have you got anything in black?'

Mariah shook her head.

Dora went on, 'Didn't I see a green one in your box? Dark green?'

'That one? That's was my mother's Sunday best when she was alive.'

'It's a nice, softly draped one and not too heavy. A bit formal for a barn dance but very cleverly cut, I thought, when I wrapped it to hang in the cupboard.'

'Oh, my mother looked really lovely in that gown. I used to try it on when I fancied myself grown up. I felt a proper lady in it.'

'It would suit you very well for your first outing.'

'It's beautiful cloth. Sewn from the end of a bolt used to make a ladies' afternoon dress.' Mariah thought about the gown. 'It needs another petticoat. And the bodice is a bit tight.'

'Why don't you cut in a new front like you did for Emma? Put in one of those low necklines? You can add a piece of muslin or lace for modesty and a trimming round the cuffs. It would be perfect for the harvest supper.'

'Yes, I might do that. I have some old lace that would suit. It's yellowed a little with age, but it would go well with the green.'

Dora nodded in agreement. 'And just right for a matching lace cap. You could dress your hair higher on your head to show off your features.'

Mariah shook her head. 'I don't want to go,' she repeated.

She thought about her mother's Sunday gown

as she put the finishing touches to Dora's coat and wrapped it in calico to keep for her to wear at the harvest festival service in church. She looked forward to re-fashioning the dress even if she didn't go to the barn dance.

But she could not help thinking that Dora was right. She could not hide for ever. Dora often reminded her that her secrets were safe and she ought to face other people soon. Perhaps a festive supper and dance would give her a start? She took out her mother's gown from her cupboard, unwrapped it and laid it on the bed. Then she stood back from it for a long time with her head on one side before she picked up her scissors.

A neighbouring farmer collected them in his cart, which had straw bales and boxes for them to sit on. Dora looked cheerful wearing her brown plaid gown with a matching bow in her greying hair. Mariah, with Dora's encouragement, had made a special effort with her own hair, pinning it securely in coils at the back of her head and dressing it with a ribbon of lace to match the lace at her breast and elbows.

The barn was huge. Swept clean of farmyard debris, and lit by lanterns hanging from the wooden roof trusses, it was filled with people, noise and movement. In one corner, two fiddles and a flute were tuning their instruments and the ale-house keeper from Keppel village was preparing to call for the dancing. Servants from the Hall had set out chairs for the older people and furnished a long table they were covering with all kinds of delicious things to eat and drink.

Dora took a reluctant Mariah around to meet the people she knew from Keppel village, the butcher and his wife, the ale-house keeper and the farrier's family. They welcomed her among them. But when the dancing commenced Mariah lingered at the back, in the shadow of the barn walls, until she was dragged protesting, into one of the reels by the farrier's son whose boundless energy ensured he never missed a single dance.

After a second dance she began to enjoy herself. Who would not among such good people? Those solid, ruddy-faced country men, waistcoats unbuttoned and shirt necks wide open, flinging themselves about with wives and maids alike, restored a little of her faith in mankind.

The shouting and laughter continued after the music ceased as men, women and children celebrated the end of long days working in the fields. Two barrels of ale had been set up and tapped to slake their thirsts. One of the cooks from the Hall carved at a roasted aitch bone of beef and several game pies, which were quickly devoured with pickled vegetables and marrow relish.

Mariah and Dora were talking with the farrier and his wife when the barn fell silent and everyone looked round. Mariah recognised Mr Fitzkeppel, but not his lady companion who was dressed in a very grand gown. He was flamboyantly dressed, too, in a long-coated suit of dark blue wool with gold braid trims that gave him the appearance of a naval man. His lady matched this opulence with a gown of rich maroon silk, its burgeoning skirts so full the villagers were forced to step back as she walked by them.

247

'How does she get her skirt to stay like that?' Dora whispered.

'Crin petticoats. They're filled with horse hair.'

'Not for dancing in, then?'

'Who is she?'

'His sister. Can't you detect a likeness?'

Mariah craned her neck, but her line of vision was blocked by others who had crowded forward to get a better view of their landlord and pay-master.

'Your lace looks better than hers,' Dora whispered.

'Can you see her? I can't.'

'Come over here.'

Mariah shuffled next to Dora as Mr Fitzkeppel and his sister walked around the barn, greeting and talking to the village folk. She ducked down to peer through a gap between two men. Yes, Mariah agreed, the lace was wrong for the gown. It was too heavy for silk and much of it was wrongly placed, detracting from the beautiful sheen. Mariah would have added flounces and frills in the same silk rather than this thick cotton lace.

She stepped back to allow the enormous skirt to pass. Mariah's sharp eye noticed a crooked seam in the bodice and escaping threads where the lace was attached. The sleeves, too, did not fit as closely as they should have. Goodness, Mariah thought, Mother would have been shocked that a lady's maid had allowed her mistress to go out like that! So am I, Mariah decided. She wanted to take this lady to one side, hitch up the sleeves and adjust the lace to make the neckline fit better.

It was then that Mariah realised how much she

was like her mother in this respect, and thinking in exactly the same way when confronted with poor workmanship. She realised, also, that this was the first time she had thought about her mother without wanting to cry.

'A new face, I believe, brother dearest?' The people in front of Mariah had moved aside and Miss Fitzkeppel had not walked on.

Mr Fitzkeppel smiled at Mariah, a warm acknowledgement of their prior acquaintance, and Mariah thought he had an enchanting, almost ethereal, face. His hands too were smooth skinned and white with long fingers, and nails that were clean and tended. There was lace at his wrists, too, more subtle than that on his sister's gown and perfect against the fine weave of the wool. He was not much more than her own age and Mariah warmed to his friendly countenance.

'Christobel, my dear,' he said. 'May I present Miss Bowes. She is residing with Mrs Barton.'

Until that moment, Mariah's attention had been taken up by the details of Miss Fitzkeppel's opulent gown. She lowered gracefully into a curtsey with her head bowed. But when she looked up she was startled by Miss Fitzkeppel's arresting blue eyes, piercing Mariah's façade of gentility and seeming to reach into the dark recesses of her recent traumas. Mr Fitzkeppel's sister was, as local folk said, quite lovely. Her smooth milky complexion was lightly tinted on her cheeks with a mellow country glow rather than French rouge. Her thick fair hair was coiled high on the back of her head and dressed with peacock feathers and strings of jewels that matched a necklace at her throat.

Miss Fitzkeppel's keen eyes swept over Mariah and lingered on what she saw. She turned to Dora. 'Mrs Barton, would you call on me tomorrow afternoon?'

Surprised, Dora murmured, 'Of course, ma'am,' and dropped a small curtsey.

The Fitzkeppels moved on.

'What was all that about?' Mariah whispered.

'I have no idea. I'll find out tomorrow.'

'Do you think she's – you know – ill?'

'Heavens, no! She has a proper doctor from town to attend her. It may be for one of her servants.'

'She's not asking you about – er – what you did for me?'

'Lord, no! She doesn't know about that!'

'I thought for a second she knew about me – about what happened.'

Dora looked askance. 'Why should she?'

'That look of hers. It seemed to go right inside me.'

'It's those large eyes. They really are a brilliant blue. Everyone notices them. And they notice everything, mark my words. Miss Christobel is as clever as she is pretty.'

'Where is her husband tonight?'

'She doesn't have one. Don't look so surprised. I expect she is quite happy to remain as mistress of Fitzkeppel Hall for her brother. She is much more interested in the estate farms and livestock than he is. Mind you, *he* ought to be thinking about marriage and heirs even if she isn't.'

The interval was soon over. Brother and sister left, and the villagers quickly returned to the more serious business of enjoying themselves. Mariah, too, cheered immensely. She did not dance again, but talked with several village people, drank ale and ate well. That night, she slept soundly for the first time in weeks and woke the following day feeling refreshed.

She urged Dora to wear her new coat to visit Miss Fitzkeppel.

'I was saving it for the harvest festival in church next week.'

'You need to look your best for the Hall.'

'But I might catch it on twigs as I walk through the wood.'

'Then you will have to take great care not to,' Mariah insisted, as she helped Dora fasten the buttons down the front.

'It's beautiful,' Dora breathed. 'And it fits so well. How do I look?'

'Very handsome. Fit to be a lady's lady.'

'You are so clever, Mariah.'

'It helps to have the best woollen cloth.'

'But all those fastenings – they took you ages! And the matching braiding on the collar is beautiful. It has the look of, well, of a militia man's coat to me. Where did you find the braid?'

'I made it from the cloth,' Mariah commented absently as she stepped back with a critical eye. 'Yes, it fits you perfectly. Off you go. I'll make some nice broth for when you get back.'

But Dora did not return alone. Mariah was surprised to hear a carriage creaking and rattling down the bumpy track to the garden gate. Through the front-room window she saw a foot-

251

man helping Dora and Miss Fitzkeppel onto the grassy path to their front door. Quickly, Mariah removed her apron and smoothed her hair. Their visitor pushed her full skirts, protected by a large heavy cloak, through the front door of Dora's cottage and into the front room. It was tidy, but the table was clearly being used as Mariah's worktable and she stood in front of it to hide the mess. In the corner, Mariah's old mannequin carried the beginnings of another coat she was making for Emma.

Miss Fitzkeppel walked over to it and fingered the lovat green cloth. 'So it is true? You are more than a seamstress, Miss Bowes. Where did you learn all this?'

Mariah was proud of her heritage and answered, 'From my mother. She taught me everything.'

If this surprised Miss Fitzkeppel, she did not show it but went on, 'When I asked Mrs Barton who your dressmaker was, I did not believe her reply. She told me it was you who had fashioned the bodice of the gown you wore at the harvest supper – and also this coat that she wears today. I imagined them to have come from Leeds. Or London.'

'My mother's family were tailors from the North Riding, ma'am,' Mariah volunteered by way of explanation. She maintained a steady gaze, meeting Miss Fitzkeppel's searching expression calmly.

'And where is your mother now?'

'She is dead, ma'am.'

'I see. I am sorry.' She took a step forward and peered to one side. 'May I?'

Mariah moved aside to reveal her worktable.

The visitor picked up an illustration, torn from a printed journal Mariah had used to guide her when making the coats. There were some light sketches in the margins and, on the table top, calico toiles that Mariah had made as models for herself, Dora and Emma.

Miss Fitzkeppel turned swiftly. 'I should like to discuss a commission with you, Miss Bowes. Will you come to the Hall on Tuesday? I shall send my carriage for you after luncheon.'

The excitement Mariah had felt during this visit threatened to bubble to the surface. Miss Fitzkeppel might be the most beautiful and powerful woman in this part of the Riding, but she was still a woman, and one who appreciated a well-made gown when she saw one. At that moment, Mariah felt herself to be Miss Fitzkeppel's equal and replied clearly, 'Of course, ma'am.'

'Very well. Good day to you.' She gave a brief nod in Dora's direction, adding, 'Good day, Mrs Barton,' and swept out as elegantly as she had entered.

Mariah stared at Dora with raised eyebrows. 'A commission? A commission! Dora did you hear that? A commission!'

'I did, indeed.' Dora's face softened as she saw the delight on Mariah's face.

'Just think! The lady at the Hall will wear something I have made! Mother would be so proud of me. Oh, Dora, I can do so much for her. Her shape is very womanly, like mine. I know how to fashion the cloth to improve her form, instead of detracting from it as her gown last night did.'

'Well, you have done it for me right enough.

You should have seen the looks I got at the Hall!'
Dora thought this could be Mariah's salvation. It
could help her climb right out of the abyss of her
despair. At last, Dora saw a glimmer of hope for
Mariah's future.

Chapter 23

'A fine morning, Havers.'

'Oh! You startled me, Miss Christobel.'

Bel's eyes lingered on the patchwork fields
which rolled away and disappeared into the
valley in front of her. On the far side the hills rose
again towards the high moor, obliterated by an
early morning mist. She had walked through the
kitchen wing of the Hall, and on past the stables
to breathe in the fresh autumn air. 'We are indeed
lucky to live in the South Riding, are we not?'

'If you say so, miss.'

'Do you not agree, Havers?'

'Depends which way the wind is blowing when
the smoke rises from the furnaces in the valley.'

Bel laughed. 'Yes, indeed. You are quite right.
But they are our future.'

'Aye, miss. Are you taking Chestnut out this
morning?'

'I am. Is he ready?'

'Joe's bringing him round now.'

'Whoa, boy.' Joe held tight onto the bridle as
Chestnut tossed his head and pranced across the
stable yard, clattering his hooves on the cobbles.

'He's a bit frisky this morning, Miss Christobel. The farrier put new shoes on him yesterday and he likes the sound of 'em ringing on the stones.'

A cacophony of pheasants, spooked by the noise, rose from a nearby hedgerow and scattered over the fields. 'Your birds have bred well this year.'

'They have that. There'll be plenty for the larder this winter if I can keep away the poachers.'

'Do we lose many to the poachers?'

'Not if I can help it, miss. They take rabbit as a rule an' we've allus got plenty o' them.'

Joe held the bridle as Bel climbed the mounting stone and settled herself in the sidesaddle spreading her new riding skirt to cover her boots. She held herself well, head high and with a straight back, her fair hair hidden by a black snood and tall hat. She pulled at the cuffs of her gloves and took up the reins. Her new riding jacket fitted perfectly. It was the most comfortable she had ever worn. Miss Bowes certainly knew how to cut cloth to fit the female form. She must talk to Mrs Havers about further commissions for her.

Havers checked the buckles and smoothed the horse's neck. 'You'll soon ride that friskiness out of him this morning, miss.'

As Bel turned the horse's head towards a wooded hillside she had a sudden thought and called over her shoulder, 'Havers! Why don't we have a shoot sometime? Like Father used to have when I was a child? What do you say?'

She did not wait for his answer. The morning air beckoned and she urged Chestnut to a canter across the fields. At the top of the hill, Bel reined him in and he slowed, his nostrils steaming in the crisp, fresh air. She pushed up her veil, inhaled deeply and marvelled at the early autumn colour of the woodland. In the valley, the chimneys were already smoking and she could hear the whine of winding gear at the pit head on Keppel Hill as a group of miners descended to their long day of toil at the coal face.

She wondered what it was like down there in the cold damp dark. Years ago she had asked her brother's trustees if she might see what a coal seam looked like and they had laughed at her, telling her that only men and boys went down the mines. She remembered that day when she had wished she was her brother. Not that she really wanted to be him, but she would have liked to be allowed to do some of the things he did, instead of spending her days with a governess learning to sing and play the pianoforte.

Her irritation with this state of affairs made her angry and the horse, sensing her tension, fretted under the reins. Why shouldn't she care about the estate and its mines and manufactories? She wanted to know about these things and no one would tell her! Why did people think this such an unsuitable, unladylike concern? It annoyed her that, as Nathan grew older, he became less interested in his estates and the industries that it supported. He spent his days reading poetry and painting and his only contribution to running the estate was to redesign the parkland to improve the view from drawing rooms – although she had to admit that the park was beautiful now. Even so, Bel looked forward to the day when she would leave the Hall as a bride.

She had hoped to find a suitor among her brother's university friends. But they shared Nathan's artistic tastes and none of them had really interested her. Besides, they showed no more than a passing politeness towards her and this vexed her. She did not wish to be a spinster and spend her life playing second fiddle to whomsoever Nathan chose to be his wife and mistress of Fitzkeppel Hall.

'Come on, Chestnut,' Bel murmured to her mount, tugging at the reins. 'It is time I had a proper conversation with that brother of mine.'

She found Nathan in the north-facing conservatory where he had set up his easel and paints. He was dressed casually in an open-necked shirt and corduroy breeches, eating boiled eggs and bread at a small wickerwork table.

'Good morning, Nathan. Is Henry not taking breakfast with you?'

'No, he has ridden into town to meet his father. They have business at the bank.'

Excellent, thought Bel, we shall not be distracted by that boy. 'I wish to speak with you,' she began.

'What about, my dear?'

'About you, Nathan. About your plans for your future here at the Hall.'

Nathan put down the teaspoon he was using to tackle his second egg and looked at Bel with raised eyebrows. 'My plans? Why should I have any plans? Withers takes care of everything.'

'Then, are you and I to stay here together, like this, for the rest of our lives?'

'I don't see why not. Really, Bel, what on earth

257

has got into you?'

'I am not getting any younger, brother dear. And the Hall is *your* home, not mine.'

'Bel, my dearest, darling sister, of course Fitz-keppel Hall is your home.'

'Only until you marry and bring your new wife as mistress to the Hall. Then I shall have to step aside.'

'When I marry? Why should I wish to marry?'

'Because that is what gentlemen in your position do! You have to marry. You need an heir for all this. If Father were still alive, I am sure he would insist upon it. Did your trustees not talk of this when you inherited?'

'They mentioned it once or twice, but they have not pressed me. Not yet, that is. I have only just turned one and twenty.'

'And I am three and twenty! Mama was married at nineteen. If she knew – or even cared – about me, she would be shocked.'

Nathan tipped back his head, looking down his nose at her, and responded. 'I am sure Mama does care about you. I am sure she cares about both of us and she would be shocked by the ruddiness of your complexion this morning, Bel. You are not a servant girl.'

'I have been out riding. Do not change the direction of our conversation. You must find yourself a suitable wife to run the Hall for you.'

Nathan seemed genuinely nonplussed by her suggestion. 'But – but why?'

Bel grew impatient with his languid responses. 'I have already told you why! I do not wish to remain a spinster for the rest of my days. I want to marry. If I do not marry soon I shall be the laughing stock of the Riding!'

'That does not mean that *I* have to marry.'

'Of course it does. The Hall needs a mistress.'

'But, Bel, this is *our* home. Yours and mine. We are happy here together, are we not? Why must we spoil everything by *marrying*, for heaven's sake?'

'Because that's what people do!'

'I have no intention of marrying,' he replied irritably.

'Then you should have! The Hall needs an heir!' After a pause, Bel added quietly, 'And I want a husband.'

'Really, Bel? You wish to go away and leave me?'

'No, no. Of course I do not wish to leave you. It's just that – well, why shouldn't I want to marry? If I had had a mama like other girls, I am sure she would have found someone for me.'

Bel felt her emotions rising in her throat. She really *did* want to marry. She wanted a gentleman to visit and court her, and then to wed her and give her children to care for. Most of all she wanted a husband who would cherish her and hold her close. When she was alone in her bed at night, she imagined how it might be with a husband. She would not be a shy bride, she would welcome his caresses on her tender flesh.

She knew what her body was for. One of her governesses had instructed her briefly and she knew it was being wasted as a spinster. She had learned much more by creeping from her room after dark and eavesdropping on servants as they gossiped into the night. The upstairs maids and footmen were always telling stories of things they had heard or seen in bedchambers, including the most shocking tales of her own mama and the Italian artist. Bel often wondered if she was like her mama in this respect for sometimes her body ached to be held, her skin yearned to be stroked and her mouth became dry as her imagination ran riot.

Nathan's sympathetic eyes frowned. 'I thought you were happy as we are.'

'Well, I am not,' she pronounced. 'Oh Nathan, I shall soon be too old to marry. Who will look at me then?'

'Bel, my dear, if it means so much to you, I am sure I can find someone for you.'

'I do not want one of your insipid friends! I want a man with red blood in his veins! A man who shoots and enjoys the hunt and – and shows an interest in me!'

There was an awkward silence and Nathan went back to his eggs. 'I'll thank you not to be rude about my friends. Besides, Lord Stannic rides to hounds, and so does Warrender.' He paused for a moment and then repeated the name. 'Warrender. He has a large estate in the Dales that might suit you.'

Bel thought it wouldn't, but nonetheless her pretty blue eyes lit up. 'Then you'll do it?'

'Do what?'

'Have a house party, of course! Mrs Havers will open up the empty rooms and we shall invite the best families in the Riding. We'll have a banquet to welcome them. And a pheasant shoot. And a ball, perhaps, later. With gaming tables and – oh yes, a midnight supper and, oh, you will say yes, won't you, Nathan?'

'No, no, no! Never! All those dreadful, boring people who talk about the price of corn and coal and nothing else. It's bad enough having to listen to Withers and his worthy lawyer friends without inviting others of the same kind to my home.'

Surprised by his outburst, Christobel blinked and stepped back. 'But Nathan, dearest, they are Riding people like us.'

'Like you, Bel. Not me.'

'Nathan?'

'What do they know of art and literature? What interest do they have in the antiquities?'

'What – what interest do they need to keep their country estates going, or manage their mills and manufactories?'

Nathan clicked his tongue impatiently. 'You are so like Father. There is no wonder Mother ran away. *She* understood about art.'

'Just because she fell in love with an Italian artist doesn't mean she knew anything about his art! Really, Nathan, where did you get that idea from?'

'And what, pray, do you know of Mother's inclinations?'

'Well, more than you do about her appalling behaviour and the scandal it caused our family.'

In the silence that followed, Bel experienced one of those moments of clarity in her life that she remembered for years afterwards. As she said the words, she realised why it was so difficult for her to find a husband. She was tainted by her mother's reputation. No decent fellow who knew of that would risk her as a wife. Memories were long in Riding families and her mother had behaved wickedly and unforgivably. It wasn't fair! Why should she have to suffer as a result of her mother's indiscretions!

'I was here all the time, Nathan,' she added. 'She kept the servants' hall alive with rumours for weeks.'

'The servants were loyal to Father, I am sure.'

'Oh yes. And they said Mama knew where her duty lay. Do you know that one of the footmen used to listen at doors and then tell the maids? He was very popular with them. Sometimes he hid behind the curtains if he could and watched them in the bedchamber.'

'Bel! You should not listen to servants' gossip.'

'What else had I to do when you were away at school?'

Nathan sighed. 'I suppose Father should not have married her in the first place. Marriage does not suit everyone.'

'But there was no one to inherit!'

'No. He had lost both nephews and he needed an heir. So a healthy farmer's daughter was a good choice. He gave them land in exchange for her.'

'Really?'

'Withers told me. Her family could not have all the land until she produced a male heir.'

'The servants said it wasn't easy for – for Father – to – you know, he was quite old on their wedding day. She must have been very disappointed in him. And with me as her firstborn. They said she cried when I was born. Is that why she did not take me with her when she left?'

'No, dearest. I am sure Mama loves us both. Father insisted we were looked after by nanny and her maids so she turned her attention to re-fashioning the Hall. I think she found her true self doing that. She had time on her hands and plenty of Father's money and – and she had a talent, a rare artistic talent for it. That's how she met him.'

'The Italian lover, you mean? How could she?'

'Withers said it was a meeting of minds. He was an artist who came over to paint the murals in the long gallery. They are beautiful, are they not, Bel?'

Bel expressed surprise. 'Withers has been talking to you about Mama?'

Nathan nodded. 'Since I inherited. There was such a huge scandal and I was away at school at the time. He thought I should know.'

'He thought you should know about a mother who abandoned her own children? Withers is losing his mind.' Bel felt tears welling at the back of her eyes. 'She deserted us. She left me to the mercy of others. What kind of mother does that?'

'She had no choice. Father would have locked her away.'

Bel held her head in her hands to stem the flow of tears that threatened. She recalled the twitter-ing of the maids, all those years ago, and their chattering about the handsome young Italian and the mistress. They were gossiping about her mother! Her own mother! The whole of the South Riding knew how she had betrayed their father!

Nathan gazed through the glass conservatory wall at the sheep grazing in the fields beyond the terrace. 'It wasn't all her fault, you know,' he commented.

'No, I do not know that,' Bel responded firmly. 'And neither do you.'

'Yes I do,' he said quietly.

Bel looked at him long and hard. He could be infuriatingly stubborn about some things, especially concerning his art, but, on the whole, since he had inherited he had been a good brother to her, never questioning any of her requests for gowns, horses or servants. She hoped her future husband would be as generous. Now, she realised, her brother was keeping something from her.

'What do you know?' she asked bluntly.

'She wrote letters to us. Every year on our birthdays.'

'What?' Bel sank into one of the cane chairs. 'Mama? Wrote letters to us?'

'Well, not exactly to us. To Withers. She knew Father would not allow us to receive anything from her. And neither could Withers until I came of age. He had to abide by Father's wishes as my trustee. But he has kept them all in his safe. I've read some of them.'

Bel was silent. All these years she had thought her mother did not care for her, there had been letters. Letters that her father and his lawyers had not let her see. She felt her tears threaten again.

'Nathan, is that coffee still hot?' she said at last.

'I'll ring for some more.'

'Ask for some brandy with it, would you? This is quite a shock.'

She felt better after hot coffee laced with brandy. Nathan told her Withers wanted to know what to do with the letters. Father had ordered them to be destroyed but Withers had counselled against that. Their father was elderly and Withers would soon be the children's guardian and trustee. So Withers had kept them until he could rightly hand them over to Nathan.

'Now they are mine,' Nathan explained. 'And I must decide what to do with them. They give Mama's side of events. She may not have been as wicked as we have been led to believe.'

At last she asked, 'Have you read any of the letters Mama wrote to me?'

'One or two.'

'And what do you propose to do with them?'

'They are yours if you wish. It might help you understand her.'

Understand her? Bel thought. Understand that her behaviour had ruined her childhood and was continuing to dominate her life by ruining her chances of finding a decent husband in the Riding? Understand that she might be an old maid because of her mother's scandalous behaviour when she was a child?

As Bel's silence continued, Nathan added, 'I'll ask Withers to bring them over if you wish.'

'No. I do not want to *understand* her. I do not want anything to do with her! She should have been here when I was a child, when I was growing up! She wasn't! She left me! She left us both! It is too late now.' Bel shook her head irritably. 'This is too much! After all these years! To have to wait until now to read letters sent to me as a child. I am so angry with her. It is all her fault. I blame her for the situation I find myself in now. You can do what you like with her letters – burn them for all I care. Mama's behaviour has ruined my chances of happiness and I shall never forgive her for that. Never!'

265

'I am sorry you feel like that about her, Bel.'

'It was all right for you! You had school and university and the support of your friends! I was stuck here with only a succession of governesses for companionship. They were awful! Awful! Well-bred ladies, embittered by the bad fortune that had forced them into servitude. They despised me because I had money, dirty money from coal and iron, but no family title or breeding as they had. And they pitied me because I had no reputation! Not after the way Mama behaved. Is it any wonder I preferred horses and shooting?' She began to plead with him, 'Please, Nathan, please look for a wife. If you married, we should have another family. Your wife would have brothers and sisters and cousins for me to meet!'

'I have told you that I do not wish to marry. However, if marriage is so important to you, my friend Warrender has hinted to me he might have to find a wife soon. His father is insisting on it.'

'Not Warrender, for heaven's sake! He's like you. He hates our outdoor life here, and only rides to the hounds because his father orders him!'

'How do you know that?'

'Oh Nathan, do you not notice anything? Each time he has visited here I have tried my best to engage him in all manner of conversations and he is not interested in me. Everyone thinks I'll run off like Mama did. I'll never find a decent husband. Never!'

Nathan frowned. 'I am sure that is not the case. But maybe Warrender is not such a good choice for you. His father has curtailed his visits here, anyway.'

'I am sorry to hear that. You have been friends for a long time.'

'Yes.'

'Is that why Henry Bowes visits us such a great deal, now?'

Nathan shrugged silently.

'I cannot fathom what you see in Henry.'

'He has an artist's eye for colour and for shape.'

'But he is so much younger than you are. And, if I may say so, he shows it in his behaviour.'

'Yes, I find that rather charming, don't you?'

Bel did not, but refrained from saying so. Like herself, her brother had grown up without the care of parents who loved him. Friends were more precious in their circumstances as Bel knew only too well. If he was upset at losing his friend Warrender to the responsibilities of his estate, then she was happy for Nathan to have found a replacement in Henry Bowes. Nonetheless, she found Henry's 'charm' a little too brash for her tastes. She did not want her brother's good nature to be exploited.

'Well, he is several years younger than I am, so perhaps I cannot judge. But, forgive me, dearest, he is not really of our status.'

'He has no family of note, I agree. Henry's origins are humble, but his father is prospering as an ironmaster. Withers says the future of my estate, indeed the future of the Riding, is in manufacturing and not farming. Besides, Henry is a gentleman now, he is educated, he was at my school, the same one as our father. He understands my art and we share the same tastes.'

Bel nodded in agreement. Nathan knew more

267

of London fashion than she did and Henry's dress, when she had seen him at the Hall, demonstrated that he did too. Well, perhaps she would surprise them both with her new gowns when they held a banquet or a ball at Fitzkeppel Hall! South Riding society may have had no interest in her at seventeen. But she would show them she was not to be ignored now!

She remembered the last chaperone Withers had found for her when she was nineteen, a well-connected dowager who was employed to get her invitations further afield from the Riding, even into Derbyshire society. Bel had thought her dreadful. She had dressed her in the fashion that had been popular when she had been a young lady, in gowns she had decided were elegant and aristocratic. Bel remembered the stifled giggles from behind the fans of other young ladies at her first ball. No wonder she had not found a suitor! For a whole season Bel had trailed around house parties and balls with this lady, who insisted that she behaved like a silly young girl in an effort to attract the right sort of gentleman. Invariably they were gentlemen who were as stupid as the dowager and Bel grew impatient with their ways. Heavens, if she ever had the opportunity to launch her own daughters into society she would certainly do better than that!

Surely it was not too late for her? There must be other unmarried men like Warrender in the Riding and she would find one to suit her! Nathan must help her in this. He must!

She said, 'Then I am happy that you have found a new friend in Henry Bowes. But, Nathan

268

dearest, do you not see that I have not had your advantages of school and university for my friends and that I am lonely?'

'You have me.'

'I cannot marry you. If I am to marry anyone at all, you have to do something about it. Now.'

Nathan heaved a great sigh. 'Must I have these parties in my own home?'

'Yes, you must. As you say, for the present it is my home, too. Do you not wish to show off your artistic tastes?'

Nathan sighed again.

Bel would not be put off. 'There will be new furnishings to buy and rooms to decorate for our guests. Perhaps Henry would like to help you?'

'You would not mind that?'

'I should be delighted for you. You can invite his father to our first house party. Please say yes, Nathan. Please.'

'If that is what you really want.'

'I do. It is as much for you. You really should look for a wife.'

'I have already told you I do not want a wife. Now go away, Bel, and plan your party.'

'There is one other thing.'

Nathan sighed and pushed aside his egg. 'This has gone quite cold now.'

'I shall need to spend much more of your money on myself. For gowns and extra maids, you know.'

'Yes, yes. I'll tell Withers when he calls. Have as much as you want.'

'Thank you, my darling brother.' She kissed him lightly on his forehead. 'You should not be so casual with your wealth. It may run out.'

'Withers says not. He says it's piling up and I should put more of it to good use.'

'Do your bankers not do that for you?'

'Yes, they do. But Withers wants me to build more furnaces and buy more machinery. He has a mission to get me interested in my coal mines and ironworks.'

Bel laughed. 'He never gives up on you, does he?'

Nathan smiled back at her and she bent to kiss him again. She wished he would behave more like the landowning industrialist that he was, but it was not in his nature. Perhaps if he married and had heirs, he would take his estate responsibilities more seriously. And not spend so much time with that boy Henry. But he seemed quite firmly set against the notion of finding a bride for himself.

Well, that was not going to stop Bel making a match for herself. There was much to be done. She gathered up her mud-splattered riding skirt and headed for the kitchen wing, calling, 'Mrs Havers! Mrs Havers! Where are you, Mrs Havers?'

Chapter 24

'Good God! What are you doing here?'

Mariah was waiting outside the housekeeper's private sitting room across the stone-flagged passage from the Hall kitchen. It was after luncheon and the servants were busy with their cleaning tasks. At the end of the passage the back door stood open, letting a shaft of light into the darkness.

'Henry!' Mariah recognised his affected vowels and looked up, as startled to see him as he was to see her. He was dressed for riding in a brown hacking jacket, moleskin breeches and brown leather boots, and carried a brown bowler hat in his gloved hands.

His clothes were new and he looked handsome in them. Mariah had felt confident in her appearance when she had left Dora's, in her dark grey gown and heavy outdoor cloak. But now, beside Henry, she knew she looked shabby.

'Is this what has become of you?' he demanded. 'A kitchen maid? Father is right when he says you are not worthy of our name.' He leaned forward and lowered his voice. 'I'll thank you not to mention our former relationship in these corridors. Just remember I know the truth about your birth.'

Mariah pursed her lips angrily. 'Go away, Henry. You need have no fear I shall own you as a brother, or Ezekiel as a father!'

Mrs Havers opened her sitting-room door. 'What is going on out here? Oh! Mr Bowes, sir! What are you doing in my kitchens?'

Henry stepped back. 'Taking a short cut to the stables, ma'am.' He turned to leave and then changed his mind, adding, 'I hope you are not giving employment to this person, Mrs Havers. I am sure your master would not approve. She is known to be wilful and disobedient.'

Mrs Havers knew better than to respond to this and simply explained, 'A visitor to the servants' hall, sir. That is all.'

'See that you check her pockets before she leaves.'

Humiliated, Mariah looked down at the flags and clenched her fists. She wondered what else he was going to say. No doubt Ezekiel had been quick to disassociate himself from her. She had caused him great embarrassment by her refusal to marry Mr Smith and she understood why he would not own her. Henry had agreed with his father about her marriage. But his main concern, she realised, was his reputation with the Fitzkeppels. Fortunately for her temper, Henry left as hastily as he had arrived without giving her another glance.

'Well, Miss Bowes?' Mrs Havers sat imperiously in her fireside chair and her chatelaine of keys rattled as she arranged her skirt. 'While you are here, working on Miss Christobel's new gowns, I shall be responsible for your conduct. I am waiting for an explanation.'

Mariah did not know what to say. She had no wish to be connected with Henry or his father in any way. But he had acknowledged a familiarity with her.

After a short silence, Mrs Havers went on, 'You are Miss Bowes? He is Henry Bowes, of Bowes Ironworks. A cousin of yours perhaps?'

'No,' Mariah replied truthfully.

'Well? From where does he know you?'

Mariah inhaled deeply. She had hoped that Mrs Havers would ask no more questions.

'We are related, ma'am. But there has been a – a difference between us and I no longer – er – reside with them.'

'And why should he make that comment?' Mrs

Havers had raised her voice.

Spite, probably, Mariah thought and replied defiantly, 'I really do not know, but it is not true!'

'Hmmm. He is right about you being wilful.'

'I am not a thief!' Mariah denied hotly.

'No, I do not believe you are. Mrs Barton would know if you were and she would not have you in her house. Her recommendation is enough for me. Nonetheless, I have enough to do looking after the Hall servants. Truman, our butler, is too old to cope now and the responsibility for them is left to me. I expect honesty and obedience at all times. Is that clear?'

'Yes, Mrs Havers.'

'Miss Christobel has insisted that only you will fashion her new gowns. Since you made that riding habit for her she has talked of nothing else. Nanny will help you with her sizings. Nanny has been looking after Miss Christobel since she was born. And we will find one of the servants to help you.'

'Yes, Mrs Havers.' Mariah was thrilled at this opportunity. To work at the Hall, with rich silks and satins, and to have a seamstress to help her – it was all she could wish for. 'I shall need somewhere to work,' she said. 'The laundry room–' Mariah stopped as Mrs Havers glared at her.

'It is in hand. My laundry mistress is fully aware of your requirements. Now what is all this she tells me about you wanting leftover silk and trimmings?'

'Only that I should like to purchase it out of my pay. Good wool and silk is so difficult to come by.' Mariah waited anxiously for Mrs Havers to reply. She planned to make shoulder capes and trim bonnets to sell at the market as her mother had done before her.

'Well, you can have them. On one condition.'

'Yes?'

'They are not to be made up into any garment for a whole year.'

'Oh.'

'Come now, Miss Christobel does not wish to see some village girl dressed in the same silk as herself, even if it is only a frill or a flounce! As soon as she has passed her outfits to her maids, you may make up the remnants into whatever you wish.'

'Thank you, Mrs Havers. When shall I start?'

'Today. Master Nathaniel's valet is run off his feet. Mr Bowes is a constant visitor and both gentlemen have extensive wardrobes. Their riding clothes will need sponging and pressing later today and you will take over the repairs.'

'Does Mr Bowes stay here, then?'

'He has his own bedchamber and dressing room.'

And Master Nathaniel's valet, thought Mariah. 'How pleasant for him,' she observed. 'I did not know that he was so well acquainted with Mr Fitzkeppel.'

'He is assisting the master with the Hall refurbishments.' After a pause, she added, 'They share the same tastes.'

Mariah pondered silently on this. She hardly knew Henry, but his early ideas for Ezekiel's house at the ironworks yard seemed, to her, to be far too grand for them. Mariah was sure that Bowes Ironworks was not prosperous enough to provide for the silk embossed wallpaper and carpets from the Orient that were to his taste. Clearly, he was more at home with a house the size of the Hall. And an income to match!

In the brief meetings that Mariah had had with Miss Fitzkeppel, she had found her to be most civil. She hoped Henry was not going to sully her name at the Hall. She thought he would not, for he would not wish to disclose that a close relative of his was working as a servant at the Hall. Why, Henry may even learn some of the Fitzkeppel civility while he stayed at the Hall!

'Miss Bowes, are you listening to me?'

'S-sorry, Mrs Havers. Yes. You were saying that I may wear my own gown and need not dress as a servant.'

'Quite so. The carrier from the village will bring you here each morning and you will take luncheon with myself and Truman. Now, I have to inspect the plate and china and after that I shall show you to your workroom.'

By the following week, Mariah had made a good start in her new workroom. Mrs Havers brought in the seamstress and then left to return quickly to her own duties. The girl hovered in the doorway.

'Come right in and tell me your name.'

'Maltby, Miss Bowes.'

The little girl took a step forward. She wore a dark brown housemaid's dress covered by a large calico pinafore and her hair was tucked out of sight beneath a close-fitting calico bonnet. She had bright eyes and was not timid in her manner.

'Maltby? That's the name of a village near

town, is it not?'

'Yes, miss. It's where they found me when I was little. In a ditch by the turnpike.'

'I see.' Mariah inhaled. 'Do you have another name?'

'Sarah, miss. After the lady who found me. She took me to the poorhouse, miss.'

'Do you know how old you are?'

'Twelve, miss.'

'Mrs Havers tells me that your mending work in the laundry is very good.'

Sarah did not reply, but Mariah detected a flash of light in her eyes and slight upward movement of her head and neck. She guessed nobody had told her that before and asked, 'Do you know why you are here?'

'Mrs Havers said to go and work with you from now on and to do as you told me.'

Mariah noticed Sarah's eyes beginning to stray, taking in her huge worktable, cutting shears and threads, the new mannequin already padded with horsehair to Miss Christobel's shape and the pieces of calico Mariah was preparing for the toile she would use as a pattern for her outfits.

'Show me your hands.' Mariah examined the girl's nails and palms. 'Good. Keep them clean and smooth and never, *never* come in here with rough nails or salve on the skin. And never make up the fire. A footman will tend to that. Now, let me see what you can do with this calico.'

Mrs Havers had chosen the room well. It was on the first floor and had a large, north-facing window with inside shutters that folded back against the wall. There were no curtains and only a marble washstand remained to indicate it had once been a bedchamber. A large china bowl stood on the washstand, and a housemaid had brought up a ewer of hot water and clean linen towels that she had hung neatly on the brass rails at either side.

The window looked out onto a walled fruit garden, and directly beneath it was a conservatory. Through the roof Mariah could see one or two large-leaved green plants, wicker furniture and an artist's easel with canvases stacked against the wall behind it.

Mariah sat at her sewing table, working at her creation and examining every detail of Sarah's stitching. She was determined not to be satisfied with anything less than excellence. But when a brewing storm darkened the sky she allowed herself to stand and stretch, walk about the room and linger by the window.

She took a minute to grimace at the dark clouds and then looked down at the conservatory roof. Lamps had already been lit and she was startled to see Mr Fitzkeppel there, standing by his easel. He must have sensed her eyes on him for he suddenly looked up and saw her watching. Mortified that she had been caught snooping, Mariah jumped back into the room with a cry.

'Oh, miss, you startled me. Oh dear, look, now I've drawn blood.' Sarah sucked at her stabbed finger.

'Come over here to the washstand.'

'What is it, miss? What did you see?'

'Oh nothing, nobody. Sarah, come away from the window.'

'There is somebody down there in the conservatory. Did that worry you, Miss Bowes? It's only the gardener tending to his plants, I expect, or the master doing his painting. Good at that, the master is, Mrs Havers says. He can draw a likeness as well as anybody.'

'Yes, I am sure he can. Let me look at your finger.'

'It's nothing. Just a needle prick.'

'Best stop for now. It must be nearly time for the servants' dinner. Off you go.'

Outdoor servants, housemaids and footmen, some of whom got up at 5 o'clock in the morning to get the fires going, had their dinner at half past eleven. Mariah ate later with Mrs Havers, her husband who was the estate's gamekeeper, and Truman, the Hall's ancient butler. The master's valet joined them as well as nanny who, to Mariah, appeared to be as elderly as Truman. Nanny's wits, however, had remained sharp and she questioned Mariah every day on aspects of her work to report back to her mistress.

Mariah fell easily into a routine. She welcomed such an orderly and regular existence. She felt safe working at the Hall, far away from the town and her stepfather, far away from the canal bank and her tortured memory of those horrible men. Even Henry seemed a distant relative to her now. She used the back staircase to get to her workroom and her path at the Hall rarely crossed his unless he chose to visit the kitchens.

She rose early at Dora's, dressed and walked down the lane where she met a horse and cart taking estate workers from Keppel village to the

Hall. Mariah sat next to the driver and wrapped her cloak closely around her to keep out the cold.

When they reached the Hall there was hot porridge on the kitchen range for breakfast and, if it was raining or there was a hard frost on the ground, cook laced their porridge with West Indian rum to warm them.

At the end of their working day, there was mulled ale in the kitchen before making the journey home. They were cheerful, friendly folk, from the same families she had met at the harvest supper and Mariah began to feel as though she belonged.

Mariah was checking Sarah's seams after she had gone downstairs for her dinner, when she was startled by an unexpected visitor. The door to her workroom opened, quite suddenly, and Mr Fitzkeppel walked into the room. She stood up hastily.

'So this is where Mrs Havers has hidden you?' he said. 'I remember you were at the harvest supper with Mrs Barton, and my sister told me you were here.'

He was casually dressed, looking more like an estate worker than a landowner, in corduroy breeches and a flannel shirt. But he wore a distinctive flamboyant waistcoat, made from an elaborate brocade. Mariah noticed smears of oil paint on his shirtsleeves.

'Good morning, Mr Fitzkeppel.' Mariah pushed aside Sarah's work and dropped a curtsey.

He approached her worktable and she jumped forward. 'Oh no, sir. I am so sorry, but you have oil paint on your clothes. I cannot allow you near to my worktable.'

279

He turned to her with a smile. 'Not even to look?'

'No, indeed.'

'You mean it, don't you?'

'Yes, sir.'

He gazed at her for a minute. 'Do you know you have the look of Henry when you are vexed like this?'

'I – er – that is... Henry, sir?'

'Henry Bowes. You are related to him, are you not?'

'Yes, sir. Distantly.'

'I think not, Miss Bowes. I shall ask him. Or will you tell me?'

Mariah guessed he already knew and resigned herself to the truth. 'He is my half-brother, sir. Since our mother passed on we have become estranged.'

'So I hear. He does not like you, does he? He became angry when I spoke of you. He says you are headstrong.'

'I have quarrelled with my stepfather, sir. I do not wish to speak of it.'

'Wilful, too. I have a sister just the same. Dear me, Miss Bowes. Think on. At least you have a father to quarrel with. My sister and I have no such luxury.'

'No, sir.'

'I have painted a portrait of your brother. Has he told you?'

'We do not speak much.'

'I should like to paint a portrait of you as well.'

'Of me? Why?'

'I believe I can bring out the resemblance

between you. Will you let me try?'

'I have work to do here. You know I have.'

He walked about the room from door to window and then turned. 'I shall sit quietly in this corner and draw sketches of you as you work and when I have my canvas ready on the easel I shall ask my sister if I may borrow you to sit for the final touches. Only if you agree, of course.' He raised eyebrows. 'Do you?'

'I believe you must ask your sister, sir.'

'And she will ask me if you are willing.' He sounded impatient.

'Very well. If Miss Fitzkeppel has no objections.'

'I shall speak to her today.'

Mariah sat and stared out of the window after he had left. Mr Fitzkeppel was indeed a charming man. Gentle too, and concerned for her wishes. He was so very different from the man she had grown up with. She began to understand why Henry came to the Hall so often and why he had formed an apparently strong bond of friendship here. Mr Fitzkeppel would be a good friend for anyone to have and Mariah felt a sense of relief that, for Henry, the attraction was not only the Fitzkeppel wealth and position.

Miss Fitzkeppel, on the other hand, did not echo her brother's gentle charm. She had a reputation in the servants' hall for being more demanding and quite frightening sometimes, especially to very young maids who had known only their own doting parents before they came into service.

She did not frighten Mariah. Nothing could frighten her now, except perhaps her own anger if she ever met up with those Cluffs again. In her dark moments she imagined facing them in the street or market place and fearing they might come after her. Rage bubbled through her to such an extent she did not know what to do with herself. She no longer wanted to scream at the memory, but she still wanted to kill them.

'Miss Bowes? Mrs Havers is wondering if you have forgot your dinner?' A young footman came into her workroom to make up the fire.

'Is it that time already? Thank you.' She draped calico over the fabric on her table. 'You will be careful with those ashes, won't you?'

'Yes, Miss Bowes. I have my orders.'

Mariah smiled and thought how lucky she was to have been given this commission at the Hall. She was comfortable and safe here. And the fees Miss Fitzkeppel had agreed to pay her meant that, for the first time in her life, she would have real money in her pocket, money of her own. She inhaled heartily and hurried down the back stairs for her dinner.

The following afternoon, Mrs Havers told Mariah that Miss Christobel wished to see her in the small drawing room overlooking the west terrace. A weak sun silhouetted the distant woods and brightened the parkland below.

'Miss Bowes. How are you finding your workroom? And your seamstress, is she satisfactory?'

'Thank you, Miss Fitzkeppel. I am well suited and Maltby is a good worker.'

'Mrs Barton told Mrs Havers you left town for the country air. You have suffered a recent bereavement and have been ill.'

'Yes, ma'am.'

'I am sorry. Are you quite well now?'

'Yes, ma'am.'

'I advise a walk every day, after luncheon.'

'Yes, ma'am, thank you. Mrs Havers has asked me to accompany her. Her husband will show us the glasshouses.'

Miss Fitzkeppel nodded as though satisfied with the arrangement. 'My brother wishes to make sketches of you at work. Did you know of this?'

'Yes, ma'am. He came to see me yesterday.'

'He told me that you are Henry Bowes' sister. Is this true?'

'Half-sister.'

'But you do not live with him? Or with your father?'

Mariah swallowed. If she did not explain, Miss Fitzkeppel would believe she had something to hide and be suspicious. She would rather any information came from her than from Henry via the master.

'He is my stepfather, ma'am. I do not live with them.' When she saw Miss Fitzkeppel was waiting patiently for her to continue, she went on, selecting her words carefully. 'My stepfather wished me to marry – someone – someone of his choosing. I did not care for his choice and we quarrelled.'

'You mean the gentleman he presented to you was not to your liking? Your stepfather is a successful ironmaster, I am sure he chose well for you.'

Mariah stayed silent.

Bel considered some of the suitors who had been selected for her at nineteen and did not press for further detail. She said, 'You are exceedingly lucky Mrs Barton took you in.'

'Her nephew and niece are employed at Bowes Ironworks. They were aware of my – my circumstances.'

'I see. You should have told Mrs Havers who you were.'

'I am sorry, ma'am. I did not know you were so well acquainted with my – with Mr Henry Bowes. And I have a settled situation in Keppel now with Mrs Barton.'

'Very well. Be seated. You will take tea?'

Mariah watched Miss Fitzkeppel as she poured and offered her milk and sugar. Poised and confident, she appeared to Mariah to have so many attributes desirable in a wife that she wondered why she was not yet married. Perhaps she was considered too strong-willed? Certainly, she had had no domineering stepfather to curb her behaviour and her trustees were, no doubt, only interested in preserving her brother's fortune.

Christobel's appearance was that of a woman older than she was. Her tea gown, in a soft dove grey with a darker braiding, did not fit as well as it should and Mariah was irritated that such good fabric had been wasted in this way. She was determined that Miss Fitzkeppel would look so much better in *her* gowns.

As she poured the tea and handed a cup and saucer to her visitor, Bel considered the independent nature of the woman in front of her. Miss Bowes appeared to be in improving health and was, indeed, very becoming to the eye and, most definitely, was the best needlewoman she had ever known. She was already using the tailoring methods the gentlemen were so taken by. And, since she first wore the riding habit Mariah fashioned for her, Bel realised the value of tailoring for ladies' outfits. What Henry Bowes had achieved with his suggestions for the Hall refurbishments, his sister was more than capable of echoing in Bel's wardrobe.

She said, 'You may spend the time with my brother that he requires for the painting. However, if the gown you are making is satisfactory, I shall require more for the winter season. And a shooting habit. So you may have another seamstress from the laundry. I shall instruct Mrs Havers that you may choose any girl you wish. Now, let us sit at the table and take a look at these illustrations.'

Bel opened a portfolio containing pages from a ladies' journal and some sketches of gowns, showing the form and detail of necklines and trims. Mariah almost fell on them with delight.

'Miss Fitzkeppel, are these the new fashions? They are magnificent. You will look very beautiful in them!'

'Do you think so? They appear splendid enough in the drawings but when they are made up and I see myself in the glass I am not so sure I shall.'

'May I suggest a solution, ma'am?'

'That is why you are here.'

Mariah held up two of the journal pages. 'Take the bodice from this gown and the skirt from that one.'

'Combine the two as one, you mean?'

'I can make the bodice separately from the skirt. That way the waist will fit more closely, as

285

it does in the drawing.'

'Will it? Will it really? I do like the skirt on that one.'

Mariah nodded. 'With those flounces for extra fullness, oh yes. You will need more petticoats, though. They must be made with more crin to stand out like that.'

'You have worked with crin?'

'Of course. Mother used it for sleeve-heads.' Mariah was studying the pictures closely, noting how much lower the necklines were. 'Have you considered this one, ma'am?'

'I have. The bodice is very – er – revealing, don't you think?'

'Mmm,' Mariah murmured, 'the neckline is indeed wide. I do not see how you can move your arms if it is cut so low on your shoulders.'

Miss Fitzkeppel took the drawing from her and studied it. 'I shall not care for my comfort. Make it. I need a gown that ensures I am noticed.'

'You will certainly astonish your guests in that gown, ma'am. No other lady in the Riding would be so daring. If you choose a heavy silk, I can tailor a waistcoat for your brother in the same colour.

'A gentleman's waistcoat as well? You *are* clever!'

'What an entrance you two will make at your banquet!'

'Yes!' Miss Fitzkeppel's bright blue eyes shone. 'You will make the waistcoat in secret and I shall surprise him!'

Mariah smiled and nodded. She would have plenty of time to stare at Mr Fitzkeppel as he worked on her portrait. His valet would tell her which of his existing waistcoats was the best fit so she could fashion one to the same measure.

'I shall make you the envy of all other ladies, ma'am.'

'Yes!' Miss Fitzkeppel had taken her eyes off the sketches and was gazing out of the window. 'My brother and I will show the Riding that we are people to be reckoned with,' she said. 'We are ourselves, not our parents. We shall make a very fine entrance at our first Fitzkeppel ball, and we shall be the talk of the whole Riding.'

Mariah returned to her workroom elated. She was certain that, in her gowns, Miss Fitzkeppel would be a true belle. Every head would turn when she walked into the room. And every lady would surely wish to know who made her gowns! A shivering excitement began to run through Mariah. It was her responsibility to ensure Miss Fitzkeppel became the most beautiful woman in the Riding. She would not fail her. Long after Sarah had gone for her tea, Mariah studied the designs in the failing light. She brought the candle close and made sketches of her own. She could not wait to get started on the silk.

Chapter 25

'I told you I had completed one of Henry. Come and look.'

Mariah followed Mr Fitzkeppel to the back of his conservatory where his paintings were stacked against the wall. He reached down with his long white fingers, extracted a framed portrait and turned it to the light.

'Is your brother not a handsome fellow, Miss Bowes?'

Mariah stared at the picture. It was indeed a good likeness, but it was in a flattering light, making Henry look innocent and boyish, dressed as he was in a summer jacket and the necktie of his former school-house colours. She wondered what Henry thought of it now he preferred cashmere and velvet for his jackets. He had tried so hard of late to dress as a gentleman, to look the part of a man of means who rode in a carriage and conversed with gentry.

'It is as I remember him,' she replied. 'But I fear he has lost some of this young charm now he has left school.'

'How perceptive you are, Miss Bowes. Now come over to my easel and sit for me.'

He had made three visits to her workroom with his charcoal and paper, sitting quietly as he sketched, speaking to her only when Sarah left the room. He was so quiet that after a while Mariah forgot he was there and was able to concentrate as before. Sarah had shown herself to be an able and willing pupil and soon she would be joined by another young maid from the mending room.

Mariah was confident that her gowns for Miss Fitzkeppel would be the most stylish in the Riding. But she was unsure what Mr Fitzkeppel wanted from her as she arranged herself on an ornate gilt chair in the conservatory and stared at the back of his easel.

He walked over to her, examining her face

288

closely. 'There is a furrow on your brow; this will not do,' he commented. 'You have no such expression when you are sitting at your worktable.'

'I am on familiar ground in my workroom, sir.'

'I see. So you are concerned when you are here. Not because of me, I hope, Miss Bowes?'

'I – I am not sure what you require of me, sir.'

'I require you to sit still, of course. Do you think you can do that?'

'Yes, sir.' Mariah made a supreme effort to relax. She was dressed in her dark grey gown, the one she wore to the Hall every day. It fitted her perfectly and she kept it very clean and in good repair. It was plain with a close-fitting bodice and sleeves. She had cut in a fashionably low neckline filled with a sprigged muslin, echoing this in a neat cap for her hair and the sleeve frills at her wrists. Since working at the Hall, she had added an extra crin petticoat to give the skirt more fullness.

He did not ask her to remove the muslin at her neckline as she had feared he might, or pull down the shoulder of her gown. But she was startled when he walked over to her and touched the skin of her face gently with his knuckles.

'And now the furrowing is worse. Really, Miss Bowes, I cannot paint you with lines on your face.'

Mariah inhaled deeply and forced a smile.

'I do not wish you to smile, either. I want the calmness you have when you are at work.'

'Then perhaps I should have some work to do?'

'Of course! An excellent suggestion!' He went out of the conservatory into the adjoining room and pulled on the bell sash by the fireplace. 'I shall send for some of your work,' he said.

Mariah was horrified. She wanted none of her sewing in here, picking up any of the strange-smelling pigments and spirits that Mr Fitzkeppel used. He might not care about a smear or two on his flannel shirts and corduroy breeches, but she did!

A footman came in and he said, 'Fetch the maid from Miss Bowes' workroom.'

When he had gone, Mr Fitzkeppel approached her again. 'This bright hair must be your mother's for Henry and your father are dark. Is that not so?' He removed her cap and began to unpin her hair so it fell about her shoulders.

He stood very close to her and she could smell the heavy musky scent that wafted from him. She did not recognise it, though she was certain it was not lavender or rose water. The gentle touch of his hands on her hair sent an unexpected shiver down her back. As he arranged it around her throat, his fingers stroked her skin, but she did not feel frightened or threatened in any way, and she was amazed that this was so. She marvelled that his gentlemanly civility towards her helped her relax, instead of causing her the anxiety she had felt in the presence of any man after the attack.

She said, 'My mother's hair had the same colouring before it turned white due to her illness. She told me it came from her father's family.'

'Mmmm.' He stood back and considered her appearance. 'Do you have a riding habit?'

'No, sir.'

'I shall ask Bel to give you one.'

'I do not ride, sir.'

290

'For the painting, Miss Bowes,' he explained patiently. 'With white lace at your throat, Bel's black riding jacket will be a perfect foil for your hair. Such a colour. Such a challenge.'

Mariah had never met a gentleman like Mr Fitzkeppel before. He revered her appearance and when he was obliged to touch her for the purposes of his work, he handled her as though she were a piece of expensive porcelain. No man had ever treated her like that before and she felt cherished by his actions. She realised Dora was right. There were good men in this world and Mr Fitzkeppel was one of them.

The next afternoon Mariah was sitting in the same north-facing conservatory wearing Bel's jacket over her gown and with a white lace jabot at her throat. Her copper-coloured hair cascaded over one shoulder and she worked peacefully on a piece of embroidery. She felt at her most serene and continued to marvel that she was in the presence of a gentleman, a fine gentleman, who seemed to admire her appearance.

After a couple of hours a footman brought her refreshment in the form of a tiny cup of hot sweet chocolate. Eventually, Mr Fitzkeppel laid down his brushes and draped calico over his easel.

'Enough for today,' he said.

'Sir?'

'You may rest now, Miss Bowes. You are an excellent sitter and I thank you for that. Off you go, now.'

She removed the jacket and jabot and went back to her workroom, elated by such praise. The light was fading already and it was time to go down the back stairs to the kitchen for the cart back home.

Mariah was excited when she related the events to Dora that evening. 'He is such a kind and considerate gentleman. So civilised, so charming. I never thought I would feel this way in the presence of a man again.'

'He is not just any man, Mariah. He is the pinnacle of our local society.'

Mariah was not listening. She twisted round to look at the back of her skirt, 'Can you see any paint or spirits on my gown, Dora? Bring the lamp and look carefully.'

'There is a little mud around the lower part at the back. And on your boots, too. Wait until it dries before you brush it off. Well, I must say it is good to see you so cheerful.'

'The servants at the Hall are so kind to me. Although they do make fun of Mr Fitzkeppel's interest in me.'

'Do not forget his interest is only to paint your picture.'

'But he behaves in such a friendly manner towards me! He does not treat me like a servant.'

'I am pleased you find your situation so comfortable, but do take care with your affections for him. You are from a different position in life.'

'Surely most of the people in the Riding are? He is the biggest landowner around here, but Henry went to the same school as Mr Fitzkeppel and Ezekiel has visited him at the Hall for dinner. Mr Fitzkeppel told me so.'

'He has talked to you about your family?'

'I told you, he does not treat me as a servant.'

'I see. Then perhaps his interest in you is more than politeness. I do remember that he was quite taken by you that first time he saw you crossing the parkland.'

'I am to sit for him every day this week, in his conservatory. It is just below my workroom at the Hall. The light is good there. He is determined to capture my hair. That's another thing. He does not despise or make fun of my colouring. Ezekiel always hated it. And we speak of other things, just as you and I might.'

'You *do* seem to have made an impression on Mr Fitzkeppel.'

'Why are you so surprised, Dora? I am not a freak and he does not know of my – my recent misfortunes. He knows only that I have quarrelled with my stepfather.'

'I am very happy for you, Mariah. It appears that I am wrong and he has a genuine affection for you. Be careful you do not lose your heart to him.'

'Why not?'

'He is gentry and you are not.'

'You told me yourself that his mother was a farmer's daughter.'

'And her marriage was a disaster.'

'You mean they did not love each other? To know love in a marriage is a luxury, Dora. My mother did not know it and I do not expect to have that luxury in mine.'

'Then you should!'

'How can I? What gentleman could ever love me if he knew the truth about me?'

'I hope there will be forgiveness in the

gentleman who loves you. If he truly loves you, he will understand and not love you any the less.'

'I think a knowledge of what happened to me and – and what I did would test even the strongest affection, don't you?'

'Yes, I suppose it might.'

'Well, it is my secret and a secret I shall keep to myself. I shall not let it stop me from accepting a proposal of marriage, should I ever receive one.'

Dora asked lightly, 'Do you suppose you could go forward into marriage without telling your betrothed the whole truth?'

Mariah fell silent. Perhaps not. How could she keep a secret like that from a husband? Besides, he would know she was not a maid on their wedding night. Dora was right. Dora was always right.

'I am not talking of *marriage* to Mr Fitzkeppel. Only friendship.'

'As long as you are sure about that, my dear.'

No one could deny he had a genuine and sincere interest in her, Mariah reflected. And she was becoming increasingly enchanted by him as she sat quietly assessing his shape and movement for the waistcoat, while he mixed pigments and oils to capture her colouring.

Nathan considered Mariah a good sitter. She was patient and good humoured and had a maturity her brother did not possess. She reminded him of Bel in that respect. He worried about Bel. Since her outburst about wanting a husband he realised that she was lonely. Perhaps marriage was a solution for her. It was certainly not for him. Although Withers had mentioned at their last

294

meeting that he ought to be thinking about heirs.

As he studied and painted Miss Bowes, he thought she would make some ambitious artisan or worthy clerk a decent wife. She had attributes of energy and good sense, exceptional skill with a needle and was personable. Too wilful, though. Unless you wanted a lady like Bel to run your estate for you.

He realised, suddenly, that if Bel did marry and leave the Hall, he would need someone to take care of his domestic affairs. He toyed idly with the idea of marrying Miss Bowes. She was a comfortable companion, easy to talk to, and would be ideal for the task. He amused himself by imagining Withers' reaction to a match that was so obviously beneath him. Yet his father had done just that to produce his heirs. He sighed. Henry would be so distressed to know he had been thinking such thoughts.

'Thank you, Miss Bowes. I shall not need you to sit for me again. My painting is finished. You may look.'

She had thought his earlier sketches of her were a good likeness. But when, at last, she saw his canvas on the easel, she blinked at it with surprise. He had caught her features well, but it was her likeness as she had been before her mother died and before her ordeal. It was not a likeness of her as she was now, as a grown woman with maturity in her face. It was a portrait of her as an innocent maid. Her features were angular and undeveloped as they had been when she was younger. She looked more like a boy, a young boy.

She stared at it, swallowed and said, 'I had no idea I looked so much like Henry.'

'But of course you do. You have his bone structure if not his skin tone. The hair, too, is different. I have captured the colour, have I not?'

Mariah thought not. He had not secured the true copper colour. Rather, he had painted a paler version, and he had given her hair more waves than were actually there, so the portrait had a misty, dreamlike appearance. It was not unattractive. And it was clearly her. But not as she saw herself at all, or indeed as she believed others saw her.

He traced her features tenderly with the back of his knuckle and smiled at her gently and said, 'Ethereal, my dear Miss Bowes. That's what you are.'

In the painting, yes. Her skin was too pale and he had completely disregarded the freckling across her nose that was evident to any casual observer. In the painting, she was ghostlike in her appearance.

Well, she thought, I expect that is what ethereal is. But the sight of such fragility alarmed her. She may have looked like that when she first arrived at Dora's but not now, surely? She must take more exercise in the fresh air to improve her colour!

That evening as she sat in the cart home, she asked the driver to stop and let her down at the path that ran across the Hall parkland and led to the woods, so she could walk home.

'Are you sure about this, Miss Bowes?' the driver asked.

'My feet are quite cold from sitting, and my fingers are stiff. A brisk walk is exactly what I need.'

'If you say so. But I 'ave no lamp to lend you.'

'The moon is rising already and I know the way through the woods. Will you collect me from here in the morning?'

'Right you are, miss.'

When Mariah arrived at Dora's, she was slightly out of breath.

Dora frowned. 'Was somebody chasing you?'

'No, I came by the woods. Tell me, Dora. Are my cheeks a little pink?'

'Yes, they are. What on earth were you doing cutting through there in the dark and on your own?'

'I am familiar with the track now, and it's so much quicker than going round by the village and the lane.'

'Even so, after dusk and without a lamp? You could have easily taken the wrong path, or stumbled over a root.'

'There's a good moon tonight. I could see my way well enough and the leaves are soft underfoot.'

'But what if there were poachers about? If they heard you they might have shot you for a deer.'

'Oh, I thought I saw one or two, but they didn't have guns. They had ferrets and were flushing rabbits out of the warren on the long meadow. They were near to where the sheep graze, I think.'

'As long as they keep well away from the birds. Mr Havers doesn't miss a rabbit or two, but he won't stand for losing any pheasants or partridges. Mrs Havers should let you off before it gets dark now the nights are drawing in.'

'I sew as long as there is enough light. Besides, the cart for the villagers doesn't leave until their work is done, and there's so much to do now to get ready for the visitors. I know it's dark but it is still quite early and I am safe enough.'

'All the same,' Dora said, 'you should take care. What's all this about visitors?'

'The Hall servants and villagers talk of nothing else. It is Miss Fitzkeppel's wishes. She is to have a house party with a pheasant shoot and a ball. She has asked me to make her outdoor dress and a silk gown to impress her guests with two bodices. One of them has a very low neckline. And I am to make Mr Fitzkeppel a waistcoat in the same silk for him to wear at the banquet.'

'So I shall see less and less of you?'

'But we are going to be rich by Christmas, Dora! I have built Miss Fitzkeppel's mannequin and Sarah has made up the toiles. And Mrs Havers has given me another girl to train as a seamstress. A child from the laundry with good eyes and nimble fingers who has already shown her uses in my workroom.' Mariah's eyes shone and her cheeks glowed as she hung up her cloak on the hook in the hall.

'I think this commission at the Hall may well give you a new direction in life,' Dora commented.

'Oh, I do hope so! I am so much recovered now, Dora! Miss Fitzkeppel has been very kind. I shall make certain she is the most beautiful lady at her gatherings. Her guests will not forget her gowns and there will be other commissions, I am sure.'

'So my front room will become a gown maker's workshop?'

For a moment Mariah closed her eyes and dreamed of that image. Her own workroom. As big as the one at the Hall, with seamstresses to work for her, and a pony and trap to visit clients. Dora's front room was only a beginning!

She opened her eyes and bit on her lower lip. 'Will you mind? I can give you proper lodging money now. Every week. Look.' Mariah hoisted up her skirt and fished inside the pocket of her drawers. 'A guinea. A whole guinea. Mrs Havers gave it to me for Miss Fitzkeppel's riding habit. She told her it was the best-fitting one she has ever had!'

'Like the coat you made for me. You really are very clever with a needle and thread.'

'My mother was the clever one. I shall always be grateful to her for teaching me. Here, take the guinea for coal and food. Are you going to the beast market in town next week?'

'Aye. We need flour and salt. I shall see the butcher there too, and ask him to call and stick the pig before he starts losing his fat to the cold weather.'

'You can pay the butcher with real money now instead of giving him one of the legs.'

'Yes, Fanny can have that. Salted down, it will be champion for her Christmas feast. I'll get the pickling trough ready in the outhouse.'

'I'll do it, Dora. I am leaving all the household tasks to you these days.'

'Aye, well, you do better with your sewing and I am happy for you to get on with that. Will you come to market with me?'

Mariah inhaled sharply. 'I cannot. I cannot take a whole day away from my workroom until Miss Fitzkeppel's new habit and gowns are finished. I'll meet the carrier at the end of the lane and help you carry the flour and salt.'

'All right, lass.' She hesitated. 'I'll be seeing our Daniel, I expect.'

There was an awkward silence.

'Shall I tell him you are on the mend?'

Mariah nodded. 'If he wants to know.'

'Of course he does!'

'Do you think he has said anything about me to Ezekiel?'

'Don't you trust him? He wouldn't say anything to anybody about what happened.'

'I'm sorry. It's just that, well, he is Ezekiel's supervisor and that is where his loyalties lie now.'

'Our Daniel is nobody's lackey. He is his own man. I realise you may blame him for your attack...'

'No, I don't blame *him*. He didn't know about Mrs Cluff's past. Those men are to blame. No one else. They should be hanged for what they did to me. What is it that makes men do those things?'

'Some men are just bad. Remember that.'

'I cannot imagine Mr Fitzkeppel behaving in that way. I suppose that's what wealth and education do for gentlemen.'

'He's different. It's the way he is. Do take care with him. It does not do to move out of your class.'

Mariah shrugged. 'Henry and Ezekiel have done. Why shouldn't I?'

When Dora did not respond, she let the matter

drop and said, 'Fire's getting low and there's a clear sky. That means another frost tonight. I'll put a couple of bricks in the oven to warm for our beds.'

Chapter 26

The following week, Mariah stayed later than usual at the Hall. Miss Fitzkeppel's elderly maid had asked for help with cleaning and mending her day gowns. Nanny's eyes were too tired for detailed work, even though she did have spectacles. Mariah was feeling so much better now that, when she had finished, she declined the offer of a governess cart to take her round to the lane.

It was a fine night and Dora knew she would be late. There was a half moon, which gave a little light to her walk. She left the main driveway and cut across the fields on the now familiar path. As she neared the edge of the woods, she heard sheep bleating and their hooves beating as they scattered.

Mariah slowed her pace. Something had disturbed them. A fox, maybe? Unlikely, as it was not lambing time. Perhaps the flock had been spooked by a deer? One single sheep continued its plaintive bleating and Mariah guessed it had been caught up in brambles. Drawn towards the trouble, she strained her eyes in the darkness. The bleating stopped suddenly and as she crept closer she heard subdued voices, rough male voices, and she suddenly felt afraid.

Silently, she slipped into the cover of the trees, but she was drawn to the noises and by a sickening feeling that these men were not the usual rabbit poachers about their dubious business. They were sheep stealers. Instead of hurrying away along the path, she hesitated and strained her ears to listen.

The flickering of a lantern, in the thick of the wood led her to their deed. One of them was dragging the dead animal with blood oozing from its throat into the trees and away from the chance sight of any passing rider. Mariah watched their movements in horror.

'Bring it round 'ere. Gerron with it, lad, we a'n't got all night.'

'A' tha gunna skin it first?'

'That'll tek too long. By the time I've gutted this 'un, t'others'll 'ave quietened and we'll fetch another.'

As soon as she heard the voices, Mariah became rigid as though frozen to the spot. There were two of them and they had a handcart, a small wooden affair stacked with old sacking and straw. The younger man held the lantern as the older man took his knife and slit the sheep's belly until its steaming sagging innards spilled out onto the leaf-littered ground.

'Keep that lamp high, I tell yer!'

'That's good money we're leaving behind, Dad. Yer can allus flog sheep's guts.'

'Aye, I know, lad. But it'll lighten our load. This lot'll be heavy enough ter push as it is.'

'Yer got a buyer, then?'

'A buyer? They've got labourers sleeping on clothes lines over Sheffield way! We'll get a good price fo' this from somebody.'

As she crept a little closer and her eyes became used to the flickering lamplight her stomach sickened at what she saw. But it was not the sight of butchery that turned her, nor the stench of spilled guts – she recognised the Cluffs.

Mariah pushed her knuckles between her teeth to stifle her cries. Her recollection of her degradation was so clear it could have happened yesterday! As she watched them go about their foul deed, she re-lived that night of horror and her heart turned to stone. She knew exactly what she must do.

When they had loaded their first quarry onto the handcart, they would go back to the meadow for a second kill. She had time. She silently retraced her steps to the familiar track and then ran as fast as she could across the parkland and all the way to the Hall. She went straight to Mrs Havers' sitting room, and fell against the door, her heart racing and her breath coming in short urgent pants.

Mrs Havers herself answered her urgent thumping and calling. 'Miss Bowes! What on God's earth is wrong?'

Mariah leaned on the door jamb to steady her shaking body. 'Sh-sheep stealers. Got a handcart in the woods at the edge of the parkland. Two men. Ruffians, by the look of them.' She did not say their name, nor that she knew them.

'Go into my sitting room. Mr Havers is there.'

Mr Havers had been dozing with an empty ale

tankard in his hand. As Mariah entered the room he was already on his feet and reaching for his gun in its resting place by the fire. 'I heard. Good work, Miss Bowes.'

'They said they were taking them over to Sheffield, to lodging houses there.'

'Mrs Havers, send one of the stable lads for the constable right away. Jed and Joseph are just finishing their supper. I'll take them with me now.' He checked his pockets for gun cartridges.

'Take care, Mr Havers.' Mrs Havers stretched up to kiss him on the cheek.

He gave her a rueful smile and strode purposefully out of their small, cosy sitting room.

Mariah slumped down in a chair to recover her breath. 'Will he shoot them?'

'Only if they try to get away. Wait there until I get back from the stables.'

Mariah's breathing had subsided but she was still feeling nervous when Mrs Havers returned.

'Mr Havers will catch them, won't he?'

'He'd better! He has been losing too many of his sheep lately.'

'What if he doesn't, though?' Mariah asked anxiously.

'He'll get them, don't you fret. And he will have you to thank. He'll be right pleased, he will. Now, why not take a piece of shortbread and a glass of mulled wine to refresh you?'

'No, thank you. I'd better get off now, Mrs Barton will be worried and she might set out to meet me. I don't want her coming up against them.'

'Don't be daft! You can't go out there until Mr Havers has 'em handcuffed and taken away.'

'I can't let Dora–'

'Sit down and drink some wine. Jed's brother has taken our fastest horse to fetch the constable. I've told him to go to Mrs Barton's as well to tell her what's going on. When we know all is safe out there, he'll take you round in the trap. Now, lass, while we're waiting we can talk about this house party Miss Christobel is having. I am going to need as many hands as I can find when the guests arrive.'

Much later and safely home, Mariah related the events of the night to Dora over a cup of tea by the kitchen fire.

Dora said, 'Well, the judge won't have any trouble finding them guilty. You saw 'em and they were found with the sheep's blood on their hands and the carcasses in their handcart.'

A sudden fear gripped Mariah. 'Will I have to go to the assizes?'

'I shouldn't think so. Not if Havers and two of his men caught 'em at it and the constable's men took 'em away, sheep an' all.'

'Where? Where have they taken them?'

'Sheffield, I expect. They'll be locked up in the town hall until the magistrate decides what to do with them. He'll most likely send them to the gaol in York to wait for the next assizes. You've seen the last of them around here, Mariah.'

'I hope so, I really do. Will the judge hang them?'

'I can't say. He might favour transporting criminals to the Australias. They say the prisons here cost too much already and our colonies out there need the labour.'

'I heard that some buy their freedom and come back.'

'Not many, lass. Even when they're free, they are better off out there. The governor encourages them to stay. They can have a bit o' land if they want.'

Mariah did not like the idea of the Cluffs being free men again, even if they were on the other side of the world. She would prefer them to be incarcerated for life in a stinking gaol. However, either way, she would not see them again around here and that gave her a measure of redress. She sank back into her chair. 'I can't believe it. They're gone. Gone for good.'

'And we're all well rid if you ask me. Them woods'll be safe for the rest of the winter. As soon as news gets around about this, all the poachers'll stay well clear, you mark my words.'

At last Mariah felt a door close on her past. She could not undo what they had done to her, but she felt some satisfaction she had been able to play a part in their downfall. They were gone! Locked up. They would never threaten her or anyone else again. In time, she hoped their faces would become distant memories. She would never forget the ordeal they put her through, but she felt a kind of release from the torment that had lingered within her. For so long she had wanted punishment for those men and their wickedness. And now she had got it.

'It was them,' she said quietly.

'Them? Who?'

'Those men. Cluff and his son. Stealing the sheep.'

Dora glanced sharply at Mariah. 'The ones who attacked you?'

Mariah gazed into the fire. 'I recognised their voices and I saw their faces in the lamplight. I have never forgotten those faces, those evil mouths sneering at me. Or their hands, their hands and bodies doing unspeakable things to me. I hope they both hang. I'll go and watch them if they do.'

Chapter 27

'Come into town with me tomorrow, Mariah.'

'Yes, I will. It's time I put in an appearance, don't you think?'

'You have no idea how I have longed to hear you say that.'

They were in the outhouse, turning the flitches of bacon in their trough of brine. They would be ready to dry soon, though the hams needed a bit longer to cure. Autumn had been chilly and the ripening holly berries promised a cold winter. The ground froze early and their store of logs and coals had dwindled so quickly Dora had to order an extra cart load from the pit head.

Mariah took to wrapping a shawl around her head when she was sitting sewing by candlelight in the front room after tea. Her commissions at the Hall were finished and Miss Fitzkeppel had paid her well. She had money left over after paying Dora for food and fuel.

'I couldn't be sure until now that the Cluffs

wouldn't show up again.'

'Well, you were right. They didn't stay in Manchester. There were too many rich pickings round here for them.'

Mariah straightened her back and heaved a sigh. 'Since they were put away, I feel I have turned a corner. I can hold my head up and face people again. If folk do shun me, I shall smile and turn the other cheek.'

'Why would they shun you?'

'Ezekiel will have blackened my name at the lodge to save his own.'

'Their womenfolk will understand. There's a beast market tomorrow. You can sell your hand muffs to the farmers' wives.'

Mariah heaved over the fitch, splashing her jute apron. 'Yes, I'd like that. If we go on the early carrier I'll get a good pitch.'

As well as muffs, Mariah had sewn rag dolls from scraps of fabric and stuffed them with soft wool gleaned from the hedgerows. She had also made several ladies' shoulder capes, woollen ones, fashioned with two layers of cloth for protection against the biting winds that whipped across the valley.

'We can go to our Fanny's for dinner. What do you say?'

'That would be nice. I'd love to see them all again. Won't Arthur mind you going there?'

'I've called once or twice since you came to stay and he's not been too bad about me. Fanny says he's going soft in his old age.'

'When I was there, I always thought he was good with baby Victoria.'

'He's a good man,' Dora said sincerely. 'Our Fanny's lucky.'

Mariah took her hands out of the icy brine and dried them on a cloth. Her fingers were shrivelled and red with cold and a graze on her skin was stinging. She did not complain. The salt in the water would help the healing.

'I'm looking forward to seeing your nieces again,' she said.

'Our Daniel might be there, as well. Will you mind?'

'About seeing Daniel? No, I don't think so. Not now.'

'He may have news from Sheffield about the assizes.'

'I'm not interested any more. It's over for me but I hope the Cluffs rot in hell.'

Dora nodded silently to herself.

They set off for the market before dawn, walking down the lane to catch the early carrier's cart, which soon filled to capacity as they trundled nearer to town. Dora and Mariah held her bundle between them sharing the precious space with village folk and squawking poultry in wicker baskets.

Dora helped Mariah spread out her square of calico on the cobbles and weight it down with stones. Then she went off to do her own marketing while Mariah arranged her dolls, muffs and capes to sell. She wrapped her cloak closely around her as a keen wind whipped up her appetite. She looked forward to going down the hill to the Thorpes for her dinner when she had done.

The wintry weather favoured her and she had sold everything long before dinner time. She folded up her pitch and went off with a spring in her step to spend some of her gains on a news sheet for Mr Thorpe, lavender water for Mrs Thorpe and spice for the girls, all of which she placed carefully in pockets on the inside of her cloak.

When she could not stand her hunger any longer she bought some hot chestnuts, roasted on a smoke-shrouded coal brazier. Her mother used to buy them for her when she had a copper to spare. Mariah blinked back a tear, blaming the smoke and thought her mother would be pleased she had found friendship with the Thorpe family. In those last few years of her life, her mother had taken to young Emma, and had often said what a good lass she was.

Mariah sat on a low stone wall waiting for her chestnuts to cool and thought how much stronger she was. She straightened her back and held her head high. Whatever Ezekiel had told his friends about her and whatever the town folk were saying she knew that she had been right to leave his house. The last few months and this morning had shown she could earn her keep by her own hand. Her mother would have been proud of her.

Despite the bitter weather, there was a general air of cheerfulness about the beast market as trade was good. Furnaces and forges were thriving, boosted by the new railways and talk of an empire across the seas. Yet another butcher's shop had opened in the town. The cobbled streets were familiar ground to Mariah and she scanned the bustling crowd for faces that she knew. One or two looked in her direction and gave her a nod, but did not stop to speak.

Across the square she spied the traveller from Leeds with his horse and cart and went over to see what he had for sale. He remembered her and was pleased to meet her again. She bought wool flannel for winter petticoats, cotton for new drawers and stockings for Dora and herself. He wrapped them up in her calico square and tied up the corners so she could sling the weighty bundle over her arm for the walk down to Canal Bank Cottages.

She felt confident at the top of the hill, but as she turned into the alley and the place where she had first encountered the Cluffs, her self-assurance deserted her. Her boots clattered on the cobbles as she began to hurry. She bent her head to her breast and pulled up the hood of her cloak.

The memory was not far below the surface of her mind and it shoved itself forward, quickly and painfully. She pushed it away. I'm all right, she thought, it's daylight and there are people around. I passed two women back there. There is no need to panic.

'Oh!' Someone, a man, had overtaken her and was barring her way. She kept her eye on his boots. They were good boots, she noticed.

'Mariah?'

Her body went rigid and her voice rose to a squeak, 'Oh, it's you.' She relaxed a fraction and raised her head. Daniel Thorpe's serious face searched hers.

'I did not mean to startle you. Aunty Dora called in at the works. I am invited home for my

311

dinner. She said you would be there too.'

Somehow, he was not as she remembered him when they had first met in his parents' kitchen. Since then, she had never really looked at his face properly, even when he came to mend Dora's table. She had been too distraught and embarrassed for her eyes to engage with his. But she recalled how shaken she had been by the sight of him chopping wood in Dora's back yard. And now she remembered that first meeting, and how she had thought then that he was a striking-looking man. She had warmed to his manner at first, until she had realised his mission was for her to do Ezekiel's bidding, return home and marry Mr Smith. He had been so very sure of himself. Too sure, she reflected, for her liking. His command of her affairs had reminded her of Ezekiel's ways.

She still found his manner and appearance striking. Dark hair and stormy-grey eyes, thick eyebrows and strong angular features like his father. But now there seemed to be an underlying sadness shadowing his expression. It had not been there before and it belied the lightness of his voice when he spoke.

'Shall I carry your bundle?' he asked.

She thought there was an older, more worn look about his face now. He had fine lines around his eyes and mouth where before there had been none. Ezekiel was, no doubt, working him hard and he would be feeling the burden of his employer's domineering ways. But she knew he had spirit and backbone to carry such responsibility and wondered what else might be ailing him.

When Mariah made no move, he took the

bundle from her, saying, 'You must be tired after a morning at the market in this weather.' He offered her a supportive arm which she ignored. After a few steps he added, 'A lesser person than you would stay indoors on a brisk day like today.'

'I have been indoors for long enough these past months,' she responded stiffly.

They walked on in silence until he asked, 'How are you, Mariah?'

He always asks me that, she thought, as if it mattered to him. She did not think it did. No, he felt the guilt of his complicity in her degradation, that is all. Well, let him suffer! If Daniel Thorpe chose to blame himself, it was his worry and not hers.

She said simply, 'I am quite well.'

'I mean how are you – er – after your ordeal. Have you–'

'I know what you mean,' she interrupted sharply. 'And I have told you I am well.' After another awkward pause, she added, 'Thank you.'

'I am concerned for you.' He sounded superior, like Ezekiel used to be with her and she felt her anger rising. Heaven forbid that he should grow to be like Ezekiel! But, she conceded, Daniel Thorpe was not an angry man in the same way Ezekiel was. Ezekiel had a bitterness about him. But Daniel, well, Daniel carried guilt and pity for her, that was all. He felt sorry for himself, and for her at the same time.

The silence lengthened as they walked and Mariah wrestled with her thoughts. Of course she was grateful to him for finding her that night. She may well have perished in that cold wet field if he had not. But there had been times during her

313

recovery when she had wondered if it would not have been better to let her die, for what kind of life had she to look forward to now? A defiled and degraded woman with a guilty secret. A spinster's life like Dora's, with no husband and children. It was an existence of sorts, but Dora would never know the joy of a family like her sister Fanny, of the love of a husband and children. Mariah did not want Dora's life for herself.

When Ezekiel had insisted that she marry Mr Smith, she had been resolute in her refusal, but it was not because she was opposed to marriage itself. Indeed, she would welcome the opportunity if she met a gentleman she wished to marry. Though she could not, for the life of her, imagine any gentleman would ever wish to marry her now. How could he, if he knew the truth about her?

Mr Fitzkeppel had shown more than a passing interest in her. She was not of the same standing as he, of course, but that had not seemed to matter to him when she sat for the painting. And meeting him had helped to restore some of her faith in mankind. She did, however, wonder if Mr Fitzkeppel would have shown such interest in her if he had known everything about her.

Even some of the ladies in town, if they knew, would think she had brought her suffering on herself. Decent girls did not put themselves in the position of offering such temptation to men, for, as all women knew, men were men. And much, much worse than that, she had killed her unborn child. Deliberately. A conscious decision, made for her own sake, and she guessed she would suffer for that for the rest of her life.

The Lord had found His own way of dealing with her, she realised. He had made it impossible for any man to love or marry her, impossible for any man to want her to have his children. She would never have a husband and family now and that was the cross she must bear.

She grew angry as she walked, irrationally angry with the man who walked beside her and carried her bundle. Daniel Thorpe did not know what he was talking about when he said he was concerned for her! His concern was for himself and his own guilt, that was all! She found it difficult to talk to him.

However, when they reached the cottage, Mariah's irritation faded as she was drawn into the Thorpes' happy, noisy family. Meg and her younger sisters delighted in their small gifts from the market and Mr and Mrs Thorpe showed a genuine pleasure in seeing her again. Only Emma could not be with them as she was too busy looking after Ezekiel and Henry.

Fanny hugged her tightly. 'We have had news of you from Dora, but it is not the same as seeing you here in the flesh. Let me look at you.' She stepped back. 'Yes, I do believe that country air suits you better than the town. You look well, my dear. Very well indeed.'

'Your sister has cared for me like one of her own and I shall always be in her debt.'

Mariah realised that Dora did not have one of her own. Mariah wondered if all the family knew about her lost baby or if it was a secret shared only by Fanny and Dora. Did Arthur know he had had a child born out of wedlock, a child that

315

had died?

Dora looked across at her sister, who was slicing a piece of boiled bacon at the table, and then down at the blackened iron pot she was tending on the fire. Arthur had not heard. He and his son were distracted by a headline from the news sheet. Mariah frowned at her mistake and then saw Dora smiling at her so she smiled back.

'Dinner's ready,' Dora announced. 'Everybody sit at the table and let me and your mother dish up.'

It was a good dinner. Fanny had boiled the bacon with barley and lots of vegetables. Only baby Victoria did not join them – sleeping soundly in a chair by the fire. They had tankards of Fanny's own ale to drink and hunks of fresh baked bread to mop up the gravy.

'Mariah has been working as a gown maker to the gentry,' Dora announced proudly, and described their meeting with Miss Fitzkeppel at the harvest supper.

Liddy and Lizzy clamoured for details of Mariah's visits to the Hall and demanded to know if the rooms were as big as everyone said. Meg was more interested in Miss Fitzkeppel and her brother.

Mariah obliged her. 'Well, Miss Fitzkeppel, being the elder, seems to take charge most of the time. She runs the household and even talks to the estate manager about the horses and the farms. She likes being outdoors and it was a new riding habit she wanted me to make at first. You know, for the hunting season. I have seen her up and about very early in the mornings when the servants from the village arrive for the day. Her brother is just the opposite. Very cultured and artistic. He occupies himself with paintings for the walls and curtains for the windows.'

Meg and Liddy giggled and Mariah sprang to his defence. 'He is very skilled himself at drawing and painting likenesses! What is wrong with that? He is fortunate in that he has the means to indulge his talent.'

Surprisingly, Mr Thorpe supported Mariah in this view. 'Aye, it's food for the mind, that sort o' stuff. I knew a miner who could draw good likenesses wi' on'y a bit o' chalk on a slate. And another who went to the Institute and wrote poetry that were printed up and sold.'

Dora added, 'Mariah has an artistic eye herself, so she recognises it in others. She can tell you more about Mr Fitzkeppel's own paintings. He was quite taken by you, wasn't he, Mariah?'

'He – he asked to paint a picture of me. He made sketches while I worked and then I sat for him in the conservatory.'

'Really?' Fanny responded.

'Oh yes,' Dora said, 'and I do believe that Mariah has fallen for him.'

'Dora!' Mariah glared at her across the table.

Dora was not to be put off. 'Well, you talked about him all the time when you were working at the Hall and you yourself told me that Miss Christobel allowed you time to sit for the painting. She gave you a second seamstress for your workroom to help out while you were sitting.'

'Is this true?' Daniel, who had been quiet so far, was quite demanding in his tone.

317

He had heard tales from his drinking companions at the Lion about Nathaniel Fitzkeppel, and they were not stories he could repeat in the presence of his family. They came from the footmen and the gardeners at the Hall and told of the antics the young master indulged in with his university friends. They played games that never included ladies, dangerous games that could land them in prison or worse. It was not for him to question the ways of the gentry. But what they did together was not right and he could not stand by and let Mariah believe that Fitzkeppel might ever care for her as a man ought to care for a woman.

'Well, is it?' he repeated.

'Why should it not be true?' Mariah exclaimed. 'He wished to capture my – my colouring – my hair. We talked about Miss Christobel's new gowns as well and we became quite friendly.'

'From what you said, my dear, he *was* interested in you. Take my word for it.'

'Aunty Dora,' Daniel said firmly, 'I do not think you should be encouraging Mariah like this. She is his sister's gown maker, that is all, and he was being kind to her, as I would expect of any gentleman.'

'Daniel?' Now it was Fanny's turn to query Daniel's high-handed tone.

But Daniel was not to be quietened in this matter. His concern for Mariah overrode any consideration for his parents' dining table. He continued, 'Mariah, do not lose your heart to Nathaniel Fitzkeppel. He'd never be interested in you.'

'Daniel! Do not be so unkind!' his mother scolded.

'I – I meant that he, that is–' Lord, he thought! 'He – he is not interested in ordinary Riding folk.'

'And you think you know him better than the rest of us?' his father asked.

'Yes!' Daniel replied stubbornly, and then tried to think of a way to explain his outburst. He could not and added lamely, 'I am saying that he is gentry and Mariah is not.'

'No, she was a servant there, like me and Dora,' Mrs Thorpe added sharply.

'It's quite all right, Mrs Thorpe.' Mariah turned to face Daniel. 'I never suggested that I was losing my heart to Mr Fitzkeppel, as you say. Or that his interest in me was lasting. However, despite our differences in status, he has shown kindness and friendship towards me at a time when my own family, such as it was, has shunned me.'

'Mariah, you must not be fooled by his charm.' This time, Daniel's overbearing tone was stronger.

Arthur and Fanny looked at each other with raised eyebrows. The girls looked down at their plates.

'I am not fooled!' Mariah responded valiantly. 'Will you not allow me a little pleasure, Daniel? May I not indulge in an occasional fanciful dream as other young ladies do?'

'He will never return your affection.'

'Not even as an acquaintance?' Now Mariah grew angry. 'Neither Mr Fitzkeppel, nor his sister, are as rigid as you may think in their choice of companions. My brother Henry is a frequent visitor to the Hall. Why should I not be their friend also?'

Daniel despaired. She did not understand and why should she? Yet he could not see her hurt more than she already had been and felt he must warn her away from Fitzkeppel and his ways. Somehow. He said, 'Do you not see that his position in the Riding demands that his friends should be from a similar standing?'

'Of course I see! But I may have a little enjoyment, may I not? After all, my life so far has not been much fun.'

'I – I – I am sorry, Mariah. I did not mean to suggest...' Daniel hesitated and glanced at his younger sisters who, to a girl, had stopped their hungry chewing and were waiting, with their forks poised and their mouths open, for him to continue. 'I am concerned for you, that is all.'

'So you say,' Mariah responded dryly. Dear me, she thought, he *is* becoming like Ezekiel in his ways. He believes he knows what is best for all the womenfolk around him.

Dora acknowledged Daniel's sisters with a tilt of her head and said, 'Little pigs have big ears. If you two have more to say to each other, why don't you go for a walk after dinner? Have you enough time, Daniel?'

He nodded.

Mariah said, 'Oh, I should help Mrs Thorpe with the pots—'

'No need. I've plenty of hands today,' Fanny interrupted. 'You two need a proper talk.'

Daniel looked from his mother to his aunty and saw Dora give a tiny smile. He pursed his lips. 'We came down from the town together. Mariah may have had enough of my company already.'

Dora did not give up. She smiled at him and said, 'Why not ask her and be certain?'

He said stiffly, 'Will you walk with me after dinner, Mariah?'

Mariah felt obliged to agree. The Thorpes were such good people and she owed it to his parents and his aunty to try and clear the air. After their apple pudding, Daniel shrugged on his heavy coat and Mariah shrouded herself in her warm cloak.

It was overcast and cold outside, but, well wrapped and fortified by a good dinner, they walked down the towpath towards the wharf, their boots crunching on the spilled coal and iron. It was the first time Mariah had retraced those steps since – since that night.

She hesitated for a fraction, regained her resolve and continued. As they passed by the empty end cottage, she suddenly realised what was ailing Daniel and why his manner was so brusque. His heart was shattered. It had been broken by Mrs Cluff and he was pining for her. He must have loved her if he had asked her to marry him as Dora had said.

They walked in silence until Mariah heard him inhale deeply for a second time, so she said, 'I am sorry about Mrs Cluff. Dora told me that you thought she was free to court and marry.'

'It was all my fault! Can you ever forgive me, Mariah?'

The anguished tone of his reply startled her. 'But did she not lie to her husband's family as well? You cannot blame yourself for that!'

'They would not have extracted such revenge if I had not been...'

321

He faltered as though the words had failed him and Mariah frowned to herself. This did not sound like the Daniel she knew.

She continued, 'Your intentions were honourable. I do not blame you for her family's wicked actions. However, I do not, indeed I *cannot*, understand why they should have behaved in such a terrible way for what *you* did. It beggars belief. But it is over, over and done with. I do not hold you responsible for their evil deeds. I am only vexed by the means they used to take their revenge on you.'

She thought that would have eased his conscience, cheered him even, but the dismay on his face became more agonised until he stopped in his tracks and turned to face her.

'Mariah,' he began, 'you do not know everything. I cannot go on with this duplicity until you know the whole story. Lily and I were–'

'Sweethearts. I knew that, Daniel. Emma told me.'

'More than that! Oh, much more than that! I had been seeing Lily since the early summer. Every week. I visited her on Sunday afternoons. She was – is – older than me...' He hesitated again and Mariah's own heart shrivelled a little as she realised how deeply he had loved and had gone on loving Mrs Cluff. His voice lowered to a hoarse whisper. 'I knew what I was doing. When I visited her we were – we were as man and wife. I gave her money for coal and food. Her brother did not know at the time that I wished to marry her.'

Her head reeled at this revelation. 'You were as man and wife and you gave her money! Oh God, now I understand.'

She turned away from him, covered her face with her hands and remembered the argument at the door of Mrs Cluff's cottage. The dark alley where she sent Emma off to fetch Daniel. Their fingers on her arms like iron bands as they dragged her along the path, the crunch of the coal grit underfoot, the cold air on her thighs and breasts and...

We'll make a whore out of you like he has done our Lily.

Now she understood his crushing guilt. Now she understood why their revenge had been so personal.

He put out his hand and she flinched.

'No! Do not touch me.'

She did not know whether it was the taint of coal dust in her mouth or the pain she had in her heart that made her feel ill. The hurt was in her heart not in her stomach or her nether parts where the physical damage had been worst. This was a different kind of wound. A wretched aching despair for what she had lost because of what he had done.

While he had tasted the pleasures of marriage, she must forgo them! A normal existence with a husband, children, a happy dinner table, like the one they had just left, was not for her. How unfair life was! How desperately she wished she had someone to hold and care for her. Someone who did not know about her past grief and therefore did not feel sorry for her. Someone like Mr Fitzkeppel. Certainly not someone who pitied her or who needed to dispel his own guilt. Certainly

323

not Daniel Thorpe. Never Daniel Thorpe.

She said, 'Well, the Cluffs will hang for sheep stealing, so I have justice of a kind. The matter is finished with now.'

'Is it, Mariah?' he asked.

His tone told her that he did not believe her.

'You really do not have to worry so on my behalf. I am not made of china. You heard Dora. I have started a new life making gowns for the gentry.' As she said the words she thought, And though I cannot have marriage I can have freedom and independence from my own hands. She added, 'I shall gain more commissions when Miss Fitzkeppel wears my gowns at her parties.'

'Yes, indeed. She has become something of an icon to the Riding of late. She has grown into a beautiful lady. I have seen her out on horseback in the hills. Once, when I had to deliver papers to the Hall, I was quite close to her. She did not notice me in the shadows but I thought then that she was most handsome.'

'Oh, did you?' Mariah's voice came out in a surprised squeak.

'The town is fortunate to have such a mistress at the Hall. She takes an interest in her brother's estates and will soon be acknowledged as the most elegant lady in the Riding.'

'Really? I did not know.' She wished she had thought to lower her voice.

'You sound surprised. Do you not agree?'

'Er, yes. I – I was not aware that you knew her.'

'I don't. But most gentlemen in the town who have seen her have a similar opinion of her beauty.'

Mariah did not reply. Miss Fitzkeppel had the

same kind of attractive features Mrs Cluff had possessed: the tiny waist that was becoming so fashionable nowadays, and that enhanced her womanly proportions; fair hair that waved and curled in tiny tendrils around her face; wide blue eyes and a generous smile. Daniel sounded as though he was as smitten by Miss Fitzkeppel as he had been by Mrs Cluff. She felt an irrational irritation and, feeling an obligation to break the ensuing silence, changed the subject.

'It is such a pity Emma cannot be here with us today. How is she managing on her own in that large house?'

'As best she can. Henry wants a cook like the gentry have, but his father has refused.'

'I hope he's not too hard on her.'

'You have taught her well. Mr Bowes is pleased with her and she has Meg to help out on laundry days. Now that you are recovered, Mariah, will you not at least consider coming back to your proper home?'

'Oh you, too, would have me marry Mr Smith, then? For that is the price I should have to pay!'

From her furtive glance sideways, Mariah saw Daniel looked uncomfortable with her outburst.

'Surely it is your home as much as Henry's?' he said quietly. 'Your father–'

'I do not wish to discuss my father. Or my brother.' She heard him sigh again and added, 'Shall we walk back? Dora and I are catching the afternoon carrier.'

As Dora and Mariah bumped along the track out of town, muffled up in their shawls and cloaks,

325

Dora said, 'You didn't stay out long with our Danny. I am sorry about what he said at dinner. He's a changed man lately. He's different somehow, so touchy about everything and high-handed in his ways. He used to be such fun and now he's not.'

'It must be Ezekiel's influence.'

She wondered how similar they really were and if Ezekiel had rejected her mother's affections because he had kept a lady like Mrs Cluff somewhere in the Riding. For as long as she could remember he and her mother hardly exchanged a word between them, let alone a kiss. They had separate bedchambers, separate mealtimes, and separate conversations with her.

Mariah's thoughts and feelings were jumbled. For despite his role in her misfortune, she had a grudging admiration for Daniel Thorpe. He had had the courage to tell her the truth about his relationship with Mrs Cluff. He was not a man to flinch from duty and that was why he had achieved such a lot already in his life, and would, no doubt, go on to greater heights in the Riding.

She thought back to their first meeting and the feelings he had aroused in her. She had felt like a normal young woman then and had been charmed by his concern for her, even though she had been obliged to reject it. But he had been Ezekiel's supervisor for only a short while at the time and had already shown signs of his influence. She hoped he was not going to turn into a tyrant like Ezekiel.

She had come away from their short walk with a feeling that he was lonely without Mrs Cluff.

Her father had also seemed to her to be an isolated man. Surely such a handsome and successful man as Daniel need not be alone? She guessed she had been right in her assumption and he was still pining for Mrs Cluff. Certainly, he had been unusually distressed when they had walked past her cottage. Well, he could not marry her now, that was for sure. But, Mariah reflected as the cart carried her away from him, despite their unsatisfactory exchange and her increased animosity towards him, she owned he had many good qualities. More, even, than Mr Fitzkeppel.

Mr Fitzkeppel did not have the strength that ran through Daniel's veins. A strength that was in his character as well as his body. Despite her anger and resentment, Mariah could see that whomsoever Daniel Thorpe chose to be his wife would be a very lucky woman indeed.

She wondered who that might be.

Chapter 28

'Now then, Thorpe. What's to do with this wages bill?'

It was Ezekiel's habit to visit the works office at the end of every day, and on Saturdays he paid his men their dues.

'I've put an extra man on at night, sir. That cementation furnace is old and without him the temperature was dropping and it was taking longer to cook the steel.' Daniel turned over the page of a ledger on the desk. 'If you look at the output, you'll see we need all the blister steel we can make to keep our customers supplied now that we have the crucibles as well.'

'That crucible shed cost me enough without all these extra wages.'

Ezekiel gazed out of the window to his new building across the yard with its flight of stone steps up to the crucibles and wide brick chimney that gave the updraught needed to draw the fires. He called it a shed but it was much more than that. Six crucible furnaces were dropped into the floor. By, when they were at full stretch, he'd be making a pretty penny and no mistake!

'I need another teemer as well, Mr Bowes. I can't do all the teeming and run the works for you. And he'll cost. Pouring red-hot steel from the crucibles into the moulds is dangerous and it takes practice. Young Ned is nowhere near ready for that kind of work yet.' Daniel waited patiently for his employer to reply.

Ezekiel had watched Thorpe teeming and knew he was right. The crucibles were heavy when full of molten steel. They had to be gripped with great long tongs and tipped at arm's length. The heat was so fierce that Thorpe had to bite on an old rag to stop his lips burning as he poured. Mind, he'd got such a good price for his first load of ingots that Ezekiel would have tackled the teeming himself if he had been a younger man. But not now, not with his shoulder the way it was.

'Aye,' he agreed grudgingly. 'Don't forget I've the bank to pay too. If I don't pay them there'll be no house to live in and we'll be sleeping under the crucibles with the coal.'

Daniel was satisfied. He knew just the man at the Fitzkeppel works – steady and strong and looking for a gang-leader's job. He stepped aside so Ezekiel could inspect the ledger.

'When can I take him on, sir?'

Ezekiel grunted. 'I don't want to talk about that now. Have you heard they're having a pheasant shoot at the Hall? Big affair, with visiting gentry and the like.'

Daniel nodded. 'I knew there was work going on at Keppel Hall.'

'Aye well, Master Henry and me, we shall be there at the shoot. Master Henry has been invited by Mr Fitzkeppel himself. They are well acquainted, those two. They know each other from school.'

Daniel was aware that Henry often stayed at Keppel Hall and he thought it high time that Ezekiel stopped indulging his son and made him take a proper interest in his works. The furnaces would belong to Master Henry one day and he would not have the slightest idea what to do with them. But Daniel did not say any of this as he waited patiently for Mr Bowes to continue.

'Havers has asked for you to lead the beaters. He says you used to beat for them reg'lar when you were a lad and he wants a good man in charge.'

'I can't leave the works for a whole day, Mr Bowes.'

'You can if I say so. You're the gaffer down there now, so you see to it. I've told Havers you'll do it.'

'Right, sir.'

'That's settled, then. You'll answer to Havers on the day. Now, step aside, man, so I can get to the safe.'

Ezekiel knelt in front of the heavy iron box that sat in a corner of his office. It was decorated with an ornate brass plate on the door that carried the name of the manufacturer. He took two large keys out of his waistcoat pockets. The thick metal hinges creaked as he opened the safe and reached inside to extract his leather money pouches. One contained folded banknotes. The other, heavier one was more bulky and it grated with coins as he dropped it on the desk top. By gum, it took up a lot less time to pay the men their wages these days now he had Thorpe to make up the ledger and count out the coins.

The men's boots were already ringing on the stone steps outside as they lined up outside his office door. When he was ready, Ezekiel sat behind his old wooden desk and Daniel stood behind him holding the heavy ledger and calling out the names of his gang one by one, and the amount that he was due. Ezekiel picked up a pile of coins for each man and handed it over.

'Thank you, sir,' each one said, turned and pushed quickly past the men behind him to clatter down to the yard with his earnings.

Finally, Ezekiel gave Daniel his wages, inspected the household bills and added an amount for the butcher's boy and grocer's lad when they next called at the house.

'Anything else this week?'

'Just a dozen sacks of oats for the horses, sir. And your stable lad has asked for some more of that West Indian molasses to mix in their morning feed.'

'That's dear, that stuff is.'

'It gets 'em going of a morning, Mr Bowes. Especially if they do the Sheffield haul instead of us having to wait for a barge. Saves us time, sir.'

'Go on, then.'

'Thanks, Mr Bowes. I'll get off back to the warehouse now. We're loading for the next firing on Monday.'

'Aye.'

Alone in his office, Ezekiel placed his money bags back in the safe. He considered whether he could trust Thorpe with the keys to it yet. While he was on his knees he shuffled the papers, checking they were all there. His order book, bills of sale, a copy of his new will, and now the mortgage deed on the house. He wondered if he'd have to ask the bank for more to pay his next wages bill. At the rate young Henry was spending, it looked likely. He was going on about his own horse and carriage now and moving the heavy horses and cart from the stable at the back of the house down to the works yard.

His hand fell on some old papers. Damn! He would have to move them out of the safe if he gave Thorpe the keys! Where would he put them? He dare not risk Henry finding them if he took them into the house. But he could not give the safe keys to Thorpe until he had removed those papers. Should he destroy them? No, he would not, could not. However much he despised them, and himself for owning them, he coveted them and was not capable of burning them. Henry had suggested he purchase another safe for the house and put it in the study. One of the new models Mr Smith had in his shop. Perhaps he would.

Henry would never make an ironmaster like Thorpe. But he was his son and he thanked God for that blessing. Henry made all his grafting at the furnace face worth while. Everything he had worked for was for Henry. And, while Henry might not be good at the hard work needed to make steel, he would better the family name and become proper gentry. In fact he was virtually gentry, for he had been schooled with them and was invited to their houses and to the Fitzkeppel shoot and ball, securing invitations for them both.

With his new supervisor chosen for head beater, Ezekiel, too, was socially accepted. Respected. This was as it should be. As soon as Henry became of age he would find him a bride. He was a handsome lad with good manners and graces. There would be ladies at this party. Young ladies of breeding and charm just right for his Henry.

Ezekiel smoothed the sheets of thick paper lovingly and placed them carefully in the bottom of the safe, away from prying eyes. It was all for Henry. He had endured his silent sufferings for years now. He could continue to bear them when he thought of Henry and Henry's reputation. What did his own feelings matter now? Henry was his future.

Chapter 29

A flock of heavy birds squawked and flapped and broke cover from the trees. The air split and cracked and a few fell like stones to the meadow below. Blue smoke swirled from the butts and the stringency of gunpowder and hot metal assailed Mariah's nostrils. A second volley of shot brought down more birds and then there was quiet while the guns reloaded and the dogs were sent out to retrieve their prey, carrying the birds back in their soft mouths.

'Not many of the ladies here,' Dora commented. 'I suppose they are still in their beds after yesterday.'

'I reckon so. The servants were already busy with breakfast trays when I arrived at the Hall this morning. Apparently last night was pandemonium in the kitchens.'

'I heard about that too,' Dora commented. 'Truman said some of the guests were dropping asleep at the dinner table because they were so tired from their journeys.'

'The maids and valets too. They were exhausted. It's too cold to travel in carriages at this time of year. They were glad of my help.'

'You were very late back last night.'

'There was so much to do! All the unpacking and pressing of gowns and gentlemen's dress for dinner. We were all yawning when we'd finished!'

Mariah and Dora were well back from the butts, in a clearing Havers had prepared especially for this occasion. Mrs Havers had asked Dora to help Truman but, in spite of his advancing years, Truman was clearly in his element and had declined Dora's offer.

'Is that Lady Grassebrough over there?' Mariah asked.

'It looks like her,' Dora replied. 'But I can't see her maid around.'

'No. I'm standing in. She is helping the visiting maids to clean up all the travelling clothes and prepare the dinner gowns for tonight's ball. It's just as well not many of the ladies are here this morning or else they'd have all the shooting habits and walking boots to deal with as well.'

Mariah and Dora sat on the stump of a newly felled tree and watched as footmen set up wooden trestles and boards on a level piece of ground. They had a good view, too, of the woods and fields as the birds were flushed out into the open when the beaters closed in on them.

There was only one other lady shooting with Miss Fitzkeppel. Her brother was there, but he was not shooting. He was talking to Havers as he supervised the loaders and stewards. There were twelve butts and, Mariah noticed, Henry and Ezekiel were positioned at one of them. They were sharing a loader and, quite obviously enjoying their sport.

Truman shook out a white cloth over the wooden boards. Then he tapped a barrel of ale on the cart and began filling metal tankards with the foamy brew. The footmen were busy setting up a shiny new spirit warmer under a large urn of soup that had been carried out from the kitchens. A group of kitchen maids began slicing an assortment of raised game pies and opening stoneware jars of pickle and chutney.

Although tired, the servants were cheerful and there was an air of festivity about the occasion. Mariah became caught up in this atmosphere. She relaxed and began to enjoy herself as the morning progressed towards luncheon.

Havers signalled the guns to cease and all went quiet as the dogs ran for the last of the birds, rushing back with wagging tails. He supervised his keepers as they checked the pheasants and tied them in braces on wooden racks for hanging in the outdoor larder at the Hall.

A straggle of beaters emerged from the undergrowth and trees, flushed and scratched, to join the loaders and keepers for pork pie and ale served from the cart. The clearing and beyond was soon filled with a noisy, hungry crowd, marvelling at the morning's bag as it was displayed for all to admire.

Truman was pouring tots of whisky, very carefully, into tiny thick glasses. He placed one on a silver salver and took it over to Mr Fitzkeppel who was stamping his feet in the cold and looking miserable.

Miss Fitzkeppel, in contrast, was talking and laughing with her guests. She was a good shot and her cheeks glowed with excitement. She helped herself to a tot of whisky, swallowed it in one and reached for another, not caring about sideways glances from some of the gentlemen.

'You're wanted, Dora.' Mariah saw a footman waving and gave her a nudge in the ribs. 'Over there. One of the maids has tripped up by the look of it. Shall I come with you?'

'No. You wait here in case Miss Christobel needs you.'

Mariah stayed at the back of the clearing, warming her mittened hands in the folds of her cloak, content to watch the activity. It was her first experience of a shoot and she was interested in the way masters and servants mingled and enjoyed the delights of the crisp outdoors.

She saw Mr Fitzkeppel pick up two whiskies and hand one to Henry. They wandered over to the wicker tables and chairs where a footman brought them soup and pie. She faltered as she caught sight of Ezekiel talking to a man of similar age to himself. Hobnobbing with the gentry! she thought irritably. It was all he wanted to do now her darling mother had gone. Her anger began to simmer and she tried to repress it. Her instinct was to hide in case he saw her and made a scene, for she would retaliate with as good as he gave and that would never do here. But if he had noticed her he did not acknowledge it and Mariah was grateful. She was enjoying the party and did not want him to spoil it for her. Dora returned from her task with two stoneware mugs of thick oxtail soup and they sat back to back on the tree stump to drink it.

'What happened?' Mariah asked.

'She fell in a rabbit hole and hurt her ankle. I had to take off her boot and stocking and wrap a wet flannel round it.'

'Poor girl.'

'She seemed cheerful enough. Two of the footmen are carrying her back to the kitchens.'

Mariah chuckled. A weak winter sun was beginning to push through the clouds. 'Look, Dora, one or two more ladies have walked out from the Hall for luncheon.'

'And there's our Daniel. Can you see him? Over there with the beaters.'

Mariah started and spilled her soup.

'Careful, lass. I should have warned you it was hot.'

'No harm done. Did you say your Daniel was here?'

'He's with young Ned from the works.'

'Has he seen us?'

'I don't think so,' Dora answered. 'Who's that handsome young fellow sitting with Master Nathan?'

'That's Henry Bowes. Ezekiel's here, too. I saw him earlier.' Mariah looked about her. 'Can't see him now. Oh, yes I can. That's him, Dora, over by the bird racks, talking with – do you know who that is?'

Dora strained her neck. 'Oh yes, he's the manager from Keppel pit. Useful man for him to know, I should think. Want some pie?'

'I'll fetch it. Mustard pickle or marrow chutney?'

As she pushed through the servants, milling around their dinner cart, Mariah glanced over to where she had last seen Daniel. He had a metal tankard of ale in one hand and a slice of pie in the other and he was laughing. Mariah had not seen him laughing like this before. She stared at him for a moment and her heart gave a flutter. He had a noticeable presence, even in a crowd. As he laughed he seemed to come alive and she thought how very attractive he was when he was not being serious and overbearing. She wondered what had made him laugh. Suddenly she really wanted to know what it was. She wanted very much to be a part of the small circle of people that stood around him and whose company he was enjoying.

'Miss Bowes, there you are.' Miss Fitzkeppel threaded her way through her guests towards her. Her face carried a healthy ruddiness, whether from the cold winter air or the whisky Mariah could not tell, but clearly she was thrilled that the shoot was going so well. 'Where is your workbox? Lady Grassebrough has torn her skirt with the heel of her boot.'

She followed the hostess over to one of the wicker tables where her titled guest was twisting in her chair to examine the damage. She was relieved Henry had moved away. Mr Fitzkeppel, also, had gone. This did not surprise her for the two of them had always had their heads together, talking about something, when she saw them at the Hall.

Mariah knelt on the damp grass beside Lady Grassebrough. 'Nothing serious, your ladyship. The edging has broken free and is trailing as you walk. It will get worse if I do not stitch it now.'

Mariah's mittened fingers, warmed by her mug of soup, chilled again to the bone as she strained her eyes to insert tiny stitches into the dark wool. Her knees, also, felt the damp through her own woollen skirt and she was glad when she was finished and able to get up. She blew on her finger ends and wrapped them in the folds of her cloak.

Alarmed, she noticed Ezekiel moving towards them. His face had darkened and he looked angry. She did not want a scene with him here where she was surrounded by her new friends from Keppel village and the Hall staff. But he had reached them before she could move away.

She need not have worried; he ignored her and walked straight past. She felt an irrational hurt as he looked through her. They had lived as father and daughter for nineteen years and he behaved as though she did not exist! In spite of the traumas she had experienced since their quarrel, she would have acknowledged him with a bow of her head. Now she was glad she hadn't!

Yet she was impressed by his appearance. He certainly looked the part of a country gentleman out shooting, dressed in new woollen breeches and waistcoat with a smart tweed jacket and hat. He carried a polished gun over his arm and a new leather hunting bag across his shoulders.

'Miss Fitzkeppel,' he called as he swept by Mariah, 'I am looking for my son. Henry, my son, have you seen him?'

'He was here earlier. I believe he took luncheon with my brother.'

'Then where are they now?'

'I really have no idea, Mr Bowes. Would you excuse me?'

Miss Fitzkeppel moved away with Lady Grassebrough and Mariah followed them, checking her sewing had done its job.

Ezekiel was not happy. He was standing alone talking to the air around him. 'Where is that son of mine? Where has he gone?' He became more agitated as he moved among the guests. An acquaintance hailed him to talk but he would have none of it. He pushed him aside and strode off. 'He should be here with me. He is *my* son...'

Ezekiel noticed people looking at him and quietened. He had been enjoying the shoot until Henry had gone off to talk to their host. Fitzkeppel had so many others around him to talk to, without taking Henry away from him today. He needed Henry beside him on these occasions. He was beginning to think that perhaps Henry spent too much time at Fitzkeppel Hall. Henry's visits had served their purpose. They were now accepted in the upper circles of Riding society and invited to all the right gatherings. And Ezekiel was on good terms with several forge masters and pit owners. Their house too, was looking grander every month.

It was time for Henry to stop squandering his father's money so he could invest in more pig iron and men for his furnaces. That young Thorpe fellow was proving to be worth his weight in gold, and he had done an excellent job with the beaters today. All the guns had told Havers so.

Next time Thorpe would be a gun himself. Ezekiel would see to that. He had influence now. Fine man, young Thorpe. He was going to make Bowes Ironworks sing with new steel.

That nice Fitzkeppel lady was here today, as well. Braving the cold, not like most of the other ladies. They were too nesh by half, were womenfolk. He had seen Amelia's girl with her needle and thread. Where she belonged. On her knees at the feet of the gentry. Silly woman, just like all the rest. She could have been mistress of her own house by now if only she'd done as she was told. She could have had Mr Smith's young daughters waiting on her hand and foot. Just like her mother; didn't know when she was well off. If the pair of them only knew what he had given up for them, for their sakes, for this life of respectability. He rebuked himself silently. Stop it, man! Don't think of what might have been. Not today. Not here.

But suppressing his memories and his desires was becoming more difficult since Amelia had passed on. Her presence had been enough to separate him from his past. But when he was alone, he often thought of those times before Amelia and her bastard and how much he wanted to go back there. And how he could not. Not now. He had spent twenty years of his life gaining respectability in this town and he meant to hold on to it.

Ezekiel became more agitated. He wanted Henry by his side.

He marched about with his gun over his arm, asking after Henry until one of the beaters told him he had seen Mr Fitzkeppel with a well-dressed young gentleman go down the keeper's track through the trees. Ezekiel set off after them.

He came across the old keeper's hut in a small clearing and gazed at it uneasily, ignoring the thoughts tumbling through his mind. An assignation? He had heard tales of young gentry and the women who pleasured them. Was this why Henry was so attracted to the Hall? Were the two of them with some willing wench from the servants' quarters? The woodland was still, but there was a noise coming from the hut.

It was solidly built of rough timber with a stone chimney wall at the back and a heavy door at the front, slightly ajar. The hut was large enough for a gamekeeper to stay in for days and nights on end when chicks were hatching or poachers were about.

There was a shuttered window and, as Ezekiel crept closer, he recognised the sounds within. His heart began thumping in his chest. He had not heard grunts and groans such as these for many a year. He prayed it would not be Henry with some kitchen maid from the Hall. He wanted better for his only son. He crept to the door and listened. Whoever she was she was quiet about it. But it would not do. He would not have his son the object of any servants' gossip at the Hall. He must stop this now. He swallowed and pushed the door with the barrel of his gun. It swung wide open and banged against the wall.

Light flooded into the dusty, sparsely furnished room, illuminating two fused figures rutting on an ancient couch. Their boots and breeches were scattered over the table and chairs, their long white legs exposed to the chilled air. Both their heads turned as daylight streamed in and then was blocked by Ezekiel's figure looming in the doorway.

Henry's strangled, painful cry was muffled by the fusty couch under his face. Fitzkeppel yelped with surprise and slowed the rhythmic movements of his rump. Ezekiel stared at this horror before his eyes. No, this could not be. Not Henry. Not *his son* Henry, coupling with a man who called himself *gentry*. Not Henry, please not Henry, complicit in this shameful act.

Despair and torment engulfed Ezekiel.

Was this why Henry was always at the Hall? Nothing was secret there. The servants knew everything and they gossiped. The single barrel of his shotgun clicked into place. 'Get off my son,' he growled.

Nathan Fitzkeppell heard rather than saw the gun. He peeled himself away from Henry's back, allowing his shirt to fall and cover his nakedness.

'Calm yourself, Father. Put down your gun.' Henry struggled to a sitting position on the couch.

'How long?' Ezekiel demanded through the mist that was clouding his eyes. 'How long has this been going on? *How long?*'

'Come, Father. You know how it is—'

'How long, I said?'

Henry inhaled deeply. 'Since school days. I was his fag.'

'No! No!' Ezekiel let out a long and anguished cry, like that of a dog in pain. Not Henry. Not his son. He felt as though he had been sliced in two and he doubled over, crying and groaning. He swung about, backwards and forwards, pointing his gun in all directions, hitting the barrel against the wooden walls and eventually aiming at Fitzkeppel.

Henry leapt to his feet. 'Give the gun to me, Father.'

But Ezekiel was not listening. He turned

343

towards his son, then back to Fitzkeppel. His mind was in turmoil and a descending blackness was engulfing his reason. This could not be happening to him. Not his Henry. He had tried so hard, so hard to do things right by Henry and that – that *Fitzkeppel* had undone it all. He could not live with this, he could not...

Henry took a step forward. 'Father, stop this. You have to understand, I love Nathan. I was willing, am willing. I have loved him since–'

But the remaining words were lost to everyone's ears as the shot blasted through the air, a deafening crack that sent the birds flapping from their roosts, cawing and calling, disturbing the quiet afternoon sky.

Daniel detached himself from his group of friends to speak to Mariah who was standing alone by a felled log.

'Good day, Mariah. You are looking very well, if I may say so.'

'Thank you,' she said simply.

'Your father seems troubled. Is something wrong?'

'I believe he is missing Henry.'

Daniel surveyed the mix of guests and servants in the clearing. 'Henry is here somewhere.'

'Oh yes. I saw him earlier. He was at the luncheon tables with Mr Fitzkeppel. They are very good friends, you know.'

'Very good friends, did you say?' Daniel's body went rigid with alarm. Fitzkeppel and Henry? 'No, I did not know. I understood Henry visited the Hall for business, to cultivate trading contacts for his father.'

'Well, yes, that too. But they have known each other since their schooldays.'

'I see.' Daniel schooled his features into still-ness, raised his head and, again, looked about. He must be calm about this, but a sickening feeling was spreading though his veins. 'Mr Fitz-keppel is not here either.'

'I expect they have gone back to the Hall. Mr Fitzkeppel hates shooting.'

'He is the host. He would not leave before the shoot is over.'

'Then perhaps they have gone for a walk?'

'Perhaps.'

'I am sure they will be back soon. Ezekiel has gone looking for them.'

Daniel's face remained expressionless as though it was of no consequence. He stared at her for a moment, then said calmly, 'Yes of course.' Without leave, he took her elbow. 'Aunty Dora is looking for you, Mariah.'

She drew away from his touch, startled at first, but nonetheless allowed him to steer her through the throng towards Dora who had collected small cups of steaming chocolate for them.

Daniel kissed his aunty on the cheek. 'Sorry I cannot linger, I – er – after the shoot there's a tea laid on for the beaters in the old barn. Why don't you two come and join us?' He did not wait for a reply but hastily withdrew and Mariah watched him disappear through the trees down the track Ezekiel had taken.

It must be something to do with the ironworks, she reasoned. She took the small cup gratefully

345

and inhaled the rich aroma. 'Mmm, this is delicious. I've tried this before at the Hall, when I was sitting for the painting. Are you sure we're allowed to have it out here?'

'Truman ordered it to be sent out for the ladies. But there aren't many of them braving the cold today, and the footmen have refused to carry a full urn all the way back to the Hall.'

'At least they keep warm dashing backwards and forwards. This is fun, isn't it?'

'Oh aye. It's like in my younger days when old Fitzkeppel was alive. My father was a beater for him and I used to come along for the tea afterwards. All the beaters' families did if they could. There was always a good spread, and cake for the children. I used to love the cake, the cook put plenty of butter in it and eggs and sugar. Ee, lass, I never thought I'd see the day when I would be able to afford to make my own cake. That's because of you, Mariah, my love.'

'Nonsense. You managed very well on your own.'

'Aye, but much better now I get regular money from you as well.'

'I am very grateful for all the help you have given me. I think I would have sunk so low I would never have recovered if it had not been for you.'

'You're a strong lass. Strong in mind as well as body. You had the worst of it, though.'

'I don't dwell on it now if I can help it. Shall we talk of something else?'

'Of course, I– What was that?'

The air was shattered by the crack of a gun going off, quickly followed by a cacophony of

346

birds flapping through the trees. Every person in the clearing stopped what they were doing and looked around.

'Someone gone down to shoot early?' a male voice asked.

'Surely they haven't started for the afternoon already? The beaters are still here and they haven't drawn for the butts yet.'

'Some young blood can't wait to get going again?'

There was an air of disquiet from the guns and their loaders punctuated by a shrill voice in its midst. 'Havers! Havers! What was that?'

'I'll just go and see, Miss Christobel.'

Havers had a face like thunder. If someone was fooling around at his shoot, they'd have him to reckon with and no mistake. These jumped-up ironmasters and factory owners didn't know the form. He raised his voice, 'Ladies and gentlemen, would you all stay where you are, if you please?'

Mariah's eyes widened. The shot had not come from the butts. 'It came from the woods,' she whispered. 'Daniel is in there, Dora. He went to look for Ezekiel.'

Dora looked frightened. 'Daniel didn't have a gun with him. I'm off to see what's going on.'

'You can't! You heard what Havers said!'

'Just watch me. Danny might be hurt.' Discreetly, she picked up her battered leather bag and followed Havers down the track into the wood.

'Do be careful, Dora. Oh heck, you're not going on your own. I'm coming with you.'

'There's a keeper's hut down here,' Dora said breathlessly over her shoulder. 'They sleep there when the chicks are hatching.'

Mariah hurried after her, holding her cloak and skirts tight to her legs to avoid the worst of the brambles. Her heart was thumping in her chest. As the trees thinned and they approached the old hut, they heard a male voice, a raised and anxious voice. There was a faint whiff of gun smoke pervading the air. Some of the trees blocked Mariah's view but she could see the side of the hut and two men standing in the open doorway. Havers appeared to be in a state of high agitation, and Daniel was leading him away, trying to calm him.

Daniel heard the women crashing through the undergrowth and looked round. He immediately left Havers, who slumped against an oak tree, and came to meet them.

'What's happened, Daniel?'

'Go back.' He stood in front of them with his arms outstretched as though to embrace them both. 'Go back to the party. Take Mariah with you.'

'Is Ezekiel here?' Mariah demanded.

'Mariah, do as I say. Go back now.'

'What is going on?' Mariah looked past Daniel to where Havers was sagging against the tree. His knees were giving way under him. He had dropped his gun to the floor and his hands covered his eyes.

Daniel was saying, 'Please take Mariah away.' His voice lowered with intensity, 'Do as I say. Please.'

But as he spoke Mariah darted past him saying, 'Is Havers injured, Daniel? Dora, come and help me.'

'No, Mariah, come back!'

Daniel turned rapidly and caught her arm. She snatched it away, so he grasped the fabric of her cloak and pulled her back sharply.

Mariah heard the stitching give and turned on him. 'What do you think you are doing? Can you not see that Havers is not well?'

'Mariah! Stop!' he called as she broke free again.

But by then it was too late. Mariah had crossed the front of the keeper's hut and had glanced through the open door. She had a clear view of the motionless figure lying on the earth floor inside. A man, half clothed, his pale legs and feet bare to the elements and his shirt, his once white shirt, darkened by torn flesh and congealed blood.

Mariah choked on a strangled cry of shock. The vomit rose in her throat and she could not stop it spilling forth on the ground. Her legs buckled beneath her.

Daniel caught up with her and his arms reached around her, supporting her. 'Come away, Mariah. Don't look.' He turned her to face him and held her close against the coarse wool of his jacket.

She wanted to stay there for ever, leaning against his solid body, embraced by arms so strong they had once carried her for a mile over rough ground to safety, arms that now held her firmly so she could not fall. She fumbled in her skirt pocket for a handkerchief to wipe her mouth as Daniel attempted to steer her away from the hut.

'Who – who is it?' Mariah choked.

349

No one answered.

'Who is it?' she cried.

Dora stood by the lifeless form. She had seen blood many times before. She was used to blood. Animal blood and human blood. But not blood like this, oozing from an inert body torn apart by shot. A close-range shot, if she was any judge.

She gazed at the wounds, shaking her head in disbelief. His face was peppered too. Contorted and peppered, but recognisable. She looked anxiously at Mariah and said, 'Come along, my dear. This is no place for you.'

'No!' Mariah struggled with Daniel until he was forced to release his hold or risk hurting her. She tore herself away from him and went into the hut.

She bent over the body, swallowing hard to keep down the bile rising in her throat. Dark blood spattered his still, pallid face.

Her voice was weak and small. 'No. Not Henry? This cannot be Henry.' She dropped to her knees, not caring about the blood, desperately trying to wipe away the spatters on his face. 'I know we quarrelled, but you were all I had left.'

Tears fell from her eyes and rolled down her face. She sat back on her heels. Her hands were smeared with blood. Her own brother's blood. Her head fell back and a prolonged low wail escaped from her throat.

Daniel picked her up and carried her out of the hut. He gently lowered her to the woodland floor, with a tree to support her back, and made her swallow some brandy from his hip flask. He called for Dora to fetch a blanket from the hut and laid it over her, tucking it around her back and legs. Two of his beaters had followed him to the hut.

Mariah's head began to swim and her mind became muddled. What was Henry doing, half clothed in the gamekeeper's hut? She had seen discarded breeches, fine gentlemen's breeches. Were they his? Mariah moved her lips to speak but no words came out.

Daniel handed Dora his flask. 'See she takes some more of this,' he directed. 'And keep her as warm as you can. I'll ask one of the beaters to bring round a dog cart and take you home. The other can fetch the constable.'

'Was it poachers again?' she asked. 'Revenge, perhaps, for the sheep-stealing business?'

'I doubt it. The Cluff clan never use guns. Knives are more their style. Besides, since that night, things have gone quiet over Mexton way.'

'Do you know what happened here?'

'No. Neither does Havers. But I have found a gun. Abandoned in the undergrowth.'

'Whose is it?'

Daniel glanced at Mariah. 'I don't know.' A straggle of Hall staff had appeared in the clearing and someone called his name. 'Look after Mariah.'

On hearing her name, Mariah looked up at Daniel. 'Don't go,' she whispered.

He did not hear her. He was already distracted by a beater asking him what he should do about Havers. Mariah stared after him. She didn't want him to leave her. Not now. Not ever.

351

Chapter 30

Bel was concerned for her party. 'Where is my brother? Where is he?' She circled around the clearing, surveying her guests. 'Has anyone seen him? He should be dealing with this. Not me.'

Their shooting party had been going very well until then. Now it was in danger of falling apart. Some young blood had fired off early, trying to impress one of the ladies, no doubt. But Havers would sort that out. If only Nathan were here to help her calm their guests.

A ripple of concern was spreading, as a result of that single wayward shot. A few of the gentlemen had detached themselves from the group and followed the track to see who it was. How tiresome! Impatiently, Bel stamped over to where the Hall servants and beaters were lounging, heads together in speculation. They ceased their murmurings as soon as she approached them.

She marched up to a man that she recognised as a gardener at the Hall. 'Find Havers for me. He went after that loose gun.'

The man scrambled to his feet and scurried away. She watched him go, then on impulse followed him down the track. Perhaps Nathaniel was with Havers dealing with the incident?

There were several gentlemen clustered around the gamekeeper's hut when Bel arrived. Her head gardener was bending over a figure sitting propped against a tree. As she approached she realised it was Havers and his face was as white as a bedsheet. The gentlemen were standing about with serious expressions and murmuring to each other.

But it was the figure of the man who was commanding events that riveted Bel's attention. Who was he? She had not noticed him before. Judging by his dress he was not a guest. Not one of Havers' keepers either. She knew most of them by sight.

No, not one of the Hall's regular staff. He must be a beater. Had she seen him earlier, she wondered, having a drink with Havers? As she stared at him, taking charge and organising, she saw the kind of outdoor man she thought her brother should be, the man she hoped that, one day, he would become.

She could not take her eyes from him and became fascinated by his movements on the opposite side of the clearing. He was tall with dark hair and a well-built form. She could see he was a very capable man. A rugged man dressed in rugged clothes. She wanted to know who he was and why he had assumed command of the situation. She wished she could hear what he was saying.

Slowly she walked across the clearing until he noticed her. As soon as he did he came towards her, his arms outstretched to bar her progress.

'Miss Fitzkeppel! You should not be here. Please return to your party.'

Ignoring his request, she demanded, 'Who are you? What do you think you are doing?'

'Daniel Thorpe, miss. I am the supervisor at Bowes Ironworks. You really should be with your guests.'

She gazed at him. His clothes were scuffed and rumpled but they could not detract from his air of authority. He had a handsome face too, although his features were marred by a frown that darkened his eyes to the colour of smoke.

When she made no effort to respond, he continued, 'Your brother must cancel the afternoon shoot.'

'And who are you to tell my brother what he should do?' Bel demanded.

As she moved closer to converse with him, she examined the detail of his face, and wondered why she had not noticed him before. This curiosity distracted her from the surrounding disarray and an unfamiliar flutter began to spread through her veins. The murmurs and mutterings of bystanders faded in her ears as Mr Thorpe became the centre of her vision. This man was exciting to be near, she realised, and she had to try very hard to concentrate on his words.

'There has been an accident. A shooting,' he said.

'Yes, I heard the shot. We all did. Was it a poacher?'

'A guest, miss.'

'A guest? A loose gun? After one of the deer, no doubt. Is the quarry dead? Or has the poor thing fled to lick its wounds? We must find it quickly and put it out of its misery.'

He did not answer her but lifted his hands as though he were about to grasp her upper arms and hold her. Startled by his boldness, Bel's blue eyes widened, but she did not shrink back from him and was shocked to acknowledge a fleeting disappointment when his hands stopped short of her.

'Is your maid with you? You should have someone with you.'

'What are you talking about, Mr Thorpe?'

'There has been a shooting, miss.'

'Yes, yes. You said.'

'One of the guests has been shot.'

Bel's hand went immediately to her throat and her face contorted in horror. 'No! This cannot be? But who – how–?'

'An accident, I believe. Henry Bowes. My employer's son. He is dead, miss.'

'Dead? Henry, dead? No, surely not? Where is he? Let me see!' Bel moved to walk around him, but he stepped smartly to one side to stop her.

'No, Miss Fitzkeppel. Stay where you are, I beg of you. We shall be taking him away from here as soon as the constable arrives.'

'We?'

Daniel nodded in the direction of Havers, still slumped by a tree trunk. 'Havers asked me to take charge. As you can see, he is not well.'

Bel's eyes narrowed and she assessed the scene in front of her. The gamekeeper's hut with its door swinging open. One or two gentlemen were standing about, avoiding looking at her and speaking in low voices. Havers was clearly unable to answer any of her questions. She chewed her bottom lip. Whatever the explanation, Havers would blame himself for this accident.

Her expression deepened to a frown. 'I do not understand. Who shot him?'

'We do not know.' Daniel kept his hands

355

hovering by her shoulders as though to protect her from the surrounding air. He took a deep breath. 'We must find your brother, Miss Fitzkeppel. No one knows where he is.'

'Nathaniel? You don't think he did this, do you? No, he would never – not Henry, never. You do not understand, they were friends, the very best of friends...' Then the implication of what she was saying overwhelmed her. Hysteria began to bubble up in her throat. 'But Nathan may be injured and dying somewhere!' She swayed. Not her beloved Nathan! No!

Mr Thorpe's hands supported her, held her. She felt their power through the close-fitted jacket of her shooting outfit. She was thankful he was there, solid and strong and keeping her steady as a nervous panic began to spread over her. 'I must find him. I must!' She began to struggle out of his grip, but he held her firm.

'Please calm yourself, Miss Fitzkeppel. I am sure he is not seriously injured. There was only one shot and poor Henry Bowes took the full force of that. But your brother may have been peppered and, like yourself, miss, he may well be very agitated and shocked. We need to find him quickly.'

His commanding tone sounded confident and she slowed her struggle. She stood face to face with him, acutely aware of his hands on her arms. The steely determination in his eyes made her blink.

No gentleman had ever looked at her like that before. In fact, if one had she would have been offended by his audacity, and told him so! But

Mr Thorpe was different. And she felt different, too. An unfamiliar tingle coursed through her. She felt it spreading, making her insides tremble. Her mouth became parched and her vision became hazy. Try as she might, she could not move her limbs. She was going to faint! Here, in the woods. In front of her guests and the servants. Her eyes rounded and she appealed to him, mouthing the words, 'Help me.'

He gave her a gentle shake. 'Are you all right, Miss Fitzkeppel? Do you feel unwell? Will you sit a while?'

The movement revived her and her faintness ebbed. But she struggled to regain her composure. In a daze she answered mechanically, 'Quite well. Nathaniel, my brother, where is he?'

'We shall find him, have no fear. Indeed, he may have returned to the Hall already, and be waiting for you. Why don't you take your guests to the warmth of your drawing room? Let me call one of the gentlemen to walk you back to your party.'

Bel allowed herself to be steered away by Mr Thorpe's guiding arm. 'He was with Henry,' she muttered absently. 'I saw them together, at luncheon. He is all right, isn't he, Mr Thorpe?'

Daniel did not respond. Ezekiel Bowes had disappeared as well, and this worried him greatly. In the short time he had worked for him, Daniel had come to realise that Ezekiel Bowes, underneath his tough exterior, was a very troubled man.

Bel clutched at Daniel's thick, coarse jacket. 'You must find him, Mr Thorpe! You must find Nathan!'

Daniel managed a smile. 'I am sure he is not far

357

away.' He gently removed her gloved hand. 'We shall search for him all afternoon.'

'Then you will come to the Hall this evening and tell me what you know.'

'I am afraid Mr Ezekiel Bowes will need me tonight.'

'Tomorrow then. After breakfast.'

'I have a furnace to fire up tomorrow. Your man Havers, I am sure, will be fully recovered by then.'

'Oh, look.' Bel heaved a great sigh. 'He is on his feet already.'

'He will be needing orders, miss, for the remainder of the day. Until we find your brother, you will have to talk to him.'

'Oh, oh yes, of course. I do that anyway. Nathan does not involve himself greatly in estate matters.' Bel turned on Daniel and clutched at his coat again. 'You will find him quickly, won't you? He is all I have in this world.'

Again, Daniel carefully detached her strong grasp from his clothes. 'Come along, Miss Fitz-keppel,' he said gently, 'your guests will be waiting for you.'

Across the clearing, the brandy spread through Mariah's veins and revived her. She watched this meeting between Daniel and Miss Fitzkeppel. She saw a robust man take charge of a difficult situation, and a beautiful lady clutch at him for support. A lady who seemed unwilling to let him go. A lady who looked as attractive as she did because of her new shooting outfit, an outfit that she, Mariah, had fashioned for her to accentuate her womanly contours. She noticed how Daniel stared after Miss Fitzkeppel as she was led back to her party and, at that moment, Mariah envied her beauty.

A pony and trap trundled into the clearing accompanied by the constable on horseback and Daniel's attention was distracted.

Mariah staggered to her feet. 'I want to go home. Will Daniel take us?'

'I don't think he can until he's spoken to the constable,' Dora replied. 'I'll ask the driver.'

Mariah clambered into the trap. She watched Daniel talk to the constable and hand over a shotgun, the gun that had killed Henry. He came over to the driver and stood by the pony's head while Dora climbed in beside her. Then he retrieved the blanket and handed it up to them.

As he did, Mariah asked, 'Where is Ezekiel? Have you seen him?'

Daniel shook his head ruefully. He wished he knew.

'Try not to worry,' he said. 'I'll be round to see you later.'

He signalled to the driver to move on and frowned deeply as he watched them trundle away.

By nightfall, Bel was exhausted. She had stood on the front steps of the Hall as the carriages, one by one, had taken her anxious guests away. She would not see them here again. Her plans were ruined. Fitzkeppel Hall would not recover from this. No wonder Nathaniel had fled. What vestige of a reputation she had tried to salvage for herself and her brother had disappeared with the smoke from that gun.

Havers was devastated. She did not blame him, though most of her guests did and, for that reason, would never visit the Hall again to hunt or shoot. Forlorn and rejected, Bel retreated to her bedchamber, where her luxurious new gown was laid out for the evening ball.

She sat there, too tired to climb into bed. She tied the ribbon fastenings on her nightgown and stared at her image in the glass. Her old nanny had unpinned her hair and brushed it for her until, after a second stifled yawn, Bel had sent her to her bed. The candles on either side of her looking glass were burning low. In the flickering light, she took a long, critical look at herself and shook her head slightly. Her party was over before it had begun.

But it was not all bad news. Nathan was alive. In shock, perhaps, and probably with friends by now, she guessed. She had not spoken with him herself. One of the grooms at the stables had seen him, blood-spattered and agitated, but not bleeding so much that he was unable to ride. He asked for a saddle on his best mount and left as soon as the horse was ready. He had many friends across Lincolnshire and Derbyshire from his school and university days.

Bel could not believe that Nathan had shot Henry, though others did, she knew. Talk was rife, especially among the gentlemen, who became silent as soon as she approached them. Nathan had disappeared without leaving a message for her. Perhaps he would write a note to her when he was recovered.

She would not get any answers from him for a

while, so Ezekiel Bowes was her only hope to throw some light on the incident but he was nowhere to be found. Did he know his son was dead? Or was he dead himself? Shot by the same gun as his son? The gun that had been hastily discarded at the scene. By whom? she wondered. She sighed. Poor Henry. She did not wholly approve of him as her brother's confidant, but they were the closest of friends and she grieved for that loss.

She hugged herself and closed her eyes. How she wished she had someone dear to hold her now! Mr Thorpe's image swam under her eyelids. A proper man, like Mr Thorpe, to hold her in his arms and soothe her agitation, a man she could cling to for support.

She wondered where she might find a man such as he to marry her. Certainly not among the suitors her chaperones had found! Or, indeed, at her shoot. Those who had shown an interest in her were already settled with wives and children. Was waiting for a widower all she could hope for now?

She wished Mr Thorpe were here, comforting her as he had done earlier. She had never met a man such as him before, so strong and so capable, and with eyes the colour of a leaden winter sky. She wanted his arms instead of her own around her.

She remembered how sturdy he had felt beneath his rough clothes and wondered how his firm body would feel beside her, dressed only in his night-shirt and she in her nightgown. She blew out the candles and removed the warming pan from her bed, placing it carefully in the hearth. The room would grow chilly quite soon as the fire was low. In the light of its embers she noted the sleeping draught left beside the bed by her physician.

She imagined Mr Thorpe climbing into bed beside her, his fine body, hard and strong. Perhaps he had a scar or two from his labours? He would lean over and kiss her on the lips, then cover her body with his. She imagined his weight pressing her into the feathers of her mattress. And then what? What? What came next? She was three and twenty and did not know. Perhaps she would never know? But her body yearned to be touched by Daniel Thorpe, to be adored by him, caressed by him. To be loved by him.

With a small, anguished cry she rolled over, picked up her draught and swallowed it in one.

Chapter 31

'It's only me, Aunty Dora.'

Mariah and Dora were sipping hot ale by the kitchen fire when Daniel came in through the scullery door.

Mariah was on her feet straightaway. 'Have you found out what happened?'

He shook his head. 'Ezekiel has not shown himself since the shooting. We must wait for the constable to speak with him.'

'I am sure it was an accident. I cannot believe that either he or Mr Fitzkeppel would have shot Henry,' Mariah declared. 'Do you think he had an assignation with a girl?'

'Possibly.'

'Does that mean the girl's father may have shot him – and the others as well?'

Daniel shook his head. 'The constable thinks not. There was no trail of blood and, apparently, Fitzkeppel was well enough to ride, but there has been no sign of Ezekiel apart from–' He stopped and looked uncomfortable.

'What? Tell me, Daniel.'

'It was his gun that was fired.'

'*Ezekiel*'s gun?'

Daniel's discomfort continued. 'I am worried about him, Mariah.'

'I am sure you need not be. He is tough and–'

'He is a troubled man!'

'What do you mean?'

'Something ails him. I cannot explain it, but I know he is not at ease with himself.'

'Well, yes, he was a difficult person to live with. For me, anyway, because Henry was always his main concern.'

'That is why he will need you now.'

Mariah laughed harshly. 'You do not know him as I do! I am the last person he wants.'

'Can you not forget your quarrel with him? You are his daughter.'

'No, I am not.'

'I don't understand.'

Dora, who had been listening quietly until now added, 'Neither do I.'

Mariah inhaled deeply. 'I told your mother when I moved in with your family. I am not his child. My real father died before my mother could

363

become his wife and she wed Ezekiel instead.'

'Does he know you are not his?'

'Oh yes. He was paid by her family to marry my mother. He never really wanted her. I have often thought his true love must lie elsewhere. But he chose money. Perhaps that is why he is so troubled.'

'Perhaps,' Daniel conceded.

Dora looked across to her nephew. 'What do you mean by troubled?'

Daniel shrugged. 'Tense and agitated all the time. He tries hard to suppress it, but then he becomes angry for no obvious reason.'

'Yes, that's him, all right,' Mariah responded dryly. 'I am really, truly sorry about Henry. Of course Ezekiel will be devastated by his death. But I am sure you will find him in his office at the ironworks. That is where he always goes when he is – er – troubled, as you say.'

'Will you not, at least, attempt a reconciliation?' Daniel pleaded. 'You carry his name.'

'A name he wishes me to be rid of! That is why he arranged for me to marry Mr Smith. He wants me off his hands and so I have obliged him. He cares only for Henry and his profits from the ironworks!'

'And now there is no Henry, will his profits from the ironworks matter to him?'

Mariah did not answer him. Without Henry, Ezekiel would have no one to leave the ironworks to and his lifetime of labour would have been in vain.

'You are his only kin now,' Daniel added gently.

Mariah shook her head. 'He has disowned me.'

'But the – the shooting has changed everything.'

There was a weariness in Daniel's voice that reached Mariah's heart. She met his eyes with sadness in her own. Why did circumstances between them have to be so difficult? She wanted to accept his help but did not know how.

Dora interceded. 'I do not think you should be pressing Mariah in this way, Daniel. She has just lost her half-brother.'

Daniel saw the anguish on Mariah's face and immediately regretted his actions. In desperation, he shook his head wordlessly.

'It's all right, Dora,' Mariah responded. 'Daniel is right. Ezekiel is a wealthy man because of my mother's money. I have some questions of my own to ask him. If Ezekiel is willing to speak to me I shall come to his office.'

Daniel heaved a sigh. 'I shall send word as soon as he returns.'

'Will you have some warmed ale?' Dora asked.

'I cannot stay. There is too much on at the works.' He embraced his aunty and without thinking did the same to Mariah.

Surprised, Mariah allowed herself to be taken into his arms and let her hands creep around him, feeling the roughness of his jacket on her face and inhaling an unfamiliar masculine smell that quickened her pulse. She lingered, welcoming the solid strength of his body against hers. His hug tightened as though he did not want to let her go.

She did not know how long she stayed there, only that it felt right. Eventually he stepped back and when she looked at his face his eyes were

365

brighter and searched hers with an enquiry she could not fathom.

And then he was gone and she wondered if she had imagined the warmth she had felt for those few seconds in his arms.

'Enter.'

The foreman at last, thought Daniel. He was in Ezekiel's office, completing the billing for the week and anxious to keep the furnaces going until Ezekiel decided to show his face at the ironworks again. He was sure to return by Saturday. For the men had to be paid on that day and the keys to the safe were always with Ezekiel.

The rustle of silk made him look up sharply. He closed the heavy ledger with a snap and hastily scraped back the chair to stand up.

'Miss Fitzkeppel! I was not expecting you!'

'Mr Thorpe.'

She stood motionless on the threshold, framed by the light from the open door. Her full skirts, partly covered by a plush velvet cloak, filled the doorway. He walked around the desk, repeating, 'Miss Fitzkeppel!' then adding, 'I am sorry, but Mr Bowes is not here.'

She stepped forward. 'I have come to see you, Mr Thorpe. May I come in?'

'Of course. Sit by the fire. It is a frosty morning. Will you take a little wine to warm you?'

'Thank you, yes.'

She sank into Ezekiel's buttoned leather armchair while Daniel closed the door against the cold and asked, 'Is there news of your brother?'

'I believe he is unharmed, thank God.'

Daniel took the cork out of Ezekiel's sherry wine and poured some into a pewter goblet. 'Then he is safe?'

'I can only assume so. He was well enough to ride.'

'Does he know where Mr Bowes has gone?'

'I have not seen my brother, Mr Thorpe, or spoken to him. I – he...' He saw her swallow and take a deep breath. 'On the afternoon of the shoot, he took one of the best horses from our stables and left.' She paused. 'I expect to hear from him – eventually – but,' she turned her pretty face upwards, 'I have to know what happened, Mr Thorpe. Why did my brother leave so hastily? You must tell me.'

He listened to her silently, noticing a few tendrils of fair hair escaping from her fine velvet bonnet. Her delicate skin glowed from the cold air, enhancing her features with youthfulness rather than coarseness. Beside her, he felt very much an artisan in his working clothes. He poured himself a goblet of Ezekiel's wine and sat opposite her by the fire.

'Miss Fitzkeppel, I do not know any more than your man Havers. I cannot help you.'

'You do, you do! You must know something. It was something between the three of them, I am sure! You lived with Henry. You live with his father–'

'I work for Mr Bowes and I am here at the works more than I am in their house. I hardly knew Henry and he spent much of his time with you at the Hall, I believe.'

'Not with me. With my brother. Do you know

367

of a quarrel, Mr Thorpe?'

Daniel covered his eyes with his hands for a moment and then faced her.

'I do not *know* anything, Miss Fitzkeppel. Except that Henry is dead and your brother has disappeared.'

'But Mr Bowes was there! He must know what happened!' she responded shrilly. 'Where is he?'

'Mr Bowes has not yet returned home. He may have witnessed the shooting. He may have–' Daniel stopped. Speculation was of no use here. The less Miss Fitzkeppel knew of this sad and sorry business the better. There were enough stories about Henry and Fitzkeppel going around the works already. He stood up and continued, 'I would like to help you, but I have to keep the ironworks going, and I–'

He stopped again as she rose and crossed the hearth to stand close to him. In the heat from the fire a female scent assailed his nose, a nostalgic mixture of womanliness and lavender. Not since Lily had he inhaled such an aroma.

She placed her gloved hands on his forearm. 'Mr Thorpe, I have no one else to turn to. At the shoot you were so – so – *capable*. Please help me. Please.'

He stared at her wide blue eyes, glistening with unshed tears, and frowned. 'Very well. I shall do what I can for you, Miss Fitzkeppel. Please do not distress yourself.'

'Will you really? I shall be so very grateful.'

'I am sure Mr Bowes will return to his ironworks soon. If he witnessed the accident, he will be in some distress himself. Henry meant everything to him. He had such plans for him.'

'An accident, you say? You are sure this was an accident?'

'The constable would like to speak to Mr Bowes and your brother to assure himself it was so.'

'I am sure it was. Nathan would never harm Henry!'

'No, of course not.'

He watched her pretty face darken as she considered that he may have. Eventually she said, 'May I have a little more wine, Mr Thorpe?'

When she took the goblet from him, he noticed she was watching him carefully. She grasped the cup with both hands and held on to his fingers. Their heads were close together and she looked directly into his eyes. He gazed back evenly, his face expressionless and unemotional. But he felt stirrings that reminded him forcefully that he was a man, stirrings he had not experienced for some time.

For a fleeting moment he remembered the indulgence of those Sunday afternoons with Lily. Miss Fitzkeppel had a similar look about her, with hair the colour of honey, finely boned features and delicate skin. The soft kidskin of her gloved fingers rested lightly on his hand and he did not wish to withdraw it from her touch. It had been so long since he had considered a woman in this way that he had almost forgotten the desire. Until now.

Miss Fitzkeppel broke the lengthening silence. 'You will bring me news when you have it, Mr Thorpe? You will come to the Hall yourself?'

'I cannot leave the ironworks.'

'Then, may I visit you? I hear so little out at the

Hall. The servants know more than I do. Please allow me to visit your office, sir.'

'That would be a little unorthodox, if I may say so, Miss Fitzkeppel.'

'At the least until I have news from my brother?'

'Very well.' He stepped back and gave a short bow. 'If you would excuse me, I have my duties to attend to.'

'Of course, Mr Thorpe. Thank you.' She took her leave gracefully, leaving a cloud of feminine scent that was hitherto unknown in Ezekiel Bowes' office.

Mariah arrived at the ironworks in time to see Miss Fitzkeppel walk carefully down the outside steps from the office to her waiting carriage. Her rich blue velvet cloak and matching bonnet were as incongruous with the grimy surroundings of the yard as were her elegant coach and matched pair of well-groomed horses. Mariah stayed outside the gates until the visitor had left. She guessed that Miss Fitzkeppel had wanted answers from Ezekiel too.

Inside the yard, Mariah was taken aback by the sight of the new crucible furnace and its wide brick chimney already smoking. She realised how long she had been away and wondered briefly if Daniel was working there, labouring and sweating in the heat. But as she looked up at the office window she saw his face, and not Ezekiel's, staring down. He had, no doubt, been watching Miss Fitzkeppel leave and she was reminded uncomfortably of the intimate exchange between this elegant lady and Daniel she had witnessed after the shooting.

He clattered down the stone steps to meet her. She wore her good green gown with flannel petticoats underneath for it had been cold on the morning carrier cart. But her bonnet was plain and her cloak was old and worn. Its shabbiness would not have concerned her so much if the vision of Miss Fitzkeppel's blue velvet was not still clear in her mind.

She remembered Daniel's warm embrace and wondered if he did too. She thought not for he seemed agitated. 'Ezekiel has not returned,' he said. 'Where do you suppose he is?'

'I have no idea. Unless he has gone to one of his friends.'

'Of course! He may be with Mr Smith.'

'Or Mr Withers, his lawyer,' Mariah suggested.

'I'll send Ned to find out.'

'No, you need him here. I'll go.'

'Try Mr Withers first. He knows everything that goes on in this town.'

They stood for a moment staring at each other. Mariah realised this was the first time that she had felt a true bond with Daniel. They were united in their task. She was glad he was her friend in this respect but it was a strange feeling. She hurried out of the yard to the lawyer's office on the High Street.

'Wait there, Miss Bowes.'

The outer office of Mr Withers' High Street chambers was filled with very old heavy oak furniture and piles of documents. Two young gentlemen, dressed in dark jackets and high-collared white shirts, were seated at tall tables by the window carefully copying documents with quill pens and ink. They looked up at her as she waited, then exchanged murmurs and smirks until Mr Withers' clerk came to fetch her. He led her upstairs to a large chamber overlooking the street. The furniture here was newer, polished and lighter in colour and form, and there were cupboards around the walls instead of open shelves.

'Please be seated.' Mr Withers took off his pince-nez and stared at her from across his desk. 'May I offer you my condolences, Miss Bowes. Master Henry was a fine young man.'

'Thank you, sir. Have you spoken to the constable? Do you know how he died?'

'I cannot say.'

Mariah felt her patience dwindling. 'What do you mean? You do not know or you will not tell me?'

'I cannot say.'

'Then perhaps you can say something about my father, Mr Withers? Mr Bowes has not returned home since the incident. Have you knowledge of his whereabouts?'

'Do not travel this road, Miss Bowes. I cannot tell you anything about your father's affairs.'

'We both know he has disowned me.'

'Do not press me! Would you have me break a client confidence?'

She half rose from her chair. 'Henry was my brother!'

Mr Withers looked uncomfortable. He must know she had lost her last blood relation in the

Riding. However, she had not meant to become so agitated and sank slowly back into her seat.

He said, 'Are you destitute, Miss Bowes? Is that why you are here? I believe you have a comfortable home outside town and – and have obtained work at the Hall? Besides, your father did his duty and found a gentleman of means for you. You could have married Mr Smith, my dear.'

'Just as my father married a woman of means! I know it was my mother's dowry that bought him the furnace in the first place! Please tell me where I can find him.'

'I have given you my answer.'

'But you do know where he is?' she persisted.

Mr Withers heaved a sigh. 'No, I do not. I should like to speak with him as much as you do. Now, if that is all, would you kindly leave me to my work?'

Annoyed and frustrated, Mariah got up and walked to the door. As she opened it, he added, 'If ever you do find yourself destitute, Miss Bowes, you will come to these offices and speak to me.'

Surprised and puzzled, she shook her head irritably and left the building. She imagined herself making gowns for stout Mrs Withers to earn her keep and thought she might earn herself a good living doing so. If only she had premises! A room as large as her former workroom at the Hall. It would not take much of Ezekiel's money to purchase a lease. It galled her to think her mother had provided him with the means to prosper and she could not reap the benefit. She became even more determined to ask him about his plans for the future of the ironworks.

The warehouse man told her Daniel was in the crucible shed when she got back to the yard. She stood at the bottom of the steep stone steps as the bright glow of molten metal lit the interior. A nipper appeared from the coal store underneath the floor. His task was to keep the flues clear and make sure there was a good updraught for the furnaces. He was as black as the soot he swept.

'I must speak to Mr Thorpe.'

'Don't go up there, now, miss,' he advised. 'It's too dangerous.'

'But he is in there?'

'Aye. But 'e's big and strong and knows what 'e's doing.'

She caught a glimpse of Daniel through the doorway as he stepped back and carefully lowered the empty crucible to the floor. He wore a long leather apron and had a rag stuffed in his mouth. His face was darkened and reddened with the smoke and heat. He did not notice her.

'Don't distract him, miss. Not right now.'

'No, of course not. Would you give him a message from me? Tell him I could find out nothing. He'll understand.'

Mariah bought provisions before she went back to Dora's, a sack of flour, a cone of sugar and some sewing notions from the draper's shop. She heaved the sack onto her back to wait for the carrier. Dora would be pleased with the sugar and Mariah planned how she would decorate her plain bonnet with ribbons for her next visit to town, and make braiding to smarten up her cloak. She would be back. Ezekiel would have to show himself sooner or later and she could wait.

Chapter 32

When the gun had fired in that fetid hut, Ezekiel had seen only a cold blackness descending on him, enclosing him in its own private cage. He had thrown the gun away from him as though it were a serpent, and had lumbered away, his mind filled with the sights and sounds of his own private hell. He had not known where he was going, only that he must get away from that hut. He ran, stumbled and walked blindly, crashing through trees and brambles, unable to feel, hear or even think of the world around him.

Where had he gone wrong with Henry? He had tried so hard to leave his past behind and make something of himself for Henry's sake, to provide a way of life to be proud of. And now that life had crumbled before him. He had no son to be proud of any more, no future in the Riding. He should never have married Amelia, should never have been tempted by the money. He was just a boy then, obeying his elders and betters who knew what was best for him...

As a youth, Ezekiel had been a strong, handsome lad – everyone said so. A natural son whose mother had died in childbirth.

She had been a servant in an ironmaster's house in the North Riding and never told a soul who his father was. But he had been lucky. His mother had been a good worker, a favourite in the servants' hall, so she had not been sent to the poorhouse as others in her unfortunate position had been. She bore a healthy, robust lad, and lads were always useful in the quarry or the foundry. He was brought up in the servants' hall, spoiled by attention from young maids and older matrons alike.

Well fed and properly shod, he grew straight and sturdy and at the age of ten was sent to work in the quarry, extracting the sandstone that was used in foundry work for iron-casting moulds. On Sundays, he went to school with other youngsters from the families who worked for the ironmaster and learned to read and write. When he was fourteen he was moved to the foundry, working on the steam hammers, forging the iron into cannon to fight the Frenchies. He was a good lad, loyal and willing, and he was favoured. On Wednesdays and Saturdays he was allowed to join the ironmaster's own children at their lessons with the rector.

The rector was one of the gentry, the second son of their local landowner, and he took his church responsibilities seriously. An educated man, he encouraged learning for all the children in his care. Ezekiel learned the Bible, right from wrong and the way of things. Most of all, he learned his place. He had no right to anything, he was a natural son, a bastard the men at the foundry called him, and he must be grateful to his masters, the ironmaster, the quarry master, the foundry master and the schoolmaster. Ezekiel *was* grateful and he felt proud to be allowed to learn. He was able and earned praise from his masters.

The rector gave lessons in the church vestry and the ironmaster's children scampered off for their tea as soon as they were finished, but Ezekiel was a servant and stayed to clear away the books. He became the rector's right-hand help in the classroom, setting out the books and cleaning up the vestry afterwards.

At sixteen the rector trusted him enough to leave him with the keys to the vestry when he went back to the rectory for his supper. Ezekiel polished the table and swept the floor before returning the keys.

One evening the rector asked Ezekiel to join him for supper and conversation. He cut him a generous slice of pie, offering him pickles and relish and sliced the bread himself. There was cheese, too, and ripe pears in a bowl. And wine. The rector kept Ezekiel's glass topped up with wine until its warmth spread through his veins down to his toes and he smiled and relaxed. He gazed at the polished wood of the table, littered with crumbs and debris from the meal, and thought how much he could enjoy the life the gentry led. He felt special. He watched the red and yellow flames leaping from the coals in the fire and felt an affinity for their destiny. Burning, yearning, reaching through the blackness of the unknown for their freedom. The rector's arm crept around Ezekiel's shoulders and his fingers probed the muscles of his arm.

'So young and so strong,' the rector murmured. 'Take off your jacket.'

Ezekiel's private flames searched through their darkness. His heart began beating strongly in his

377

breast. He obeyed.

'And your waistcoat.'

Ezekiel did so, then loosened his tie.

The rector's hand stilled his. 'No. Allow me to do that.'

The desire racing through his young body was almost unbearable. He was aroused in a way he had not known possible. His skin felt alive as the rector removed his shirt and undershirt and caressed his chest. The rector led him to the rug before the fire and kissed him. Their mouths joined and he tasted wine and mustard as their tongues entwined and his arousal pushed inside his breeches.

He was overtaken by a rising urgency as the rector's hands and mouth moved downwards. Kissing and caressing until Ezekiel thought he would burst. He had suppressed this desire for so long, telling himself it was wrong. How could this be wrong? They were as one, united in their fervour. In all his young life Ezekiel had never felt so happy, so fulfilled, and so loved.

He hardly remembered what happened afterwards, except that the rector had said, 'We shall not talk of this. You will tell your master I wish to give you extra tuition, so you may help me with lessons in the schoolroom. Every Wednesday and Saturday. Do you understand?'

'Yes, sir.' Ezekiel felt his excitement rise again. The rector wanted his body as much as he coveted the rector's. There would be a next time. And another after that.

He was in love.

How could Ezekiel imagine it would last? The

other youths at the foundry, already jealous of his favoured treatment, began to push him around and call him names. Encouraged by older men in the works they set about him one night, beating him viciously until he lay senseless on the ground. The ironmaster found him and sent for his own surgeon. While Ezekiel lay, barely conscious, in his bed, the ironmaster made his own enquiries among his men.

'You listen to me, lad,' the ironmaster said later. 'You've been a good 'un so far and I reckon you've been led astray by them who should know better.' For a moment his face softened. 'Aye, you've been led astray like your ma was afore you. Any road, you're going away from 'ere.'

Going away? From everyone and everything he knew and loved?

'I'll set you up with a wife and child and enough to buy a share in your own concern.'

A wife and child? He did not want a wife and child.

'There's one condition.'

When he did not respond, the ironmaster went on, 'You never show your face or theirs around here again. Never visit, never write, never ask for nowt else.'

'I don't want to go away,' he protested miserably.

'There'll be no argument. You'll not go near my children, or the schoolroom again. And you won't be safe at the foundry or the quarry either. You'll pack a box and marry this lass as soon as I can arrange it.'

'What lass?' he muttered.

379

'It just so happens that my wife 'as a cousin who 'as a problem she needs sorting. The lass is not wed and she already 'as a bairn in her belly. So you won't have to touch her if she's not to your taste. With any luck the bairn'll be a lad to inherit your works, but you'll have to take that chance. You're to go over to her parish and be wed, then take the stagecoach south.'

'And never come back here?' he asked quietly.

'Never! You were not an innocent in this. If you had not been willing, none of this evil would have happened.'

Tears welled in Ezekiel's eyes.

'And don't look so miserable. You're a lucky devil, that's what you are! Without my connections you'd be on the gallows for what you've done!'

It was twenty years ago now. As Ezekiel prospered, he tried to forget about those earlier times. Amelia was no help to him. If his firstborn had been a son, his life would have been more tolerable. But Amelia's baby was a girl.

'A girl!' He had shouted when Mariah was born. He had wanted a son so much. A son would have given him a proper reason for marrying Amelia, but he was tied to her now. It was God's punishment for his sins. He hated the Church for what it had done to him! He managed to lay with her the once and she bore him Henry. After that she had served her purpose and he wanted nothing more to do with her.

The ironmaster had been a man of his word, and gave him papers including a banker's promissory note that had bought him a share in a rundown cementation furnace. He was too young to hold the stake himself and it was held by a legal man, until he was twenty-one. He and Amelia lived with one of the partners in the house by the furnace yard and Ezekiel worked hard.

He laboured every waking hour at the furnace to make the best blister steel in the South Riding. He bought good Swedish iron and cooked it long and slow with charcoal, checking the fires himself until it was ready. His steel was reliable and his reputation grew. He sold it to big forges with contracts for the new railways.

His partners were old men and the one he lived with was already dying when he arrived. He planned to buy them out one day with a mortgage from the bank. It was a decent house to live in, built for an ironmaster and he settled well. He had insisted on separate bedchambers when he wed Amelia as she was with child. Anyway, he knew the gentry lived like that, and he was going to live like the gentry. One day...

Ezekiel forced his way through the undergrowth of Keppel wood, the brambles tearing at his smart new tweeds. He could not go on like this. He had tried. Lord, how he had tried! He had tried to bury his sinful ways when he had left that forge in the North Riding. He had not tolerated any such behaviour or inclination in his men. He had kept away from temptation and had rid his works of anyone who might test his resolution.

But his befuddled mind was overcome by how he had felt when he had opened the door of the gamekeeper's hut. He had faced a scene of manly love within, a love he had rejected. No one knew how desperately he had battled with his desires.

He had had such plans for Henry. And that – that, oh God, that *fop* of a man who called himself *gentry*, had used his son in the same way that the rector had used him. Not Henry! Please, not Henry! What had he done? What had he done to Henry? Without Henry, his life was empty, a deep, dark void of hollowness and sorrow.

Ezekiel stumbled on, in blackness and despair, until he came to the cut, the narrow waterway from Keppel pit to the canal and ironworks in the town. He sank to his knees by the silent brown water and grieved. He grieved for his son and for himself. He grieved for the way he was – a sinner who could not repent and who had to pay the price for his sin.

When he came to his very own Rubicon he knew what he must do and he did not flinch. The devil spawns devils. He would be welcome in hell.

Chapter 33

'I thought I heard a horse in the lane, Dora?' Mariah continued to knead her bread dough.

Dora looked up from plucking a fowl in the scullery. The hen had been a good layer, but was past it now and she would make a rich stew with some barley and field mushrooms. 'I'll go and look.' She put aside the half-plucked hen and went to peer out of the front-room window.

'It's our Daniel!' she exclaimed, as she hurried

back to the kitchen. 'Very smart he looks too. On a black hunter. Is that Ezekiel's horse?' She took off her apron. 'Have I got any feathers in my hair, Mariah?'

'Come here.' Mariah took a damp cloth from the scullery and wiped away the down from Dora's bodice. 'There. Shall I get him some refreshment?'

'Please. It's a cold morning so you'd best mull some of that ale to warm him through.'

Mariah quickly took off her pinny, dusted the flour from her grey gown and straightened her cap. When Daniel followed Dora into the kitchen she was heating ale over the fire.

'You'd better let me finish that,' Dora said, elbowing her out of the way, 'it's you he wants to see.'

Mariah turned around with an enquiring expression. She thought he looked very handsome in his brown riding boots and hacking jacket and guessed Ezekiel had lent him his hunter to come over here. So her stepfather had returned home at last! Her hopeful air faltered when she saw his face, serious, unsmiling, sombre even. She became alarmed.

'What is it? What news have you?'

'Sit down, Mariah. I am afraid it is not good.'

'Is this about Ezekiel? Henry's death *was* an accident, wasn't it?'

His composure wavered and the silence lay heavy in the air as he tried to find the words. Mariah sat down by the kitchen table, frowning, and said quietly, 'Tell me what has happened.'

He inhaled deeply. 'There is no easy way to say this. Ezekiel is dead.'

'Dead? No! But how? When?' Mariah rested her brow on her hand. Not Ezekiel! He was a strong man, hard working and always in good health. She had not expected him to die. Had he been injured himself in the shooting? Her shoulders sagged. Even in her quarrel with Ezekiel and in her condemnation of his ways, she had never wished him *dead*. Her head felt hot but tears did not threaten. A dull emptiness crept over her. He had been a hard man but he had been the only father she had known and now he was gone.

'How?' she repeated. 'How did he die?'

'He was drowned. In the Keppel cut.'

'I do not understand,' she frowned. 'He was a man of sober ways. How could that happen?'

Daniel half rose to his feet and stretched out a hand towards hers. When she made no similar move he thought better of his actions and sank back into his chair. 'You must be strong about this, Mariah. He – he was found downstream, caught up in the lock where the cut meets the canal. He – he had–' Daniel stopped and inhaled again. 'He had filled his pockets with rocks.'

'No! Surely not? Ezekiel would not have done such a thing! I do not understand,' she repeated. 'Ezekiel was strong in mind and body. How could this be so? Why would he *do* that?'

Daniel went on, 'Of course, we cannot be sure. But the constable believes he was, somehow, to blame for his son's death. It was his gun, you see, that fired the shot. And – and now, now, this.' Daniel exchanged a grimace with his aunty. 'The constable has concluded your brother's death was an accident, but one that he, your stepfather, had caused and – and he could not live with his guilt.'

'Then he has spoken, also, with Mr Fitzkeppel? Did *he* see what happened?'

'Mr Fitzkeppel has left the Riding. He is with friends in Lincolnshire.'

'Oh.' He has run away, Mariah thought. Why would he do that if he was not to blame in some way? He was Henry's friend. He should have stayed and talked to the constable.

'Mr Withers has sent a message asking him to return.'

Dora poured the hot ale into a tankard for Daniel and said, 'I'll fetch Mariah a drop of brandy. I could do with one as well.'

Mariah felt a weariness take over her. Now she could never ask Ezekiel about the future of the ironworks. Mr Withers was her only hope and his lips were firmly sealed. What would happen to the works now?

Mariah gazed at Daniel. The furrows in his brow and the downturn of his mouth aged him. But he was watching her closely and she thought that his anxiety, now, was not for himself; it was for her. She was grateful he had taken the trouble to ride over here, even though this news was so dreadful, and managed a small rueful smile of gratitude. A light came into his eyes that seem to burn right through her and, somehow, it gave her strength.

Dora returned with the brandy and the moment was lost.

But Mariah did not forget it and she knew she was fortunate to count Daniel as her ally. 'What will happen to the ironworks?' she asked.

'I am to see Mr Withers in his offices this afternoon.' He stood up and as she raised her head she saw again, for a brief moment, the fire in his eyes. 'You will think about coming home, Mariah?' he said.

'It is not my home,' she answered dismally, 'and whoever is fortunate enough to inherit it will not want me there.'

'Who will inherit?' Dora queried.

'I have no idea.' Mariah shrugged. 'I am sure Mr Withers will tell Daniel later, and I am certain that, whoever he is, he will not wish to know me.'

'It should be yours,' Daniel said quietly.

'Yes, it should!' Mariah suddenly felt angry. 'Without my mother and the child she was carrying, there would have been no Bowes Ironworks!'

'I am so sorry—'

'Don't be! My mother may not have had an income of her own to leave me, but she left me a far greater gift and one that nobody can take away! Miss Fitzkeppel continues to give me commissions. Only last week she sent over a length of woollen cloth and a plain bonnet for me to make a shoulder cape and bonnet trimmed with matching ruches and bows. It is to be a gift to Mrs Havers from her mistress. Others will follow her example and I shall earn my keep quite well here in Dora's front room. I am happy living with Dora.'

Daniel pursed his lips and nodded. He left shortly afterwards to keep his appointment with Mr Withers. Dora followed him to the front door and spent several minutes talking to him before he rode away. When she returned to her kitchen,

Mariah's cheeks were bright spots of pink and her eyes were bright.

'It does help to weep at times like this,' Dora suggested.

'I wept for my mother and for Henry, but I cannot weep for him. Let his friends lay Ezekiel Bowes to rest and remember him at his wake,' she said.

'A funeral is no place for a woman anyway, so they'll not expect you.' She poured Mariah more brandy and added, 'Do not make any hasty decisions, though. Mourning is a useful retreat for reflection.'

Mariah drank quickly and set down her glass. 'I have had enough of mourning. I have spent too many months grieving. The bread will be ready for the oven and I have Mrs Havers' cape and bonnet to finish.'

As Mariah busied herself with these tasks, her anger simmered. Why should some distant cousin or local worthy be given what was rightly her own inheritance? It was not unheard of for women to inherit when there were no male descendants. But, she reflected, those ladies were, no doubt, good-living wives and daughters who had not been disowned or discredited in any way. It was ironic, she fumed, that obedience was the price a woman had to pay for such independence.

Mariah found it difficult to concentrate on her tasks. Daniel's words echoed in her head. She had a right to know what would happen to the ironworks! Surely Mr Withers could not refuse to impart his knowledge of Ezekiel's affairs now. He may have disowned her during his life, but whether he liked it or not she was his daughter in the eyes of the law.

After two days of useless fretting, her patience gave way and she took the carrier into town to call on Mr Withers again.

He was not at his offices. He had just left to call on Mr Thorpe who was reluctant to leave the yard while the new crucible furnaces were firing. If she hurried she might catch him there. She was out of breath when she reached the top of the steps outside the warehouse at Bowes Ironworks. She opened the heavy door and almost fell into the office, her cloak half off her back, her cheeks pink from running and her bonnet and hair awry.

'Mr Withers! I must speak with you,' she gasped.

'Mariah, what is the matter?' Daniel was standing by Ezekiel's desk. His face was sooty and his hair dishevelled as though he had just left his furnaces. Mr Withers was handing him some keys, the ones Ezekiel had always carried with him. Daniel put the keys onto the desk and came towards her. 'Calm yourself. Come, sit by the fire and catch your breath.'

She shrugged away his proffered hand and approached the older gentleman.

Mr Withers smiled at her. 'You have saved me a journey, Miss Bowes, for I was coming to see you this afternoon.' He steered her towards a chair by the fire.

'Are those my father's keys?' she asked as she untied her cloak.

Daniel answered. 'Yes. They were on his body when he was found and the constable has just

388

released them. I need them urgently to pay the men's wages, and – and the bank is calling for payment.'

Withers addressed Daniel, 'Are you able to deal with that?'

'Yes, sir. Mr Bowes gave me full responsibility for the accounts.'

Withers turned his attention back to Mariah. 'Miss Bowes, you should know that I have your father's will in my possession and he has appointed me as one of the trustees for his estate. I was about to explain this to Mr Thorpe when you burst in on us.'

'Please continue, sir,' Daniel asked, 'I have no secrets from Miss Bowes.'

Mariah flashed him a grateful smile.

Mr Withers continued, 'Mr Bowes' intention was to leave a thriving ironworks to his son in the hope that he would wish to continue to make steel and, eventually, pass on the works to his grandsons. But Henry, God rest his soul, did not have the makings of an ironmaster and Mr Bowes harboured concerns about his future. With this in mind, he added a clause to his will after he employed Mr Thorpe. Should Mr Bowes be taken from this world before Henry came of age, he appointed Daniel Thorpe as a second trustee for the ironworks, as long as Mr Thorpe remained employed as supervisor at his works.'

'Daniel! Did you know this?' Mariah exclaimed.

'No. It is as big a surprise to me as it is to you. Mr Withers, is there provision for Mariah?'

'He believed Miss Bowes would be married,' Mr Withers answered warily.

'I did not care for his choice of suitor.'

Withers shook his head slowly and Mariah sighed. Ezekiel's legacy to her had been Mr Smith. Mr Withers would view marriage to a well-set-up widower like Mr Smith a good match for the daughter of a man with no background or connections.

'Yes, he told me you were headstrong,' Mr Withers added, as though it explained her misfortune.

'Well, I am not destitute, sir. I can provide for myself and I shall not be a drain on the parish.' But even as she said the words, Mariah realised how close she had come to the poorhouse. She had known what it was like to see it as her only solution. Without Dora, she would have had to go there, in her degradation and shame. She stared into the fire.

Mr Withers arranged to return and talk further with Daniel after he had been to see Ezekiel's bankers. Before he left he said, 'Miss Bowes, as you are in town, I should be obliged if you would call on me at my offices later. Good day to you both.'

When he had gone, Daniel picked up the keys. 'This does not seem right to me. You should have these. Here, take them and open the safe.'

'No.' Mariah was emphatic. 'Please do not taunt me with what could never be. It was Mr Smith or nothing for me, and I chose nothing.' She held her head high but there were tears in her eyes.

Daniel's face took on a hurt and haunted expression. 'Tell me how I can help you, Mariah?' he pleaded.

He could take me in his arms and hold me as he had done at Dora's, she thought. That would help, but it was not what he meant. There was nothing he could do for her now. She had made her choice and she must live with it. She said, 'You are not responsible for me. Your duty is to the ironworks and the new owner.'

He became impatient with her and demanded, 'Why do you always reject my friendship so?'

Mariah frowned. Is that what he thought? Perhaps she had in the past because she did not want his pity. But she, no *they,* were through that now. The past was gone. She welcomed his friendship. She wanted to reach out her hand and touch him and say so. But she feared that she wanted more from his friendship than he was prepared to give and hesitated.

'Forgive me,' she said, 'I am overwrought by these events.'

He took a step forward. 'Of course. I understand.'

He reached towards her with his hands. She looked at them. Large, capable hands, grimy from his morning's work. His shirtsleeves were rolled back and his forearms were sooty. She thought that, more than anything, she wanted those arms around her, holding her close to him, so close she would be able to feel the beating of his heart against hers.

But he would never want to hold her so, knowing what he did about her shame. Friendship was all that she could hope for and her face fell. She shrank from his touch and he noticed.

He gave a nervous laugh and stepped back. 'I

am forgetting my manners. You do not want soot on your gown.'

Would he have taken her in his arms? She would never know. But she thought even if she were dressed in one of Christobel Fitzkeppel's silken ball gowns she would not have been bothered by a little soot. The image in her head excited and shocked her at the same time. She wanted to feel the strength of his back under her exploring hands, and to kiss him. She wanted so much more from him than he would give her and she was stupid even to contemplate the idea.

She said, 'I shall detain you no longer. I came here on impulse and it was foolish of me. There is nothing here for me now. Except...'

'Yes?'

She thought of Henry's patronising ideas about her, of Ezekiel's domineering ways and of Mr Smith and said, 'Except bad memories.'

'Does that include Emma?'

'No, of course not.'

'Then stay for your dinner. Emma would be pleased to see you.'

'Thank you.' She looked around the office, with its cupboards full of ledgers and its battered furniture. 'I wonder who will inherit,' she murmured.

He said abruptly, 'Whoever it is, you are always welcome here while I am employed as supervisor.'

He was being kind, and Mariah felt her emotions threaten to overcome her. Daniel and his family were everything Ezekiel and Henry had not been to her. They had taken her into their home and into their hearts without question. She took her leave quickly and went to the house to see Emma.

The kitchen was warm and smelled deliciously of a simmering stew. A wave of sadness swept over her as she remembered her childhood days, kneeling on a stool at the table and helping her beloved mother cook the dinner.

Emma was washing up her mixing bowl in the scullery. 'Mariah, how are you? Such dreadful news about Mr Bowes, I am so sorry.' She came through the open door drying her hands. 'This is all too much for you. Take off that cloak and sit by the fire. Will you have some dinner with me? There's mutton stew nearly ready. Daniel will have his later. He's staying in the yard today. That new crucible shed takes up all his waking hours nowadays.'

Mariah told Emma about the will. 'There is to be a new owner. Mr Withers is calling back after his visit to the bank and I am to go to his offices later.'

'Perhaps Mr Bowes remembered you after all?'

'I doubt it. Mr Withers did not give me any hope.'

Mariah draped her cloak over a chair and sat on the fender warming her hands. The kitchen had not changed much since she had left. Unlike the rest of the house. After they had eaten, she toured the rooms with Emma and marvelled at the beauty and craftsmanship of the new furnishings. She recognised the influence of Fitzkeppel Hall in Henry's choice of carpets and curtaining. The ironworks must be making much more than she realised to afford all this.

'What happened to the old furniture?'

Emma grinned at her. 'The attics are filled with

it. Do you want to see them?'

'Not today. I've got to meet Mr Withers and do some marketing before the carrier leaves.'

Mariah collected her cloak and set out for the High Street.

Mr Withers saw her approaching through his upstairs window, and called down the stairs when she opened the outer door. 'Come straight up, Miss Bowes.'

A formal document was spread out on his polished desk and a second glance told Mariah it was Ezekiel's will. She sat opposite Mr Withers, composed herself as best she could, and waited for him to speak.

'Your father made changes to his will after your mother died,' he began. 'He provided for a trust in Henry's favour. He came to see me when Henry finished his schooling as it was clear his son did not aspire to be an ironmaster. He wanted to be sure Henry would inherit a profitable concern and Mr Thorpe was essential to that end. Hence his trusteeship. Do you understand this, Miss Bowes?'

'Yes, sir. Though I do not see any relevance to me.'

'A gentleman of Mr Bowes' standing would not have wished for you to become a burden on the parish and an embarrassment to his son. Your father took my advice and allowed for the trust to provide for you, should you become destitute.'

'I see. However, as you know, sir, I am not destitute.'

'No, Miss Bowes. But the will acknowledges

you as his daughter. So you were not disowned in the end.'

She shrugged. It was small comfort to her if the ironworks went to someone else.

'You are therefore his heir, Miss Bowes.'

'I beg your pardon?' The surprise was evident in Mariah's voice.

'You are his only surviving relative.'

'There – there's no one else? No cousins in the North Riding?'

'No one, I assure you.'

'Do you mean I shall inherit the house and yard?'

He nodded.

Her mother's dowry had not been in vain! The ironworks were hers. She would make sure they thrived. With Daniel's help she would make the best steel in the Riding. She could hardly believe it! 'Surely Ezekiel would not have wanted that?' she ventured.

Mr Withers got up and crossed the room to a small table. 'I tried to explain that Henry could die first, but he would not even contemplate it. Will you take a glass of sherry wine, Miss Bowes?'

'Thank you. Is this true? Bowes Ironworks really do belong to me?'

'Not exactly. I am afraid it is not all good news.' He handed her a small glass half full of amber liquid. 'It is, of course, in trust until you are one and twenty.'

'Yes, I understand that. Mr Thorpe and your good self are my trustees. Does he know I am to inherit?'

Mr Withers nodded. 'I spoke to him first.'

She wondered how Daniel felt about this. She guessed his new responsibility would change his attitude towards her. His dutiful concern for her would likely make him even more paternal. Just as she thought they might have become closer; the fancy evaporated. That's all it was, she thought sadly, a fancy.

She did not want Daniel as her trustee, being a dutiful guardian and watching over her. She wanted to be his equal. She wanted to be a part of the ironworks with him. She could not make the steel as he did with his labourers, but she could work with him in the countless other things he did to keep their output flowing.

Their output. Hers and Daniel's.

She looked up at Mr Withers as she took the wine. His face was sombre and she realised this was not a celebration.

'You have more to tell me, sir.' She frowned.

'I am afraid so. I visited your late father's bankers today. He borrowed heavily to build his new furnace and has not been making any repayments. Unless cash is forthcoming immediately, the bank will foreclose on the mortgage. Your ironworks are bankrupt, Miss Bowes. I am sorry, but, as your trustee, I shall be selling them, and the house, at the earliest opportunity.'

Mariah's heart sank into her boots. She had come so close to her dream. 'But there must be a way to keep them! Can you not sell the house? The furnishings alone will surely–'

'I have considered all the options. Many of the new fittings have not been paid for and will be removed by the suppliers immediately.'

'The house?'

'It is of little value without the works. I agree it is a fine house, but who would live there unless they had an interest in the adjoining yard? Mr Thorpe has said he will stay on without wages and keep the furnaces firing in the hope we can find a buyer soon.'

'But he cannot work without pay! He supports a sick father! He has a mother and sisters—'

'Do try and stay calm, Miss Bowes. I am optimistic about a sale. If all goes well, the works will continue to make steel and there will be monies over to provide you with a small annuity.'

'I don't want an annuity. I want the ironworks,' she said stubbornly.

And Daniel, she thought. I want Daniel as well. This realisation surprised her. But the more she thought about it, the more determined she became that he must be a part of her future.

Mariah hardly remembered buying soap and beeswax for Dora, or her ride home. Her head was too full of tumbling thoughts. She could not, *would not,* let her trustees sell the works that had begun with the wealth her mother had brought to the Riding. It was her birthright and she wanted them. She had to find a way to keep them. And Daniel.

Chapter 34

'Fetch the horses, Ned. Have you got the harnesses?' Daniel was supervising the men as they loaded a shipment of crucible steel onto a dray for the start of the journey to Sheffield. The rain that had begun before noon had persisted and it was already growing dark.

'Right you are. The stable lad is just on his way. But Miss Emma called me over and sent me to tell you there's someone to see you at the house. A lady.'

'Who is it? Did Emma say?'

'Only that she wished to see you personally.'

Mariah, he guessed, come to talk about the future of the works.

'All right, Ned. I'm relying on you to keep that canvas in place and get those ingots loaded onto the barge. See you get a signature on the docket when the bargeman takes delivery at the wharf. Do you hear me, lad?'

'Yes, Mr Thorpe.'

'And don't forget to lock the warehouse.'

'No, Mr Thorpe.'

Daniel surveyed the scene in front of him. His steel was as good as any man could get from crucibles, and his output, though low, was reliable. But he had seen the figures and Mr Withers was right. Ezekiel had overstretched his credit. He had borrowed to fund Henry's ambitious plans as well as the new furnace. Bankruptcy was looming.

He feared for the future of the yard and the livelihoods of the men he supervised. With his present output, he could pay the bank or pay the men but not both. He was trapped. He could not afford enough men to work the crucibles to full capacity. Damn Ezekiel and his social-climbing son! If no buyer for the works came forward soon, he'd have to lay off his gang.

'Emma said not to keep the lady waiting, Mr Thorpe.'

'Right you are. Get yourself off, then.'

Daniel sprinted across the ironworks yard, past the warehouse and office and through the gate in the wall to the garden. He stopped in the scullery to take off his waistcoat and wash his face and neck. He kept a jacket for the house on a peg behind the door and shrugged into it, raking his fingers through wet hair and smoothing down his damp trousers. Emma was slicing cabbage at the kitchen table.

'Where is she, Em?'

'In the study. There's a good fire. She said you were expecting her.'

'Did she?' He stopped outside the door to draw breath and then opened it with a flourish.

For a second, he was speechless. 'Miss Fitz-keppel! I – er – I had not expected *you*.'

She rose to her feet in a rustle of blue silk and petticoats. 'You agreed that I may call on you?'

'In my office. I agreed to see you in my office, at the works.'

'I recall, sir, that you found my presence there a little uncomfortable.'

'I am a busy man, miss. What do you want of me?'

'Mr Thorpe, please do not vex me. My servants were whispering in corners this morning. I understand there is news of Mr Bowes. What have you to tell me?'

Daniel sighed. Emma had taken her cloak and Miss Fitzkeppel swished restlessly around the small study, fingering her silken cape and bonnet. 'Please sit down, Miss Fitzkeppel. I am sure Mr Withers will tell you all you need to know.'

'That is my point, Mr Thorpe. Withers communicates only with my brother. Who is in Lincolnshire, if you please. He does not think *I* need to know anything.'

'Your brother would be very wise to stay there until this sorry affair is forgotten,' he snapped. He regretted it the moment he had said it, having no desire to increase Miss Fitzkeppel's agitation. 'However,' he added, 'I believe his reputation is safe. The body of Ezekiel Bowes was found in – in your cut, and the constable has concluded that he was responsible for the accident to Henry.'

Miss Fitzkeppel seemed to shrink before his eyes. She sank into one of the chairs and whispered, 'So it is true, then? Henry's father really is dead?'

'Yes. And your brother, apparently, is cleared of any involvement.'

This seemed to cheer her a little and she murmured, half to herself, 'Perhaps Nathan will come home now.'

Daniel had no more to say to her and hoped she would leave. But, after an awkward pause,

400

she inhaled deeply and continued, 'So, what will you do, Mr Thorpe? Will you continue at Bowes Ironworks?'

'Why should I not?'

'Why, because, without Henry to take over, I imagine it will be sold, of course!'

So that was why she was here. He watched the flames licking and cracking round fresh coals. He said, 'Well, I am sure that Bowes Ironworks is too small to be of interest to your brother.'

'I have not come to see you about the ironworks.' She began to loosen the ties on her cape. 'It is warm in here. Do you not find it warm?' She took off her blue silk and white lace cape to reveal a matching bodice, close fitted and decorated with pleats and lace trims. The neckline was cut very low and she wore no lace to cover the swell of her breasts. Neither had she adorned herself with a necklace and her smooth ivory throat moved slightly as she swallowed. She leaned forward to stand up and, for a moment, Daniel was captivated by the fluidity of her body.

Her bonnet carried the same pleating and white lace as her bodice and slowly she undid its ribbon fastenings until they fell softly onto her white skin, skin that trembled gently as she moved towards him in a warm haze of womanly scent.

He hoped he was mistaken by her demeanour, but when he noticed a gentle smile playing around her lips he knew he was not. The heat was rising in his cheeks and he held his breath.

'The fire is high. Are you not warm, sir?' she said again.

Daniel did not respond. He was momentarily

401

mesmerised by the pale velvet of her throat, the swell of her breasts and the dark valley between them that descended beneath her gown.

'May I call you Daniel?' she suggested softly. 'I do hope so because I have a proposition I believe will interest you. Shall we sit down?'

Her wide blue eyes reminded him of Lily. He had never experienced such behaviour in a woman of her standing.

'What do you want of me, Miss Fitzkeppel?'

'You are so formal, Daniel. Will you not at least address me as Miss Christobel?'

'Do you have business to discuss with me or not?'

'I do. Daniel, I am sure you are ambitious for success as an ironmaster. I can help you achieve that and become a very rich man.' She chose the couch to sit on and extended a graceful hand towards him. 'Come, sit by me and listen to what I have to say.'

She was so near him he could see the sweep of her lashes against her skin and a tiny scar on her temple. He wondered how she had come by it. The last time they had been this close he had hardly noticed anything about her, but now he saw everything.

As she settled by the fire and arranged her silken skirts he caught a glimpse of soft kid, buttoned boots, tailored neatly round her narrow ankles. He wanted to kneel at her feet, take off those boots and peel away the white stockings that lay beneath them. He wanted to touch her legs, stroke the skin, gently, upwards. She was a woman any man would covet and he did.

Bel saw the light awaken in his eyes and felt a thrill of triumph. She was right. This man was no milksop around a lady, as so many of her brother's friends were. He had red blood in his veins and a hard strong body. She tried to imagine its contours beneath his clothes, but she had only stylised pictures, painted by artists, to guide her. How long would it take for her to know his body properly, to feel his hands exploring her as his eyes now did?

She patted the couch beside her but he settled in a chair, stretching out his legs and watching her closely. She leaned forward a fraction to accentuate the swell of her breasts, and smiled again.

'Daniel, you are an unmarried man of five and twenty, I am told. Handsome, clever and ready to become an ironmaster in your own right.'

'If you say so, Miss Fitzkeppel.'

'Bel. Do please call me Bel. We are not so far removed in status that we cannot be friends.'

'Yes, we are, *Miss Fitzkeppel*. Your father was a landowner. My father was a coal miner.'

'But we are in the middle of the nineteenth century! There has been a revolution. I am told that coal and iron, and not land, will be our future.'

'Your brother has both in abundance.'

'And I have none. Like you, sir, I have none. I have nothing save what my brother chooses to give me.'

'Make your point.'

'Very well. My brother will not marry. He has told me so. We have no uncles, no cousins that we

403

can trace. Therefore it is left to me to provide heirs for the Fitzkeppel estates.'

'Will that be such a hardship for you?'

She detected a mild sneer in his voice and panicked. She did not wish to lose his sympathy. Those who did not have land and wealth thought it a blessing. They did not know the responsibilities that it entailed.

'Of course not. I know my duty. However, I had been brought up to believe that I would leave Fitzkeppel Hall when I married. But my brother seems so set against his own marriage I feel it is my duty to stay.'

She detected a slight nod from Daniel and hoped she had regained his respect. She so desperately wanted him to like her.

'And – and to marry,' she added. 'I plan to marry quite soon.'

His face relaxed a little. He seemed relieved and genuinely pleased for her. 'I had not heard this news. May I wish you every happiness, Miss Fitzkeppel.'

'Do you not wish to know whom I shall marry?'

'I am sure I shall not know the gentleman – unless he was at the shoot?'

'Indeed he was.' She took a very deep breath. 'I plan to marry you.'

'What!' He rose to his feet and Bel prayed she had not alienated him with her boldness.

'You are being quite ridiculous! I believed you wished to have a serious conversation with me. But if all you want is to play parlour games at my expense, you are wasting my valuable time. I have an ironworks to run.'

'Please sit down. I do not play games. Truly. I mean what I say. You will be a great asset to the Fitzkeppel iron and steel works and ... and to our ... our blood line.' She watched him absorb these words and hoped she had not shocked him.

He sank back onto his chair and muttered, 'You really mean this, don't you?'

'Yes, I do. Of course, my brother will always own the estate, but he is not interested in its future. I am. And I believe you are too. Between us we can ensure the pits and the ironworks thrive.' She saw this had impressed him and carried on recklessly. 'And – and produce Fitzkeppel heirs to carry on.'

'Fitzkeppel heirs? Heirs called Thorpe?' He laughed and, again, she detected the derision in his voice. 'I think not.'

'No of course not. I have not come here on a whim, sir. I have thought about that. You will change your name to Fitzkeppel. Withers will do that for us. It is not unheard of in well-born families.'

She hesitated. His face was a picture of disbelief. This plan was not being received as well as she had thought it would. Anxiously, she added, 'And our firstborn son will be called Thorpe.' After a moment she put her head on one side and said softly, 'Thorpe Fitzkeppel. That has rather a nice ring about it, do you not think?'

'Out of the question. Your brother would never consent to such a match.'

'He would if I asked him. He knows I wish to marry and he cares for my happiness. I am three and twenty and time is running out for me. My brother is not a tyrant. He will welcome my marriage, I am sure. He will increase my income, as well. You have not said no, Daniel. You have only found practical difficulties to our union. May I assume then, that you are considering my offer? Think of it, wealth and position in the South Riding and making the best steel in the world. Think also of the advantages for your own family. You have sisters, I understand? They will need husbands. Imagine the choices they will have when they are my sisters too.'

Daniel thought all right. All his ambitions would be fulfilled by one single word. He would be a fool to turn away such an opportunity. But he would also be a fool if he did not consider the difficulties they would both have to face.

'It won't work,' he said. 'Gentry needs to marry gentry. Your own mother's conduct should have taught you that.'

'But that is precisely my point. I am only half gentry. My mother was a farmer's daughter.'

'Aye, and look at the trouble she caused. Working folk are best wedded to other working folk.'

'But do you not see? *I* come from yeoman stock. My grandfather was a Dales man, a sheep farmer. I have money from my brother's estate, yes. But everyone in the Riding knows I do not have the breeding to be welcome as the wife of a baronet or lord.' She looked directly into his eyes. 'Or, indeed, the inclination.'

His expression stilled as he waited for her to continue.

'Daniel, I am sincere in this proposal. I am my mother's daughter and I have her desire to make

406

the best of my life.' Her voice dropped to a murmur. 'And I have her needs as a woman. Do I not please you as a woman should please a man? Would you not care for me as your wife?' She fingered her throat and then very quietly added, 'In your bed?'

She saw his eyes darken as he contemplated this. He would have no misgivings about her wayward mother, or any scandal associated with her. She had no doubts about him. He was a strong, ambitious man. He would not allow her to stray from the marriage bed as her father had her mother. And she was sure she would never wish to, for, judging by the look in his eyes, he was already contemplating the experience. As she was. Imagining their first coupling. She could not wait and her body twitched with anticipation.

She swallowed nervously. 'You – you would be willing to take me to your bed? It – it would not be an – an ordeal for you?'

'No, it would not be an ordeal.'

It was what she desired more than anything. Her heart began to beat quickly and she became hot and damp under her skirts. She fidgeted nervously on the couch, but did not lose her courage. 'I believe it is the custom among the working classes for the future bride to – to prove her value in the marriage bed before the ceremony. Sh-should you wish that of me, I – I shall not resist.'

She stared at her hands folded on her lap and tried to keep them still. She had gone too far. He would be scandalised. But how else was she to ensure their union? If she became with child, his child, he would marry her. His sense of honour and responsibility would not let him do other-wise. Suddenly she felt an excitement surge through her. She wanted that more than anything. A baby. Daniel Thorpe's baby.

His silence made her uneasy and she dared not look at him, but she was unrepentant. What if she had shocked him? She had no reputation to lose, her mama had seen to that, and she had much to gain from this handsome and capable man. She wanted his flesh against hers, his body entwined with hers. She would learn what to do so he would enjoy her so much he would want her over and over again. Her insides began to melt at the prospect. When she found the courage to meet his eyes, she was startled by their dark intensity.

Finally, he spoke, slowly and deliberately, 'Miss Fitzkeppel – Bel – I–'

'No, do not say anything now. I know I have astonished you with my forwardness.' She bit her lip and frowned. 'You must think me wanton and I hope you will forgive me. Please, take time to reflect on what I have said. Come to luncheon at the Hall after church on Sunday and give me your answer then. Mr Withers will be there with his wife. But afterwards – after they have left we shall be alone. Most of the indoor staff have a half day and go out. If – if it is your wish, we may really get to know each other. Properly. In private.' She continued to look directly into his eyes and knew he had not mistaken her meaning. 'You will join me at luncheon on Sunday?' she repeated.

Such an invitation! The temptation stirred his desires. He had been celibate for so long – too long. If he visited her as she asked him to, he doubted he would be able to say no to her. And why should he? He had no wish to refuse her; he had an awakening hunger to satisfy. But the outcome of his previous carnal attraction towards Lily was still raw in his mind.

'I think it will be wise for you to go now,' he said.

'But you will visit me on Sunday?' she pressed anxiously. 'I shall not leave until you promise to be there.'

'Yes, Bel. I shall be there,' he replied.

Neither said another word.

When she had gone, he went to the stable at the back of the house and saddled a horse, the large black one Ezekiel had kept for himself and that was fretting from lack of exercise.

He rode the hunter hard, out of town and up onto the Keppel hills. From there he could see the Hall and its lands across the valley and smoke from the ironworks and forge chimneys down by the navigation. Most of what he saw was Fitzkeppel land.

He guessed Nathan Fitzkeppel would never marry. His inclinations were not towards ladies. He knew why Henry Bowes and Fitzkeppel had gone to that keeper's hut in the woods, and it sickened his stomach to think of what they did together. Over the years, the Fitzkeppels had been a sorry lot, to be sure. Except for Miss Fitzkeppel. She was a bold and determined woman. And clever. She knew if the estate was to thrive it would need a sure hand directing its manufacturing affairs.

He could do it and he would welcome the challenge. He could make crucible steel in abundance, go to all the lectures he wanted and learn about new processes, visit Manchester, London even, and meet great men like Stephenson and Brunel. And – and possess a pretty, intelligent wife who understood the ways of the industrial world. All this in front of him would belong to his sons. Any man of sense would not hesitate.

As he sat alone on that bleak and windy hillside, holding on to the reins of Ezekiel's horse, he tried to imagine a future living at the Hall with Bel as his wife. He would have to give up his job and all that it entailed. Mr Withers would probably sell it to the Fitzkeppels anyway and it would be absorbed into their estate. An estate he would be able to treat as his own. An involuntary cry escaped from his throat and reverberated across the valley, causing the horse to whinny and shy away. He soothed the animal and rode him less urgently back to his stable.

Chapter 35

After her Sunday dinner Mariah wrapped the finished bonnet and cape and placed them carefully in a box. 'Dora,' she called from the front room, 'I'm going to walk over to the Hall with this. Will you come with me?'

'No thanks, love. I'm taking that mutton pie over to Mr Shaw in a minute.'

'How is he keeping these days?'

'Not too good. The vicar has a place for him in the almshouse. He's moving quite soon.'

Mariah had walked through to the kitchen. 'Oh? I didn't know. What will happen to his house?'

'One of his sons will live there with his family. He needs the land for storing the stone and such like he uses in his building work.'

As she walked across the parkland in her hooded cloak, enjoying the crisp cold air, Mariah passed Mr and Mrs Withers in their pony and trap heading for the gatehouse and village. They acknowledged her as they clattered by. Mariah thought they appeared quite jolly and guessed they had eaten and drunk well at the Hall.

Since Mr Withers had told her about the financial plight of the ironworks she had racked her brains to think of a way to save them. Daniel was the best steel maker in the Riding. There must be an answer somewhere!

Miss Fitzkeppel had instructed her to bring the cape and bonnet directly to her when they were finished, so she could present the gift herself. Mariah hoped Mrs Havers would be taking a nap in her sitting room.

Everywhere was unusually quiet. Mariah found a footman, a young lad, without his livery jacket, sitting on the floor eating a piece of cold Yorkshire pudding.

'Where is everyone?' she asked, pushing back her hood.

'Mrs Havers gave most of 'em the afternoon off. They've all gone out in one of the farm carts to listen to a travelling preacher. There's on'y a

411

few of us 'ere. Can I help you, miss?'

'I have this box for Miss Fitzkeppel.'

'I'll keep it safe, miss. I'll give it to Mrs Havers when she comes in.'

'No, you can't do that. Is Miss Fitzkeppel here?'

'In the drawing room, miss.'

'Well, would you go and ask if she'll see me?'

'Oo, I couldn't do that, miss. Not until she rings for me. She was very firm about it. I was not to disturb her.'

'Tell her it's Miss Bowes.'

'I know who you are. You used to make the gowns here. Sarah's always going on about you. But I daren't go in there, miss. She 'as a visitor, y'see. She'll ring for tea when she wants it. I'll ask her then.'

'All right.' Mariah was reluctant to leave the cape and bonnet with such a young servant and decided to wait until the visitor left. 'Would you fetch me a chair from the servants' hall?'

'Right you are, miss.'

Mariah settled in the wide flagged passageway that ran between the kitchens and storerooms and connected the front of the Hall to the stable yard at the back. A solid, but worn, oak door separated the servants from the gentry. The door edge was so knocked about that there was a gap where it closed. As she sat, Mariah wondered what it was like to live on the other side of that door.

The unusual silence lengthened. But after a while she heard a door open and voices in the hallway. They were muffled at first, and then they became more distinct as they moved closer to the servants' door. There were two voices, a gentle-

412

man and a lady talking urgently to each other in a heated, passionate way, and they were getting louder.

Mariah instinctively rose to her feet as the door half opened, pushed by the man's shoulder. She heard him clearly.

'I have given you my answer, and I must make haste to return. If I do not make steel to sell, my men will have no wages.'

Mariah recognised Daniel's voice immediately. He was Miss Fitzkeppel's visitor! The door opened wider. He had his back to her and beyond him she caught a glimpse of Miss Fitzkeppel's face, shiny eyes and pink cheeks.

'Do not go! Stay with me, Daniel, and I shall show you how much I love you.'

Mariah had never seen Miss Fitzkeppel so agitated. She pressed her back against the wall as the door opened wider and Daniel turned to walk down the passage. He was very smartly dressed and held a riding hat and crop in his hand.

'Mariah!' He stopped abruptly and stared at her.

She saw him look from her to Miss Fitzkeppel and back again. There was an anguish in his face, a despairing anguish she had seen before but now it tore at her heart. She wanted to smooth it from his brow and take away his pain, no matter what it was. He started to say something to her, then must have thought better of it, for he stopped and turned back to Miss Fitzkeppel.

'Good afternoon, Bel,' he said. He gave the briefest of nods to Mariah and marched off down the passage towards the stables.

Bel? He had called Miss Fitzkeppel, Bel! A name she had previously heard only from the lips of Miss Fitzkeppel's own brother. She had no idea Daniel and Miss Fitzkeppel were so close. Miss Fitzkeppel was standing in the open doorway. Although she appeared vexed and was frowning, Mariah thought she looked quite beautiful in her blue silk gown with the delicate lace trims. She appeared not to have noticed Mariah and her voice dropped to a whisper as though the words were only for herself. 'He *is* going to marry me. He *is!*'

Mariah's eyes widened and she sat down again with a thud. Daniel and Miss Fitzkeppel? She was speechless. This could not be! Her heart was pumping loudly in her throat and her head began to spin.

'Miss Bowes? I did not see you there.'

Mariah rose to her feet instantly. 'I – I – er–'

'What is it, Miss Bowes?' Miss Fitzkeppel demanded irritably.

'The – the bonnet and cape for Mrs Havers. They're finished.' She picked up the box from the floor.

'Oh that. Yes. Where is my footman?'

'Here, miss.'

The young lad loomed out of the shadows buttoning on his jacket.

'Take this to the small drawing room.'

He grabbed the box and scuttled past her, leaving the two ladies alone.

'Was there anything else?'

'No, Miss Fitzkeppel,' Mariah answered.

Without another word, Miss Fitzkeppel walked away in a rustle of silken skirts and Mariah was left staring at the open door. She closed it gently and made her own escape to the stable yard, in time to hear the hooves of a horse galloping away. She broke into a run herself, in a different direction, across the parkland until she was forced to slow down, catch her breath and re-pin her loosening hair.

Miss Fitzkeppel and *Daniel?* It defied credibility. Surely Dora would have known of his affections? Unless it was a secret? Had she unwittingly stumbled on a covert liaison between Daniel and Miss Fitzkeppel? Mariah did not want to believe what her own eyes and ears had told her.

This would change everything for her. Mariah leaned against the stump of a recently felled tree. She had harboured ideas of keeping her ironworks afloat with Daniel's help but all was truly lost now. Marriage to Miss Fitzkeppel would bring him comfort, wealth, respectability in the Riding, and a grand house to live in with his pretty, clever wife. Why should he not marry Miss Fitzkeppel if she desired him? And desire him she did. Mariah had seen the passion in her eyes.

She did not know why she felt so angry. She kicked so hard at the felled tree trunk that she hurt her toes, and she was obliged to sit until the pain eased. How could he marry Miss Fitzkeppel when *she* needed him so badly? When her ironworks needed him so badly? Without him she had no hope of rescuing them from bankruptcy. She would lose everything: her mother's inheritance; a house she could make into her home; a man who, somehow, for her, made everything possible by his very presence.

She sat for a long time, growing chilly in the weak afternoon sun, until the sound of a horse galloping towards the Hall roused her from her thoughts. She was quite a distance from the drive, but as the rider levelled with her he slowed, turned the horse's head towards her, and cantered across the grassland. She recognised the elegant dress style and fine-boned features of Mr Fitzkeppel.

Nathan had been tired when he spurred his mount through the lodge gates. He had suffered a great shock at Henry's death and continued to grieve for his loss. He acknowledged that he had not loved Henry in the same way he had loved Warrender, but their friendship had been constant and he mourned his passing deeply.

The letter he received from Withers gave news of Bowes' death and the constable's decision. And it urged him to return. But Withers warned that there was talk about his friendship with Henry. If he came back to the Riding he must marry and staunch the rumour. He must assure the respectability of his family name and produce heirs for the estate. It was his duty.

Nathan had reluctantly agreed. He did not want to end up in gaol, or worse, for the life he led, so he resigned himself to this fate. He could surely find *someone* to be his wife? He wanted to be home, to be with Bel and to be painting again. The sight of Fitzkeppel Hall raised his spirits, as did the figure sitting alone on a tree stump in the middle of his parkland, her copper-coloured hair making her so easy for him to identify.

He dismounted, holding lightly onto the reins. 'Good afternoon, Miss Bowes.'

'Good afternoon, sir.'

She sounded forlorn. He stood in front of her and thought how much she reminded him of Henry. 'I heard about your father,' he said, 'may I offer you my condolences? So soon after Henry, too.' His voice cracked a little and he swallowed. When she raised her head he saw the sadness in her eyes, and added, 'I am truly sorry, Miss Bowes.'

'What happened that day, sir? Please tell me.'

'It was an accident, as the constable said.' After a short silence, he asked, 'What will you do?'

'I do not know. The ironworks are mine, but they are almost bankrupt. I have to find a way of keeping them going.'

He gazed at her and recalled his idle musings about her when she sat for him. A good match for an ambitious artisan, he thought. But that was before she became an ironmistress in her own right. The Bowes were far beneath him in status, to be sure. But Henry had been accepted as his friend, and Henry's father by the Riding's other factory owners. Why not the daughter? This might be a way forward for both of them.

She had a look of Henry about her that he coveted. She was personable and would be polite in civilised society. Bel spoke highly of her character. He wondered if it would work? And if it did not, would that really matter as long as she agreed to his terms?

'I could help you,' he said. 'I could pay off your creditors.'

'Why would you do that?'

'For a favour in return.'

'Sir?'

'From you. A favour from you.'

He saw a guarded expression cross her features. 'What would be the nature of this favour?' she enquired warily.

'Nothing immoral, I assure you. Just the opposite. Would you, by any chance, consider becoming my wife?'

'Your *wife?*' She sounded as taken aback as she looked. 'I do not understand, sir. Why would you wish to marry *me?* I can bring nothing to a marriage, no dowry, no connections.'

He remembered how well she had adjusted to sitting for him and how pleased Bel had been with the gowns and habits she had fashioned. 'My sister would approve of you,' he said. 'She would welcome you to the Hall.'

'And what of *your* feelings, sir?'

'We are comfortable in each other's presence, are we not?'

'I do not love you.'

'Nor I you. I have my art. You have your ironworks. We shall manage quite well without love.' She looked doubtful, so he added, 'I am sure your bankers are insisting you pay your debts immediately. Give me your promise and I shall instruct Withers to settle them.'

Until then, she had responded to him out of politeness without taking his proposal seriously, but now he saw a light in her eyes as she considered the possibilities.

'I see,' she said. 'And after our marriage my ironworks would become yours and you would have the best steel maker in the Riding working

418

for you again.'

He had not anticipated this response and hastened to reassure her. 'I have no hidden motive for my proposal, Miss Bowes. I do not want your ironworks. I want a wife because I need heirs.'

'And you think I will do for you?'

'I think you will do very well. Why else should I ask you? You are resourceful and intelligent. If you are so attached to your ironworks, you may continue to treat them as your own and put them in trust for – for any daughters of our union.'

The light in her eyes intensified as she gazed at him steadily. 'Do you want my answer now?' she asked.

'Do you think you might get a better offer, Miss Bowes?' he responded impatiently. He prepared to remount. 'You may have a week to consider.'

She watched him ride away, hardly believing that he had proposed *marriage* to her. But he *had* meant it and it *was* a way out of her troubles. She could keep the ironworks, take on more men and have both furnaces going all the time. She would be a woman to be reckoned with in the Riding!

But she would not have Daniel by her side and it was he who stirred her passion, a passion that was more than equal to Bel's. She would not give him up to her! Not until Daniel himself said he would marry her. Only then could she be certain she had lost him and would accept Mr Fitzkeppel's offer. And, like her mother before her, she would not know love within her marriage.

As she hurried through the woods she thought also of her workroom at the Hall. No one in the Riding made gowns as well as she did and she

419

wondered if Mr Fitzkeppel would consider that a suitable occupation for his wife. He must care for her. He did not love her, but gentlemen in his position did not offer marriage lightly. This was more than, as Daniel had warned previously, 'only being kind to her'.

When she reached Dora's she could not settle. She flung aside her cloak and paced back and forth across the kitchen.

'What *is* the matter?' Dora asked, mixing her pikelet batter at the table.

'Daniel was at the Hall,' she said. 'He was visiting Miss Fitzkeppel.'

'Really?'

'Did you know that they were friends?'

'No. Are they? I think he might have mentioned it to me.'

'They are more than friends.'

'Are you sure? I can't see our Daniel–'

'I saw them together! Oh!' Mariah's elbow caught on the dresser and the china rattled.

'Will you please sit down, Mariah! I expect our Daniel was there on ironworks business.'

Bel's behaviour had indicated otherwise. She said, 'I – I don't want him to sell my ironworks.'

Dora put down her spoon and heaved a sigh. 'Then why don't you go into town and tell him.'

'I think I might. I shall stay for a few days. I'll go now.'

Dora put her head on one side and stared hard. The relationship between Mariah and Daniel had changed since the shooting. She said, 'Go tomorrow, dear. There's no cart on a Sunday.'

Mariah sat up front with the driver, the hood of her cloak thrown back to show off her new bonnet of ruches and bows. When he set her down, she hired a boy with a barrow to carry her box and walked home with her head held high. She no longer had time for self-pity and she stood proudly on the front doorstep of the house she was determined to keep. She reached up and dropped the heavy brass knocker against the door with a satisfying thud.

Later, as she was helping Emma prepare a tea of hot boiled ox tongue and greens from the garden, she asked casually, 'When will Daniel be in? I want to talk to him.'

'I haven't seen him all day. He went down to the furnaces straight after breakfast with some snap for his dinner. When he comes back tonight, I'll take hot water up to his chamber for his wash, and then he'll come down for tea in the kitchen.'

'What does he do after tea?'

'Sometimes he goes back down to the yard, or out to a meeting or a lecture at the Institute. He reads a lot as well. That new study is full of books now.'

'Is he going out tonight?'

'No. I'll make some of that coffee stuff for him. I don't like it, but our Daniel has a taste for it. I generally take a pot into the study.'

'Will you make enough for us both tonight?'

'Are you having tea in here with us, then?'

'No, I had a good dinner with Dora before I set off here. I shall unpack my box instead and come down afterwards.'

She had travelled in her green gown that so

enhanced her colouring. This, she had decided, was to be her day dress and she would make a new Sunday gown with a matching bonnet and cape as soon as she could. Now she had made up her mind to talk to Daniel, she was determined to be strong, whatever the outcome. She had to know if he would be leaving the works to marry Miss Fitzkeppel, and she continued to wonder what she would do without him.

As the time to speak to him drew near, Mariah fretted about the outcome of their conversation. The last time she had been in the study had been for that embarrassing interview with Mr Smith. It seemed long ago now and she had suffered much worse since then.

He was not sitting by the fire reading, as she had expected, but standing by the window, drinking out of a tiny cup. When she opened the door, he turned swiftly. 'Mariah! Emma tells me you are staying?'

'Yes,' she answered coolly. 'Though not for long, I expect. Have you spoken to Mr Withers again?'

He nodded. 'We shall keep going while we can.' He moved to the centre of the room, to the desk where candles burned, and set down his cup. 'I shall make immediate plans to move out.'

Her coolness began to evaporate. He could not wait to get away from her and into Miss Fitzkeppel's waiting arms. Her teeth clenched as her irritation grated. 'You will do no such thing!' she replied. 'The men need you here.'

He looked surprised at her agitation. 'People will talk. I cannot stay and be the reason for that.'

'Of course, I should have realised,' she answered tightly. 'Now you move in grander circles you must guard your own reputation.' She stopped suddenly, embarrassed by her outburst.

'Mariah?' His voice was soft and full of concern. 'I am thinking only of *your* reputation.'

'My reputation? My *reputation!* You of all people should know that I have no reputation in this town.'

'That is not true. Town folk know of your misfortunes, and many have a good deal of sympathy for you. They, as I, will be pleased to see you return to your home.'

'Oh yes, so they can continue to entertain themselves with idle chatter and—'

'Stop this at once! I shall not listen to you speak like this. I was talking of your bereavements. Folk know nothing of other events.'

But you do. You know almost everything. She said, 'Well, I shall not insist that you stay. You have less than one year to serve as my trustee and then you may sever all connections with me.'

'Sever all connections? Why should I wish to do that?'

'To marry Miss Fitzkeppel, of course!'

His face darkened. In the candlelight he looked angry. The coffee was forgotten and hopes for a pleasant evening were shattered. 'So you have decided how I shall live my future life?'

'I recall you were once just as sure I should not marry her brother!'

'I had my reasons!'

'Oh yes, I remember. It would never do for working folk to marry above themselves. Does

423

that not apply to you also?'

He sighed. 'You are quite worn out and are acting like a petulant child. You are overwrought by events and – and, somehow, spoiling for a fight. I shall not continue this conversation with you. We may talk tomorrow after you have rested. Come over to the works, to your father's office, after breakfast. There is much for you to learn there.' He handed her one of the candles from the desk and said pointedly, 'Goodnight, Mariah.'

She took the candle from him ungraciously and demanded, 'When are you going to marry her?'

He sighed again and said firmly, 'Go to bed.'

She left, knowing she had behaved badly. She had not been able to help herself. She wanted him to stay here. With her. To be by her side, making steel instead of living at the Hall with *her*. She could not imagine the ironworks without him. She understood, now, what her mother meant when she had talked of love. She loved Daniel. Miss Fitzkeppel might be fair and pretty with wealth and position, but she was not right for Daniel. Miss Fitzkeppel did not, *could not*, love Daniel as she did.

Emma had gone to her bed, leaving hot water on the washstand in Ezekiel's room, where the stable lad had put her box. It was the largest bedchamber, furnished with an ornate wrought-iron bedstead. The quilt was new, she noticed, made in a heavy dark red satin and there were matching curtains at the window. Henry's influence, she guessed. She did not want to sleep here, in Ezekiel's bed. She took her nightgown, neatly folded on the carved oak chest, undressed and

424

washed, then picked up the candle and crossed the landing to her old bedchamber.

The number of books around the room told her this was where Daniel still slept and, for some reason that she could not fathom, she wanted to weep. She wanted to fall into the feather mattress and pour out her heart to him.

It was the first time since her attack she had wanted to be this close to a man, lying together, her body against his. Mr Fitzkeppel's kind and gentle ways had not aroused such feelings in her. But Daniel did and this made her want to cry.

She heard a door open downstairs and retreated to her mother's former sickroom. This had been Henry's dressing room until recently. It still contained some of his things. There was a couch against the wall. Mariah dragged the feather quilt from the bedchamber next door, wrapped herself in it and lay down. She remained awake for ages listening to Daniel's movements downstairs, checking locks and bolts, raking and damping down fires. He belongs *here*, she thought. Not at the Hall. He belongs here with me.

Her ears strained for his heavy footsteps on the stair treads, but none came. Perhaps like her he could not sleep. She heard again the squeak of a door hinge. Perhaps he was reading. He read a lot. That was why he knew so much, she thought. Eventually, she drifted into a restless sleep imagining Daniel, his long legs stretched out in front of a dying fire, a candle by his head, turning the pages of a book.

Chapter 36

It was dark when she woke, but the noises from downstairs told her it was morning. She dressed carefully, spending more time than usual with a candle in front of Henry's looking glass smoothing her coiled hair. Her hands and feet had become quite chilly when she went down to the kitchen.

Emma was standing at the kitchen table, rubbing dripping into some flour in a bowl. 'Oh, you're up early. Fire's drawing well, I was just waiting for the water to heat.'

'I'm going over to the works this morning. What time does Daniel leave the house?'

'He's gone already. Wi'out 'is breakfast, an' all.'

'But it's not properly light yet!'

'He likes to make sure the fires are going for the crucible steel. He makes that every day now.'

'I'll go over there straightaway,' Mariah said.

'Can you wait while the kettle boils and take a can o' tea for him? I'll cut some bacon and bread too.'

Mariah carried the basket of food and drink into the yard. There was smoke curling from the wide brick chimney of the crucible furnace and the men were already working, loading the cementation furnace for the next firing. The sky was overcast and the air was cold, but it was fully light. She hovered by the warehouse until Daniel saw her and came over, striding across the cobbles, his waistcoat flapping in the crisp morning breeze.

He stopped a few paces from her, taking in her gown and hair and how they complemented each other. Her clear, hazel eyes were challenging.

'It was a bad start last night,' he said. 'We ought not to quarrel.'

'Quite so,' she replied. 'What have you to tell me?'

He detached the keys from his belt. 'Come into the office.'

Mariah followed him up the outside stone steps. 'I've brought you some breakfast,' she said.

'Champion. The fire should be going well by now.'

The office was tidier than she remembered. The hearth was swept and the worn desk top cleared and polished.

Daniel poured hot tea into two metal tankards. 'Will you share this with me?'

'Thank you.' She handed him some bread and bacon in a cloth and took a piece herself.

'Did you sleep well?' he asked.

She shrugged, her mouth full of food.

He looked sympathetic. 'You have been through too much of late. The worst is over now.'

'Is it? I have inherited debts and this yard is a millstone around my neck.'

'I shall salvage what I can for you. Mr Withers will get a good price for the house and yard. The furnaces are sound. Ezekiel had plans to expand once the new crucible shed was finished. We talked of taking on more men. Even now we need a manager to replace Ezekiel.'

'But surely you are that person?'

'I am the only teemer for the crucibles and if I do not keep up output we cannot pay the men's wages. They have wives and children to feed.'

'Can you not employ another teemer?'

'I know of such a man eager to join us.'

'Then why do you not proceed?'

'I have no funds to pay him. Ezekiel borrowed too much to build the new shed.'

'But surely there is money for the men's wages? Ezekiel always had banknotes in his safe.'

'That was before Henry came home from school and started spending on the house and his new carriage.'

'New carriage?'

'It's in the stable at present. Henry had chosen a pair of matching horses to draw it. They are in the stables too.'

'But he was not gentry! He did not have the income for a carriage! Or indeed a life that demanded such an extravagance!'

'He had other ideas.'

'I suppose he wanted it for travelling to the Hall and Ezekiel indulged him. Have I any money at all?'

Daniel shook his head. 'Not after paying for bar iron and coal.'

'Is there any way you can keep going?'

He heaved a sigh. 'The bank is taking everything.'

'What does Mr Withers say?'

'The same as I do. We must sell up to pay off your creditors.'

'But if you did not have that burden, could you

take on more men and increase your output?'

'Oh yes. Bowes Ironworks would be making the best steel in the Riding! It would have a future. The price of crucible steel is rising all the time.'

Mariah thought she saw a glow in his eyes for a moment as he spoke. Then it disappeared as he added quickly, 'I am afraid it is not a possibility. Mr Withers and I have racked our brains to find a way.'

She gave a rueful smile. 'Is Henry's carriage paid for?'

Daniel nodded.

'Sell it. And the horses. And anything else we don't need. Will that pay the men's wages?'

'For a while.'

'With enough for another teemer?'

Now he shook his head and gave a harsh laugh. 'I would not take a man from another yard only to have to lay him off when the money runs out.'

She tipped the rest of the cooling tea into his tankard. 'Then I must find a solution. Bankrupt or not, these are my works, after all.'

'Do not be fanciful, Mariah. We cannot play games with men's livelihoods.'

'Mr Fitzkeppel has offered to pay off my debts.'

'Fitzkeppel? Is he not in Lincolnshire?'

'He returned to the Hall yesterday. After you left. Mr Withers has kept him informed of events. He wishes to marry.'

'Is that what he told you? I do not believe it.'

Mariah was startled by the scorn in his voice and she retaliated sharply. 'Well you had better believe it. He wishes to marry me.'

Daniel stood up, knocking back his chair. His

voice resonated around the office like a clap of thunder. 'No!' He repeated the word twice, loudly and with anger, adding, 'Do not do this, Mariah. It will bring you only grief and unhappiness.'

Mariah stood up to challenge him. 'How dare you? How dare you presume to tell me what to do? Mr Fitzkeppel's generosity will allow these works to continue to employ men and make steel. They will be mine, in trust for my children, my daughters. My daughters will not have to suffer the humility of dependence that my mother and myself endured.'

'He will never love you.'

'Now who is being fanciful! Is love such a prerequisite of happiness? We are friends. We shall grow to love each other.'

He was shaking his head and his eyes had taken on that haunted, anguished look that tore her heart. He leaned over the desk, resting both his hands on its surface and stared at her. 'I forbid it. I am your trustee and I forbid it.'

For a moment she was dumbfounded. How had she ever considered she could have had a future with this man? She had thought he would be pleased. She pursed her lips and frowned. She would just as soon have Ezekiel back, ordering her life than this – this tyrant that Daniel had become. She said, 'I am sure Mr Withers will not share your view.'

'You do not understand.'

'I think I do. I think you have lived and worked for so long with Ezekiel that you have grown to be too much like him.'

'No!' he roared.

She gazed at him. Had he lost his mind? 'I shall give Mr Fitzkeppel my answer tomorrow. You may tell the men that Bowes Ironworks are safe from their creditors. I shall rename them Bowes Steelworks as soon as I can.'

She would have left that minute if he had not caught her arm. 'Stay,' he demanded of her. 'There is something you should know.' He stepped back, breathing heavily as though attempting to compose himself and then went to the safe and drew out a sheaf of thick papers that he placed on the desk.

'What are these? Are they the drawings for the new crucible shed?'

'No. They are nothing to do with the works.'

'What are they, then?'

Daniel did not reply.

'Well, are you going to show them to me?'

He covered his face with his hands. 'You must prepare yourself, Mariah. These are not for – I mean, they are only for – they are meant for gentlemen.'

'Yet they do not concern the furnaces?'

He hesitated, picked them up again and shook his head. 'I cannot do this. I have made a mistake. I shall return them to the safe.'

'Daniel? What intrigue is this?'

'I am sorry. This is wrong. Please do not press me.'

'But I do. What secrets do you have that you must keep them in the safe?'

'They are not my secrets. They were there before I came here.'

'Then they were Ezekiel's?'

431

'Yes. They are – were – his.'

'Where did they come from?'

'Who knows?' he shrugged. 'Do you understand what I am saying? They are for – for gentlemen.'

'Ezekiel kept these drawings in his safe? No, I do not understand. Show them to me.'

He shook his head again. 'I should have removed them and destroyed them when I found them.'

'But they belong to me now.'

'Let me burn them in the fire. They are not for your eyes.'

'Nonsense. I am a grown woman. And I, of all people, know that men have these needs.'

Daniel shook his head emphatically. 'No, you do not know about this. You cannot see them.'

'But they are mine.'

'And I am your trustee.'

They stared at each other silently for several seconds.

'Do you think I cannot deal with these things now? Do you think I am some weak and whimpering woman who will faint at the sight of unclothed bodies? Do not misjudge me so.'

'I don't. I–'

'No, Daniel. Let me speak. My mother was an unhappy woman as Ezekiel's wife. I need to see the kind of woman Ezekiel wished my mother was. I have to try and understand why Ezekiel behaved towards her as he did. He treated my mother and myself abominably. He was successful but you believe he was a troubled man. Did you not say as much when you came to tell me of his death? For heaven's sake, he died by his own

432

hand! Please Daniel, don't you understand? I need to know!'

She was half crying now, hiccupping with anger and frustration. Her voice had risen to a squeak. She had never understood Ezekiel, but she hoped some answers might lie in the drawings. Sobbing slightly she beseeched him, 'Let me look on them once, Daniel, and then you may destroy them.'

Daniel wrestled with her need to understand Ezekiel and her brother's friendship with Fitzkeppel, and his desire to protect her from the truth.

She was whispering to herself, 'Why? Why? Why was Ezekiel always so angry with Mother?'

Agitated, he ran his fingers through his hair and muttered, 'Very well, I'll show them to you.'

He cleared the top of the desk and laid out the drawings. He grimaced as he stepped to one side, gesturing for her to inspect them. 'I shall pour you a brandy. You are going to need it.'

The only sound was that of Mariah's skirts rustling as she walked around the desk and gazed at the papers. At first she was puzzled. She had expected ladies, foreign ladies, from the Orient or the West Indies, showing off their breasts and bottoms. As she studied the drawings incredulity crept over her.

Mariah choked and coughed, and then began to shake. She took the brandy that appeared in front of her and sank, speechless, into Ezekiel's battered old office chair. 'But – but these are young gentlemen.'

'You did not know about this, did you?' Daniel asked quietly. 'You did not know that there are men who prefer to look on other men?'

She shook her head wordlessly and drank. 'Did he – did Ezekiel...?'

Daniel grimaced. 'He hid his preference well. He had to. The men would have found out and they would have talked. It is my belief he suppressed his inclinations and these drawings were his substitute.'

Mariah shook her head and spoke very softly. 'It's – it's – it's...' at last she got out her words, 'it's not natural.'

'Not to you or I, but it happens. I have seen it among farm animals.'

'What do you mean?'

'It's not unknown that sometimes a boar or a stallion won't do his duty at stud and prefers to run with other males.'

'You mean, it's not only that they prefer to look on gentlemen, but they do not have urges for ladies?'

He nodded.

'Mother told me Ezekiel did not love her. Now I know why. He was not able to. They had Henry though, didn't they?'

'Perhaps he tried to be a dutiful husband and found it too difficult. He lived the life he wanted through Henry and, I guess, when he found him with Fitzkeppel in that old keeper's hut–'

'Henry? Henry and Mr Fitzkeppel?'

'Fitzkeppel will never love you in the way he loved Henry. In time, he will find a substitute for Henry, but it will never be you, Mariah. Never. You must not marry him.'

'No, I see that now. Do other folk know about them?'

'There have been stories going round the works about those two for a while now, but not about Ezekiel. He buried his nature well and that was his trouble. I suppose he felt he could not go on.'

'Poor Ezekiel.'

Daniel began to scoop up the offensive papers. 'Ezekiel would not have wanted anyone to know about these. I'll burn them, as I should have done when I found them.'

'Thank you. I understand now why he was such a difficult man. It must have been impossible to reconcile this part of him with his ambitions to be so well-respected.'

She watched Daniel tear up the sheets one by one and feed them to the burning coals. She stared across the room at him, and thought what a fine gentleman he was. He had wanted to protect her from this knowledge for the very best of reasons. She finished her brandy and realised how very, very special he was to her.

She glanced at the open safe. 'What else is in there?'

'Well, no money, I am sorry to say. But I have paid the men for last week. The title deeds to the house and ironworks are with your bankers. The papers in there are orders, bills of sale and ledgers, just the usual.' He took the poker and broke the burned drawings into ash that fell among the glowing coals. 'And something of yours,' he added.

'Mine?' She did not leave any of her possessions with Ezekiel.

He crossed to the safe, reached inside and retrieved a small package wrapped in calico.

'For you,' he said, handing it over.

435

The wrapping fell away to reveal a silver frame, the silver frame that had held her mother's likeness, that Dora had sold for her in town and bought woollen cloth to make a winter coat. The silver frame that had also given her money to buy notions and fabric to make the things she sold in the market.

Mariah gave a small laugh, her mouth widened into a smile and her eyes lit up with delight, a delight that lifted Daniel's heart more than he could tell.

'But how did you know? Where did you get it?' Mariah burbled, as she stroked the figured surface and turned it over and over in her hands.

'Dora came to see me when she brought it into town to sell. So I knew all about your plans. I would have bought it from her then if I had had the money. Instead, I went with her to the silversmith on the High Street and secured it with a payment and a promise to buy it over the following months. I took him the final sum last week and placed it in the safe for you.'

'Oh Daniel, it's the most wonderful thing you could have done for me. I still have my mother's likeness, between the pages of my Bible. Now it can resume its rightful place on the mantelshelf in the morning room.'

'I shall move my books out of there as soon as I can.'

'No, it is better as your library and study.' A plan was beginning to form in her mind. A plan to keep her steelworks going. If only Daniel would stay.

'When will you marry her?' she asked quietly.

He did not answer and look pained.

'I saw you together. She says you will marry her.'

'Does she? She presumes too much.'

Mariah's heart turned over in her breast. 'You are not betrothed? You won't be leaving here, then?'

He gave her a long level stare. 'No.'

The word hung in the air and Mariah could hardly contain her joy. But she dare not hope for too much. Not yet. Her mind raced. 'We must find money for the men's wages every week.'

'If I could make more crucible steel, I could make more profits.'

'And you need another teemer to do that?'

'I *need* to be sure I can pay him.'

'I may have a solution. I have been thinking about this since I worked at the Hall. I shall make gowns. Fashionable silken gowns for the wives of manufacturing and professional gentlemen in this town. I shall need needlewomen, of course. If Emma is comfortable in the small attic, there is room for two girls in the large attic. Will that help?' Even as she said it, she was planning how to use Henry's bedchamber for her workroom, and the adjoining dressing room to receive her clients.

'You mean in the house?'

'Do you think Meg would join me in this venture? I shall ask her. I shall be set up in no time, and surely make enough to pay for your teemer.' She wondered if she could persuade Mrs Havers to let Sarah Maltby go from the Hall and become a seamstress alongside Meg.

Daniel's eyes widened and met her steady gaze.

437

'I think it might. In fact, I do believe it would. I'll talk to Mr Withers tomorrow.'

Mariah began to pack the basket with the debris from their breakfast. He would stay at the works and give them a future. Give her a future, too. They would be together. She had hope. She noticed him watching her silently with his head on one side, the way Dora did sometimes. She was glad she wore her green gown and had spent time on her hair this morning.

'Will you ever truly forgive me?' he asked quietly.

She did not pretend she did not know what he was talking about. 'There is nothing to forgive.'

'It was my fault it happened.'

'No. The fault lies with others.'

'But, don't you see, it was because of my actions, my weakness for–'

'For Mrs Cluff. I know. You told me.'

'I was such a fool. I believed her.'

'But why should you not believe the woman you loved?'

'Because I did not love her. I know now that I did not love her. It was a physical craving for her, that is all. Love is more, it means more.'

'Did you love Miss Fitzkeppel?'

He shook his head slowly and deliberately.

'But you craved her in the same way as you did Lily?'

'I did. Briefly, yes I did. What do you want me to say, Mariah? That I am not a man with a man's desires?'

'I am sorry. I did not mean to cause you anger.'

'I am not angry!'

Clearly he was.

'I wanted the truth, that is all.' She shrugged.

'Truth? The truth is that no amount of wealth or position will take me away from here. Away from you.'

'Do not say that!' It was what she wished to hear. But, now, she had to tell *him* the truth. 'You do not know everything about – about what those men did to me that night.'

His anguish etched the fine lines on his face deeper. He looked haggard and grey in the pale morning light. For weeks he had despaired about Mariah's future, until he realised that her future was with him. It was not blame or guilt that drove him. He wanted her by his side. His woman. He was fired with a desire for her stronger than anything he had experienced. And yes, part of it was for the bedchamber, but he realised that he must proceed with caution at her pace.

He said, 'It is the past. To be forgotten. If you can.'

Quietly, Mariah replied, 'Some things may not be forgotten.'

The naked pain in his eyes was distressing for Mariah to witness. He turned to face her, his voice low and intense. 'Why do you torture me so? Do you not know that I would give my *life* for it never to have happened?'

The hopeless despair on his beautiful, strong face brought tears of sadness welling in Mariah's eyes. They stood, silent and still, facing each other.

Mariah's voice came out in a whisper, 'And if you did, my life would not be worth living.

Without you I have nothing, I have no strength, no desire, no passion. Without you I *am* nothing.'

There was no need for further words as they stepped closer and clung together in a mutual possession that wanted no kiss or passionate searching to satiate their unfulfilled desires. Daniel had wanted this for so long and had not dared hope she could ever return his feelings. It was an embrace that swelled his heart and told him they were as one, united in their need for each other and in their satisfaction that they had found each other.

But for Mariah, there remained one last truth that would test all her strength. She put him away from her, stepping back and swallowing hard before she continued.

'You do not know everything about me and you must.' She swallowed again. 'There was a child. After the attack I was with child.'

'A child? You had a child?' Yes, he agreed. A child may not be forgotten. 'Where is he?' he asked, spreading his arms to hold her again.

'No, please don't touch me. Let me finish. You must know everything.' She sank into a nearby chair. 'You see, I did not know which of those two men—' She stopped and choked on the words. 'I could not live with the fruit of their evil seed inside me. It felt as though the devil had invaded my body and was growing within me, corrupting me. I wanted to die.'

Mariah looked at Daniel's face, searching for his rejection of her. But all she saw was sadness and hurt in his eyes, eyes that were shiny with unshed tears. 'I – I would have killed myself, if

Dora had not helped me – helped me rid my body of their wickedness. But when the deed was done I knew, too late, that a part of me had died with my unborn child.' She stopped and inhaled deeply and shakily. 'That is my punishment, you see, my suffering for condemning my child, my innocent child, and I cry every day for the life I took. I have sinned, Daniel. I am unchaste, and tainted for ever by my own actions. I am not worthy of you. Go to Bel instead, live at the Hall and be a wealthy gentleman. For if you stay with me you will become tainted too.'

'No. Never. We have both made mistakes we cannot undo and we must live with them as best we can. But don't you see, Mariah? If we have each other we can survive.'

'You still want me, knowing this?'

'I love you. Do you love me?'

'Yes.'

'Then we can face the future together. When we marry, our vows to each other will be stronger because of what we know about each other.'

'It will always be there. Coming between us.'

'Only if we let it. You will have more children, *our* children, and they will bring you the joy and happiness you deserve. The bad memories will fade. I shall look after you and protect you so no one in this world will ever hurt you again.'

He held her so close and kissed her with such a passion she could barely breathe. She could taste fresh tea in his mouth. She could smell the smoke of the furnace on his skin, mingling with the leather of his waistcoat. Her arms crept underneath it and around his firm strong back. She wanted to tug away his shirt and kiss the naked skin of his chest. His hands roamed the surface of her bodice, exploring her contours hungrily, her waist and breasts, her shoulders, neck and head, tangling and disturbing the smooth coils of her hair.

When they pulled apart, breathless and eager for more of each other, he whispered, 'You *will* marry me soon, won't you?'

'I will. Yes, I will.'

Chapter 37

Bel sat alone in her small sitting room and stared out of the window. Even on this grey and overcast day, the parkland looked lovely. Nathan had been right to plant more trees. She had missed him so much after the shooting. Mrs Withers had suggested as much when she had come to luncheon with her husband. Bel remembered her surprise at Mr Thorpe's presence. The two gentlemen had conversed well. When the ladies left them to their port and cigars, Mrs Withers had made another suggestion to Bel, which she had taken seriously and to which Nathan had agreed. The door opened, bringing her back to the present.

'You wish to speak to me, Miss Christobel?'

Bel turned and pasted a smile on her face. 'Yes, Mrs Havers. The master and I are quitting the Hall for the remainder of the winter. Perhaps for longer.' Saying it made it seem more real. She would feel the loss of her horses and her morning rides more than anything. But, no doubt, there would be compensations where she was going. She added, 'We shall be in Italy with our – our mother.'

'Yes, miss.' Mrs Havers hid her surprise well.

'You may close up the main rooms. You will not need all the servants when we are gone, but do try and keep them gainfully occupied. If any of them wish to leave us, I should be grateful if you would help them find suitable positions elsewhere.'

'Yes, miss.' The older woman hesitated a moment, then continued, 'Forgive my boldness, Miss Christobel, but I shall miss you both. Very much.'

'Yes.' Bel sighed. 'We shall miss you too, Mrs Havers. You have been a loyal and faithful servant to us. However, it is for the best. Withers will keep you informed. We may decide to lease the Hall.'

'Yes, miss.'

When Mrs Havers had left, Bel returned to the window. She knew she had made a fool of herself in front of Daniel Thorpe and he would never marry her. She really would have relished him as her husband. But now there were other matters to occupy her thoughts. Withers had presented her with her mothers' letters last Sunday. She hadn't read them yet. She would do so on the journey. It was going to be a long journey for her, but one she must make.

Later that month, Fanny went to visit Dora and they walked over to Keppel village.

'She's a grand lass, isn't she?' Fanny said.

'Mariah? Oh aye. The longer she stayed with me, the longer I thought of her as the daughter I never had.' Dora took her sister's arm. Neither needed the physical support, but the unspoken bond between them had not broken. It had been tested over the years, twisted and strained by events that had served only to strengthen it. 'I'm really glad they are going to wed, aren't you?'

Fanny nodded. 'Arthur's as fussy as a dog with two tails. He says she's just what our Daniel needs to steady him down.'

They walked through the wet grass, towards Keppel churchyard where it bordered the woodland, and stopped in front of a mossy headstone. The chiselled names of their mother and father were already weathered. But the names of Fanny's children, Thorpe children taken before their time, were still sharp, and reading them brought tears to the eyes of both women. One name, the first of the children, had been there longer than the others and the edges were wearing just as their parents' names were.

Also Matthew Barton, aged two weeks, grandson.

'Poor little Matthew.'

Tears welled in Fanny's eyes and ran down her cheeks. She bent down and laid a posy of winter jasmine on the grassy mound. When she straightened, Dora began to cry as well. She put her arm around Fanny's shoulders and said, 'He was a little fighter and I did my best for him, but he was born too early.'

'Did we do a wicked thing?' Fanny asked.

'No. It was for the best.'

'Do you think Arthur ought to know about him?'

'He does know. He thinks, like everyone else, that Matthew was my child,' Dora replied. 'Why? Do you want to tell him otherwise?'

'No. It would upset him. I can't tell him now, he would never forgive me for deceiving him so. When I lied to him and told him your baby had died, he shed a tear, you know. He cried! I had not seen a man cry before. But he said it was God's will and asked if you were all right. And after that he said we should not speak of it again.'

Dora gave Fanny a brief hug. 'He was right. Is right. Daniel has a mother and father who love him and that is all he needs to know.'

'But what about you, Dora, love? Yours was the greater sacrifice. You gave me your healthy baby when mine died. I'll never forget what you did for me.'

'I had to. It was the only way I could make good the wrong I had done you. And Daniel has a proper name and family. I could not have given him that.'

'Even so,' Fanny insisted, 'it doesn't seem right not to tell him.'

'Some secrets are best kept for ever.'

'From Arthur, yes. But not from Daniel,' Fanny replied. 'He should be told you are his true mother. He should know what you did for Arthur and me.'

'If you tell Daniel, you'll have to tell Arthur as well. Don't do it, Fanny.'

'You know as well as I do that Arthur does not

have many more winters on this earth. If God spares me and Arthur goes first, I shall tell Daniel the truth. So I want you to promise me something, Dora.'

'Yes, of course.'

'Promise me that if I go before you, you will tell Daniel you are his real mother. You will not take this secret to your grave.'

'Yes, I'll promise you that, Fanny. It will be a shock for him, though.'

'He'll be all right. He has Mariah, now.'

'Aye, you're right. I'm glad they're together. I knew they cared for each other. I could tell that from the beginning,' Dora added.

'Yes, I do believe he loves Mariah more than us at home.'

'Our Daniel has a big heart. There's enough to go round. And look what a lovely new daughter you will have in Mariah.'

The sisters bent down together to pull out a few weeds from the grassy mound.

Fanny added, 'I think they could spend more time with you from now on. A lot more time.'

'I should like that very much.'

This Large Print Book for the partially sighted, who cannot read normal print, is published under the auspices of

THE ULVERSCROFT FOUNDATION

THE ULVERSCROFT FOUNDATION

... we hope that you have enjoyed this Large Print Book. Please think for a moment about those people who have worse eyesight problems than you ... and are unable to even read or enjoy Large Print, without great difficulty.

You can help them by sending a donation, large or small to:

The Ulverscroft Foundation, 1, The Green, Bradgate Road, Anstey, Leicestershire, LE7 7FU, England.
or request a copy of our brochure for more details.

The Foundation will use all your help to assist those people who are handicapped by various sight problems and need special attention.

Thank you very much for your help.